"Francis aficionados ... other Felix chooses to carry on the family tradition on his own."

—*Publishers Weekly*

Rave reviews for

DICK FRANCIS AND FELIX FRANCIS

"With wit and an expert's understanding of both horses an...

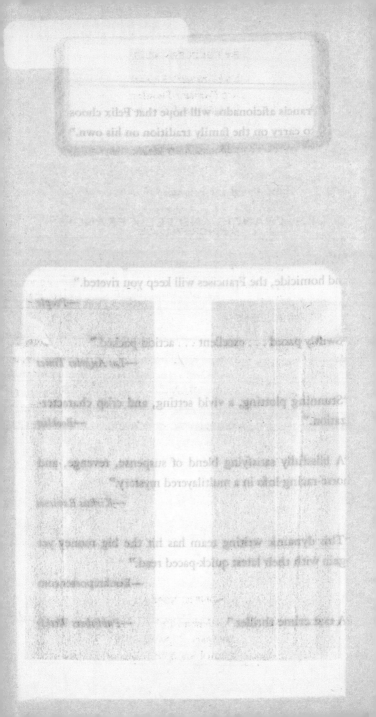

...Francis aficionados will hope that Felix chooses ...to carry on the family tradition on his own."

...and homicide, the Frances will keep you riveted."

"...swiftly paced ... excellent ... action packed."
—*Los Angeles Times*

"...Sounding plotting, a vivid setting, and crisp characterization."

"A blissfully satisfying blend of suspense, revenge, and horse racing lore in a multilayered mystery."

"This dynamic writing team has hit the big money yet again with their latest quick-paced read."
—*Bookreporter.com*

"A taut crime thriller."

DICK FRANCIS'S

BLOODLINE

FELIX FRANCIS

BERKLEY BOOKS
NEW YORK

PB
FRA

17 Aug 7
B+T
9.99 (6.49)

THE BERKLEY PUBLISHING GROUP
Published by the Penguin Group
Penguin Group (USA) Inc.
375 Hudson Street, New York, New York 10014, USA

USA | Canada | UK | Ireland | Australia | New Zealand | India | South Africa | China

Penguin Books Ltd., Registered Offices: 80 Strand, London WC2R 0RL, England
For more information about the Penguin Group, visit penguin.com.

DICK FRANCIS'S BLOODLINE

A Berkley Book / published by arrangement with the author

For information, address: The Berkley Publishing Group,
a division of Penguin Group (USA) Inc.,
375 Hudson Street, New York, New York 10014.

ISBN: 978-0-425-26135-4

PUBLISHING HISTORY
G. P. Putnam's Sons hardcover edition / October 2012
Berkley premium edition / July 2013

PRINTED IN THE UNITED STATES OF AMERICA

10 9 8 7 6 5 4 3

Cover art by Ben Perini.

ALWAYS LEARNING   PEARSON

With my special thanks to
Mike Cattermole,
race caller and TV presenter,
to all my friends at
Channel 4 Racing
and
BBC Radio 5 Live
for their help and encouragement,
and, as always, to Debbie

1

T hey're off!"

I looked down at the image of the horses on my
TV monitor and shielded my eyes from the bright
September sunshine. An unremarkable straight, mile-long
sprint for maiden two-year-olds at Lingfield Park with
twelve runners—just another horse race, one of more than
fifteen hundred such races I would watch live this year.

But this particular race was to change my life forever.

THE HORSES broke from the starting gate in a fairly
even line, and I glanced down at my handwritten sheet
that showed the runners in their draw positions as they
faced me almost a mile away.

The mile start at Lingfield was slightly obscured from

the grandstand by some overhanging trees, so I leaned closer to the monitor to get a better view.

"They're running in the Herald Sunshine Limited Maiden Stakes, and Spitfire Boy is the early leader," I said, "with Steeplejack also showing early pace. Sudoku is next on the rail, tracked by Radioactive, with Troubleatmill running wide. Postal Vote is next, then High Definition and Low Calorie, with Bangkok Flyer on the far outside in the green jacket, followed by Tailplane with the white cap and Routemaster in the orange hoops. The back-marker at this stage is Pink Pashmina, who is struggling and getting a reminder as they pass the three-quarter-mile marker."

I lifted my eyes from the monitor and looked down toward the horses using my high-powered binoculars. At three-quarters of a mile I could now see them all clearly as they raced directly toward me, the foreshortening effect of the binoculars making the horses' heads seem to bob up and down unnaturally.

Races like this, with the horses running headlong down the straight track, nearly always made life difficult for race callers, and this one was no exception. The twelve runners had split into two groups, with eight horses running close to the nearside rail and the four others making their way right down the middle.

The punters in the grandstands understandably wanted to know which horse was leading, but the angle from which I was looking did not make it an easy task to decide.

"The red jacket of Spitfire Boy leads the larger group on the nearside, with Radioactive making a challenge. Troubleatmill and Bangkok Flyer are running neck and neck in the middle of the course with half a mile to go."

I looked intensely at the field as they galloped toward me. It may have stated in the race program that Bangkok Flyer's colors were dark green, but, silhouetted in the sunshine, they looked very black to me, and I didn't want to confuse them with the navy jacket of Postal Vote.

No, I was sure. It was Bangkok Flyer, with his sheepskin noseband, and he was living up to his name.

"Bangkok Flyer, with the sheepskin noseband, now stretching away on the far side. He has opened up a two-length margin over Troubleatmill, who seems not to be staying the distance. And on the nearside, Spitfire Boy has been caught by Radioactive. But here comes Sudoku between horses under Paul James in the white jacket, who has yet to move a muscle."

I lowered my binoculars and watched the horses unaided.

"Sudoku now sweeps to the front on the nearside as they pass the eighth-of-a-mile pole, but he still has the short-priced favorite, Bangkok Flyer, to beat. Sudoku and Bangkok Flyer come together as they move into the closing stages. Sudoku in white and Bangkok Flyer in dark green, it's a two-horse race." The tone of my voice rose higher and higher as the equine nostrils stretched for the finishing line beneath me. "Bangkok Flyer and Sudoku stride for stride. Sudoku and Bangkok Flyer." My pitch reached its crescendo. "Sudoku wins from Bangkok Flyer, Low Calorie runs on gamely to be third, Radioactive is fourth, followed by the longtime leader Spitfire Boy, then

Routemaster, High Definition, Troubleatmill, Steeplejack, then Tailplane and Postal Vote together, and finally the filly, Pink Pashmina, who has finished a long way last."

I pushed the button that switched off my microphone.

"First, number ten, Sudoku," said the judge over the PA. "Second, number one. Third, number four. The fourth horse was number eight. The distances were a neck, and two and a half lengths."

The PA fell silent.

The race was over. The excitement had come and gone, and the crowd would already be looking forward to the next contest in thirty minutes.

I looked out across the track and felt uneasy.

Something there hadn't been quite right.

It wasn't my commentary. I hadn't confused the horses or called the wrong horse home as the winner—something that every race caller had done at some time in his life. It was the race itself that hadn't been quite right.

"Thanks, Mark. Great job," said a voice in my headphones. *"And well done mentioning every horse, and thanks for the finish order."*

"No problem, Derek," I said.

Derek was a producer for RacingTV, the satellite broadcaster that was showing the racing live. He would be sitting in the scanner, a large blacked-out truck somewhere behind the racetrack stables, with a bank of television images in front of him, one for each of the half a dozen or so cameras, and it was he who decided what pictures the people at home or in the betting shops would see. The TV company didn't have their own race caller, so they took the course commentary—namely, me. But they liked it if all the horses were mentioned at least once, and they were pretty insistent on the full finishing order being given. That was fine with twelve runners, but not so easy when there were thirty or more, especially in a sprint like this when the whole thing was over in less than a minute and a half.

"Derek?" I said, pushing a button on the control box.

"Go ahead," he replied into my ears.

"Could you make me a DVD of that race? To take home. Every angle."

"But she didn't win."

"I still want it," I said.

"OK," he said. *"It'll be ready."*

"Thanks," I said. "I'll collect it after the last."

"We'll still be here."

There was a click and my headphones went silent once more.

"But she didn't win," Derek had said.

"She" was my sister—my twin sister, to be precise, Clare Shillingford—a top jockey with more than six hundred winners to her name.

But that race had not been one of them. She'd just come second by a neck on Bangkok Flyer, and I thought it was her riding that hadn't been right.

I LOOKED AT MY WATCH. There were twenty minutes before I needed to be back here in the commentary booth for the next race, so I skipped down the five flights of stairs to ground level and made my way around behind the grandstand to the weighing room.

I put my head through the open doorway of the racetrack broadcast center, a small room just off the main weighing room that was half filled with a bank of electronic equipment all down one wall.

"Afternoon, Jack," I said to the back of a man standing there.

"Hi, Mark," said the man, turning around and rubbing his hands on a green sweater that appeared to have more holes in it than wool. "Everything all right?"

"Fine," I replied.

Jack Laver was the technician for the on-course broadcasting service that relayed the closed-circuit pictures to the many television sets throughout the racetrack, including the monitor in the commentary booth. His dress sense might have been suspect, but he was an absolute wizard with electronics.

"Fancy a cuppa?" he asked.

"Love one," I said, and he disappeared into an alcove, reemerging with two white plastic mugs of steaming brown liquid.

"Sugar?"

"No thanks," I said, taking one of the beakers.

Weighing-room tea would never have won any prizes for its taste, but it was hot and wet, and both were good for my voice. A race caller with a sore throat, or—worse—laryngitis, was no good for anything. Peter Bromley, the legendary BBC race caller, always carried with him a bottle of his special balm—a secret homemade concoction containing honey and whisky. He would take a small swig before every race to lubricate the throat.

I was never as organized as that, but I did like to have a bottle of water always close at hand. And tea was a bonus.

"Jack, can you show me a replay of that last race? Just the last quarter mile will do."

"Sure," he said, moving toward the electronics. "Did you get something wrong?" he asked, glancing over his shoulder at me with a huge grin.

"Get stuffed," I said. "And, no, I didn't."

"You'd never admit it anyway. You bloody commentators, you're all the same."

"Perfect, you mean."

"Ha! Don't make me laugh."

He fiddled with some of the controls and the previous race appeared on one of the tiny screens on the front of his equipment.

"Just the last quarter mile, you say?"

"Yes, please."

He used a large ball-type mouse to fast-forward the race, the horses moving comically along the track at breakneck speed.

"There you are," said Jack, slowing the runners to a normal pace.

I leaned forward to get a closer look.

I hoped I was wrong. In fact, I wanted desperately to be wrong.

"Can you show me that again?" I asked Jack.

He used the ball to rewind the recording to the quarter-mile pole.

I watched it once more, and there was no mistake.

I had absolutely no doubt that Clare Shillingford, my twin sister, had just been in contravention of rules (B)58, (B)59, and (D)45 of the Rules of Racing, rules that state, amongst other things, that *a rider must ride a horse throughout the race in such a way that he or she can be seen to have made a genuine attempt to obtain from the horse timely, real, and substantial efforts to achieve the best possible placing.*

Put more simply, Clare had not won the race when she could have done. And, furthermore, I believed she had not won it on purpose.

THE NEXT HOUR passed in somewhat of a blur. Good commentating requires solid concentration to the extent that all other thoughts need to be excluded. No one actually complained about my race calling in the next two races, but I knew that I hadn't been at my best, and Derek made no further appreciative comments into my ears.

I made another trip down to the weighing room between the third and fourth races. Clare had a ride in the fourth, and I wanted to have a quick word with her, but it was nothing to do with my unease over her riding Bangkok Flyer. We had a long-standing arrangement to have dinner together that night, and I wanted to confirm the plans.

"Hi, Clare," I called out to her as she exited the weighing room in a set of bright yellow silks with blue stars across her front and back. "Are you still on for tonight? I've booked a table at Haxted Mill for eight o'clock."

"Great," she said, smiling up at me as I walked alongside her. "But I'm going to see Mom and Dad first, so I'll meet you there."

"Fine," I said.

I slowed to a halt and watched her walk away from me and through the small crowd into the parade ring.

I wondered whether I really knew her anymore.

We had arrived into this world by cesarean section just thirty seconds apart, she being born first, as she never failed to remind me.

Our childhoods had been totally intertwined, with us sharing first cots, then bedrooms, schools, and finally a rented apartment on the outskirts of Edenbridge in Kent when, aged nineteen, we had together summoned the courage to tell our overbearing father that we no longer wanted to live under his roof.

That had been twelve years ago, but our sharing of an apartment had lasted barely six months before she had moved out and gone north to Newmarket.

We had both wanted to be jockeys for as long as we could remember and had ridden imaginary races and stirring finishes, first on rocking horses and then on ponies in the paddocks behind our parents' home in Surrey.

Twins we might be, but we didn't have all the same genes.

While Clare remained short and slight, I became tall and broad.

She ate heartily and stayed annoyingly thin, while I had starved myself half to death but still grew heavier by the day. While we both became jockeys, we never rode against each other as we had done so often on our ponies. Hers became the life of a featherweight flat jock at racing's "headquarters" in Newmarket, while I rode precisely five times as an amateur over the jumps before my battle with my ever-increasing body mass put paid to that career path.

So, instead, I had rather pretentiously announced my desire to be a racehorse trainer and had moved briefly to Lambourn as an assistant to the assistant at one of the top steeplechase training stables. By this time I was twenty years old but, somehow, my body had still been growing at an age when everyone else's had stopped. When it decided that enough was enough, I stood at six feet two inches in my socks, with shoulders to match, and, in spite of severe undernourishment, I was too heavy even to ride out with the string.

Riding had been my passion, and I had soon discovered that driving a Land Rover up onto the Berkshire Downs each day to watch the horses at work was not what I'd had in mind as my future. I missed the adrenaline rush of riding a Thoroughbred racehorse at high speed, with the wind and rain stinging my face, and watching others do what I craved somehow made the agony all the worse.

Strange, then, that I had ended up as a race caller doing just that, but the adrenaline rush was back, in particular on big race days when my audience could be millions.

"Hello, Mark," a voice said behind me. "Are you rooted to that spot?"

I recognized the voice and turned around, smiling. "Hi, Harry," I said. "I was just thinking."

"Dangerous stuff, thinking."

As far as I could tell, Harry Jacobs was a man of leisure. Only twice over the years had I asked him what he did for a living and both times he'd replied in the same way: "Nothing, if I can manage it." He was too young to be of retirement age. I estimated him to be in his late fifties, but he would've hardly had time for any paid employment as he seemed to spend every day of his life satisfying his passion for racing.

I'd first met him when I'd been an eighteen-year-old budding amateur jockey and he had agreed to me riding one of his horses in my first-ever race. I hadn't expected it to be the beginning of a firm friendship, especially as I'd missed the start, never recovered my position, and finished tailed-off last. But Harry hadn't appeared to mind, and he had slapped me reassuringly on the back. We'd been firm "racetrack" friends ever since, although I'd no idea where he lived and, I suspect, he had no idea where I did either.

"Fancy a drink?" he asked.

"Harry, I would have loved to, but I'm commentating, and they're almost on their way out of the paddock. Some other time."

"You workers." He laughed. "No sense of priority."

I wondered again where his money came from. He had a sizable string of racehorses, both jumpers and flat, and there was no shortage of readies available for entertaining in private boxes around the country's racetracks.

I made it back into the commentary booth just in time to describe the horses for the fourth race as they emerged onto the course and made their way to the one-mile start.

"First going down is Jetstar, in the red jacket with the white crossbelts. Next is Superjumbo, in white with a red circle and black cap." I looked down at my notes and also at my folded copy of the *Racing Post* with its diagrams of the jockeys' silks. "Rogerly comes next, in the blue and white quarters and hooped cap, followed by Scusami, the favorite, in the yellow jacket with the light blue stars and cap." I watched Clare cantering Scusami down the course and wondered again what was going on in that head of hers underneath the light blue cap. "Lounge Lizard is next, in the green and white stripes, with Tournado—in the pink with dark green epaulettes and cap—completing the lineup for the John Holmes Construction Limited Stakes over a mile, the big race of the day here at Lingfield."

I clicked off my microphone.

Six runners over a mile on the round track. Easy-peasy.

I pushed a button on my control box and the latest betting odds for the race came up on my monitor.

"Scusami is still the favorite, and his price has shortened to five-to-four. Superjumbo is at threes, as is Rogerly. It's five-to-one for Tournado, sixes Lounge Lizard, with Jetstar the rank outsider at twenty-five-to-one."

I turned off my mike and switched the monitor to show the horses as they circled at the start.

For a race with a very large field, like the Grand National, I would have spent some time the previous evening studying the colors, but mostly I learned them in the last few minutes before the off. If I tried absorbing six or seven races' worth all together, I would simply get them confused in my head.

So I learned them race by race and probably couldn't describe them ten minutes after each had finished. I started each race with a clear mind, and describing the silks as the horses cantered to the start was as much part of my learning routine as it was for the benefit of the racegoers in the grandstands. Now I watched the horses circle on the monitor and put my finger on the image of each animal in turn while saying its name out loud. With more runners I might have gone to see them in the parade ring to give me more time, but with six . . . piece of cake.

"Going behind the gate," I told the crowd. "Scusami is still the favorite at five-to-four, Rogerly now clear second at three-to-one, with Superjumbo at seven-to-two; five-to-one, bar those."

I flicked the monitor back to the horses and went on, putting my finger on their images and saying aloud each horse's name.

"Now loading," I said.

Derek spoke into my ear. *"Mark, coming to you in five seconds. Four. Three. Two . . ."* He counted down to zero while I described the horses as they were being loaded into the starting gate. As he reached zero, I paused fractionally so that I wasn't actually speaking as the satellite viewers came online.

"Just two to go now," I said. I briefly flicked back to the odds on my monitor. "Scusami is still favorite but has drifted slightly to six-to-four, with Rogerly still at threes. Just Superjumbo now still to be loaded."

I took a small sip of water from my bottle.

"Right, they're all in. Ready. They're off!"

Easy-peasy indeed. Even my grandmother could have called this race.

Scusami jumped out of the gate first and, as an established front-runner, he never relinquished the position. He was only briefly challenged in the home stretch by Superjumbo, but when Clare asked him for a response it was instant and dramatic. She raised her whip only once, riding the horse out mostly with hands and heels, to a comfortable three-length victory, with the others trailing past the winning post in line astern.

"I'll make you a copy of that one too," said Derek into my ears. *"What a great horse. Must be a good bet for the Guineas."*

"The opposition may have made him look better than he really is," I replied. But I did agree with Derek. Perhaps I'd make a small investment in the ante-post market. The 2,000 Guineas was not until May, and a lot could happen in the next eight months.

Indeed, much would happen in the next eight hours.

LINGFIELD WAS my local course, and I was home by half past six, even though the last race didn't start until five twenty-five. And I had remembered to collect the DVD from Derek with the two recordings on it.

I sat on my sofa and played them back over and over.

The difference between a moderate jockey and a great one is all about weight management and timing. All jockeys stand in their stirrup irons and lean forward, placing their weight over the horse's shoulders, and all jockeys move their weight back and forth slightly with the horse's action, but the greats are those who use this movement to bring the most out of their mounts. They dictate to, rather than just follow, the horse beneath them.

Riding a finish with "hands and heels" has far more to do with the positioning of weight than anything actually done to the horse with the hands or the heels. Most jockeys, especially those on the flat, ride far too short to be able to give the animal a decent kick with their heels anyway, and the hands on the reins move back and forth with the horse's head.

I watched again the recording of Clare riding Scusami to win that afternoon's fourth race. As Superjumbo came to challenge, Clare gave her mount a single smack with her whip down its flank, then she rode out a classic finish, lowering her back and pushing her hands back and forth along the horse's neck and moving her weight rhythmically to encourage it to lengthen its stride, which it duly did to win easily.

I compared that with her riding of Bangkok Flyer in the first when she was beaten by a neck by Sudoku.

In the final eighth of a mile she appeared to give the horse three heavy backhanded smacks with the whip, but the head-on camera showed that these strikes were, in fact, "air shots," or superficial hits at best, with her hand slowing dramatically before the whip made any contact with the flesh. As on Scusami, she had lowered her back, and there had also been plenty of elbow motion, but little of this had actually transmitted to her hands, the elbows going up and down rather than back and forth.

But the most telling thing was what had caused me to question her riding in the first place. Clare's body movement had been all wrong. Instead of encouraging the horse to lengthen its stride as she had done on Scusami, her actions had had the opposite effect. It was like in a car engine: if the combustion in the cylinder occurred when the piston was moving up and not down, the effect would be to slow the engine rather than to speed it up.

So it had been with Clare's riding, and hence Bangkok Flyer had been easily caught and passed by Sudoku.

But she had been very clever. It was a real art to make it appear that she was riding out a finish for all she was worth while actually doing the opposite.

Indeed, the only reason I had been suspicious was because of a game we had loved to play when riding our ponies as kids.

The "Race Fixing Game," we had called it—pulling up our ponies to a halt while looking like we were riding a tight finish. We had practiced for days and days so that even our aged great-uncle couldn't tell what we were doing, and he'd been a regular steward for decades at racetracks all over the country.

There had been no inquiry, so the Lingfield stewards obviously hadn't spotted it. And the racing press clearly hadn't noticed anything either, as there had been no difficult questions asked of me in the press room when I'd visited there after the fifth race.

But I could see only too clearly that Clare had definitely been playing the Race Fixing Game on Bangkok Flyer.

2

I was at Haxted Mill on time, at eight, and I chose a quiet corner table inside the restaurant, although they were still serving dinner on the terrace alongside the River Eden. The day may have been unseasonably warm for September, but the temperature was dropping fast with the setting sun.

Clare arrived at ten past in faded blue jeans and a pink polo shirt.

"Sorry I'm late, Marky," she said, sitting down opposite me.

"No problem. What would you like to drink?"

"Fizzy water."

"You can have a bed for the night if you want to drink."

"No, thanks," she replied. "I have to get back. I'm riding work in the morning, then racing."

"Newmarket?" I asked.

She nodded. "I've got three rides including one in the Cesarewitch Trial."

"I'll be at Newbury so I'll watch you on the television."

A waitress arrived with the menus, and I ordered a large bottle of sparkling mineral water.

"Don't let me stop you from having something stronger," Clare said.

"You won't. I'll have some wine with my dinner."

We perused the menus in silence for a while.

"How are Mom and Dad?" I asked.

"Oh, god-awful as always. They're getting so old."

The waitress returned with the water and poured two glasses.

"Are you ready to order?" she asked.

"Just the haddock for me," Clare said. "And without the mashed potato."

"No appetizer?" I asked.

"No, thanks. I'm riding at one hundred and ten pounds tomorrow."

"My," I said. "That is light."

"Too bloody light."

"I'll have the steak," I said to the patient waitress. "Medium rare, but no fries." I could hardly eat fries with Clare watching enviously. "And a glass of the red Bordeaux, please."

The waitress took our menus and left us.

"I found it really depressing going home," Clare said.

"Why?"

"Dad's lost all his sparkle, and Mom's not much better. I swear Dad gets more grumpy every day."

"But, as you said, they're getting old. Dad will be seventy-eight next month, and Mom's only a couple of years behind him."

Both our parents had been in their mid-forties when we had unexpectedly come along. We had three much older siblings.

"Getting old's a real bugger," Clare said. "I've decided I'm never getting old."

"It's better than the alternative."

"Is it?" Clare replied. "I can't imagine a time when I couldn't ride anymore. I wouldn't want to go on living."

"Willie Shoemaker was nearly sixty when he stopped riding."

"Yeah, I know," she said. "And he was fifty-four when he won the Kentucky Derby for the fourth time. I looked it up."

My, I thought, she's really worried about retirement and she's only thirty-one. In my experience, when jockeys started thinking about it, they usually retired pretty quickly. Lots of them would say they would in five years and then stop in about five months, some in five weeks or even less.

The waitress brought me my glass of wine and offered us bread, which we both declined.

"And the house is looking old too," Clare said.

"Well, it would, wouldn't it?" I said. According to the datestone on one of the gables, it had been built in 1607.

"You know what I mean," she said. "It needs some TLC."

"A lick of paint on the windows," I agreed, nodding.

"But Dad's a bit too old to do that himself. He may be quite fit, but I don't think ladders are a good idea anymore, not at his age."

"I think they should move," she said decisively. "Into somewhere smaller, or into an old folks home. I told them so."

"I bet that didn't go down too well."

"No," she agreed. "Dad was angry—as usual. But they have to be practical. That house is too big. I think they should go into a home now while they still can."

"Don't be daft," I said. "They don't need to yet. And where would they put all their stuff?"

"What worries me is what the one will do when the other dies. That place is far too big for both of them, let alone just one. The one left will have to move, then."

"I hope that'll be years away. Anyway, we'll cross that bridge when we come to it."

"That's typical of you," Clare said, pointing her slender left forefinger at my chest. "Always burying your head in the sand and doing nothing."

"That's not fair," I said.

"Yes, it is," she said defiantly. "You always put things off. That's why you still live in that dreadful rented apartment in Edenbridge."

"You liked it, once," I whined.

"I did when I was nineteen, but life moves on. You should have bought yourself a house years ago. You must be earning enough by now."

She was right. She usually was.

Our meals arrived, and we ate for a while in silence.

"How's your love life?" Clare asked finally.

"None of your business," I replied, laughing. "How's yours?"

"Absolutely wonderful. I have a new man. Three months now. What a lover!" She grinned and then laughed. He clearly made her happy.

"Who is it?" I asked, leaning forward.

"Now, that's none of *your* business," she said.

"Come on, Clare. Who is it?"

"I'm not saying," she said seriously, drawing a finger across her mouth as if zipping it shut. She opened it, however, to pop in a bite of her haddock. "Are you still seeing Sarah?"

"Yes," I said.

She looked down at her plate and shook her head.

"And what's that meant to mean?" I asked.

"Mark, it's high time you had a proper girlfriend."

"I do."

"Sarah is not a proper girlfriend. She's someone else's wife."

"She's working on it," I said defensively.

"She's been working on it for five years. When are you going to realize she won't ever leave Mitchell? She can't afford to."

"Give her time."

"God, Mark, you're so weak. For once, do something about it. Tell her it's now or never and you're fed up waiting. You're wasting your life."

"You should talk," I said. "Your love life has hardly been a Hallmark Romance." Clare had dated a string of what my father had rather generously called "unsuitable young men," and not all of them had been that young either. "Which misfit is it you're seeing now anyway?"

"I told you, that's none of your bloody business," she replied curtly, and without the humor that had been there earlier. "But at least I'm not living a lie."

"Aren't you?" I said.

"And what is that meant to mean?" she asked belligerently.

"Oh, nothing."

We ate again in silence.

Why did we always seem to fight these days? When we were kids, we had been so close that we didn't even need to speak to know what the other was thinking. But recently our twin-intuition had waned and faded away, at least for me. I wondered if she could still read my mind. If so, she probably wouldn't like it.

The waitress reappeared to collect our plates.

"Dessert?" she asked.

"Just coffee," Clare said. "Black."

"Same for me, please."

The waitress went away, and we sat there awkwardly once more.

"Good win on Scusami," I said.

"Yes," Clare replied, keeping her eyes on the table.

"Do you think he'll win the Guineas?"

"I doubt it. That Peter Williams colt, Reading Glass, he'll take a lot of beating. But Scusi's good, and it would be nice to be the first lady jockey to win a Classic." She looked upward wistfully. "One year anyway."

"But you'll ride him?"

"Maybe," she said thoughtfully. "That'll be up to Geoff."
Scusami was trained by Geoffrey Grubb in Newmarket.

The coffee arrived.

"Shame about Bangkok Flyer," I said.

Clare sat in silence and looked down at her cup.

"Don't you think?" I prompted.

"I'd forgotten you were commentating."

"You don't deny it, then?" I asked.

More silence.

"Why, Clare?"

"It's complicated."

"How can it be complicated?" I asked incredulously.
"You fixed the bloody race."

"Don't be silly," she said, looking up quickly. "I didn't
fix it. I just didn't win it."

"Don't split hairs with me," I said sharply.

"Ooh! Look at you, getting on your high horse."

"Be serious."

"Why should I?"

"Because it's a serious matter," I said. "You could lose
your license, and your livelihood."

"Only if I get caught."

"I caught you."

"Yeah, but what are you going to do about it?"

I sat and watched her. I could tell that she already knew
the answer.

"Nothing. But someone else will be bound to notice if
you do it again."

"No one has done so far."

I looked at her in disbelief.

"Are you saying this wasn't the first time you've done this?"

She smiled at me. "Of course not."

"Clare!"

The couple at a table nearby looked over at us. I lowered my voice but not my anger.

"Are you telling me that you regularly don't win races you should?"

"I wouldn't say regularly," she said, "but I have."

"How often?"

She pursed her lips.

"Three or four times, maybe five."

"But why?"

"I told you, it's complicated."

I didn't know what to say. She was so matter-of-fact about it all. If the British Horseracing Authority knew she had "stopped" horses three, four, or five times, they probably would have taken away her license for good and banned her from all racetracks for life.

And she didn't seem bothered.

"Well, don't ever do it again," I said in my most domineering tone.

"And what will you do about it if I do?" She was mocking me.

"Clare, please. Don't do this. Don't you understand? I love you, and I don't want to see you destroy all that you've built up."

I glanced around to make sure no one was listening.

"Don't be so patronizing," Clare said.

I sat there, stunned.

"I've had to claw my way up in this business," she said with feeling, leaning across the table. "No one gives you an inch. Lady jockey—ha! Don't make me laugh. Half of those in racing think we're no bloody good and should leave it all to the men, while the other half are a bunch of dirty old men who fantasize about us wearing tight breeches with whips in our hands. I've had to bow and scrape to them all, and sweat blood, to get where I am today, and now at last it's me who's in control of them."

"Is that it, then?" I asked. "Is this all about control?"

"You bet. Control over the bloody trainers, and the owners."

Control, I thought, could be a powerful force. What was that old adage? *Power corrupts; absolute power corrupts absolutely.* Absolute power and unbridled control over others had led to the Nazis, and a world war was needed to wrest control from their fingers. Control over others was a dangerous concept.

"I thought I knew you," I said slowly, "but I don't."

"I've changed," she said, "and I've hardened. I've had to climb the slippery pole while others kicked me in the teeth. Success didn't just fall into *my* lap by chance."

We both knew what she meant.

I had been in the right place at the right time.

It was now eight years since that day at the Fontwell Park races when the paddock presenter for RacingTV had been taken seriously ill with a heart attack just before he was due to go on the air. The backup presenter, the much respected wife of an up-and-coming young trainer, turned out to be the main presenter's mistress, and she had insisted on going with him to the hospital in the ambulance.

I was only there as a guest to watch because I'd carelessly put my hand up at a charity auction to spend a day with the RacingTV team. But I found myself putting up my hand again and volunteering to stand in.

"Do you know the horses?" the agitated producer had demanded while pulling out clumps of his already thinning hair.

"Yes," I'd replied.

And I had. As my sister had so correctly pointed out, I tended to drift rather a lot, and I hadn't actually acquired a proper job since returning from my brief sojourn in Lambourn two years before. Rather, I'd decided to earn my living as a professional gambler and had consequently spent most of my time studying the form. I knew the horses very well.

"Only for the first race, then," the producer had said. "I've sent for a replacement, but he won't be here until two o'clock."

I had talked easily to the camera about each horse in the first race and had even tipped the winner. When the replacement had arrived, he'd just sat and watched me all afternoon as I'd tipped the winner in three other races as well.

"What are you doing tomorrow?" the producer had asked as they were packing up.

"Nothing," I'd replied honestly.

"We're at Wincanton. Fancy a job?"

Since that day, I had never looked back, spreading into

commentating again by accident when the race caller at Windsor had been held up by a big car crash on the local highway and I had been asked to stand in.

Nowadays I split my time three ways—commentating at the racetracks, paddock presenting for RacingTV, and also hosting the TV coverage on Channel 4, the terrestrial broadcaster of horseracing in Britain.

But Clare firmly believed that I still didn't have a "proper" job and that I would soon drift off into something else.

Maybe she was right.

"I much preferred the old you," I said to her.

"Oh God!" she said. "Don't start all that again. I live in a competitive world. I have a competitive job. I have to compete. Otherwise I'd be trampled on."

"Do you have to compete on everything?"

"What do you mean?" she asked.

"I just feel that whenever we have a conversation these days, it's a points-scoring exercise."

"Don't be ridiculous."

I wasn't going to argue with her. There was no sense in it. For whatever I might say, she would have a riposte. Losing was not an option for her, except, of course, when she clearly lost on purpose.

I paid the bill, and we went out together to the parking lot.

"Is there anything I can say that would stop you from doing it again?"

She turned to me. "Probably not."

"I might report you to the authorities."

"I don't think so."

"Don't bank on it," I said.

"Mark, don't be such a prat. You know perfectly well that you won't tell anyone. For a start, it would reflect badly on you. So just keep your eyes and mouth shut."

"I can hardly do that in my job."

"Then you'll have to turn a blind eye instead."

"Clare, seriously, if you do that once more when I'm commentating, I'll never speak to you again."

She opened the door of her silver Audi TT.

"Your loss, not mine."

She climbed into the sports car and slammed the door shut.

Again, I was stunned. Maybe it had been a careless thing to say, but I hadn't expected such a brusque answer.

What had happened to my lovely twin sister?

She gunned the engine, and spun the rear wheels on the gravel, as she shot off without a wave, without even a glance.

AS I ARRIVED back at my apartment, the phone in the hallway was ringing, and the caller ID on the handset showed me that it was Clare calling from her cell.

I wondered what else she had to say to hurt me some more. Maybe she had thought up another barbed comment to thrust into my heart.

I let the phone go on ringing.

Eventually the answering machine picked it up, and I

stood there in the dark listening for any message. There wasn't one. Clare had hung up.

My own cell phone started vibrating in my pocket, but I also let that go to voice mail.

I didn't want to talk to her. I was hurting enough already. Even if she was ringing to apologize, which I doubted, she could wait. It wouldn't do her any harm to feel guilty for a while.

I flicked on the light and looked at my watch. It was still only nine-twenty. Far from enjoying a leisurely dinner with my loving twin sister to mull over our news and catch up on family gossip, I was back home less than an hour and a half after leaving.

I felt wretched, and cheated.

I walked into my sitting room–cum–kitchen–cum–dining room–cum–office.

Perhaps Clare was right about my apartment. Maybe it was time to move on.

We had initially found the place through a student accommodations company, and, looking at it now, I had to admit that it certainly still had a "student" feel about it.

Once I had talked the landlord into redecorating, but that had been about eight years ago, and the cheap paint he had used had faded and cracked. I knew I should ask him to do it again, but I didn't relish all the upheaval that would be produced moving my stuff. Better to live with a few marks on the walls and a slowly yellowing ceiling.

I sat down at my table and opened my laptop computer. I logged on to the *Racing Post* website and looked through the cards for the following day's racing at Newbury, where I would be presenting for Channel 4.

As hard as I tried to concentrate on the horses, looking up their form and making notes, my mind kept drifting back to Clare and our conversation over dinner.

How could she be so stupid? And for what? Did I really believe she was stopping horses from winning just to play some weird game of control over trainers and owners? There had to be more to it than that. Surely there had to be some financial implications.

"It's complicated," she had said.

It sure was.

My phone rang again, and I went on ignoring it. I was sure it was Clare, but I was angry and upset and I wouldn't speak to her. It stopped ringing, and, as before, there was no message.

I forced myself back to the horses running at Newbury the following day and spent the next hour going through all eight races in detail. Only three of the eight were due to be shown live on Channel 4, but, as I still tried to supplement my income with some winnings, I was looking for horses that I believed showed especially good value in the prices currently offered on the Internet betting sites.

One particular horse, Raised Heartbeat, running in the third race, was quoted at decimal odds of 7.5; in other words, if I placed a bet of one hundred pounds, I would get seven hundred fifty pounds back altogether, including my hundred-pound stake. That was equivalent to fractional odds of thirteen-to-two. I felt sure that the horse would actually start at maybe six-to-one or even five-to-one. If I placed a bet now at the longer price and then "layed" the horse at shorter odds tomorrow, I would effectively have a bet to nothing. If it won, I would win a little, but if it lost I wouldn't lose anything.

It was a technique I had employed for some time with considerable success. But the system wasn't foolproof. The horse could drift in the market, making my bet seem rather undervalued. I could then still lay the horse to limit my exposure, but that would guarantee a financial loss whether the horse won the race or not.

However, due to my job, I watched the same horses run day after day, week after week, even year after year, and I knew them as well as anyone. Experience had proven that I was more often right than not about the way the odds would change.

I logged on to my account and placed my bet on Raised Heartbeat—a hundred-pound stake to make six-hundred-and-fifty profit.

If I was right and the price shortened to, say, five-to-one, I would then lay it. That is, I'd take a hundred-pound bet from someone else for them to win five hundred. Now, if the horse won, I would win six hundred fifty on my bet and pay out the five hundred on the bet from someone else, giving me a profit of a hundred fifty pounds. If the horse lost, then I would lose my hundred-pound stake, but I'd also keep the hundred from someone else, leaving me even. Whereas it wasn't quite win/win, at least it was win/not lose.

The phone rang once more. I looked at my watch. It was ten past eleven. I was tempted to answer it, but I was still smarting from earlier and I didn't want another row. I would speak to her in the morning when we had both cooled off a little.

I closed the lid of my computer and went along the corridor to bed.

The only significant change I had made when Clare had moved out to go to Newmarket was to transfer from the smaller bedroom into the larger one. Now I lay awake on the double bed in the darkness and thought back to those months we had spent here together.

Undoubtedly it had been the happiest time of my life. We had escaped the nightmare of living in a house where our father had become so prescriptive about what we could and couldn't do that he had refused permission for us to go out to a friend's New Year's Eve party in spite of the fact that we both were over eighteen. When we had defied him and gone anyway, we had found the house locked and bolted on our return. We had rung the bell and battered on the door, but he wouldn't let us in, so we had spent the night shivering in Clare's Mini and planned our getaway.

This apartment had seemed like a palace—somewhere we could leave the lights on without being shouted at, and where we didn't have to account for our every waking minute.

How I longed for a return to those halcyon days.

Perhaps I should call Clare after all.

I turned on the bedside lamp and looked at the clock.

It was a quarter to midnight. Was it too late to call? It was a good half hour since she had last tried me. Would she be asleep?

I tried her anyway, figuring that she could always turn her cell phone off if she didn't want to be disturbed.

It went straight to voice mail.

"Clare, it's Mark," I said. "I'm sorry this evening was such a disaster. Call me in the morning. Love you. Bye."

I hung up and then turned my phone off. I needed to sleep and didn't want her calling me again tonight.

I WOKE to the sound of someone hammering on my front door.

My bedside clock showed me that it was just past three o'clock in the morning.

The hammering went on.

I turned on the bedside light and collected my dressing gown from its hook on the back of my bedroom door.

"OK, OK, I'm coming," I shouted as I walked down the corridor.

Bloody Clare, I thought. Go home.

I opened the front door, but it wasn't Clare. Someone shone a flashlight right into my face so I couldn't see anything.

"Mr. Shillingford?" said a voice in an official tone. "Mr. Mark Shillingford?"

"Yes," I said, holding my hand up and trying to see past the light. "What is it?"

"Kent Police, sir," said the voice. "Constable Davis." He held out his warrant card.

My skin went cold. Personal calls from the police at this time of night were never good news.

"I'm sorry, sir, but I have some very bad news for you," the constable went on. "It's your sister, Miss Clare Shillingford." He paused. "She's dead."

3

D ead?" I said, my voice box seemingly detached from my body.

"Yes, sir," said PC Davis. "I'm afraid so."

"Where?" I asked in a croak.

I felt weak and swayed somewhat.

"Shall we come in, sir?" he said, stepping forward and supporting me by the elbow.

There were two of them, the other a female officer, and they guided me into my sitting room and down onto the sofa.

"Liz, get some sweet tea," the policeman said to his colleague.

I watched as she went over to the kitchenette and opened cupboards, looking for mugs.

"Top right," I said automatically.

Time seemed to stand still as the kettle boiled and a cup of hot tea was pressed into my hand.

"Drink it, sir," said the constable. "It will do you good."

I took a sip and winced. "I don't take sugar."

"You do tonight, sir. Drink it."

I drank some of the sweet liquid, but it didn't make me feel noticeably better.

"Where is she?" I asked.

"Sorry, sir," he said, "what do you mean?"

"Where is she?" I asked again. "I must go to her."

"All in good time, sir. We need to ask you some questions first."

I just looked at him.

"Are you, in fact, Miss Shillingford's next of kin?" the female officer asked.

"I don't know," I said. "Her parents—our parents—they're still alive. Does that make them the next of kin?"

"No husband?" she asked. "Or children?"

"No."

I drank some more of the tea.

"How did you find me?" I asked.

The two police officers looked at each other.

"We had your address, sir," said the man.

"How?" I asked again.

"It was amongst Miss Shillingford's possessions," he said.

"Where was she killed?" I asked.

"In central London. Park Lane."

I looked up at him. "How odd."

"Why odd, sir?"

"She wouldn't normally drive up Park Lane going from here to Newmarket."

"Was she here this evening?"

"Yes," I said. "Well, she was at Haxted Mill, down the road. We had dinner there together."

The policeman made a note in his notebook.

"But she didn't drink and drive, if that's what you're thinking. She only had fizzy water."

"What time did she leave?" he asked.

"About ten past nine," I said. I thought back to her spinning the wheels of her sports car as she left the parking lot. "I always said that bloody car would be the death of her."

"Oh no, sir," said the female officer. "It wasn't a car crash that killed her."

I stared at her.

"What, then?" I asked.

The police officers looked at each other once more.

"It appears that Miss Shillingford may have fallen from the balcony of a hotel."

I sat there with my mouth open.

"Where?" I said finally. "Which hotel?"

"The Hilton Hotel on Park Lane."

"But when?"

"At half past eleven."

Oh God! She had tried to call me twenty minutes before that.

"How are you sure it was her?" I asked in desperation. "It must be someone else."

"I am told, sir, that it is definitely Miss Clare Shillingford."

"But how can they know for sure?"

"I don't know that, sir. But I am told it's one hundred percent certain. Maybe there were witnesses."

"But it was an accident, right?" I asked forlornly.

"The incident is still under investigation. It will be up to the coroner to determine the cause of death."

There was something in the way he said it that gave me no comfort.

"Are you implying it wasn't an accident?"

"As I said, sir, that will be a matter for the coroner."

"But what was she doing at a hotel anyway?" I asked. "She said she had to go straight home to Newmarket."

"I can't say, sir," the policeman replied. "The investigating officer will no doubt look into that."

I sat on my sofa not knowing what to think or what to do. How could Clare be dead? It didn't seem real. She had been so alive just a few hours ago. I found I couldn't even cry. There were too many unanswered questions in my head.

"Now, sir, do you have the address for Miss Shillingford's parents? As next of kin, they need to be informed. There will also be a need for an official identification."

Oh God, I thought. That would kill my mother.

"How exactly did you have my address?" I asked.

"Apparently it was written on an envelope found in Miss Shillingford's hotel room."

"What was in the envelope?" I asked, perhaps not wanting to know the answer.

"I can't say, sir."

"Can't or won't?" I asked.

"Can't," he said. "I was not at the scene and was simply informed about the presence of your address on the envelope. My colleague and I are not from the Metropolitan Police, we're from Kent headquarters at Maidstone. Now, where do your parents live?"

"Oxted," I said.

"Surrey," the policeman said to his colleague with obvious displeasure. "We'll have to contact Guildford."

"It's only five miles away."

"Still outside our patch," said Constable Davis. "What address in Oxted?"

"I'll go and tell them," I said.

"Fine, sir. But I will still need their address as they will have to be officially informed. There are procedures to follow."

"Yes, of course." I gave him the address, and he wrote it in his notebook as well as relaying it over his personal radio. "Tell them to give me time to be there first."

He spoke again into the radio, but I couldn't hear the reply.

"The Surrey Police will be in no hurry, sir," he said. "They will probably visit your parents later in the morning."

"Thank you," I said. I bet the Surrey Police would be delighted not to have to perform what must be a dreadful duty. I certainly didn't relish the task. "I'll go and see them right away. I'd also better call my two brothers and my other sister."

"I would recommend that, sir. The incident is already being reported on the BBC radio news, and it will only be a matter of time before Miss Shillingford's name is mentioned, her being something of a celebrity and all."

"You've heard of her, then?" I was pleased.

"Oh yes, sir. I follow the horses a bit. Like to have a flutter now and again. And I've watched you on the telly lots of times. I saw you last Saturday on Channel 4."

Last Saturday suddenly seemed like a long time ago.

"Will you be all right now, sir? We can stay awhile longer if you'd like."

"No, thank you. I'll be fine. I'll get dressed and drive over to Oxted."

IT WAS the worst journey of my life. Afterward I could hardly remember a single yard of the five miles from my apartment to my parents' house.

Lots of questions struggled to get a hearing in my consciousness.

What was she doing in a Park Lane hotel in the first place when she'd told me she was going straight home to Newmarket? Had our row at Haxted Mill somehow caused her to change her plans? Had she gone to the hotel to meet someone? How could she have fallen from a balcony? Why? Why? Why?

I couldn't get out of my head the image of her driving off from dinner without even a glance at me. I didn't know whether to be angry or sad.

And then there were the phone calls I had ignored.

Had she been calling me for help?

I should have answered them, I thought. What had I been doing? She was my sister, for goodness' sake, my darling twin sister. And she had needed me.

The tears started, and I had to pull over as I couldn't

see the road. I sat in the driver's seat of my trusty old Ford and sobbed.

How could she be dead? She had been more full of life than anyone I had ever met. It must be a mistake.

I HAD SAT there for a full fifteen minutes before I had been able to continue, but it was still just before four when I pulled my Ford through the gates and down the sweeping driveway in front of the familiar Jacobean pile on the southern edge of Oxted.

My parents had moved here when Clare and I had been babies, my mother inheriting the place from her parents, but they had never had the money to decorate and furnish the house in the manner that its architectural grandeur demanded.

Dad had been a banker before his retirement. At least that is what he regularly told everyone. In fact, he had spent his working life in the accounts department of a City of London investment bank, doing the paperwork for all the deals that other people had made.

I sat now in my car and looked up at the imposing façade lit only by the glow from the streetlights on the road at the far end of the drive. I suppose I must have had some happy times here when I'd been a young boy, but all I could remember were the fights of my teenage years.

By then, Dad had been in his late fifties, but he had somehow seemed much older. In spite of him having been only twenty-five at the start of the Swinging Sixties, pop music had passed him by, and he had regularly shouted at

Clare and me for playing it at anything above a whisper, even in our bedrooms with the doors closed.

The thought of having any of our school friends around for a bit of a party was completely out of the question. For a start, he'd say, they would then know what we had in the house and would send burglars around when we were away. The fact that we had nothing much in the place that anyone would want to steal anyway seemed to have been beside the point.

By the time Clare and I had moved out to the apartment in Edenbridge, which we had done in secret one day when Dad had been in London for a reunion lunch at his bank, I had come to hate this house so much that I'd not returned to it for the next five years.

But I suppose as time moves on and we grow older, family ties become more important. Or maybe it's that our unhappy memories fade. Either way, I was now a regular visitor here, helping in the battle against dry rot and damp inside and organizing a man to assist with the garden outside.

Not that Dad and I had become close. He still liked to boss me around. The difference now was that I took no notice of him and went home when I could stand it no longer. Nowadays instead of rows, we simply had long periods of noncommunication. Clare had been right when she had said I'd rather put my head in the sand than do something more constructive. I had found it to be the recipe for a quieter life.

Well, now I *had* to do something, although I would

have happily found some sand-hole in which to hide my head.

I turned on *BBC Radio 5 Live* and listened to the four o'clock news bulletin. Clare was the lead story, but they didn't mention her by name. "Police are investigating how a thirty-one-year-old woman fell to her death from the balcony of a central London hotel late last evening."

I clicked off the radio and got out of the car.

I decided that standing on the step and battering on the great oak front door, as I had done with Clare all those years ago, was not the right approach. Knowing my father, he would probably think I was a burglar, trying to get in, and call the police.

Instead, I used my cell to call their number.

I could hear the phone ringing in the hallway and, presently, my father answered it in the bedroom.

"Yes," he said, sounding very sleepy.

"Dad," I said, "it's Mark. I'm outside. Could you come down and let me in?"

"What do you want?" he asked, clearly irritated.

I could hear my mother in the background, asking who it was.

"Dad, just come down and open the front door."

"It's Mark." I heard him telling my mother. "He's outside and he wants to get in."

I didn't hear her reply, but he came back on the line. "OK," he said. "I'm coming down." He had that tone which implied he was doing me a huge favor.

If only he knew.

How, I thought, am I going to tell him that Clare is dead?

I USED THE POLICEMAN'S TRICK and made them both hot sweet tea.

My mother sat in an armchair and wept, rocking back and forth with a tissue pressed to her nose, while my father expressed any grief he might have with anger, most of it directed toward me as if abusing the messenger could somehow change the message.

"How did this happen?" he demanded, standing full square in the middle of their drawing room.

"I don't know," I said.

"Well, you bloody well should know," he bellowed. "Why didn't you ask the police?"

"I did," I said. "But they couldn't say."

"Nonsense!" he shouted at me. "You just didn't ask them in the right way."

"Would it make any difference?" I shouted back. "Knowing exactly what happened won't bring her back."

My mother uttered a whimper, and I went over to comfort her as her stupid fool of a husband marched around the room, bunching, then relaxing, his fists. I suppose grief affects people in different ways. He clearly wanted to lash out at something—to have someone to blame, someone to hit.

In truth, part of me felt the same way.

"We had better call James, Stephen, and Angela," I said. "Before they hear it on the radio."

"You do it," my father instructed.

Oh thanks, I thought.

"I'll ask them all if they'd like to come here. Is that OK?"

"Yes," my mother said between sobs.

I thought my father was about to say something, but he obviously had second thoughts and kept quiet, just nodding.

I went into his study and used the phone on his big oak desk in the bay window to pass on the bad news to our siblings, waking each one in turn.

"Oh God, Mark," said James, my elder brother, "I'm so sorry."

He made it sound like it was more of a loss for me than for him, which, I suppose, was true. Losing one's twin, I was discovering, was like losing half of oneself.

They all agreed to come to Oxted, although in Stephen's case it would take all day to get here as he and his wife, Tracy, were on holiday near Saint-Tropez in the south of France.

"Just come as soon as you can. We all need to be together."

I wondered why I had said that to him. Did we all need to be together? We had hardly been together in the past. Other than Clare, Stephen was the youngest of my siblings, but he was still some sixteen years older than me. I had no memory of him living at home because he had also flown the nest as soon as he'd been able, just as we all had.

Once or twice over the years we had gathered together for Christmas, but they had never been great social successes, mostly descending into bitterness and recrimination rather than uplifting us all into happiness and goodwill.

The last time all five of the Shillingford children had been under the same roof had been at a London hotel where we had gathered two years ago to commemorate my parents' golden wedding anniversary.

Now we would never all be together again.

I sat at my father's desk and was again close to tears. But I made one final telephone call, to Lisa, the producer of *The Morning Line*, the Saturday racing program on Channel 4. I knew she wouldn't still be in bed. She would already be at Newmarket racetrack getting ready for the live broadcast that started just before eight o'clock.

She answered on the second ring. "Lisa here," she said.

"It's Mark," I said.

"My, you're up early," she said. "And you're not even on the show. Aren't you at Newbury today?"

"That's partly why I'm calling," I said. "Can you tell Neville I won't be able to make it to Newbury today?"

"You tell him," she said with some humor in her voice.

"Lisa," I said. "My sister's been killed."

"Not Clare?" she asked.

"Yes," I said. "Have you heard the radio news this morning?"

"Yes," she said slowly.

"Clare was the woman who fell from the hotel balcony."

"Oh my God!" She paused. "Can we use it?"

Always the journalist.

"Yes," I said. Why else had I rung her?

"Any details?"

"No, nothing other than you'd know from the news. And be kind."

"Of course," she said. "Mark, I'm so sorry. And leave Neville to me."

"Thank you, I will. And Lisa, no one else knows."

"Right," she said. "Thanks."

A POLICEMAN arrived at the house at eight o'clock, but he wasn't from the Surrey constabulary; he was from the Met.

"Mr. Shillingford?" he asked when I opened the door.

"Yes," I said.

"Detective Sergeant Sharp," he said, holding out his ID card.

"Detective?" I said.

"Every unexplained death is investigated by a detective. Can I come in?"

I took him through into the drawing room where my mother was still sitting in the same armchair, wearing her dressing gown. My father had been upstairs to dress, and we had also been joined by Angela, my elder sister, and her husband, Nicholas, who had arrived from their home in Hertfordshire. I made the introductions, and the sergeant sat down facing us.

"I am very sorry for your loss," he said to the five expectant faces. "Can any of you suggest why Miss Shillingford would take her own life?"

4

Suicide?" my father said loudly. "But that can't be so."

"I'm afraid it appears to be," said the detective sergeant. He opened his briefcase and removed a clear plastic folder containing a single sheet of paper. "This was found in Miss Shillingford's room at the hotel."

He held out the folder and, as I was nearest, I took it, which was appropriate because the sheet of paper inside was a brief, handwritten letter addressed to me on Hilton Hotel–headed notepaper.

Dear Marky,

Thank you for dinner tonight. I am sorry it was such a disaster. You are right—you're always right. I don't

know what has been happening to me these last
few months. Please don't think badly of me.
　　I am so sorry

There was no signature, but I recognized the handwriting, and only Clare had called me Marky. I couldn't stop the tears running in streams down my cheeks. I passed it to Angela, who also sobbed.

"What was it you were right about?" the detective sergeant asked.

"Just something about her riding at Lingfield yesterday," I replied, wiping my face with my fingers.

Suddenly it didn't seem to be that important.

"Was there anything she said at dinner that might have indicated she was troubled?"

"No," I said. "Quite the reverse. She was looking forward to riding today at Newmarket. And she was hopeful of being the first lady jockey to win a Classic next May. I can't believe she would kill herself."

"She wouldn't," my father said decisively from over by the window. "Clare was here only yesterday, and she was talking about coming back to see us in two weeks. Why would she do that if she was contemplating suicide? It's all nonsense."

"And," I said, "she hardly ate anything at dinner last night because she was due to be riding very light today. Why would she bother?"

The phone vibrated in my pocket. In my business, ringing phones on the air were severely frowned upon, and I had been caught out too often in the past. Nowadays I permanently left mine on "vibrate only."

It was Sarah, the lady Clare had called my non-proper girlfriend.

"Excuse me a moment," I said, walking out into the hallway.

I answered the phone. "Hello."

"Mark, my darling, I've been watching *The Morning Line*. I can't believe it. Oh my love, I'm so sorry." She was crying.

"Thank you for calling," I said inadequately. "I'm at my parents' house, and it's a bit bloody here at the moment."

"I don't suppose you'll be at Newbury, then?"

"No," I said. "Sorry."

"OK. I'll call you later," Sarah said.

"Right. Bye, now."

She disconnected, and I stood for a moment in the hallway, thinking. What was it that Clare had said? *When are you going to realize she won't ever leave Mitchell? She can't afford to.*

Mitchell was her husband—Mitchell Stacey—her much older husband. He was one of the country's leading steeplechase trainers, with over eighty top horses in his yard in the village of East Ilsley, north of Newbury.

It had been five years now since that Friday night at Doncaster when Sarah and I had carelessly ended up in bed, professing undying love for each other.

We had both been there for the two-day Christmas National Hunt Meeting. I had been commentating at the course, and Mitchell had had runners on both days. He and Sarah had stayed over in the same hotel as me, where we had all dined together in a large party of racing folk. Mitchell and the others had gone straight to bed after dinner, as was the norm, in my experience, with racehorse trainers, while Sarah and I had shared, first, another bottle of red wine, then a nightcap liqueur or two, followed by a passionate sexual encounter in my bedroom.

Since then we had survived on snatched hours here and there, sometimes even a night or two together whenever Mitchell was away at the sales, and I had run up huge telephone bills calling her cell.

We had been due to see each other at the Newbury races this afternoon and then for a while afterward at a carefully selected, discreet motel near Hungerford, one more fleeting assignation in our ongoing dangerous liaison.

Another of Clare's pearls of wisdom came floating into my mind—*Tell her it's now or never and you're fed up waiting. You're wasting your life.*

Was I?

I was thirty-one, and Sarah was four years my senior. Mitchell, however, was now in his sixties, having been married twice before. How he had wooed and won the then-twenty-one-year-old Sarah remained a mystery to me, but perhaps it was something to do with his immense wealth, most of which he had inherited as a baby from his grandfather, an eccentric oil magnate.

They didn't have any children of their own—Sarah told me that Mitchell had had a vasectomy before they met— but there were three boys from his previous marriages, and Sarah was being the dutiful stepmother. The youngest was about to finish school, and Sarah told me that then she would leave Mitchell and come and live with me. But, in truth, it was the latest in a long list of prospective departure dates, and maybe Clare had been right: Sarah never would leave Mitchell. She couldn't afford to.

But did I care? Was I, in fact, not content with how things were? The old joke—*I used to be indecisive, but now I'm not so sure*—seemed to have been written for me. As things stood, sex was fairly frequent and exciting, but I also quite enjoyed the freedom of living on my own.

However, there was also the worry of being found out. Mitchell Stacey was a hugely influential character in racing, and I wasn't at all sure my job would be safe if he discovered that I'd been seducing his wife behind his back. But would it be any better if we came clean and Sarah left him for me? Probably not. The best thing, I decided, was simply to carry on as before and not get caught.

Nicholas, my brother-in-law, came out of the drawing room, looking for me. "This policeman needs to ask you some more questions."

"Sorry. I'm coming."

DETECTIVE SERGEANT SHARP remained for another two hours, asking mundane questions and annoying us all. My brother James, the eldest of the Shillingford offspring, arrived in the middle with his scatterbrained wife, Helen, so much of the ground had to be covered again.

Finally, the policeman seemed content with the answers he had, not that any of us were able to give him any reason why Clare should have thrown herself to her death from the balcony of a hotel room on the fifteenth floor.

"Are you sure that's a suicide note?" I'd asked him as he'd shown it to James. "It doesn't say anything about dying."

He'd said nothing, but his expression had shown that he thought I was grasping at straws. Maybe I was.

"I'm afraid there will need to be a formal identification of the body," he said in the hallway.

To his credit, Nicholas volunteered immediately.

"It would be better to be a blood relative," said the detective, "rather than an in-law."

"Can't you do it by DNA?" I asked.

"We can, sir, yes. But that takes time."

And money, I thought.

"The coroner will likely want to open an inquest first thing on Monday, and he will want evidence of identification at that point."

"The policeman who came last night told me that you were one hundred percent certain it was Clare. He said there were witnesses. Who were they?"

The detective somehow seemed reluctant to tell me.

"Who were they?" I pressed.

"There had been a charity gala dinner in the ballroom of the Hilton Hotel. Most of the guests had left before Miss Shillingford fell." He paused. "But there were a few that had stayed on after the dinner for a drink in the bar. She narrowly missed landing on this group as they were waiting for a taxi."

Oh God, I thought.

"The gala dinner," he went on, "had been in aid of the Injured Jockeys Fund."

Of course. I remembered getting an invitation to buy tickets for the event, but, as usual, I had left it so late before deciding that all the spaces had already gone.

"And the group had included a Mr. Reg Nicholl, an ex–police superintendent who, I understand, is now the head of the racing security services. It was he who confirmed the identity of Miss Shillingford."

"I still can't understand what she was doing there in the first place," I said, "let alone having booked a room. I feel this is just a huge mistake and that Clare is at home, safe, in Newmarket."

"I'm afraid it's not a mistake, sir. It would appear that your sister turned up at the hotel without having made a reservation. There had been a cancellation, and Miss Shillingford checked in using her credit card at . . ."—he consulted his notebook—". . . ten-twenty p.m."

An hour and ten minutes after leaving me. She must have gone almost straight from Haxted Mill to the hotel. But why?

In the end it was decided that James would go with Detective Sergeant Sharp to perform the gruesome task of making a formal identification, and Nicholas would go with him for support.

I couldn't decide whether I should go as well. Part of me really wanted to in order to see Clare for one last time, but I was frightened. Fifteen floors was a long way down, and I didn't like to think about what the impact might have done to her. But, equally, I was distressed by my memory of the last time I had seen her alive, staring straight ahead in anger as she drove away from the restaurant.

THE AFTERNOON dragged by, with my mother taking herself off to bed, while my father wore a groove in the carpet, endlessly pacing up and down the drawing room. Helen and Angela, meanwhile, adjourned to the kitchen to find us all something to eat, and I settled down in the small sitting room on my own to watch the racing on Channel 4 from Newmarket and Newbury.

The program started with a short tribute to Clare, showing video clips of her winning many races on a variety of horses. The flags at Newmarket racetrack were flying at half-mast, and there was even a minute's silence before the first race, with some racegoers clearly in tears.

I watched the races, but less than half my mind was on the action. I kept coming back to the same two questions. Why had Clare gone to a hotel in central London? And why had she killed herself?

So distracted was I that I only remembered my hundred-pound bet on Raised Heartbeat when the horse was being loaded into the starting gate at Newbury. As I had predicted last evening, his price had shortened from thirteen-to-two to five-to-one, but with my computer still at my apartment it was too late now to lay the horse on the Internet exchanges. My money would just have to take its chances on the nose.

The horses broke from the gate in an even line, and I found myself commentating on the race inside my head.

However, as was always the case, my eye was drawn unintentionally toward the horse I had backed. It was why I almost never had a bet in those races on which I was commentating; it was simply too distracting.

Raised Heartbeat lived up to his name, lifting my own pulse a notch or two, as he fought out a tight finish with the favorite, going down to defeat only in the final stride.

My hundred pounds was lost, but it was a minor inconvenience compared to the greater loss of my twin sister.

I sat there alone for quite a while and wept.

I cried in grief, but also I cried in frustration. Death was so final, so permanent. There was no "undo" button like there was on my computer.

Why oh why hadn't I answered the phone when Clare had called me? Perhaps I could have prevented this disaster.

STEPHEN AND TRACY arrived from Saint-Tropez at four o'clock, just as James and Nicholas returned from the morgue, looking drawn and shell-shocked.

I didn't need to ask how it had been, and I was suddenly thankful that I'd decided not to go with them.

James just nodded at me before disappearing into the cloakroom. I wondered if he was going to be sick.

"Bloody awful," said Nicholas. "Literally, bloody awful. But it was her. No mistake."

I hadn't really expected there to be a mistake, but the confirmation of what we already knew was, nevertheless, another cause of distress, especially for my mother, who had come down to greet the new arrivals.

We sat once more in the drawing room, this time for some tea, except that my father refused to sit down, again pacing back and forth near the French windows.

None of us could imagine why Clare would have taken her own life. We speculated about what might have been troubling her but came up short providing any answers.

"I absolutely refuse to believe she committed suicide," said my father resolutely. "It had to have been an accident."

"Or murder," said Stephen.

Everyone looked at him. Even my father ceased his pacing.

"Don't be ridiculous," he said. "Why on earth would anyone want to kill our Clare? Everyone loved her."

But who would think that anyone would have wanted to kill John Lennon? People had loved him too.

"What about the note?" said scatterbrained Helen. "It certainly looked like a suicide note to me."

I watched as my father, over her head, gave Helen a contemptuous stare. He had never been slow in expressing his disapproval of James's choice of wife, and she clearly was not endearing herself to him right now.

"But why would she kill herself?" Angela wailed, putting into words once more what we were all asking ourselves.

"Maybe because living in this family is not always easy," Helen said somewhat tactlessly.

I thought my father was going to explode behind her.

"Shut up, you silly woman," he bellowed from somewhere close to her ear.

Helen instantly burst into tears and was comforted by James, who tried to defend his wife.

"It's true," he said. "Helen is right. We are all so competitive."

Yes, I suppose we were.

It was how we had been brought up. *Top of the class, top of the class, you must strive to be top of the class.* It had been drummed into us as children. *School, university, first-class degree, job in the City.* It had been like a mantra for our father.

He had been appalled and outraged when both Clare and I had announced that we had no wish to follow our older siblings to Oxford or Cambridge, or to any other university, but were determined to go straight into racing. Not that racing had been a departure for the Shillingford family.

Prior to his retirement to a villa in southern Spain, our uncle, my father's younger brother, had been a multi-Classic-winning Newmarket trainer, and he had himself taken over the stable from our grandfather. Two of my cousins were also in the racing business, one as a trainer in the family yard and the other as the owner of a racehorse transport firm. Indeed, the Shillingfords were a much respected racing family and had been owners, trainers, and occasionally jockeys, in and around Newmarket since the days of Charles II and the founding of the Jockey Club.

It had been my father who had been the one to take a different route, becoming the first Shillingford of record to get a university degree, let alone a first-class from Merton College, Oxford.

But there was no doubt that the family as a whole, whether in the City of London or on the racetrack, had a huge competitive streak in its makeup. Clare certainly had, and she'd said so at our dinner at Haxted Mill.

Only I amongst the Shillingford clan, it seemed, hadn't been born with fire in his belly to be *The Very Best of the Best*. But even I could be pretty competitive if pushed, and I didn't like it much when people said that I wasn't the best commentator in racing, although I knew what they were saying was true.

"Perhaps we drove her to it," James said gloomily.

"What utter nonsense," my father stated, resuming his pacing. This time, however, he didn't pace aimlessly back and forth but made a beeline for the liquor cabinet in the corner. "I need a drink," he said, sloshing a hefty slug of whisky into a tumbler and knocking it back in one gulp.

I looked at my watch. It was only a quarter to five, but it felt much later. I'd already been up for almost fourteen hours, and I'd had far less than a full night's sleep before that.

I, too, could have done with a drink, but I didn't say so.

And I did tend to agree with my father on one point: I also couldn't envisage how the family could have driven Clare to kill herself. Sure, we were all competitive, but, if anything, Clare was more competitive than the rest of us put together. And she had thrived on it.

People who took their own lives, I'd always believed, were driven to it by failure and rejection, not by success and widespread affection. But I knew that wasn't universally true. I could recall several high-profile suicides whose deaths had staggered the public, where an outward persona of joy, happiness, and huge achievement had masked some inner depression and hopelessness.

The real truth was that one never knew what was going on in someone else's head.

And the big question that wouldn't leave mine was whether Clare's death was related to me confronting her about her riding of Bangkok Flyer and her subsequent admission of race fixing.

Her note might seem to imply this, but her unconcerned, almost blasé reaction at dinner hardly seemed to fit with her being so tormented by it that she had thrown herself from a balcony only two and a half hours later. However, I decided that now was neither the time nor the place to introduce this new factor into the discussion.

Nothing prepares a family for death, particularly the death of one of its youngest members. But my family had responded in true Shillingford fashion, shouting one another down and refusing to countenance any opinion but their own. Only Nicholas demonstrated any real decorum, and I realized he was the only one amongst them I actually liked.

I finally escaped from this hotbed of accusation and blame, using the excuse that there were insufficient bedrooms for us all to stay and, as I lived closest, it was easiest for me to come and go.

So I went, and just as soon as I could.

5

On Monday I went to the races and back to work. It seemed like the logical thing to do.

I had sat at home alone all day Sunday, feeling miserable, answering the hundreds of e-mails that kindly people had sent, and dealing with the fifty or so voice messages on my phones. How I wished Clare had left a message on Friday evening.

Why hadn't I answered her call?

By Monday morning I'd been desperately in need of some human contact, but the thought of going back to my family in Oxted had filled me with horror. So much so that I'd invented a sudden nasty cold in order to escape from them.

"Are you sure you can't come?" my mother had asked when I'd called early Sunday morning.

"Quite sure," I'd replied while holding my nose. "I don't want to give this cold to Dad."

I'd been on safe ground. She knew as well as I did that my father was obsessive about avoiding people with colds. Indeed, he was obsessive about lots of things. How she had put up with him for fifty-two years I couldn't imagine.

"I DIDN'T THINK you'd be here today," Derek said from behind me as I climbed the half dozen steps up to RacingTV's scanner, the blacked-out production truck parked in a compound near the Windsor racetrack stables. "I've arranged for Iain Ferguson to present."

"That's fine by me," I said, turning around. "I'll just help where I can. To be honest, I don't feel up to much anyway."

"No," said Derek. He paused. "Look, mate, I'm really sorry about Clare. I can't actually believe it."

"Thanks, Derek," I replied. "I can't believe it either. Half the time I feel that life has to go on as normal and then, the next minute, I wonder why I bother to do anything at all. I think it's the frustration that's the worst, frustration that I can't turn back time, can't bring her back."

I was close to tears once more and I knew it was evident in my voice. Open displays of emotion could be unsettling, and I could tell that Derek didn't quite know what to do.

"It's OK," I said, breathing deeply. "You must be busy. You get on."

"Right," he said, clearly relieved. "I had better. Are you coming to the production meeting?"

"I thought I'd sit in at the back."

Whether I was working for Channel 4 or for RacingTV, the first task of my day was always to attend the production meeting, where the running order for the show was discussed and agreed upon. The meeting took place in the scanner at least three hours before the broadcast was due to begin.

The producer, Derek in this case, began by handing out the printout of the draft running order. That afternoon, RacingTV was covering all seven races at Windsor, and also seven from Leicester racetrack a hundred or so miles to the north, the paddock presenter there joining us via live video link.

The program was on the air from two o'clock to six, four hours of high-octane adrenaline. If things went wrong and off script, as they usually did at some point during the afternoon, then we just had to carry on regardless. The thing about live television was that mistakes were history as soon as you made them, there was nothing you could do to unmake them. There was no saying, "Let's do that again," as you might in a recorded program where you could do it over and over until it was perfect.

In all, there were three race meetings taking place that afternoon, with Hamilton being broadcast on the other satellite network. Even though a race was scheduled only every half hour at each track, the times were staggered so that, across the three venues, a race was due to start every ten minutes, from ten past two until five-thirty, which was fine as long as all of them went off roughly on time.

If a horse got loose or lost a shoe on the way to the start, or if a stirrup leather or bridle broke, the delay could throw out the whole schedule, resulting in races at different courses running simultaneously. And that gave the producer a big headache.

Added to the actual broadcasting of the races were interviews with winning trainers and jockeys, trophy presentations, video footage of prior races of the main participants, as well as comments from the paddock presenters. And somewhere there also had to be found the time to fit in a set number of breaks for advertisements and also promos for future races.

Manic, it was not, but it was full-on nevertheless, and everyone would breathe a collective sigh of relief come three minutes to six o'clock when the production assistant would say *"Shut up"* in everyone's ears, meaning the show was over and we were off the air.

Derek called the production meeting to order. "There's to be a minute's silence here at Windsor in memory of Clare Shillingford." Everyone in the scanner instinctively turned around to glance at me. "It will be before the first race at two-ten, after the horses have gone out onto the course. There will be a loud beep over the public address to start and also to finish the minute. Iain, do the introduction, please, but don't talk during the minute, your mike will stay live. During it we will show the flag on the grandstand, which is flying at half-mast, and then slowly fade to a picture of Clare after forty seconds. If we are on schedule, it should come comfortably after the first from Leicester. If there's a delay at Leicester and the silence occurs during their race, we will record the silence here at Windsor and play it back immediately after as if live. Iain, your cue to speak will be the second beep, and we'll go pretty much straight to a commercial break after a few words. Understand?" Iain nodded. "And full silence, please, everyone, for the whole minute, not even any talk-back."

Talk-back was what played continually into everyone's ear through an earpiece on a coiled wire like those worn by Secret Service agents. The producer, his assistant, and the director would all speak, giving cues to presenters, or instructions to cameramen and the vision mixer, or counting down time while the clips were shown or commercials transmitted.

One became used to listening to all the chatter but picking up only the material that was relevant to you. The art of great presenting was to absorb and react to the talk-back while speaking live on air at the same time. Only the very best could carry on an interview, listening and responding to an interviewee's answers while at the same time taking in appropriate talk-back information.

Derek went through the rest of the planned running order, assigning jobs to be done and detailing all the many expected "Astons," the captions that are overlaid pictures to give the viewers information, be it betting prices, horses' and jockeys' names, details of non-runners, and so on and so on. It was the full-time job of two staff members sitting at the back of the scanner to type Astons and have them ready whenever the producer called for them.

And then there were the video clips of prior races to be annotated and spoken about, all of which would be recorded before the program went on the air so that the clips, or VTs, were stored and ready to broadcast. *VT* stood for "video tape," and the term was still used even though the recordings were stored not on tapes these days but on a computer hard drive.

The magic of television allowed two complete afternoons of racing, one from Leicester and the other from Windsor, to be fitted into the time of just one of them.

By careful use of VTs, the runners could be shown in the parade ring while they were really on their way to the start. Interviews with trainers at Windsor might be recorded while races from Leicester were being run, then played back at a time when the trainers would have been unavailable, busy saddling their horses.

Often the only things that were "live" in the whole broadcast were the races themselves, and that was a "must do" rule. The rest didn't matter. Interviews recorded after the first race might be shown later in the afternoon, if time permitted, or dropped altogether if no slot could be found. Everything was timed and cut to fit together like a jigsaw puzzle around the immovable races, filling up four hours of television that then seemed to whiz past in a flash.

I spent the first part of the afternoon in the scanner, sitting behind Derek and getting an unfamiliar view of the production as he marshaled his troops at the two race-tracks, slotting everything together like a dry-stone waller taking irregular-sized segments and fashioning them to form a coherent, solid structure. It was an art, and Derek was one of the best.

Immediately after the third race at Windsor, I ventured out of the dark cavern of the scanner into the bright Berkshire sunlight.

As I walked across to the parade ring through the fairly meager Monday-afternoon crowd, it became apparent to me that the bereavement of others can be a disorienting and distressing experience for some. No end of people, including some I knew quite well, averted their eyes and hurried away as if they didn't want to burst some imaginary grief bubble that surrounded me. Even those who did talk to me seemed uncomfortable doing so.

I think it was the concept of suicide, rather than the death itself, that made for the embarrassment. Somehow, it seems that taking one's own life carries an even greater stigma than taking someone else's.

I was beginning to wish I hadn't left the comfort and security of the scanner, but I was a man on a mission—I was looking for Geoff Grubb, the trainer of Scusami, who had a runner in the fourth.

"Good God, Mark. What are you doing here?" said a man, grabbing me by the arm as I was walking by. "I thought you'd be at Oxted."

It was Brendan Shillingford, my cousin who trained in my grandfather's old yard in Newmarket.

"I'm working with RacingTV. At least I'm meant to be, but I don't really know myself what I'm doing here. I just had to get away from the rest of the family."

Brendan nodded. He knew all about his relations.

"I spoke to both James and Stephen yesterday at Uncle Joe's. They said things were pretty awful. What a bloody business."

"Yeah," I said. "A real bugger."

"Any news yet on a funeral?"

"Not as yet," I said. "The police have to agree."

"Police?" Brendan asked. "Why are they involved?"

"Something about all sudden deaths having to be investigated. They released a statement yesterday that there were no suspicious circumstances, so I don't suppose we'll have to wait too long. The coroner may have already said we can go ahead. I just haven't heard yet."

"Do you have any idea why she did it?" Brendan asked.

"None at all," I said. "Clare and I had grown slightly apart these last few months. But I know she'd been seeing someone she didn't want anyone to find out about. Perhaps that had something to do with it."

"Who was it?" he asked.

"I've no idea. I'm looking for Geoff Grubb in the hope that he might be able to tell me."

"That'll be a waste of time," Brendan said. He forced a smile. "Geoff wouldn't know about anything unless it's got four legs and a tail."

"I think I'll ask him anyway. Give my love to Gillian." I started to move away.

"Let me know about the funeral," Brendan called after

me. "I need time to organize flights for Mom and Dad from Marbella. And try to avoid Thursday, Friday, or Saturday next week. It's the Cambridgeshire meeting."

Good point, I thought. I had better make sure that my father or brothers weren't in the process of fixing a funeral date without first referring to the racing calendar.

I found Geoff Grubb hurrying out of the weighing room with a tiny racing saddle over his arm.

"Geoff," I said. "Do you have time for a word?"

He slowed. "Only a quick one. I've got to go and saddle Planters Inn."

"I'll walk with you," I said, falling in beside him.

"I'm really sorry about Clare. Bloody nuisance, too, I can tell you. I've had to find different jockeys for all my runners."

I considered that to be a minor inconvenience, in the circumstances, but I let it pass.

"Geoff, I know that Clare had been seeing someone recently."

"Seeing someone?" he asked.

Perhaps Brendan had been right about it being a waste of time.

"Yes," I said. "Seeing someone—you know, a boyfriend."

"Oh, right," Geoff said, nodding.

"Do you have any idea who it might have been?"

"It wasn't me," he said seriously.

"No," I agreed. Not even for a nanosecond did I imagine that my sister had been having an affair of the heart with Geoff Grubb. He might have been outstanding with his horses, but his people skills were almost nonexistent. "But do you know who it was?"

He shook his head. "Sorry."

"Did you ever see anyone coming and going from Clare's place?" Clare had lived in a cottage attached to Geoff's training stables.

He shook his head again. "Not that I recall."

"Was there ever a car parked outside?"

"That sports car of hers was there," he said unhelpfully.

"Any others?"

"A few, now and again, but not a regular one," he said. "Not that I can remember anyway."

It wasn't that his memory was bad. He could have told me in detail about every race run by every horse in his expansive yard, not just this year but throughout their whole lives. He simply didn't notice anything else going on around him, not unless it impacted on the training of his horses.

"Do you mind if I come and have a look round her cottage?"

"Help yourself," he said. "The rent's paid for the rest of the month. Will you be clearing her things?"

"Probably. Me or someone else in the family."

"There's a spare key in the yard office."

"Thanks," I said. "I'll try to be up there sometime this week."

He hurried off toward the saddling stalls, and I watched him go.

Clare had ridden as his number one stable jockey for the past four years and they had made a good team. I wondered if he had been the one that Clare had liked to control. But she hadn't ridden exclusively for Geoff Grubb. As was the case with all jockeys, she had also been engaged by other trainers when Geoff didn't have any runners.

And I knew that Bangkok Flyer wasn't one of Geoff's.

BACK IN THE SCANNER, the afternoon was progressing on schedule. There had been no significant delays in the races, and Derek was calm, which meant that everyone else was also calm, all of them working smoothly together.

I, in contrast, wasn't doing anything useful, merely being a spectator. I thought about leaving and going home. But that wouldn't make me feel any better. At least here I had something to watch, something to take my mind off Clare.

Guilt was a soul-destroying emotion and I had lain awake half the previous night, staring into the void, into the emptiness of despair and self-condemnation. Why hadn't I answered the bloody telephone? How could I have ignored her when she had needed me the most?

"There's a dog on the course at Leicester," Derek said through the talk-back while looking at the pictures coming down the line. *"Can we get a close-up?"*

Dogs on racetracks, although rare, were always good for "atmosphere" shots, provided they didn't actually delay the races and screw up the schedule. Most racing folk loved their dogs as much as they did their horses, and there was nothing like a loose puppy to provide a bit of "Aahh" appeal to a broadcast. It made a welcome change from the crying babies with runny noses that the cameramen usually found amongst the crowd.

The afternoon continued without any significant problems. I watched on the transmission screen as Iain Ferguson interviewed guests in the paddock and talked about the horses, performing the role that I should have had. He was good. Too damn good, I thought. I'd better be careful or he'd have my job permanently, and I certainly didn't want that.

I loved my work, and I specifically enjoyed the variation that came from splitting my time between presenting for Channel 4 and RacingTV, and also doing the racetrack commentaries. And I had no intention of allowing someone else to take over any of my seats. I'd better sort my head out fast and get back to my jobs while I still had them.

The production assistant counted down to a commercial break. *"Two minutes and forty seconds,"* she called, and everyone relaxed as the preset sequence was played direct from the RacingTV headquarters building near Oxford. The commercials were the only downtime during the whole four-hour broadcast, and the crew in the scanner used the break to get coffee, visit the bathroom, or just to stretch cramped legs.

"You all right?" Derek asked, standing up and turning around to face me.

"Fine," I said. "Makes a change for me to see you at work rather than just to hear it on the talk-back. It's very interesting."

"Well, don't get any ideas of taking my job." He smiled at me, but he wasn't exactly making a joke. In times of recession and cuts, everyone, it seemed, was watching their backs, and none more so than in the TV business.

"Coming out of break in twenty seconds," called the production assistant. Everyone sat down again at their places. *"Five, four, three, two, one."* She fell silent, and the whole juggernaut rolled back smoothly into motion bang on cue.

"FOUR MINUTES TO SHUT-UP," said the production assistant through the talk-back.

It was now precisely seven minutes to six, and all the races were over for the afternoon. Iain was doing the roundup, the last few moments of each race being shown in turn with his voice-over, mostly discussing possible future plans for each of the winners.

"Two minutes to shut-up," said the assistant.

Iain went on talking without a pause as the production assistant's voice spoke in his ear, not only with the countdown to the shut-up but also with those to the end of each piece of VT.

"Iain, coming to you in picture in five seconds," said Derek, adding to the chatter.

"Thirty seconds to shut-up," said his assistant at the same time. *"Four, three, two, one, cue Iain."*

"Well, that's it for this afternoon," said Iain, his smiling face now being broadcast to the viewers. "Join us later here on RacingTV for American racing live from Belmont Park in New York."

"Twenty seconds."

"And tomorrow we'll be back for live flat racing from

Folkestone, and also six contests over the sticks from Newton Abbot."

"Ten seconds. Nine, eight . . ."

"So this is Iain Ferguson here at Windsor wishing you a very good evening."

". . . two, one, shut up," said the assistant as Iain fell silent and the program titles and theme music were brought up by the vision mixer.

"Well done, everybody," said Derek. *"Production meeting tomorrow morning at Folkestone at eleven. And Iain, can you come to the scanner before you go home?"* Derek flicked off his microphone and leaned back in his chair, stretching his arms high above his head. He yawned loudly. "God, I'm tired."

So am I, I thought, yawning in sympathy, but, unlike him, I hadn't done a stroke of work all day. In my case it was probably something to do with not having had any proper sleep for the past three nights.

Derek twisted around in his chair to face me. "What do you think about tomorrow?"

I was scheduled to present from Folkestone. "I'll be fine if you want me."

"I actually think we should stick with Iain for the rest of this week," he said. "It might be construed as somewhat insensitive on your part to return too soon. But how would you feel about doing a full tribute piece about Clare for broadcast on Saturday from Newmarket?"

"Channel 4 has already asked me," I said. "I'm filming it on Thursday, and it'll be shown on *The Morning Line* on

Saturday, and also during the afternoon. I think I'd better check with them before I do another."

"It's all right," said Derek. "I'll ask Iain to do ours."

Iain, it seemed to me, was being asked to do far too much.

"You could always ask Channel 4 if you can use the same piece." Cooperation between the broadcasters was rare but not completely unknown.

"Maybe. But using Iain will give us a slightly different slant." He paused. "Sorry, I didn't mean that to sound how it did."

"It's OK," I said. "That's sensible."

And it was. I'd have done the same thing in his position.

"Do you think it'll be OK for me to use the RacingTV database in Oxford for my tribute piece?" I asked.

"I'm sure it will," said Derek. "You know we've had that new indexing system installed."

"That's exactly why I want to use it."

"It's really fabulous. Just put in Clare's name under 'Jockey' and then click on 'Winner' and it will list all the races that she's won, together with the other runners, the prize money, the distances, the prices, everything. Then you just have to click on any entry in the list to play the VT straight back. It's absolutely brilliant."

"Great," I said.

"But you don't have to go all the way to Oxford, you know. You can access everything just as easily from the scanner. Not now, of course, because the link will be down, but tomorrow from Folkestone. The link will be up by about ten and there'll be about three hours clear before racing."

"Thanks," I said. "But I still think I'll go to Oxford. Then I've got all day."

"Suit yourself," Derek said rather dismissively. He obviously thought that I surely could find the videos I needed of Clare winning races in three hours and he was well aware that my home in Edenbridge was a lot closer to Folkestone than it was to Oxford.

That was all true, but I didn't really want Derek looking over my shoulder all the time I was accessing the video database because I was actually far more interested in searching for races that Clare had purposely lost.

6

It was a bit like searching for the proverbial needle in the haystack.

During the past four months, the height of the flat-racing season, Clare had ridden almost every day, often four or five times in an afternoon, and sometimes at an evening meeting as well.

According to the database, since the beginning of June there had been four hundred and twenty-nine races run in which Clare had been one of the jockeys and she'd been on the winner in thirty-seven of them, including her last-ever ride at Lingfield the previous Friday on Scusami.

What was it that Clare had said when I asked her how often she had stopped a horse from winning? *Three or four times, maybe five*. And what had she written in her note? *I don't know what has been happening to me these last few months*.

I assumed, therefore, that the three or four races, or maybe five, would have been in the last few months. I had better start at the beginning of the four hundred and twenty-nine and just go through them all, ignoring only the ones she had actually won. That left three hundred and ninety-two races to watch. I settled myself into the studio chair for a lengthy session.

But first I watched again her ride on Bangkok Flyer the previous Friday to remind me of exactly what I was looking for. The more I saw it, the more obvious it seemed. I was sure that I'd have no trouble spotting it again in a different race. All I really needed was to watch the final eighth of a mile.

I also looked to see who trained Bangkok Flyer. I knew most things about the horses that I watched regularly, including their owners and trainers, but Bangkok Flyer was a two-year-old maiden, and Friday had been the first time I'd seen him run.

According to the database, he was trained in a New-market stable by Austin Reynolds, for a long time the "nearly man" of British flat racing. Austin was now in his mid- to late fifties, and he had never quite fulfilled his potential in the sport.

Perhaps too much had been expected of him because he'd enjoyed such phenomenal success very early, winning the Derby, the Oaks, and the St. Leger in only his second year as a young trainer. Since those heady days of more than twenty years ago, he had never again saddled a Classic winner, and he'd precious few other big-race victories to his name either.

Nowadays he mostly sent his horses north to race on the Yorkshire circuits, marketing himself to businessmen from the area—prospective owners who might appreciate his fashionable Newmarket address.

Bangkok Flyer had raced three times prior to his run at Lingfield, once each at Redcar, Catterick, and York, finishing second on all three occasions. But Clare hadn't ridden him in any of those previous outings.

Nevertheless, I watched the VTs of all three. There was nothing untoward in any of them, at least there was nothing that I could spot. In fact, the colt had run exceptionally well last time out at York, beaten only half a length by a good horse that had itself recently gone on to win one of the major two-year-old races of the season. No wonder Bangkok Flyer had started as a red-hot favorite under Clare. According to form, he should have won the race at Lingfield with ease, as he surely would have without Clare's untimely intervention.

EVEN WITH ME watching only the final eighth of a mile of each race, the first two hundred took me more than three hours to review. In them I found three "definites," as well as a further two "possibles." Perhaps Clare had been understating reality when she had said she'd "stopped" a maximum of only five.

By this stage, I had watched so many race finishes that the horses were beginning to dance before my eyes. I took a break for a coffee.

I felt absolutely wretched.

In a way, I suppose, I should be pleased to have found something, but I was seriously dismayed to have had it confirmed that her irregular riding of Bangkok Flyer had not been an isolated incident.

The phone vibrated in my pocket. It was Sarah.

"Hello, my darling," I said, answering it.

"Where are you?" she asked in a slightly pained voice.

"Oh God, I'm sorry. I've been so busy I forgot."

I looked at my watch. It was twenty past twelve, and we'd agreed to meet at noon in a pub overlooking the River Thames just west of Oxford.

"I'm on my way. Order me a glass of rosé. I'll be there in ten minutes."

I told the database technician I'd be back later and skipped out to my car. I was still excited every time I was on my way to see Sarah. If I wasn't, I suppose, I'd have moved on by now.

The lunchtime traffic was bad, and it was a good fifteen minutes before I turned into the pub parking lot and pulled my battered old Ford into the space alongside Sarah's brand-new BMW.

I hurried inside.

"What was making you so busy in Oxford that you forgot to come and meet me?" She wasn't really cross, just curious.

"I've been at the RacingTV studio."

"Doing what, exactly?"

"Oh, bits and pieces. Sorting out my work schedule for the coming months."

I wondered why I hadn't told her the truth.

"And I'm also looking at some past races that Clare rode in for a tribute that I'm making on Thursday for Channel 4."

"Well, in that case you're forgiven." She patted my hand. "How have things been?"

"Pretty awful," I said. "I seem to be wandering round in a daze. Nothing seems real."

"Have you fixed a date yet for the funeral?"

"Monday, at three," I said. "But that's another thing I'm not very happy about."

"Why?" she asked.

"I spoke to my brothers last night. The coroner has given us the go-ahead, but my father wants it to be immediate family only, and near Oxted where *he* lives."

"Why is that a problem?"

"Because Clare didn't really get on with her immediate biological family. Racing was Clare's world. They were her real family, and I think she would have preferred it if her funeral was held at Newmarket, where *she* lived, and all her racing friends could be there."

"Darling," Sarah said, turning to me, "you can always have a memorial service in Newmarket later. And, in all honesty, it isn't really what Clare would have wanted that's important now."

"I know." I sighed. "And my father can be very obstinate. But for some goddamn reason my brothers and sister seem to agree with him. I've tried my best but I've been voted down on this one. Personally, I think they only want a small quiet funeral because they're embarrassed by the manner of her death."

She took my hand in hers and squeezed it. There was nothing to say, so we sat there in silence for a while. As always, I couldn't get the image out of my head of Clare falling fifteen floors. I was again close to tears.

"Where's Mitchell?" I asked, purposely changing my pattern of thought.

"At Newton Abbot races, thank goodness." She shivered. "God, he was so horrible to me this morning before he went. He can be such a bully."

"Why don't you just leave him?"

She didn't answer, and I tried to read her mind. Perhaps she was afraid of him. Or had Clare been right and Sarah simply couldn't afford to leave?

"When will he be back?" I asked in the silence.

"Not for hours. He's got a runner in the last, so he won't be home until well after eight at the earliest." She paused. "I don't suppose you fancy coming back with me for a while?"

In spite of everything, I was tempted.

"How about Oscar?" I asked. Oscar was the youngest of her stepchildren, the only one who still lived at home.

"School play rehearsal. He won't be home until ten. Please do come." She was almost pleading. "I need you. It's been really dreadful knowing you've been in such pain and not being able to comfort you."

I sighed. "I've got to go back to the RacingTV offices to finish what I'm doing. It'll take another two or three hours at least."

"I'm only twenty minutes down the road. Come if you can."

"The offices close at six, and the technician told me he wants to be gone by half past five, so I've got to be finished by then. I could come after that for a little while, as long as you're sure it's safe."

"Safe as houses. I'll watch Newton Abbot on the television just to make sure Mitch is still there for the last race."

So would I.

Having been slightly irritated with me for arriving late, she now tried her best to hurry me away, so much so that I was back at the database studio, reviewing more of Clare's races, well before two o'clock.

IN ALL THE RACES that Clare had ridden in and not won since the beginning of June, I found what I was pretty sure were seven examples of her purposely trying to lose, even though in one of them she didn't really have much of a chance to win anyway. And there were a further four races where I thought she'd not been doing her best to win when she might have, although I couldn't be sure that she was actively stopping the horse.

I used the database system to copy the eleven races in question on a DVD, together with the information about all the horses that had run in each one.

There didn't seem to be any factors in common.

Of the seven definites, there was one pair that had the same trainer, but the five others were all different. Nine of the eleven had been trained in Newmarket, with one in

Lambourn and the other at a stable near Stratford-upon-Avon. And all had different owners.

In addition to Bangkok Flyer, there was one other horse from the Austin Reynolds string, Tortola Beach, an exciting two-year-old prospect that Clare had ridden into third place at Doncaster in August when he had looked certain to win with just an eighth of a mile to go.

One of the others was from the Newmarket stable of Carla Topazio, a large, domineering lady trainer of Italian descent who loved to sing operatic arias at every opportunity, mostly in the winner's enclosure whenever her horses had won.

In another of the eleven, Clare had ridden a three-year-old filly called Jasmine Pearls, trained by our own cousin Brendan, which had finished a close fourth in the City Plate at Chester after having led comfortably into the final eighth of a mile.

The only common thread I could see was that in none of the eleven suspect races had Clare been riding a horse trained by Geoff Grubb, her principal employer. Perhaps she had thought it would have been too great a risk. She had so much to lose if Geoff, for whatever reason, became unhappy with her riding—not just her stable-jockey job but her home as well. Even though she had mocked me, at that final dinner, for not buying a house of my own, she hadn't either, choosing to live in Geoff's rented Stable Cottage.

I stared at my list of definites and possibles, hoping that some other common denominator would leap out at me.

It didn't.

Six of the eleven had started as the favorite, three at a price less than two-to-one, but two of the other five had been relative outsiders, with odds greater than eight-to-one.

I looked up the trainers of the race winners, but they were mostly different as well. As were the jockeys and the owners. Surely the eleven horses were not simply a random selection? Was there some shared characteristic that I wasn't spotting? Maybe it was because I didn't yet have all the necessary information to look at, and I needed to look at races earlier than June.

Perhaps Clare had been playing the Race Fixing Game for much longer than just these last few months.

I glanced at my watch. It was ten past five, and the technician was hovering and clearly itching for me to go. Any further searches would have to wait.

I quickly made another DVD, with four of Clare's big race victories on it, as well as her final race on Scusami. Sadly, I couldn't find a VT of her first-ever ride or even her first winner, but I still had more than enough to make the tribute piece for Channel 4.

I collected my two DVDs, thanked the technician, and left the studio.

The one thing that was certain about every TV company I had ever known was that in the reception area you would find a large-screen television showing the current output, and RacingTV was no exception.

I stood next to the office security desk and watched the sixth, and last, race from Newton Abbot. Mitchell Stacey's horse won it easily at a canter, and the happy trainer was shown beaming from ear to ear as his victorious animal was led into the winner's enclosure.

Newton Abbot racetrack to East Ilsley was about a hundred and sixty miles. Even taking into account that most of the journey was on freeways, and also allowing for the excessive speed at which Mitchell Stacey regularly drove, there was absolutely no way he could be at home within the next two hours.

I climbed excitedly into my old Ford, sped the twenty minutes down the road, and jumped straight into bed with Sarah.

"MY POOR DARLING," Sarah said as we lay together after lovemaking, "this is such a horrid business." She lightly stroked her fingertips across my bare chest, causing shivers to go right down my legs. "It's so unbelievable."

Indeed, it was unbelievable, and I still hoped that I'd soon wake up from this nightmare and everything would be all right. Somehow it felt wrong that I could go on eating, sleeping, breathing, and even lying here with Sarah. Should I feel guilty for that too?

"What I can't understand," I said, "is what she was doing in London anyway. She told me she was going straight home."

"But people do change their minds," Sarah said.

I shook my head, not because I didn't believe Sarah but in distress at what Clare had done. "She also told me she would be riding at Newmarket on Saturday morning. How was she going to do that if she was staying in London?"

"Which hotel was it?" Sarah asked.

"The Hilton. You know, that tall one at the bottom of Park Lane."

Too tall, I thought.

Sarah suddenly sat bolt upright in bed. "But Mitch and I were at the Hilton on Friday night for that big Injured Jockeys dinner. We had a table of our owners."

"Didn't you see anything?" I asked. "An ambulance or something?"

"No. Nothing at all."

"What time did you leave?" I asked.

"Not very late. You know what racing people are like about going to bed early. The dinner started at seven, and it was over by half past ten."

"Clare fell round eleven-thirty."

"We'd gone long before then. We were back here by midnight."

"But did you see her in the hotel lobby? According to the police, she checked in at twenty past ten."

Sarah shook her head. "I would have remembered if I'd seen her because she always reminded me of you. You have the same cheekbones."

She smiled and lay back down next to me again, putting her arm around my waist.

"How many people were at the dinner?" I asked.

"Hundreds," she said. "The place was packed. They had that comedian with the funny spiky hair—you know, the one that does all those amazing impressions." She laughed at the memory. "I was actually quite surprised you weren't there. I remember spending most of the evening looking out for you."

"The tickets had all gone by the time I got round to applying."

"You should have told me. We had a spare place at our table. Someone dropped out at the last minute."

"I couldn't have come anyway. By then, I'd arranged to have dinner with Clare."

"Oh yes," Sarah said quietly, "so you had."

How different things might have been if only I'd been a bit more organized.

ON THURSDAY MORNING I drove to Newmarket and went to Clare's cottage.

I collected the spare key from the yard office, as Geoff Grubb had suggested, and let myself in through the front door.

There was a stack of unopened mail on the doormat, most of it addressed not to Clare, but to me. I knew what it would be. I'd spent most of the previous day answering condolence letters, but the people who'd sent these obviously didn't know the address of my apartment.

I collected the letters all together. There were only a couple of other items—a bill from a cell phone company and a notice from Suffolk County Council about a change to refuse collection in the area. I opened the telephone bill and scanned through the list of the numbers that Clare had called. I recognized my own, and also that of my parents, but what I was really looking for was a number that she had called regularly—say, every day—a number that might have belonged to her mystery boyfriend.

No single number stood out, but there were quite a few she had called more than ten times or so during the monthly billing period. Sadly, the bill did not include the numbers she had called last Friday night after leaving me. Perhaps I would ask the phone company for those. I put the bill down on the desk in the sitting room to look at later and went upstairs.

It was strange going through Clare's things. It felt like I was invading her privacy.

Of course I'd been to this cottage many times during the preceding four years, regularly staying overnight whenever I was working at Newmarket or anywhere farther north. But I'd been a guest, always sleeping in the guest room. Here I was searching Clare's own bedroom, pulling open drawers overflowing with what Americans would call "intimate apparel." And intimate it was too. She'd clearly had a fondness for sexy black lace underwear, and I was rather embarrassed to find it.

There was precious little else to find.

Even as a child, Clare had been frugal in the clothes department, and her wardrobe, with the exception of the lace undies, was fairly sparse, consisting mostly of jeans, polo shirts, and sleeveless puffer jackets—her usual attire.

There were only a couple of dresses hanging in the closet, one of which she had worn to our parents' golden anniversary party. It was the only time in years I could recall her not wearing pants, blue jeans mostly. She had always tried to avoid occasions where she was expected to dress up.

I knew that coming to her cottage would be difficult, but I hadn't realized just how much I would miss her. Every single thing I touched reminded me of the blissful times I had enjoyed in this place.

My heart ached and ached and ached for her.

I sat down wearily on the side of her bed and longed for her to come back, to be here once more, to laugh, to bounce up the stairs with her endless energy, to be alive again—oh, to be alive again, alive, alive.

This bout of grief lasted ten to fifteen minutes, my body plagued by both pain and guilt. There was little I could do but let it take its course, a continuous stream of tears pouring down my cheeks.

In a strange way, the session made me feel a little better. Perhaps it was the body's natural healing mechanism at work.

I would have to come back later, though, I thought. Her loss was still too recent, too raw, too painful. I simply couldn't do much sorting of her things at the moment.

I collected the condolence letters, returned the key, went out to my car, and drove away.

I WAS DUE to record my tribute to Clare at Newmarket racetrack.

Channel 4 was broadcasting both the Friday and Saturday of the Cambridgeshire meeting, and Thursday was the day that the equipment would be set up in preparation.

The tribute was to be a short piece of me talking straight to the camera in front of the Newmarket weighing room, then my voice-over of the four VTs of her major race successes, including her two Group One victories, her win in the Northumberland Plate, and also the Windsor Castle Stakes at Royal Ascot in June when her horse had won by a nose with a perfectly timed late run. Then there was to be another short piece to shoot in front of the camera, then another voice-over for her last race, on Scusami at Lingfield, then another very short piece to camera to finish. Three minutes and forty-five seconds in total.

I just hoped I would be able to get through it without breaking down.

I parked my car as always in the area reserved for the press and walked to the Channel 4 scanner, the huge blue truck that was already parked in the fenced-off compound behind the northern grandstand.

The technical team was busy laying thick black cables between the scanner and the signal-relay vehicle that was parked alongside, with its arrays of receiving domes and transmitting dishes on the roof. The images from each of the seven cameras around the racetrack, together with the pickups from the numerous microphones, would all be transmitted back here by microwave link, ready for mixing in the scanner.

It was also from where the final fusion of sound and pictures was sent via faraway satellite to the Channel 4 main studios in London for broadcast through the ether to people's televisions at home. And all in the blink of an eye, or maybe two blinks.

"Are you ready?" asked Neville, the *Channel 4 Racing* producer.

"As I'll ever be," I said, taking in a deep breath.

"You'll be fine," Neville said. "And we can always do it again."

Yes, I thought. Thank goodness it wasn't going out live.

But I needn't have worried. As soon as the camera's Cyclops-like lens pointed my way outside the weighing room, my professional instincts took over and I managed to do all the straight-to-camera pieces in just one take.

Afterward, I sat in the scanner for over an hour putting together the whole thing, editing the VTs and doing the voice-overs, shuffling things around until both Neville and I were happy with the final tribute. I played it right through from start to finish, and, once more, it brought me close to tears. I hoped that it might have the same effect on those who watched it on Saturday.

By the time I emerged from the scanner into a light September drizzle, the Thursday-afternoon races were well under way. But I'd had enough for one day and decided to take myself home to Edenbridge. If I was lucky, I'd get around London before the rush hour.

Mitchell Stacey was waiting for me in the parking lot.

Oh shit, I thought. What the hell's he doing here?

Mitchell trained nothing but steeplechasers or hurdlers, and there were only flat races at Newmarket. So why was he leaning on my car? I slowed to a halt about twenty yards away, but he came over quickly toward me, sticking his right forefinger up under my chin.

"Now, listen to me, you bastard!" he shouted at me from about ten inches distance. "Stop fucking my wife!"

There wasn't much to say, so I kept quiet.

Sorry somehow seemed inappropriate.

"If it wasn't for this business with your sister," Mitchell went on, "I'd have had your legs broken. Do you understand me?"

I remembered what Sarah had said about him being a bully. I could see what she meant.

"Do you understand me?" he said again, pushing his ruddy face up close to mine.

"Yes," I said.

"Good." He thrust a folded piece of paper into my hands.

I unfolded it. On it was printed a large colored photograph. It was rather grainy and slightly out of focus, but it was clear enough. The photograph showed Sarah and me in bed together the previous evening, and there was little doubt as to what we were doing.

"I won't divorce her, you know," he said. "And she won't divorce me either because she knows she'd end up with nothing. Not a bean. We have a prenuptial contract."

I wasn't sure that prenups were legal documents under English law, but I decided against mentioning it to him at that particular moment.

"If you ever come near my wife again, I'll kill you." Mitchell said it with real menace.

He suddenly turned and walked away from me without looking back.

My skin felt cold and clammy, and I found I was shaking.

I stuffed the photograph into my pocket and made it over to my car, sitting down heavily in the driver's seat.

Bloody hell! How did he get that picture?

I called Sarah's cell phone.

"He knows," I said when she answered. "Mitchell knows about us. He's just been here at Newmarket and he confronted me."

"I know," she said.

"Then for God's sake why didn't you warn me?"

"He threatened me, that's why." She was crying. "Told me he'd break my legs if I contacted you."

I could believe it.

"Mark, I'm so frightened."

So was I.

"He showed me a picture taken yesterday of us in bed."

"A picture?" She sobbed. "He's got the whole bloody video. He made me watch it this morning after Oscar went to school. He'd set up one of those spy cameras in our bedroom. It was awful. I thought he was going to hit me."

"Pack a bag and leave right now," I said. "Come and live with me at my place. Mitchell won't be back for a good couple of hours even if he goes straight home."

"He took my car keys."

"So what? Call a taxi and get the train from Newbury. I'll collect you at Paddington."

I could hear her sigh. "I can't."

"Why not?"

There was no reply.

"Why not?" I asked her again.

"I just can't," she said again with a resigned tone. There was a long silence on the line. "I should have paid the little shit."

"Paid who?" I asked.

"Oh, nothing," she said dismissively. There was another silence. "It might be better if we didn't talk again."

Neither of us said anything. There may have been no actual words, but the silence between us spoke volumes.

"Bye, bye, my darling," she said finally. "And thanks for everything."

She hung up, leaving me sitting there holding the dead phone to my ear.

My whole world seemed to be falling apart around me. My gorgeous twin sister had killed herself, I was arguing with the rest of my family, my lover of five years had just dumped me, and Iain Ferguson appeared to be taking over my job.

7

I sat at home all day Friday and Saturday, moping around my apartment, feeling sorry for myself, and occasionally watching the racing on the television.

I should have been at Newmarket presenting the programs for Channel 4 and RacingTV, not sitting at home watching them.

Two or three times I shouted at my TV set in frustration. I also laughed out loud when Iain Ferguson made a classic mistake, calling the trainer he was interviewing by the wrong name, not once but twice. Idiot, I thought. It was a basic rule of presenting to get an interviewee's name right because the audience at home would have it written across their screen on an Aston. They would all realize your error and think you were foolish, which indeed you were.

Perhaps Iain Ferguson wasn't such a threat to my job after all.

On Saturday, after my tribute to Clare, and shown interspersed with the flat races from Newmarket, were four others from the jumping meeting at Market Rasen.

According to my early-morning-delivered copy of the *Racing Post*, Mitchell Stacey had three horses running at Market Rasen, one in each of the first three races. I hoped they'd all lose.

I had tried to call Sarah's cell four times on Thursday evening to ensure she was all right. On the first occasion, the phone had rung a couple of times, then gone to voice mail, as if someone at the other end had declined the call. Thereafter it went straight to voice mail, as if it was switched off.

I sent her a text message. There was no reply.

In desperation, I'd called the Staceys' home number, but Mitchell himself had answered, so I'd immediately hung up. I didn't dare call again.

Now I studied the TV coverage from Market Rasen with particular attention to see if I could see Sarah, perhaps accompanying her husband into the parade ring before the first race. As always, the cameraman dwelt on the horses and not the people, and the horses were moving while the people were not. I caught a glimpse of Mitchell Stacey, his weather-beaten reddish face reminding me all too well of our close encounter at Newmarket on Thursday.

I couldn't spot Sarah, but if Mitchell was definitely at

Market Rasen, I could at least try to call her safely on their landline if she was at home.

"Please, Mark," she said, answering after three rings, "I said we were not to speak again. Not ever."

"I just wanted to make sure you were all right."

"I'm fine," she said.

"Are you sure?" I said. "You sound a bit funny."

There was no reply.

"What happened?" I asked. "Did he hit you?"

"It's nothing," she said.

It was as if she was speaking through cotton wool.

"Did he split your lip?"

"I told you, I'm fine."

"What did you mean yesterday about paying the little shit?"

"Nothing," she said.

"It must have been something. And why would you pay Mitchell anyway?"

"Leave it, Mark. Move on. Forget me. I've already forgotten you. Good-bye."

She hung up.

Dammit, I thought. Why did she let him get away with hitting her?

And, to top it all, Mitchell's bloody horse went on to win the first race at Market Rasen, his horrible red face appearing joyful once again as the horse was led in to unsaddle. Oh, how I would have loved to punch his lights out, to split his lip, and see how he liked it.

———

AS SATURDAY AFTERNOON faded into Saturday evening, I lay on my battered old sofa, drinking a can of beer, wondering where my life was going and what I should do about it.

I looked up at the peeling and cracked ceiling of my sitting room.

If the truth be told, it really was well past the "slightly yellowing" stage and was beginning to resemble the nicotine-stained walls of an East End pub before the smoking ban. Not that I smoked. I didn't. But the "whiteness" of the paint had been fairly suspect when it had been thinly applied by my landlord in the first place, and the eight years since had not been kind.

I sat up and looked at the whole room with fresh eyes.

I had to admit that it was pretty awful.

It was not just the paintwork that was overdue for a change, it was the dilapidated and soiled furniture as well. Not to mention the carpets and the drapes, both of which were unchanged since I'd first moved in twelve years ago, and they hadn't been new even then.

To think I'd asked Sarah to give up her luxurious East Ilsley mansion to come live in this squalor. Was it any wonder she'd turned me down?

"Right," I said out loud, "it is high time I made a change."

Past time, in fact.

I quite surprised myself with my decisiveness and, after about three hours of surfing the Internet, I had a pretty good idea of how much houses cost in most of the Home Counties.

By the time I went to bed at one o'clock in the morning I had a list of eight places where I might be interested in living and the telephone numbers of six realtors to call first thing Monday morning.

I found it all quite exciting, and, if nothing else, it took my mind off Sarah, Clare's funeral, and the precariousness of my employment.

ON SUNDAY MORNING I drove into central London, to the Hilton Hotel on Park Lane.

I always knew that I'd have to go there eventually, but I hadn't before felt mentally ready for the ordeal. But now seemed to be the right time, before the funeral, not that I was especially relishing the trip.

I parked my old Ford in South Audley Street, behind the hotel, and walked through to the grand frontage of the Hilton, with its overhanging stainless-steel canopy.

Not surprisingly, there was nothing to indicate where Clare had fallen to her death nine days previously. No roped-off area, no bouquets of flowers, not even a mark on the sidewalk to show the spot where half my being had disappeared forever.

I looked above me at the vertical line of balconies that stretched upward and tried to count fifteen floors. Tears filled my eyes and stopped me. Did it matter? Fifteen wasn't important. Ten would probably have been enough, or even five. According to a telephone call from DS Sharp to my father, the autopsy had established the cause of death as multiple injuries consistent with Clare having fallen a considerable distance onto a hard surface.

I approached one of the uniformed and top-hatted doormen.

"Excuse me," I said, trying to control my voice. "Where did the girl fall?"

"Never you mind," he said somewhat brusquely. "Now, move on, please, sir." He spread his arms and walked straight toward me, forcing me back.

"She was my sister," I said to him quickly, "and I need to know where she died."

"Oh, I'm so sorry," he said, stopping and holding up his hands in apology. "I thought you were another of those ghoulish creeps we've been getting here all week." He must have spotted that I was not doing too well, as he took me by the arm. I think it was his intervention that may have stopped me collapsing altogether.

He guided me inside the hotel.

"Would you like to sit down, sir?" he asked. "You don't look well."

I nodded weakly, and one of his colleagues pulled up a chair.

"I'm sorry," I croaked.

Someone arrived with a glass of water, and I slowly recovered my composure.

"Sorry," I said again to my savior. "I didn't realize how much it would affect me."

"It's no problem, sir," he said. "When you're ready, I'll take you back outside."

"Thank you."

And, in due course, he did just that, showing me exactly where Clare had met her end.

I stood staring at the unremarkable spot on the concrete paving and offered up a silent prayer for Clare's soul. Then, once more, my eyes were drawn upward toward the balconies high above me.

She had fallen quite a distance away from the building, and I wondered if she had purposely jumped outward. She must have only just missed the overhanging steel canopy. In a funny sort of way, I was glad. Its edges appeared very sharp, although that surely would have made no difference to Clare or to the outcome.

But why had she done it? Why? Why? Why?

"Will you be all right now, sir?" asked my friendly doorman.

"Yes. Thank you," I said. "I'll be fine."

He nodded at me, then moved away to help some people into a black London taxi. I, meanwhile, remained rooted to the spot for a few moments longer, even bending down to stroke the rough, cold surface, as if in doing so I was somehow offering a final caring touch to my dead sister.

Finally, I stood up and moved away. It had been a necessary journey to see where she had died, but I would always remember Clare as brimming with life. I once again thanked my lucky stars that I hadn't accompanied James and Nicholas to see her battered and broken body. That was one mental image I could readily live without.

I waved to my doorman and went back into the hotel.

I suspect that the lobbies of all the larger London hotels are busy places at eleven o'clock on Sunday mornings, and the Hilton was certainly no exception. There were several lines of guests waiting at the reception desk to check out after a big Saturday-evening event in the hotel ballroom, while a large group of brightly dressed American tourists hung around aimlessly, desperate to check in and sleep after their overnight red-eye flight across the Atlantic. And there was baggage everywhere, lined up in long snakes like dominoes waiting to be toppled.

I went over to a young woman sitting at a desk marked "Guest Relations" and asked if I could please speak with the hotel's general manager. To my eyes, she hardly looked old enough to be out of school, and she instantly became defensive, asking me what I wanted him for. Perhaps she believed that anyone who wanted to talk to the manager was going to complain about something. I told her that it was a personal matter, but she still refused to pass on my request.

"Are you sure I can't help you?" she asked with an irritating smile.

"It's rather delicate," I said. "Would you please just call the general manager."

"I'm sorry, sir, I can't do that without knowing why you need him." She continued to smile at me in her annoying way.

OK, I thought, I had tried, but with no result. Now I was getting slightly irked by her attitude. "Young lady," I said loudly and somewhat condescendingly, "my name is Mark Shillingford. And I'm trying to discover why my beautiful twin sister fell to a violent death from one of your hotel balconies. Now, can I please talk to the general manager?"

She looked rather shocked, and, in truth, I had also somewhat surprised myself by my own determination and resolve.

"He's not here on Sundays," she said, the smile now having vanished altogether.

I sighed slightly. "Then I will speak to whoever is in charge of the hotel at this very moment."

She used the telephone on the desk. "Someone is coming," she said to me, putting down the handset.

I stood and waited, looking around me. A man wearing a suit soon appeared and came over toward us.

"Mr. Shillingford," he said, holding out his hand, "I'm Colin Dilly, duty manager. How can I help?"

He was about the same age as me but shorter and with a slighter build.

"I notice you have lots of CCTV cameras in this hotel." I pointed up at the one positioned above the Guest Relations desk. "I would like to see the images for the Friday before last."

"I'm afraid that won't be possible," said Mr. Dilly. "The images are recorded on a rolling seven-day cycle. Those for that Friday will have been overwritten by this past Friday's."

Dammit, I thought. I should have come sooner.

"Didn't the police make copies?" I asked in desperation.

"I believe they did, sir, but you will have to ask them

if you want to see them." He said it rather dismissively. "Now, is there anything else I can help you with?"

"I'd like to speak with whoever checked in my sister on Friday evening nine days ago."

He pursed his lips. "I'm not sure that will be possible either. It's not hotel policy to provide that sort of information."

"Then I will spend all day, and all night if necessary, asking every member of your staff that I can find until someone tells me who did check her in. They must know. It's the sort of thing one might remember, don't you think? Being the last person to see a suicide alive."

Mr. Dilly looked at me for a few moments. Perhaps he was deciding whether to have me thrown out.

"And if you chuck me out," I said, "I promise you I'll cause a fuss. I'll call the newspapers and the TV companies. I'm quite well known in media circles, and I don't think it would be good publicity on your part."

"Perhaps you had better come into the office," said Mr. Dilly. "I am sure we can find the information for you."

"Very wise," I said.

I followed him through a door that was disguised as a wooden panel and into some offices behind.

"Please sit down," he said, pointing to a chair in front of a desk. "I'll look up the work sheets for last week."

He sat opposite me at a computer, and I could hear him tapping the keys. "Now, let me see," he said. "Friday the sixteenth. Evening, wasn't it?" He tapped some more keys. "Right. I've found it."

I stood up and went and looked over his shoulder. If he didn't like it, he didn't say so.

There were six reception staff listed for the period from three o'clock in the afternoon until eleven at night on the sixteenth, with four others for the night shift, which ran from eleven on Friday until seven on Saturday morning.

So the staff on duty when Clare had checked in had been different from those when she'd fallen.

Nothing was ever simple.

Colin Dilly wrote down the names of staff from both shifts, but he didn't give me the list. Rather, he compared it to the record of the staff currently on duty that he also brought up on the screen.

"There is one person who was on duty that night who is also working right now. If you wait here, I'll go and fetch her."

Mr. Dilly went off to find the woman while I went on studying his computer screen, but there wasn't much of interest on it.

Presently, he returned with a small, neat woman who I took to be in her mid-thirties.

"Mr. Shillingford," Colin Dilly said, "this is Mrs. Rieta Dalal. She was working on reception during the evening of Friday the sixteenth, and she says she remembers your sister arriving even though it wasn't she who actually checked her in."

"Then how do you know it was my sister?" I asked.

"Because my colleague and I talked about her," said Mrs. Dalal quietly. "Because she had no luggage. No bags at all. Not even a handbag or a makeup bag." She smiled.

"It's very rare indeed for a guest to check in with no luggage, especially a woman with no makeup. I remember her specifically because of that. It was only much later I heard that she had been the poor lady who fell from the balcony."

"Was she with anyone when she checked in?" I asked.

"No, sir, she was not," said Mrs. Dalal. "But she was talking on the telephone the whole time. That is why my colleague mentioned her to me in the first place. My colleague thought it rather rude, and she was quite cross about it."

"Which colleague was it?" Mr. Dilly asked.

"Irena."

"Irena Zelinska," he said, consulting his handwritten list. "She's not working today."

"She has gone home to Poland," said Mrs. Dalal.

It was definitely not going to be simple.

"Did my sister specifically ask for a room with a balcony?"

"I don't know, sir. Have you checked her reservation?"

"I don't think she had a reservation."

She seemed surprised. "We were very full that night, we always are when there's a big event in the ballroom. If she didn't have a reservation, we must have had a cancellation. She must have just been lucky to get a room with a balcony."

"Lucky" was not the term I would have used.

"But even then," Mrs. Dalal went on, "she would have had to ask to have the balcony door unlocked. All the balconies are normally kept locked to prevent suicides."

There was a silence as we all digested what Mrs. Dalal had just said.

"Are you saying that someone had to have gone to her room to open the balcony door?" I asked.

"Yes," said Mrs. Dalal. "We have to call security if guests request that the balcony door be unlocked. It is a common thing. It happens almost every day."

"Why do you keep them locked if you then unlock them on request?"

"The hotel policy," said Mr. Dilly, "is that there has to be a minimum of two registered guests in a room for the balcony door to be unlocked."

"The policy seems to have failed in this case," I said rather pointedly.

Neither of them said anything.

But it had also been the hotel policy not to give me the name of the person who had checked Clare into the hotel, and I'd found a way around that. Clare was infinitely more pushy than I was, and I didn't doubt that the "double occupancy" rule would have been as easy for her to circumvent.

Or had there, in fact, been two people in the room?

"Do you know who my sister was talking to on the telephone while she was checking in?" I asked Mrs. Dalal.

My question made her blush, her olive-brown skin distinctly flushing around her neck. And she looked down as if embarrassed.

"Sorry, I do not know," she replied while still studying the floor.

"Then why are you unsettled by the question?" I asked.

"It is nothing," she said, but she still wouldn't look up at me.

"It must be something," I said. "Tell me."

She looked up at Colin Dilly. "Tell him," he said.

"I am so sorry," she said to me, "we thought your sister was a prostitute. Irena was absolutely sure of it. Irena told me that she must be talking to her next client on her telephone. That is why she had no luggage. Irena said she would only have condoms, and they'd be in her pockets."

"But she paid for the room with her credit card," I said with some degree of anger. "A prostitute wouldn't do that."

She looked up again at Colin Dilly. "Sometimes they do," she said. "At least we are pretty sure they do. And Carlos then checks."

"Carlos?" I asked.

"He is one of the bellmen," she said. "If Irena gives him the nod, then he likes to check."

"How does he check?" I asked.

"When Irena gives Carlos the nod, he goes up ahead of the girl onto the same floor as her room and then waits and watches to see if a man comes."

"And did she give him the nod on that Friday night?" It was Colin Dilly who asked the question that I was itching to ask.

"Of course," said Rieta Dalal. "Especially after she'd been so rude at reception."

"And what did Carlos discover?" I asked.

"I do not know that," Rieta said. "I went home soon

after your sister arrived." She again glanced at Colin Dilly. "I always worked right through my breaks so that I could leave early. I don't like to travel home by myself on the tube after ten o'clock at night. But that was my last late shift and now I've been switched to the early one." She smiled, clearly much happier with the new arrangement. "I have not seen Carlos since that night."

"Did you tell any of this to the police?" I asked.

"Police?" she said. "No one from the police has asked me anything."

"Do you know if the police spoke to Carlos? Or to Irena?"

"I'm sorry," she said, shaking her head, "I know nothing more than I've told you. Can I go now, please, Mr. Dilly?"

"Yes," Colin Dilly said while looking at me with raised eyebrows for confirmation, which I gave by nodding. "Thank you, Rieta. You can get back to work now."

She went out of the office, and Colin Dilly closed the door behind her.

"Surely the police must have interviewed the people who saw or spoke to my sister that night."

"I don't know," he said. "I was off last weekend."

Why was I not surprised?

"I'd now like to talk to Carlos," I said. "And also to the security man who unlocked her balcony door."

"What difference will it make?" Colin Dilly asked, his tone clearly indicating that he thought I was wasting my time, only making things harder for myself.

I looked at him. "At nine o'clock that Friday evening

my sister told me she was driving straight home to New-market from Edenbridge in Kent. Instead, an hour and twenty minutes later she checked into this hotel without any luggage and without having a reservation. And just over an hour after that she was dead."

I paused and looked at him.

"I cannot believe she would have suddenly decided, after leaving me, to drive all the way into central London on the off chance that this hotel might have a free room and that that room would just happen to have a convenient balcony on a sufficiently high floor so that she could jump off it to her death."

I paused again to let what I was saying sink in.

"I think she had to be coming here to meet someone, someone she must have spoken to after she left me. I also think that committing suicide, if indeed it was suicide, must have been a last-moment decision. If she had been planning to kill herself, she would, at the very least, have made a reservation for a high balcony room."

I paused once more.

"So I'd like to talk to Carlos to find out if she did meet someone in her room here that night. And if Carlos didn't see anything, the security man might have."

Colin Dilly sat down once more at his computer and tapped away again on the keyboard.

"Carlos Luis Sanchez," he said, "the bellman. He's working today from three o'clock until eleven." I looked at my watch. It was ten minutes to midday. He tapped some more. "I can't find the details of the security men who were working that night."

"I'll come back at three o'clock to see Carlos. Can you find me the details by then?"

"I doubt it," he said, "but I'll try. I don't have access to the security company's work sheets, and their office will be shut today. I'm actually off duty at three, but I'll wait round to hear what Carlos has to say. Ask for me at reception."

"OK," I said. "I will. And thank you."

We shook hands, then I emerged through the wooden secret-panel door and back into the bustle of the hotel lobby.

"**TWO MEN,**" Carlos Luis Sanchez said. "One follow the other." He made no attempt to disguise his disgust.

"The lady was not a prostitute," Colin Dilly assured him.

"Huh," Carlos replied. "Then why she have two men in her room?"

It was a good question.

"How were the men dressed?" I asked him.

"Dressed or undressed, it makes no difference."

"No," I said, realizing that he hadn't understood the question. "What were they wearing when you saw them in the corridor?"

"Suits," he said. "You know, black suits with ties." He moved his hands back and forth at his neck. Bow ties.

"Both of them?" I asked.

"The first one. Yes. I see. The second . . ." He shrugged his shoulders.

"Did you see the second man?" I spoke slowly.

"Mario see him."

"Who is Mario?" I asked.

"My friend," Carlos said. "One more porter. He work nights. He say he see second man coming out later, during all fuss over falling girl."

"What?" I said, suddenly taking in what he was saying. "Are you telling us that the second man was in her room when the girl fell?"

"I not know," he said. "You ask Mario. But Mario say so to me, yes."

8

Clare's funeral was brief—far too brief, I would have said—but it wasn't up to me, as I had left all the arrangements to my father, my brothers, and my sister. I'd thought that was the best policy for avoiding further arguments and shouting. But as I sat in the Surrey and Sussex Crematorium chapel at three o'clock on Monday afternoon, I deeply regretted that decision.

Not that the day had started well either. I had tried to call Detective Sergeant Sharp to ask him about the CCTV from the London Hilton only to be informed that he was away on leave for the week and that no one else seemed to have any knowledge of any recordings or indeed of anything else to do with Clare's death. Call back next week, I was told most unhelpfully, and speak to DS Sharp.

Next I'd called the Injured Jockeys Fund to ask them

about the guest list for their gala dinner. Mrs. Green, the organizer of the event, was in Portugal, I was told, enjoying a well-earned break after all her hard work. She also would be back next week.

Then my father's insistence on "immediate family only" at the funeral further added to my frustration.

The arrival at the crematorium, ten minutes before the service, of my father's younger brother, my uncle George, and his wife, Catherine, from Spain had not been a welcome addition to the immediate family as my father obviously defined it. When Cousin Brendan had then turned up, along with his wife, Gillian, and their two teenage children, closely followed by his brother Joshua plus second wife, I thought my father was about to postpone the whole thing, but the minister had then made a timely appearance, ushering us all into the chapel.

So there were a total of seventeen of us who sat in the first three rows of chairs as four pallbearers from the undertaker's carried the simple oak casket past us and placed it on the high dais at the front. Five other mourners stood at the back near the door, having been banished there by my father, who had loudly accused them of invading his grief.

Not that I was particularly pleased to see one of them, Toby Woodley, the diminutive racing correspondent from the *Daily Gazette*, a tabloid best known for celebrity exposés and rumor-mongering.

As well as trying to comfort my mother, I spent time looking out for the mystery boyfriend, but none of the five non-family attendees appeared to fit the bill. Apart from

Woodley, there was an elderly couple I vaguely recognized, and two young women who told my father that they had known Clare from school, not that he had made them any more welcome for it.

Just as the minister was starting the service, the back doors of the chapel creaked open and one further individual joined the congregation. Geoff Grubb came forward and sat down in an empty row behind Uncle George and Aunt Catherine. My father stared angrily at him from across the aisle, but if Geoff noticed, he didn't react.

If it hadn't been so sad, it might have been funny.

My father couldn't see past his anger with Clare for bringing this on us all. He couldn't grasp that the death of a much-loved daughter and sister transcended the method of her passing and that her memory should be cherished for what her life had been, not vilified for how it had ended.

The service was embarrassingly short, with just a single hymn, "The Lord's My Shepherd," sung badly by us over a recorded sound track, a few prayers, and a concise Bible reading that was delivered not by a member of the family but by the minister himself.

The whole thing lasted less than ten minutes. There had been no eulogy, no family recollection of childhood, no . . . love.

I sat there fuming. How could my siblings have allowed this to happen?

I started to get up. Surely someone had to speak.

"Don't," my brother-in-law, Nicholas, said while grasping the tail of my jacket to stop me. "Trust me. Don't."

I turned and looked at him, and also at my cousin Brendan sitting next to him.

"Leave it," Nicholas whispered. "This is not the time or place."

"And not with him here," Brendan added, nodding toward Toby Woodley at the back of the chapel.

"But this is precisely the time and place and it's so wrong," I whispered back to them.

"I know it's wrong," Nicholas said. "We have all said so, but your father won't be moved."

Well, I was moved.

As the minister was starting the committal to conclude the proceedings, rather to his surprise, and mine, I stood up and went forward to stand close to the coffin.

I turned to face the Shillingford family and looked straight at my father. As was so often the case, his face was puce with rage, but I didn't care. This service was for Clare, not for him.

"I wish I had prepared a few profound words to say about Clare, but I hadn't expected to be the one speaking here. But now that I am, I suppose I'd better say something."

In all, I spoke for nearly ten minutes.

I talked at length about our childhood and the bonds of being twins, about our teenage years and us both wanting to be jockeys, about Clare's success in her career, and how we had all thought she had so much to live for.

My mother sobbed.

Finally, I turned to face the wooden box that contained the broken mortal remains of my dear twin.

"Clare, we loved you and we failed you. We should have prevented this and we are so sorry. I hope you are somewhere in a better place and you can forgive us."

I went back to my seat and sat down with a heavy heart.

Nicholas patted me on the back. He was crying. Brendan next to him was crying. In fact, there was crying going on all around me.

I noticed that even my father was now in tears. Maybe it hadn't simply been anger but guilt that had made him behave so strangely.

The minister completed the committal, and the electrically operated curtains closed around the casket, masking it from our sight.

"Well done," Nicholas said to me as we stood up. "You were right."

"But what is wrong with you all?" I said to him in frustration. "Was that really the best the collective minds of the Shillingford family could come up with?"

"There's no such thing as collective minds in our family," he replied. "You should know that by now. The truth is that no one did anything because we were all terrified of upsetting someone else, so, in the end, nothing got done at all. This funeral wasn't planned, it simply drifted into existence."

Geoff Grubb came over to me. "I thought there would have been more people here."

"It was for immediate family only," I said.

"Oh. Sorry. I didn't realize."

"It doesn't matter," I said. "I'm pleased you came."

"She was a nice girl." He, too, seemed close to tears.

"I'll miss her." He turned away from me and wiped his eyes, clearly embarrassed by his crying. "She was like immediate family to me. Looked after me, she did, since my Gloria passed away last year. We had no kids of our own."

I was quite surprised by his show of emotion, as well as by the thought of Clare in any way looking after him. Everyone thought of Geoff Grubb as a training machine with a heart of stone. But I still didn't think he could possibly have been the elusive secret boyfriend.

Geoff and I walked out of the crematorium chapel together into the watery sunshine. My father was standing there.

"Dad," I said, "this is Geoff Grubb, who Clare rode for. He also owns Stable Cottage where she lived."

My father shook Geoff's offered hand and thankfully resisted the urge to ask him why he was here.

"Well spoken, Mark," he said instead, looking me in the eye.

"Thank you, Dad," I said, looking straight back at him.

It was the first time I could remember in my whole life that my father had praised me for anything. He held out his hand to me and I shook it warmly.

"Excuse me," said a voice on my right, breaking the moment.

I turned to find the elderly couple who had been standing at the back. My father faced the opposite direction, away from them, and walked off. I actually thought he was crying again.

"Hello, Mark," said the man, holding out his hand.

"Hello." I shook his hand. "And you are?"

"You must remember us," the lady said.

I looked at them more closely.

"Mr. and Mrs. Yates," I said, smiling broadly. "How lovely to see you again."

"Fred and Emma," Mr. Yates said. "It is good to see you again, too, Mark, but it's a shame about the circumstances. Clare was such a sweet girl."

Fred and Emma Yates had been our regular babysitters when Clare and I had been kids, always coming to the house together, and even staying over if our parents were away. I hadn't seen them for nearly twenty years.

"We've always followed Clare's riding," Fred said.

"And you on the television," added his wife. "Really proud of both of you, aren't we, Fred?"

"Thank you," I said, meaning it.

The two young women who knew Clare from school were hovering to my right. I, meanwhile, was trying to look over them to see where my father had gone.

"Hello," I said, turning my eyes to the women. "Sorry about my father. He can be rather rude at times."

"We know," said the taller of the two, "from our school days."

"I'm sorry," I said, "but I don't remember you from school."

"We were in the tennis team with Clare. I'm Hanna and this is Sally."

We shook hands. "I'm Mark."

"We know," said Sally, smiling. "We always watch the racing on the telly. Mostly because of Clare. We loved it when she won. We even went to Ascot this year with some other friends just to see her ride. We were in the Silver Ring, wearing our fancy hats. We stood by the rail and cheered every time she came past. And she waved to us on the way to the start for every race." She paused. "We loved Clare."

Fred and Emma Yates, Hanna and Sally, Geoff Grubb: how many other people had loved Clare? How many were proud of her and had admired her achievements?

But what about the race fixing? Would they be proud of her for that as well?

As far as I was aware, I was the only person who knew about the seven definite cases and the four possible ones that I had found on the database.

I must use that knowledge with care. The last thing I wanted to do was to blacken people's memory of my sister.

TOBY WOODLEY spoke to me outside the chapel, coming up as I was guiding my mother back to the cars.

"Can you give me a quote?" he asked in his squeaky voice.

"I've said all I wanted to, thank you."

"You should be nice to me," he whined. "I've been good to you."

"And how is that exactly?" I replied, my voice heavy with irony.

"I was going to write all about you in last Monday's paper."

"What about?" I asked.

"Never you mind," he said. "But, luckily for you, my

editor's better nature convinced me not to kick a man when he's down."

"Well, that would make a change. I didn't realize your editor had a better nature. Now, please go away." I was doing my best to keep my temper and to remain polite.

"I wish now he hadn't been so kind," he sneered, "but he said it wouldn't make us any friends, not being so soon after your sister and all. Said it would be too tough on the family."

"Death is always tough on the families," I replied, not really knowing what he was talking about.

"Suicide, you mean. Why do you think she did it?"

I ignored him and settled my weeping mother into the front seat of my father's old Jaguar.

"Any ideas?" he persisted, coming up close to my side.

I thought about pushing him away, but, knowing the *Daily Gazette*, there'd be a photographer watching every move. Instead, I tried to ignore him.

"Come on, Mark," he whined, prodding my arm, "you must have some idea why she killed herself. You don't just jump off a hotel balcony for no reason."

I was sure he was goading me into a reaction. So I looked around for a camera and, sure enough, a man was standing half hidden in the gardens of remembrance with a telephoto lens at the ready. His editor's better nature obviously hadn't prevailed for very long.

"Sorry, Toby, you little creep," I said, unable to keep the anger out of my voice any longer, "I can't help you. Now, piss off, and leave my family alone to grieve in peace."

He didn't, of course, asking more questions of my

brothers. But he didn't really know who they were and they gave him short shrift anyway. When he asked Brendan for directions to my parents' house, he was told in no uncertain terms that he wouldn't be welcome at the family home—or anywhere else, for that matter.

At one point I thought Brendan was actually going to hit him, but thankfully, with the photographer in mind, good sense prevailed, and we all drove away, leaving Toby standing alone in the crematorium parking lot.

ONLY THE FAMILY returned to my parents' house, Geoff Grubb declining my invitation, while Mr. and Mrs. Yates, plus Hanna and Sally, had obviously thought better of it.

But so little planning had gone into Clare's funeral that no provision had been made for any refreshments afterward.

"Surely there's some drink in the house?" I said to Stephen incredulously.

"I doubt it," he said. "Dad's been knocking it back all week. I bet there's nothing left."

"I'll go and get some wine. You see if you can find some glasses. I'll try to organize some food as well."

I cleaned a local filling station out of its remaining sandwiches and also bought four bottles each of red and white wine, none of which would have won any prizes for taste, but it would have to do.

Nicholas and I stood side by side in the kitchen, cutting up the sandwiches and opening the bottles of wine.

"Will you still be coming to Tatiana's eighteenth on Friday?" he asked with a sigh.

"Of course." Tatiana was Nicholas and Angela's only child, my niece, and also my goddaughter. "Why? What's wrong?"

"Your father says he and your mom won't be coming now. He says it's too soon after all this and that we should cancel or postpone. But I think that life has to go on, and we've made all the arrangements and paid for them too. The bloody tent costs a fortune, and don't even talk to me about the caterers. I can't afford to cancel and then do it all again later. And Tatiana is so looking forward to it. All her chums from school are coming. I don't really know what to do."

"I am sure Clare would not have wanted you to cancel. Anyway, I've been writing my godfatherly speech in readiness." I smiled at him.

"But are you sure it's all right to go ahead?"

"Certain. Take no notice of Dad. I'll try and have a word with him and change his mind about coming."

"He's been very quiet since the service."

"Silly old bugger," I said. "I wonder why he gets so angry all the time."

"It's because he feels challenged by you."

I looked at him. "Don't be silly."

"I'm not," he said. "You and Clare, but especially you, you're the only ones in this family who don't do what he tells you to. Angela is all for canceling Tatiana's party simply because he says we should. But then you tell me to take no notice of him. So, you see, you are the only one who doesn't do as he says. And, what's more, you never have."

"But why does that challenge him?"

"He's the eldest male member of the family and he believes it is his role to decide on family matters and that everyone else should agree with his decisions without question. But I think he knows deep down that you are likely to make better decisions than him, and that if you feel he's wrong, to not follow his orders."

"Damn right," I said.

"That is why you should have been here this week helping him make the right decisions for the funeral. All week he's been trying to second-guess what you would have said."

"But we would have fought. It would have all ended in a shouting match and I would have walked out. Better that I kept away."

"You think that service was better for you keeping away?" His voice was full of sarcasm.

"No. I suppose not."

"No? Then you and your father will have to learn how to make compromises without fighting and to make yourselves heard without shouting."

"You should be a counselor," I said.

"I am."

"Are you really?" I asked.

"Yes," he said, smiling. "But don't tell your father. He thinks I'm a merchant banker in the City. And I do work for a bank, but I don't deal with the money. I'm the company counselor."

"Doing what exactly?"

"Counseling the staff. It is one of their inclusive company benefits."

"Counseling them on what?"

"Anything they like, but marital problems mostly. They all work so bloody hard and for such long hours, trying to earn the tons of money they need to pay their huge mortgages, and only because they think their families will be happier living in enormous houses with indoor swimming pools. The families, however, would much rather live somewhere smaller and see more of Daddy. By the time these guys get to fifty-five and are ready to give it all up to live on their accumulated millions, their wives and kids have had enough of being on their own, have left them, taken half their money, and gone to live with someone else. It's all rather sad."

"So what do you tell them to do?"

"Go home earlier and stay out of the office at weekends."

"And do they listen?"

"Not often," he said with a laugh. "In the City, money equates to testosterone. All of them are driven to get more and more of it, irrespective of the human cost."

I knew some people in racing who were just like that, people for whom winning was like a Class A drug, and they were addicted.

I took a tray of sandwiches and offered them around to the miserable bunch of my relatives who were sitting in the drawing room. Conversation topics, it seemed, were minimal, and the food provided some relief, something to talk about. Nicholas followed me with the wine that I hoped might lighten the gloom.

I went back to the kitchen to find Brendan helping himself to a large glass of red.

"Just what I need," he said, taking a sizable slug. "Perhaps I shouldn't have brought the kids. They're quite distressed by it all. Their first funeral."

"How old are they now?" I asked, not really that interested.

"Christopher is sixteen and Patrick will be fourteen next week."

"Mmm," I said, "maybe they are still a bit young." Nicholas and Angela hadn't brought Tatiana, and she was older than both of Brendan's boys.

"But the boys were so eager to come." He laughed. "Probably just to get a day off school. But I think they might be regretting it now, though. There's not much fun in this family."

I poured myself a large glass of red as well.

"How often did Clare ride for you?" I asked. I was thinking of one of the definites I had found in the database, the race when she had stopped Brendan's horse, Jasmine Pearls, in the Chester City Plate.

"Not that often," he replied. "Most of mine are ridden by Dennis Wilson, and Clare was always riding for Grubby."

"Don't I remember her riding one for you at Chester back in July?"

"Jasmine Pearls," he said, nodding. "She should have

won too. I don't think Clare was at her best that day. She went to the front too soon, and the horse stopped itself. Pearly obviously didn't like being in front. Some horses don't. She's won since, though, at Leicester, having been held up to the last moment."

"Did Clare ride her then?"

"No. Dennis. And he should also have been riding her at Chester, but he'd been thrown the previous day and hurt his ankle."

"So how many times did she ride for you altogether?"

"Maybe a dozen or fifteen over the years. Perhaps more. She last rode for me a couple of weeks ago at Doncaster on a difficult sod of a colt called Cotton House Boy. He always seems to go better with a girl up. Strange, that."

He took one of the cheese-and-pickle sandwiches off the tray I was still holding.

"Suppose I'd better get these kids back home," he said with his mouth full.

"I went to the hotel yesterday," I said.

"Hotel?"

"The London Hilton, on Park Lane."

"Oh?" he said. "And?"

"It seems that Clare met two men in her room before she died, and one of them might even have been there when she fell."

"Any idea who?"

"No," I said, "but I certainly intend to find out. The police took away some of the hotel CCTV video. I've asked them if I can have a look, but the detective in charge is on leave this week and, unbelievably, no one else seems to know anything about it. I'll just have to wait until he comes back, but it's bloody frustrating."

"Would it make any difference if you knew who the men were?"

I sighed. "I suppose not, but I'd like to understand why she did it. And I'd like to know if one of the visitors was her mystery boyfriend. Maybe they'd had a tiff, or perhaps it was something else to do with him that was troubling her."

Or, I thought, had she jumped because of what I had seen at Lingfield and because of what I'd said to her at dinner?

Oh God, I hoped not.

Perhaps I was desperate to find some other reason for her death just to relieve the burden of guilt that weighed so heavily on my chest.

9

On Tuesday morning I went back to work again, this time properly. Life, it seemed, had to continue, and Clare's death was last week's news. The world, and racing, went on regardless without her.

I was due to be the racetrack commentator at the jumps meeting at Stratford-upon-Avon, so I left my apartment early and drove clockwise around the London orbital, then up the freeway to Warwickshire. I spent the journey thinking back to the previous afternoon and, in particular, my rather strange encounter with my father at the conclusion of the proceedings.

With Nicholas's wise words still fresh in my memory, and also with his troubles over the on/off nature of Tatiana's birthday party, I had sought out my father for a quiet chat.

At first I hadn't been able to find him anywhere, but eventually I discovered him sitting in his high-backed desk chair in his study, in the quiet, facing the window.

"Hi, Dad," I said. "You OK?"

He'd swiveled slowly around to face me.

"Not really. You?"

"No. Not at all."

"I've been a fool," he said. He rotated the chair back so that he was again looking out at the garden and he sat silently for some time.

"In what way?" I asked finally. But he'd been a fool in all sorts of ways.

"Please leave me," he replied. "I'd rather be alone."

I could tell from his voice that he'd been close to tears.

"No, Dad. Talk to me."

"I can't." His whole body was shaking with sobs.

Not only had that day been a first for him ever praising me, it was also the first time I had ever seen my father cry. He had always believed, and had stated loudly and often through my childhood, that crying was a sign of weakness. Yet there he was, sobbing like a baby.

I didn't really know what to do. I was sure that he was embarrassed. Perhaps I should have left him alone to recover. Instead, I grabbed the back of his chair and spun him around to face me.

"Talk to me," I almost shouted at him. "We never communicate. We just argue."

"She didn't say good-bye," he said suddenly.

"What?"

"Clare. She never said good-bye to me."

"Dad, she was hardly likely to ring you up to say good-bye before she killed herself."

"No, not that," he said, now openly crying. "I mean, she never said good-bye to me when she left here that evening. We had argued. We always seem to, these days. I can't even remember what it was about. Something about the house, or the garden. She kept telling me I was getting too old to look after it. Anyway, it doesn't matter what we argued about—suffice to say, we did. And I told her that she was an insufferable spoiled brat who should know better than to speak to her parent like that."

I could imagine the exchange. I'd had them myself with the old git.

"She just walked out without another word," he said miserably. "She didn't even say good-bye to your mother. I followed her outside, telling her not to be so bloody stupid, but she didn't reply. She didn't even look at me. She got in her car and drove away without a backward glance." He sobbed again. "I feel so guilty."

Join the club, I thought.

IT WAS ONLY about twelve o'clock when I turned in through the gates of Stratford racetrack and parked in one of the spaces reserved for the race officials. Terence Feynman, the judge for the day, pulled in beside me.

"Hello, Terence," I said, climbing out of my car.

"Hi, Mark. I'm so sorry about Clare."

"Yeah," I said. "Not great."

"No. And just as she had made the breakthrough into the big time. Funny old world."

I didn't feel like laughing.

"Are you commentating or presenting?"

"Commentating."

"See you later, then, up top." He rushed away across the parking lot as if he were late, even though nearly two hours remained before the first race.

The judge's booth was alongside the commentator position at the top of the grandstand, his being directly in line with the winning post to enable him to accurately call the winner, assisted if necessary by the photo-finish camera that sat immediately above him.

Prior to 1949 there were no such cameras, and the judge was the sole arbiter of who had won and who hadn't.

Infamously, in the 1913 running of the 2,000 Guineas, the judge, Charlie Robinson, announced a horse called Louvois as the winner when every single other person at Newmarket that day believed Craganour had passed the post in front and won easily by a length.

Nevertheless, Louvois was declared the winner because the judge said so.

There was speculation and rumor at the time that Robinson had been influenced by the fact that he'd had friends who had died on the *Titanic* the previous year. Craganour was owned by C. Bower Ismay, younger brother of J. Bruce Ismay, chairman of the White Star Line, the company that had owned the *Titanic*. And it had been widely reported at the time, albeit wrongly, that J. Bruce Ismay had saved himself by securing a place in one of *Titanic*'s lifeboats by disguising himself as a woman.

But whatever anyone else might have thought, the judge's decision was final, and Louvois remained the official winner, and his name is still in the record books.

Not until 1983 were photo-finish cameras used at all British racetracks, and the first colored images were not available until 1989.

And it hasn't been just the judge's role that has changed due to modern technology.

The very first racetrack commentary in England was at Goodwood on July 29, 1952. For the previous eight hundred years, since the first documented racetrack at Smithfield in London in the twelfth century, races had been run in silence, the only sounds being the thudding of the horses' hooves on the turf and the cheering of the crowd.

Even as late as 1996, races at Keeneland, a premier racetrack in Lexington, Kentucky, were run without any public address other than a bell being rung when the race began. At Ascot, they still ring a bell to alert the crowd when the runners enter the finishing stretch, even though there has been race commentary at the track since the mid-1950s.

I walked into Stratford racetrack through the main entrance only to come face-to-face with Toby Woodley from the *Daily Gazette*.

"Have you seen my piece today?" he asked in a loathsomely self-satisfied manner.

"No," I replied. "I never read your rag."

"You ought to," he sneered. "You might learn something. Especially today."

He walked off toward the bar, and I watched him go. I wondered if he could have been Clare's secret boyfriend. No, surely that was impossible.

I walked around behind the stands to the press room, which fortunately was deserted long before the first. In common with most racetracks, Stratford looked after members of the press pretty well, providing them with tea and coffee, a tray of sandwiches, and occasionally hot soup. However, I was in search of the newspapers that they regularly left in a stack by the door. In particular, I was looking for a copy of the *Daily Gazette*, which I spread out on one of the wooden desks.

My blood ran cold.

CLARE SHILLINGFORD WAS A RACE FIXER, ran the headline in bold type across the back page.

However, the story beneath was speculative at best and related to a race the previous April when Clare had ridden a horse called Brain of Brixham into second place on the all-weather Polytrack at Wolverhampton. It had been at an evening meeting under lights, and Clare claimed she had mistakenly thought that a pole used to support a TV camera on a wire had been the winning post. Hence she had stopped riding hard some twenty yards short of the finish and had been subsequently overtaken and beaten by another horse right on the line.

I'd seen the video of the race at the time and I remember thinking that Clare had been rather foolish, but it had definitely not been like the others I had found. As far as I could recall, it had been just a silly, but genuine, error.

But could I be totally sure?

The stewards at Wolverhampton had accepted Clare's explanation that it had been accidental and they had given her a fourteen-day suspension for careless riding. Now Toby Woodley was claiming that she had done it on purpose and been paid handsomely by a betting syndicate for her trouble.

I heard the door open behind me.

"So she wasn't such an angel after all," said Woodley with his distinctive squeak.

I spun around. "You're a bloody liar!" I shouted. "That race was simply an error of judgment and you know it."

"How about the betting syndicate?" he said. "They made a fortune laying that horse."

"Says who?" I demanded. "This rubbish doesn't name anyone." I waved my hand at the spread-out paper.

"Sources," he said, tapping the side of his nose with his finger. "I have my sources."

"Your imagination, more like it. You've made the whole thing up."

"You may think so," he sneered, "but this story will run and run."

"I'll sue," I said.

"On what grounds?"

"Libel."

"Don't you know?" He grinned, showing me his nicotine-stained teeth. "Under English law, you can't libel the dead." He laughed. "You should have spoken to me yesterday at her funeral. I was treated like dirt."

So was that the story? Was he simply piqued by being shouted at by my father and brushed off by me?

"Not treated like dirt," I said. "More like shit."

"You'll regret that."

I picked up the newspaper and waved it at him. "And is this what you meant by saying yesterday that you'd been good to me? Ha! Don't make me laugh. You don't know what being good means."

He was about to say something further when the door opened and Jim Metcalf walked in. Jim was the senior racing correspondent for *UK Today*, one of the country's best-selling national newspapers, which prided itself on its coverage of horseracing.

"Hi, Mark," said the newcomer. "Welcome back."

"Thanks, Jim," I said, meaning it. "And thank you for your note last week."

"No problem," he said. "We're all going to miss Clare. She was a lovely girl." He shook his head slightly, as if not knowing what else to say. Instead, he turned to Toby Woodley. "What do you want, you little runt? I thought we'd made it clear you weren't welcome in the press room."

"I have as much right to be here as you do," Toby whined.

"Right, maybe," said Jim. "But we don't want you here, understand? You make the place smell. Now, clear off."

I thought for a moment that Toby was going to stand

his ground, but Jim was even taller than my six-foot-two and he'd once been a Royal Marine Commando. Toby, at about five-foot-six, would have been no match.

"Good riddance," Jim said, smiling, as the door closed. "He's a nasty piece of work."

"Have you seen his piece today in the *Gazette*?" I handed it to him.

"Is it true?" Jim asked after reading it.

"No," I said with certainty.

"Are you sure?"

"Of course I'm sure," I said.

But was I really sure? After what I'd seen on the films, could I be sure of anything concerning Clare's riding?

"What can I do about it?" I asked. "I can't sue him because it seems you can't libel the dead."

"That's right," Jim said, nodding. "But you could call him a liar on the air. Then he'd have to sue you or else be laughed out of his job. You'd then get your day in court. He'd have to prove he wasn't lying and that the facts of the story were accurate. But, sadly, even if you won, you wouldn't get any damages from the little weasel, and you might not get your costs because he'd be sure to claim it was fair comment, even if the story wasn't true."

"Do you do the legal work for *UK Today* as well as the racing?" I asked with a smile.

"Not if I can help it." He smiled back. "But if you want my advice, I would say nothing and do nothing. Everyone knows that the *Gazette* is just a rumor mill. No one believes what it says even when it's true."

"But the *Daily Gazette* sells millions of copies."

"I know they do," he said. "But millions also watch soap operas on the telly and they don't really believe those either."

I wasn't so sure. I knew people who believed all sorts of crazy things.

I left Jim Metcalf tucking in to a ham-and-mustard sandwich while I went out to wander around the parade ring and the enclosures. It was still an hour before the first, but the crowd was beginning to fill the bars and restaurants, encouraged out from their houses by the warm late-September sunshine.

It was good to be back on a racetrack. The last week had seemed to drag on forever. Things might never be the same again without Clare, but at least today, at a jumping meeting, I could get my life back on track. Clare wouldn't have been here today even if she were still alive.

I **WAS UP** in my commentator position well before the first race. I liked commentating at Stratford not least because it was one of the minority of racetracks with the parade ring in front of the grandstands. That gave me more opportunity to study the colors.

I used my binoculars to scrutinize the horses as they walked around and around. I habitually used the race cards printed in the *Racing Post*, with their colored diagrams of the jockeys' silks. Now I made notes in black felt-tip pen of which horses had white marks on their faces, or had sheepskin nosebands, or blinkers, or visors, or white bridles, or breast girths, or anything else that might help me recognize them if I couldn't distinguish the colors, something that was not unknown if the track was very muddy.

Not that that would be an issue today, I thought, not on a fine September afternoon when the problem for the racetrack had been too little water, not too much. Indeed, the dry conditions and the firmness of the track meant that the number of declared runners in each race was small. It made my life easy, but it wasn't good for racing in general.

I watched as the jockeys came out of the weighing room and into the paddock. I couldn't help but think back to the last time I'd seen Clare doing the same thing at Lingfield. If only, I thought for the umpteenth time, if only I had known then what would happen later. I surely could have prevented it.

Suddenly the horses were coming out onto the racetrack, and I had been daydreaming instead of learning the colors. Get a grip, I told myself.

Fortunately there were only eight runners in the novice hurdle and many of them I knew well from having seen them run before. It would be an easy reintroduction to commentary for me. It seemed like longer than just the eleven days since I'd last done it at Lingfield.

I switched on my microphone and described the horses as they made their way to the two-mile start on the far side of the course.

"Hi, Mark," said Derek's voice through the headphones. "Coming to you in one minute."

Derek, sitting in the blacked-out RacingTV scanner

truck, was at Chepstow racetrack, some seventy miles away to the southwest in Wales. He would be watching the same pictures that I had on the monitor in front of me, pictures that showed the eight runners here at Stratford circling while they had their girths tightened by the starter's assistant.

"*Ten seconds,*" said his voice into my ears. "*Five, four, three . . .*" He fell silent.

"The starter is moving to his rostrum," I said into the live microphone. "They're under starters orders. They're off."

The race was uneventful, with the eight horses well strung out even by the time they passed the stands for the first time. On the second circuit, three of them pulled up and the other five finished in an extended line astern with not a moment's excitement between them.

I tried my best to sound upbeat about the winner, as he strode away after the last hurdle to win by twenty lengths, but the crowd didn't seem to mind. He'd been a well-backed favorite, and most of the punters were happy.

"*Thanks, Mark,*" said Derek. "*Back with you for the next.*"

I sighed. The fun suddenly seemed to have gone out of my job.

I stayed in the commentary booth between the first two races and thought about what Toby Woodley had written in the *Gazette*. Was he just trying to get even for being humiliated by my father or was there more to his story? Did he really have his sources and knowledge of a betting syndicate or had he made up the whole thing?

If so, he was a bit too close to the mark for my liking.

I decided that perhaps I shouldn't make too much of a fuss about it. The last thing I wanted was to attract any unwelcome scrutiny of Clare's recent riding. I just hoped that the story was a one-day wonder that would quickly fade away to nothing and that everybody would soon forget about it.

Fat chance of that.

THANKFULLY, the second race was more exciting than the first, this time with seven runners battling it out over fences in a two-and-half-mile Beginners' Steeplechase.

"Beginners" were horses that had never won a steeplechase before, either on a racetrack proper or at a recognized point-to-point meeting, and it showed, with two of the seven falling at the first fence. However, the remaining five put up more of a contest, with three of them still with a chance at the last and fighting out a tight finish all the way to the wire.

That was more like it, I thought, smiling as I clicked off my microphone.

"First number, one, Ed Online," Terence the judge called over the public address from his booth next door. "Second number, three; third number, six. The fourth horse was number two. Distances were a neck and half a length."

"Well done, Mark," said Derek through my headphones. *"That was more like it. Back with you for the next."*

"OK," I replied, pushing the right button on my control box. "I'll be here."

There was a thirty-five-minute gap between the second and third races, which gave me about twenty minutes until I was needed back in my position, so I decided to go down to the weighing room for a cup of tea. However, I was intercepted by Harry Jacobs, my leisurely friend whom I'd last seen at Lingfield the day Clare had died.

"Hello, Mark," he said, shaking my hand warmly. "You must come and have a drink."

"I'm working," I said.

"I know," he replied with a smile. "I've been listening to your dulcet tones over the loudspeakers. But surely you've got time for a quick one?"

I looked at my watch. "All right," I said, smiling back. "But it will have to be quick."

"But they can't start the race without you anyway," he said, chuckling.

"Oh yes they can," I assured him. "The race will start on time, with or without the commentary."

"We'd better be quick, then."

He put his hand on my shoulder and guided me around behind the stands toward the pre–parade ring. "I've got a box," he said as we climbed a metal staircase. "In here." He opened a door, and we went into a room full to over-flowing with people who all seemed to be talking at once. The noise was almost overwhelming.

"Are all these your guests?" I asked him, shouting.

"Yes!" he shouted back. "Stratford's my local course, so I've asked along a few chums from home. Plus a few others I've sort of picked up since we arrived." He grinned broadly at me. "Now, what will you have?"

"Do you have a Diet Coke?" I asked.

His face showed that he didn't approve of any of his guests drinking nonalcoholic beverages. "Are you sure you won't have champagne?"

"Oh all right, then," I said with a laugh. "I'll force it down."

A waiter miraculously moved through the throng and delivered two slender glasses of bubbles into our hands.

"Cheers," I said, raising mine to my lips.

We were still standing close to the door, and Harry decided to dive deeper into the room. "Come on," he said, reaching out his hand and grabbing my jacket.

I didn't have much choice, so I followed him.

We struggled through and out onto the balcony on the far side, overlooking the parade ring.

"That's better," Harry said. "More air out here." He looked over my shoulder. "Hi, Richard," he shouted, and dived back into the melee, leaving me alone.

I turned to my right just as the lady behind me turned to her left so that the two of us ended up standing face-to-face, crammed together by the crowd.

"Hello, Sarah," I said.

Her irate husband, Mitchell Stacey, stood behind her, looking at me, and I swear I could see steam emanating from his ears.

I turned away from him and left, forcing my way through the mob without much finesse or consideration for toes, and I didn't look back to see if he was following. I almost ran down the metal stairs and then back to the commentary booth, where I remained holed up for the rest of the afternoon.

I LEFT IMMEDIATELY after the last race and hurried out to the parking lot, but Stacey was ahead of me, waiting at my car. I stopped ten yards away.

"I told you to stay away from my wife," he hissed at me through clenched teeth. "I warned you."

I decided to say nothing. I could have tried to explain to him that Sarah and I had come together by accident, that I hadn't even known she was at Stratford until we had ended up, nose to nose, on Harry Jacobs's balcony. But I didn't think it would help. Saying nothing was surely the best policy. Allow the volcano to subside, I thought. Don't go poking it with a stick.

He'd told me at Newmarket that he would have had my legs broken, but he could hardly do it on his own. For a start, I was half his age. I was also a good four or five inches taller than he and I kept myself fairly fit, not least by climbing stairs to the commentary booths at the top of all the racetrack grandstands.

If he was going to break my legs, he'd need help.

I glanced around, but there were no Stacey henchman lurking in the shadows. Rather, there was a group of inebriated racegoers making their unsteady way toward a row of buses.

"I warned you," he said again.

He suddenly strode toward me, so I moved quickly to

the side to put a car between us but he didn't follow. He simply marched past where I'd been standing and continued in a straight line back toward the racetrack enclosures.

I breathed a huge sigh of relief. The confrontation was over for now, but I would be naïve if I thought it would be over forever.

10

Toby Woodley's story didn't fade away. Quite the opposite.

Wednesday morning's *Daily Gazette* had upgraded it from the back page to the front with an "Exclusive" tag beneath a two-inch-high headline in bold capital letters: RACE FIXING.

The article beneath reiterated the allegation that Clare had stopped Brain of Brixham in the race at Wolverhampton, even providing details about the amount of money that had supposedly been won by those laying the horse on the Internet betting exchanges.

It must have been a slow news day, I thought, and Toby Woodley's imagination had obviously been running in overdrive to fill the gap.

But there was also an underlying tone to the piece that vaguely implied that Clare's ride on Brain of Brixham might not have been an isolated incident but rather part of a pattern.

Watch this space, it said at the end, *for further revelations tomorrow. And not only about Clare Shillingford, but also about her brother, Mark.*

I stared at it. What revelations about me was Toby Woodley going to make up now? He's told me I'd regret saying at Stratford that he'd been treated at Clare's funeral not like dirt but like shit. Now the little bastard would make me pay. Unlike Clare, I *would* be able to take him to court if he lied.

And this wasn't the first time that the *Daily Gazette* had made accusations about race fixing either. It had done so the previous May, but not on the front page. On that occasion the whole thing had quickly died away to nothing as the paper had been unable to produce any firm evidence and had declined to name any individuals, probably for fear of being sued.

Even the *Racing Post*, which should have known better, had a report following up on the *Gazette*'s story, demanding answers and challenging Toby Woodley to reveal the identity of members of the betting syndicate "for the good of racing." The *Post*'s tenor may have been more "put up or shut up," but it wouldn't help to reduce the speculation. At least Jim Metcalf in *UK Today* had refused to join the chorus.

OTHER THAN READING the newspapers, I spent most of Wednesday morning studying the brochures for the eight houses I had looked at on the Internet. The various realtors had been most efficient in sending details, each brochure arriving with a cover letter telling me, each in a slightly different way, that now was the ideal time to buy a house.

I was sure that every realtor always thought it was an ideal time to buy a house. They were hardly likely to say it wasn't, now were they?

I was particularly interested in a house in a North Oxfordshire village. I'd often thought that Edenbridge in Kent was far from being the ideal place to live for someone with my job. Lingfield Park was certainly handy, and Brighton, Plumpton, and Folkestone were pretty close as well. It was also not bad for Fontwell, Goodwood, and the London courses, but I spent much of my time at the tracks in the Midlands and the North and they were all a long way off. It was no wonder that the odometer on my old Ford had been around the dial twice.

Oxfordshire, I thought, was a good central location, one where I could get to and from almost all the English racetracks in a single day, although there were none in the county itself.

I sat and looked at the glossy pictures and wondered if I was doing the right thing. In particular, was it sensible to move away from my parents at a stage in their lives when they soon would be needing more help?

That alone, I decided, was one very good reason why I should move. As things stood, I could see that it was going to fall to me alone to look after them, as had indeed become the case in recent months. If I lived in Oxfordshire rather than just five miles down the road, my elder siblings might start believing that they also had some responsibility for their parents, especially as they would all then be living closer to them than I.

Perhaps I should call the realtor and make an appointment to go see the house. Maybe I'd do it tomorrow.

MIDWEEK RACING under the lights at Kempton Park on the all-weather Polytrack has become standard fare for punters, although during the winter months the "crowd," if that is the right term for the sparse gathering of the faithful, wisely spend most of their time inside the glass-fronted bars and restaurants.

However, in late September the weather gods had been kind, and England was enjoying an Indian summer, with hot days and balmy evenings. So much so that I left my overcoat in my car, which I parked in the track parking lot.

I generally liked commentating on racing under lights.

I had first been night racing at Happy Valley racetrack in Hong Kong as a nineteen-year-old. It probably had been the strange environment as much as anything, but I'd found the whole experience so exciting, and part of that excitement remains every time I see jockeys' silks shining vividly in the bright glow of artificial light.

But that would have to wait. The first race was at twenty minutes to six, and the sun was still well up in the sky as the ten runners were loaded into the starting gate at the one-mile start on the far side of the oval track.

"They're off in the Crane Park Limited Maiden Stakes,"

I said into my microphone. "Quarterback Sneak breaks well and is quickly into stride on the nearside. He goes into an early lead, with Waimarima a close second. Popeye's Girl is next, in the pink jacket and sheepskin noseband, with Apache Pilot alongside in the dark green. Next is Banker's Joy, with the yellow crossbelts, and then Marker Pen in the hoops, with Kitbo now making some headway on the outside in the white cap."

The race unfolded, and I continued to describe the action as they swung right-handed into the stretch as a closely bunched group, the horses spreading across the track as their jockeys searched for a clear run to the line.

And every one of the jockeys looked to me just like Clare.

I almost lost it completely, but I forced myself to concentrate on the horses and pulled myself back from the brink.

"Quarterback Sneak is still just in front, but here comes Apache Pilot, with Popeye's Girl going very well on the wide outside. Just between these three, as they enter the final hundred yards. Quarterback Sneak seems unable to quicken, and Popeye's Girl goes on to win easily from Apache Pilot, with Kitbo a fast-finishing third. Next comes Quarterback Sneak, then Marker Pen and Banker's Joy together, followed by Waimarima, who faded badly in the closing stages."

I went through the rest of the field and then clicked off my mike.

I leaned back wearily against the wall of the commentary booth and wiped a bead of sweat from my clammy forehead. I felt wretched, and wondered if I would ever again be able to commentate on a race like that without seeing Clare as one, or all, of the jockeys.

Throughout her career, and particularly in the early years, Clare had ridden often at the all-weather tracks, especially during the winter months when there was no turf flat racing in Great Britain. It was how up-and-coming jockeys nowadays learned their trade, taking rides in January and February while many of their more established colleagues were sunning themselves on Caribbean beaches or riding winners in the warmth of Australia, Dubai, or Hong Kong.

I sat down on the stool in the commentary booth and looked out across the racetrack, the lights of the aircraft landing at Heathrow now shining brightly in the darkening sky.

I told myself that the reason I didn't feel like going down to the weighing room was I didn't want to meet anyone who had read the *Daily Gazette* or who might ask me difficult questions after seeing the *Racing Post*. But, in reality, it was because I felt I had to psych myself up for the next race.

I realized that commentating hadn't been a problem the previous day because Clare had never ridden at Stratford, and never would have, since they staged just hurdle races and steeplechases. Only tonight, here at Kempton, was I suddenly struck by her absence from the track.

Staying in the booth, however, wasn't the ideal preparation for the next race, as I couldn't see the runners in the parade ring, which at Kempton was situated right behind the main grandstand.

I studied the race program and tried to memorize the colors, but there was nothing like actually seeing the jockeys wearing the silks. All too often, the pigment of the inks used in the printing bore little or no resemblance to the actual dyes used in the material.

I went out of the commentary booth and turned left.

As was the case at many racetracks, the commentary booth at Kempton was high above and behind the grandstand seating but still under its large cantilevered roof. It was one of a number of separate booths opening off a long corridor that ran behind them to a metal staircase at one end.

During the races, the various booths contained not only the course race caller but also the judge, the race stewards, television cameramen, as well as the photo-finish technicians, who were on a higher level still immediately above the judge's booth, accessed by a second metal staircase at the far end.

It was a strange world that the public never saw, with multiple cables running along the tops of the undecorated walls, each essential for carrying the pictures and sound to the racetrack crowd and beyond.

I went to the end of the corridor and climbed the staircase to the photo-finish booth. Opposite was a door that opened out onto the grandstand roof. I unlocked the door and stepped out.

The Kempton grandstand had been built in 1997, and,

like many similar projects of the time, much of its structural support was gained from a tubular steel framework that sat above the roof like a series of gigantic wire coat hangers.

There were a number of intersecting walkways that allowed access to the various air-conditioning units and the multitude of electronic aerials and satellite dishes, which were spread out all over the place. Each of the walkways had a metal grille floor and railings down either side to prevent anyone straying off them onto the roof itself.

I knew from experience that it was possible to see the parade ring from one of the walkways. I'd used it before, the previous year, when I'd twisted my ankle and didn't fancy going all the way down to ground level to see the horses.

I now spent a few moments checking the jockeys' silks. It was rare, but not unknown, for the printing in the paper to be wrong—for example, if a horse had been sold the night before a race and was running in the new owner's colors, something that was not that uncommon in the Grand National.

But on this occasion I was satisfied that all were attired as expected and I made my way back down to the commentary booth in time to describe them to the crowd as they cantered around the end of the track to the seven-eighths-of-a-mile start point on the far side of the course.

This time when the horses spread out as they entered the stretch, I was ready for the "Clare moment," as I decided to call it, when all the jockeys were facing me and each one of them reminded me of her. This time, in some strange way, I felt somewhat comforted by it rather than being overcome.

Far from trying to put Clare out of my mind in case it was too upsetting, I wanted to remember her every day, and this would be the way I would do it.

Suddenly I was more at ease with life, and I realized that, as for my father, feelings of guilt over Clare's death had overshadowed and distorted my grief. From that moment on, I told myself, I was going to rejoice in the memory of her brief existence and do my best to protect it.

Not that I didn't still feel terrible guilt over not answering the telephone calls from Clare that night. I did. And I lay awake for hours most nights rehearsing to myself what I could have done better to prevent the disaster.

But Jim Metcalf's advice to say nothing and to do nothing was for the old indecisive me. The new resolute and well-focused me would call Toby Woodley's bluff and make him prove what he was claiming was true or else admit that he couldn't.

I DID GO DOWN to the weighing room after the second race and, instead of avoiding people who might ask me questions about the front page of the *Daily Gazette* or the piece in the *Racing Post*, I started every conversation by saying how ridiculous it was and how Toby Woodley was just a little insect that needed stamping on.

"A worm is more like it," said Jack Laver, the racetrack

broadcast technician who had made me the tea at Lingfield. "Nasty piece of work, that one. He was here earlier. Always tries to snoop round the weighing room to see if there's any gossip he can use or make up. The Clerk threw him out."

The Clerk of the Scales presided in the weighing room like a judge in a courtroom, sitting behind a desk and ensuring that everything was done correctly, including keeping the press out.

His primary role was to ensure that all the jockeys "weighed out" for each race at the correct weight and also that the winner and those who placed "weighed in" again afterward, together with any other jockeys that the Clerk may choose at his sole discretion. He also had to ensure that each jockey was wearing the correct colors and had the right equipment, such as blinkers or a visor, which the horse may have been declared as wearing.

And all the jockeys called him sir.

Not that they weren't averse to trying to fool him—usually because they were having trouble getting down to the required weight.

"Cheating Boots" have been around almost since racing first began—ultralight, paper-thin riding boots used only for weighing out, which the wearer then illegally exchanges for a more substantial pair back in the jockeys' room, well out of sight of the Clerk. Weighing back in is not a problem as riders are allowed up to two extra pounds to provide for rain-soaked clothes or accumulated mud thrown up from the track.

These days, a jockey's racing helmet is not included in

his riding weight, unlike his saddle, which is. However, the colored cap that is worn over the helmet is included, but there are always those who will try to place the cap down on the Clerk's table while weighing out.

Every little bit helps.

In truth, it was all a bit of a game, and just like the schoolteacher and his miscreant pupils, the Clerks of the Scales were wise to jockeys' schemes and almost always won, but that didn't stop the jockeys from trying.

"Everything all right up top?" Jack asked. "Monitor OK?"

"Fine," I said, "as long as I can turn down the brightness a bit now that it's getting dark."

"There are some buttons on the side," Jack said. "Click the menu button twice, then use the down button on the brightness. Or do you need me to do it?"

"I'm sure I'll manage," I said. "I'll come back after the next if I can't."

I went out to the parade ring, keeping a careful watch out for Toby Woodley. I really didn't want to come face-to-face with him tonight. I wasn't at all sure I could restrain myself from hitting him and that surely wouldn't have helped the situation.

I stood and watched the horses for the third race walking around and around, noting on my race program that two of them were wearing sheepskin nosebands. Some trainers ran all their horses in nosebands. They thought it made them easier to spot, which was true as long as everyone didn't do it.

THE LAST of the eight races was not until after nine o'clock and by then many of the crowd had made their way home, not least because the evening had cooled considerably.

As my commentary of the race echoed around the deserted grandstands, I wondered if anyone at the course was actually listening to me, although I hoped that some at home might be via their televisions.

"Thanks, Mark," said a voice into my headphones as I switched off the microphone for the last time.

"Pleasure, Gordon," I replied, pushing the right button. Gordon was another of the RacingTV producers. "See you at Warwick tomorrow?"

"No," he replied. *"Derek will be back doing Warwick. I'm in the studio tomorrow, then I'll be at Haydock Friday and Saturday. You?"*

"I'm presenting for Channel 4 on Saturday at Newmarket. Friday's a rare day off for me."

"Have fun. Bye, now."

There was a click in my ears, and the system went dead. It was time to go home.

I packed my binoculars, colored pens, and race programs into my bag; went down to ground level; and followed the last remaining punters out past the parade ring in the direction of the parking lots.

By that time of night, there was a definite chill in the air, and I wished I'd brought my coat with me after all. But it was only a hundred and fifty yards or so to my car, and I hurried along toward it.

I never got there.

TOBY WOODLEY was in the parking lot, standing beside a white van.

If I'd seen him sooner, I'd have made a detour to avoid him, but as it was I came around the back of the van and there he was only about six feet away. I stopped.

"What the bloody hell do you want?" I asked him.

He didn't answer but rolled his head toward me. He was actually leaning against the side of the van with his head back against the metal.

"Are you all right?" I asked.

He didn't reply.

I stepped forward toward him just as he slithered sideways down the side of the van, catching him just before he landed facedown. Even in the relatively dim glow of the parking lot lighting, a bright red streak of blood was clearly visible on the van's white panel.

"Help!" I shouted as loudly as I could. "Help! Somebody call an ambulance."

I turned Toby on his back and looked into his face as I struggled to remove my cell phone from my pocket. His eyes had an air of mild surprise in them. I thought he was trying to say something, but it was just the sound of his rasping breath. There were flecks of bright scarlet blood in the froth coming from his mouth.

"Help!" I shouted again. "Get an ambulance."

A man came running over toward me as I finally managed to extract my phone. "Call an ambulance," I said, tossing it to him.

"What's wrong with him?" the man asked.

"I think he's been stabbed," I said. "There's lots of blood."

The man glanced at the side of the van and pushed 999 on my phone.

I looked back at Toby's face. The air of surprise seemed to have gone. Now he was just staring, but his eyes didn't see. The rasping breath was no more.

"I think he's dead," I said to the man. "He's stopped breathing."

"Has he got a pulse?"

I tried to feel his wrist, but the only beat I could detect was from my own heart thumping away.

"I don't know," I said.

"Give him mouth-to-mouth," said the man. "The ambulance is on its way."

Not surprisingly, kissing Toby Woodley had not been on my planned agenda for the day, but nevertheless I tilted his head back, put my lips over his, and breathed into him. There was no noticeable movement of his chest, so I tilted his head back farther and repeated the drill.

"Keep going," said the man. "I'll do chest compressions."

The man knelt down next to me and started vigorously pumping with his hands up and down on Toby's breastbone as I breathed into Toby's mouth.

We went on like that for a good five minutes.

"Bloody hell," said the man, pausing for a moment, "this is hard work."

"Do you want to swap?" I said.

"No," he replied. "Keep going as we are."

"Does he have a pulse now?" I asked between breaths.

"Just keep going," said the man, resuming his chest compressions.

So we kept going for what seemed like at least another five minutes until an array of bright blue flashing lights announced the arrival of an ambulance and two green-clad paramedics came running over to us followed by a sizable group of onlookers, some of them with camera phones held high.

One of the paramedics bared Toby's chest and attached some sticky patches to his skin while the other connected leads to the patches and also to a yellow box with a small screen on the front. Even I could tell that the trace on the screen was flat and lifeless.

One of the paramedics pulled another box from his large green bag and soon had two metal plates placed on either side of Toby's chest.

"All clear," he called, making sure no one was touching Toby. "Shocking!"

Toby's body convulsed for a moment, then lay motionless again. The line on the screen, meanwhile, stayed completely flat.

"All clear again," called the paramedic. "Shocking!"

He repeated the process another three times while his colleague injected something into Toby's arm. That wouldn't do much good, I thought, not without any circulation. For all their effort, the trace on the screen never even flickered.

The paramedics took over the mouth-to-mouth and

chest compressions, and they went on for far longer than I would have expected, each time they stopped, the line on the screen remaining stubbornly flat. They shocked Toby yet again and shone a flashlight in his eyes.

"No pressure," said one. "No vital signs. CPR terminated at"—he looked at his watch—"nine forty-five." He began to pack up his equipment.

"What happened?" the other paramedic asked me, all urgency having suddenly evaporated.

"He's been stabbed," I said.

"What with?" he asked while pulling Toby's shirt wider and looking down his abdomen. "And where?"

"There's blood on his back," I said. And, I suddenly realized, I was kneeling in the stuff. A great pool of it surrounded Toby's body. All those chest compressions, I thought, had done nothing more than pump the blood out of him.

The police arrived in force, and suddenly the atmosphere changed again. It was no longer just a racetrack parking lot. It had become a murder scene.

11

"Now, Mr. Shillingford, are you absolutely sure that Mr. Woodley was alive when you first saw him in the parking lot?"

"Yes," I said. "Quite sure. He was leaning against the white van, and he moved his head round to look at me when I spoke to him."

I was sitting in a cubicle in a mobile police incident room that had been parked in a corner of the Kempton Park racetrack parking lot, well away from the square white tent that now stood over the spot where Toby Woodley had died.

And I was cold.

"Can't you get me something warmer?" I asked the detective who was asking the questions. "I'm freezing in this." I fingered the white nylon coveralls I had been given to put on when my clothes had been removed and bagged for forensic purposes. Ignominiously, I had been made to stand in my underwear, shivering, as a masked forensic officer, also dressed from head to foot in white nylon, had examined my skin, hair, fingernails, and mouth for any clues.

"There's a tracksuit on its way from the station," said the detective, "and a pair of training shoes." He gesticulated at another policeman, who had been sitting quietly listening to our conversation. The second man stood up and went out of the cubicle, closing the door behind him.

If the rest of me was cold, my feet were like blocks of ice, resting as they were on the freezing metal floor of the glorified van.

"Did Mr. Woodley say anything to you?" the detective asked once again.

"No," I repeated. "I told you, he just slid down the side of the van and died."

"So why did you tell the paramedic that Mr. Woodley had been stabbed?"

"Because of the blood on the van," I said patiently. "I just presumed he'd been stabbed."

"I see," he said, making a note.

"And was he?" I asked.

"Was he what?"

"Stabbed?"

"The autopsy will determine that, sir," the detective said formally.

The second policeman came back into the cubicle and sat down again on the same upright chair as before. He shook his head, and I took that to mean the tracksuit and training shoes were not yet here. I went on shivering.

"When can I go home?" I asked the detective.

"That will be up to my superintendent," he replied unhelpfully.

I looked at my watch. It was well past eleven o'clock and nearly two hours since Toby Woodley's life had expired.

"Look," I said, "could you please tell your superintendent that I need to go home now. I've got to be up tomorrow in time to go to work."

"And what is your work, sir?" the detective asked.

"I've already told you." My patience was beginning to run rather thin. "I'm a race caller and TV presenter. I was commentating here tonight, and I found Mr. Woodley in the parking lot as I was leaving. I tried to help him, but I couldn't. He died in spite of another man and me giving him artificial respiration. That's all I can tell you. And now," I said, standing up, "I'd like to go home."

The detective, who remained seated in his chair, looked up at me.

"Mr. Shillingford," he said, "have you read today's *Daily Gazette*?"

I stood there looking back at him. "Am I under arrest?" I asked.

"No, of course not," the detective said, smiling. "We just need you to remain here a while longer to help us with our inquiries."

"And how about if I say I'm going home anyway?"

"That wouldn't be wise," he said.

No. Then I probably would be arrested.

I thought back over the interview.

"You haven't asked me why I think Mr. Woodley was attacked."

"No, sir," said the detective without elaborating.

"Why not?" I asked.

"All in good time, sir," he replied.

We sat in silence for a while, and I wondered what the police were doing that took so long. Looking for a knife, I supposed. That's it, I thought, they couldn't arrest me for stabbing Toby unless they could find the knife because otherwise there was no way I could have done it.

And maybe they wouldn't ask me why I thought Toby had been stabbed until they knew whether I could have done it. Perhaps it would affect how they asked their questions.

I sat there hoping the killer had taken the murder weapon away with him. Knowing my luck, he'd have thrown it away under my car.

Someone came into the cubicle carrying a folded track-suit and a pair of training shoes. Thank goodness, I thought. My feet had lost all feeling.

I was left alone briefly to change, but the detective and his sidekick soon returned, accompanied this time by another man who was clearly their boss—the superintendent.

"Mr. Shillingford," he said. "Detective Superintendent Cullen." He held out his hand toward me and I shook it. "I'm sorry you have been asked to stay here for so long. I hope my boys have been looking after you?" He smiled.

No knife, I thought.

"They have been charming," I said, smiling back. Two could play at this game. "And thank you for the tracksuit and shoes." We both smiled again.

Another chair was brought in, and we all sat down, although the cubicle was hardly big enough for the four of us.

"Can you think of any reason why Mr. Woodley would be murdered?" the superintendent asked.

"Other than because of today's front page of the *Daily Gazette*?" I said. There was little point in not mentioning it, and I thought it would be better if I did so first.

"Exactly. Other than that."

"Lots of them," I said.

"I beg your pardon?"

"I can think of lots of reasons why someone might want to murder Toby Woodley. He was a horrible little man who preyed on other people's weaknesses." I paused briefly. "I'd have happily stuck a knife into his back."

"And did you?" he asked seriously.

"No," I said. "Someone else seems to have done it for me."

"Is that an admission of a conspiracy?"

"No, of course not," I said. "But if you're expecting me to grieve over Toby Woodley, you'll be disappointed. I hated the little creep."

"I understand," he said slowly, "that you have been telling people here this evening that he was nothing more than an insect that needed stamping on. Is that right?"

"Quite right," I said. "Because he's been trashing my

late sister's reputation with his lies and I couldn't do anything about it."

"Someone may have."

"Well, it was not me."

"What were the revelations about you that Mr. Woodley was going to write about?"

"I have absolutely no idea," I said. "I was rude to him at Stratford races yesterday, and I expect he was planning to make up some nonsense about me out of revenge."

"How were you rude to him?"

"I basically told him he was a little shit," I said. "Because he was."

Superintendent Cullen looked down at his notebook, then up at me.

"Are you happy he's dead?"

I sat there and looked at each of the three policemen in turn.

"I tried to save his life, didn't I? I put my mouth over his—over the mouth of someone I hated and despised—and I breathed into him." I instinctively wiped my mouth with the sleeve of the tracksuit. "Of course I'm not happy he's dead. But, equally, I'm not especially sad about it either."

THEY FINALLY let me go at about half past midnight after I had agreed to and signed a full account of the incident as I remembered it. But they kept my clothes, my shoes, and, much to my annoyance, my car.

"I need my car," I said.

"None of the cars close to the white van can be moved," the superintendent said to me. "We need to search the area again properly in the daylight, and I'm not prepared to compromise any forensic evidence present by moving anything."

"But how am I going to get home?" I asked. "Especially at this time of night?"

"I'll get a car to take you."

"Thank you. How about my clothes?" I asked. "And my shoes?"

I was rather fond of those shoes.

"You'll get them back in due course."

I didn't like to ask how long "in due course" might be. Years, probably, particularly if they provided evidence that was pertinent to a prosecution.

"I'll need my car tomorrow morning," I said. "I've got to get to Warwick races."

"Don't push your luck, Mr. Shillingford," the superintendent said, but with a smile. "You're lucky to be getting a ride home. I could always change my mind. Ever heard of trains? Leave your car keys and your phone number with my sergeant and he'll contact you when you can retrieve your car."

I didn't push my luck. I gave my car keys to the sergeant.

"Thank you," he said.

I was driven in an unmarked police car by a driver who didn't say a word to me all the way from Kempton to Edenbridge. He dropped me outside my front door, still silent, and drove off.

I let myself in and then sat in my sitting room–cum–kitchen–cum–dining room–cum–office with a stiff whisky.

I didn't often drink spirits, but I didn't often have someone die with his head in my lap.

Who would have wanted to kill Toby Woodley?

Sure, there were lots of people, myself included, who might rejoice at his passing, but I couldn't imagine that anyone would actually kill him over something he had written in the paper. As Jim Metcalf had said, everyone knew the *Daily Gazette* was nothing more than a glorified rumor mill and no one really believed any of it.

So why was Toby Woodley dead? And did his death have anything to do with his pieces in the paper about Clare? Or was it totally unrelated? Indeed, were the deaths of Toby Woodley and Clare Shillingford entirely isolated incidents for which the only common factor was me?

I sat for a while pondering such questions but without coming up with any useful answers.

I knocked back the rest of my whisky and went to bed.

What I needed most was someone to talk to, someone to bounce some ideas off. In the past that would have been either Clare or Sarah.

I lay in the darkness, missing both of them hugely.

ON THURSDAY MORNING I caught a train from Edenbridge to London, and then another from London to Warwick.

I usually went everywhere by car, and it was quite a change for me to just sit and watch the world go by the window.

I bought a stack of newspapers at Edenbridge station

and mostly spent the journey reading everything I could find about the murder of Toby Woodley in the Kempton parking lot. There was precious little that I didn't know already.

Only the *Racing Post* named me as one of the two men who had tried to save Toby's life. I wondered how much flak I would get from my colleagues for that.

The *Daily Gazette*, in contrast, named me as someone who was helping the police with their inquiries, which I suppose had been true at the time the paper had gone to press late the previous evening. The paper also speculated as to why one of its "star reporters"—their words—had been so cruelly cut down in the prime of life. Was it something to do with the *Daily Gazette*'s ongoing investigation into race fixing? Without actually saying so directly, they used the obvious association of the Shillingford names to imply that it must have been me who had killed Toby Woodley to shut him up.

Perhaps I should contact my solicitor and sue them. But I knew of others who had sued the *Daily Gazette*, and even though a few of them had won sizable damages, they always lost in the end. Newspapers in general were relentless and vindictive, and the *Gazette* led the way on both counts, hounding its detractors forever, with every misdemeanor, however slight, every speeding ticket, every marital indiscretion, every faux pas, splashed across its front page in big bold type.

I took a taxi from Warwick station to the racetrack.

I was early.

I climbed up the stairs to the commentary booth and

sat silently looking out across the track. There was a good hour and a half to go before the first race, but I needed to think. In particular, I needed to think once again about why Clare might have killed herself. And also why anyone would murder Toby Woodley.

The phone vibrated in my pocket. It was Superintendent Cullen's sergeant.

"Mr. Shillingford," he said, "did Mr. Woodley have a black leather briefcase with him last night when you first saw him in the racetrack's parking lot?"

"I didn't really notice," I said. "Why?"

"Mr. Woodley was seen with it earlier in the track's press area, but now it's missing."

"So was it a robbery that went too far?" I asked.

"Possibly," the sergeant replied. "We are trying to determine if the theft of the briefcase was the reason for the attack on Mr. Woodley or whether it was taken afterward by a third party."

"I'm afraid I can't help you. I don't remember seeing any briefcase."

He thanked me anyway and then told me that my car was now ready to pick up and that the keys would be at the Kempton Park office, which was open late as they were racing that evening.

"Thanks," I said, not really meaning it. The sergeant hung up.

Not having my car was a bore. I'd better look up the return train times from Warwick to London.

So the meeting at Kempton tonight was going ahead. Just as it had been with Clare's, Toby Woodley's demise had been but a minor blip in the ever-moving symphony of life that plays on regardless. Are we each so insignificant, I thought, that our death would mean nothing more to most people than a slight inconvenience collecting a car?

Clare's death certainly meant more to me than that.

I still couldn't believe she had gone forever.

I yet again listed in my head the only reasons I could muster to explain why she would have killed herself and yet again came up with precious few.

She must have been depressed. Surely people who kill themselves must be depressed. But depressed about what?

I kept coming back to the question of the elusive boyfriend. She had definitely been seeing someone—more than that, she'd been sleeping with him. I thought back to our conversation at that last dinner: *What a lover!* she had said, and she'd grinned like the cat who'd got the cream. But she'd refused point-blank to say who it was, and I felt she'd become quite aggressive about it when I'd pressed her.

So who was Clare's great lover and was he one of the two men that Carlos, the bellman, had seen go to her room?

But why hadn't he come forward to grieve with the family?

He might be married, I thought. Or perhaps the affair had finished sometime between dinner and eleven-thirty that night. Was that the reason she had jumped?

Or had it been to do with her riding?

Had someone else spotted what I had seen in the race

at Lingfield? Maybe somebody had threatened to tell the racing authorities. I thought back again to something else Clare had said that night: *I can't imagine a time when I couldn't ride anymore. I wouldn't want to go on living.*

And how about Toby Woodley?

Were his death and Clare's connected? Had someone killed him to shut him up? Had there been more truth to his articles than I'd given him credit for? Was there indeed a betting syndicate that had made a fortune laying Brain of Brixham in April?

I didn't think there could be. For a start, the Internet exchanges would have told the British Horseracing Authority if there had been any unusual betting patterns on that race, particularly as Clare had been suspended for riding carelessly in it.

Perhaps Toby Woodley hadn't got the details completely right, but nevertheless someone had thought he'd been close enough.

Overall, I was frustrated by my lack of information. I hoped that the Hilton Hotel's CCTV film or the guest list from the Injured Jockeys Fund gala might give me some clues.

Provided I could get hold of them.

I COLLECTED MY CAR from Kempton at eight o'clock that evening, having cadged a ride from Warwick with a south-coast trainer who didn't mind a brief detour off the London orbital freeway.

"It's the least I could do," he said. "I was very fond of Clare."

He dropped me at the gates of the Kempton parking lot, and I walked through to the racetrack office. The only signs of the previous day's murder were the white tent still covering the spot where Toby had died and a very large number of police officers, standing around, holding clipboards.

"Excuse me, sir," called one of them as I emerged from the office with my car keys. "Were you here yesterday evening?"

"Yes, I was," I said. "I'm collecting my car, which was kept here. I was interviewed last night by Superintendent Cullen."

He still wrote down my name and address on his clipboard. "Is there anything else you've remembered since you were interviewed that might be useful to us?"

"No," I said. "Sorry."

He let me go, and I walked toward my car, which someone had moved over to the fence near the exit.

I felt slightly uneasy.

Less than twenty-four hours ago someone had been murdered in this parking lot. Stabbed in the back. While now there was easily enough light to see the cars, there were plenty of dark shadows in which someone could be hiding. The hairs on the back of my neck stood upright, and I spun around to check.

There was nobody there.

I laughed at myself. Of course there was nobody there.

Even a psychopath would surely think twice about murdering someone here with this many police about.

But I did walk right around my old Ford before I opened it, and I also checked the backseat to make sure no one was lurking there with intent.

They weren't. Not this time.

12

On Friday morning I packed a suitcase and drove myself to Newmarket.

My original plan had been to come there after racing at Warwick the previous day and stay for a couple of nights with Clare. But that plan had changed even before Clare's death. About a month ago we had both sort of decided during a phone call that two nights was one night too many given the current belligerent atmosphere between us.

But Clare had then laughed and promised to hide all the kitchen knives during my stay. At least, I thought, we hadn't gone too far down an irreversible path that we were unable to see the funny side and laugh at ourselves. But then the disastrous event in Park Lane had overtaken us.

Oh, how I longed again for her still to be alive. It was

like an ache that wouldn't go away. Painkillers had absolutely no effect. I'd tried.

I parked next to Clare's cottage and collected the key from Geoff Grubb's stable yard office. There must have been another key in Clare's handbag, and I presumed the police had that. I would have to ask Detective Sergeant Sharp for it on Monday. Would they also have her car? I would ask the detective about that as well.

The rent's paid for the rest of the month, Geoff had said to me at Windsor races when I'd seen him just two days after Clare had died. Well, today was the last day of the month, so I had better get on doing something about clearing out her stuff.

I let myself in and stood in her sitting room. It was only eight days since I'd last been there, but so much seemed to have happened since. Somehow, though, I felt it was a little easier being there this time.

I took my things up the narrow staircase to the spare bedroom, hanging my dinner jacket in the wardrobe.

Clare and I had planned to go to Tatiana's eighteenth birthday party together, and I had a slight emotional wobble as I recalled Clare's surprise at being asked.

"I hardly know the girl," she had said. "You're her godparent, not me."

"But you can't really blame her. If you had a celebrity aunt, you'd also invite her to your party."

"Celebrity, my arse," she replied with a laugh. "You're the celebrity. That's what being on TV does for you."

But Clare *had* indeed been quite a celebrity, as the abundant column inches of obituary that had appeared in the *Times* and the *Daily Telegraph* had proved. All the more reason why I should endeavor to defend her reputation from the slurs in the *Daily Gazette*. And, I thought, all the more reason for ensuring that I told no one of her irregular riding practices on Bangkok Flyer and the like.

I sighed. I didn't feel like going to an eighteenth birthday party. I could have done without all that noise for a start, not to mention a late night before I was due to appear on *The Morning Line* for Channel 4. But I had agreed ages ago to make the birthday speech, so I had to be there. And I wanted to support Nicholas, my brother-in-law, who was still worrying himself sick over whether or not he should have postponed the whole thing.

He and Angela had asked me if I would like to be Tatiana's godfather when I'd been only fourteen. I'd been really flattered, but, to be honest, I probably hadn't been the most conscientious of godfathers. I had no idea about her faith, but I'd always sent Christmas and birthday presents, which is what I reckoned were my main duties.

Nicholas and Angela lived near Royston, about twenty miles southwest of Newmarket, and the party was in a tent in their garden. According to the invitation, it started at eight o'clock, so I decided that I should leave at about seven forty-five in order to arrive suitably early but without appearing to be too prompt. I reckoned that if I was there pretty much at the beginning, I could get away well before the end.

I looked at my watch. It was just after twelve, midday. So I had nearly seven hours for sorting and packing before I needed to get ready. But where did I start? I wasn't even sure how much of the furniture had belonged to Clare and how much had been rented with the cottage.

I decided to deal with her clothes first. I went out to my car to collect some large blue bags and some cardboard boxes that I had brought with me just for that purpose.

I started with the overly full drawers of frilly black lace underwear, which filled up one of the blue bags to over-flowing. It made me sad that Clare had invested so much in something that almost no one saw. But I suppose it must have given her pleasure.

I managed to pack the rest of her clothes into four more of the bags, with shoes and boots filling two of the card-board boxes. I took the bags and boxes down the stairs and stacked them in the space underneath.

Next I turned my attention to the desk in the corner of the sitting room. Her phone bill was where I'd put it down last time and then forgotten to collect it. I now folded it carefully and put it in my pocket.

I sat down on the chair and started to look through Clare's papers. I wasn't sure what I was really looking for, if anything, but I couldn't just throw stuff away without going through it first. There might be share certificates or other important documents. I hoped there might even be a will.

The desk had three drawers on each side of a central kneehole, and the top two drawers on the left-hand side were full to overflowing with payment advice slips from Weatherbys, the company that administers racing's finances. They detailed all of Clare's rides, showing the riding fees paid to her bank account, along with any percentage of prize money she'd been entitled to, and she had clearly been stuffing them into the drawers for some time.

The bottom drawer on the left contained her bank statements and these were in better order. I picked up the top one, which was for the previous month.

I thought it unlikely that Clare had killed herself due to any money worries. According to the statement, just two and a half weeks before she died, her current account balance had been on the plus side of twenty thousand pounds.

I skimmed through the credits for the previous four months. Almost all were direct transfers from Weatherbys, with only a couple of small amounts paid in by checks. There were certainly no unexplained credits that matched the dates of the seven definites and four possibles, although any payment for her riding of Bangkok Flyer would not yet have appeared on a statement.

I filled another cardboard box with the statements and the payment slips and turned my attention to the drawers on the right.

The top one contained all her office supplies: a stapler, pens, notepads, stamps, and paper clips. There were also several checkbook stubs, held together with a red rubber band, and two pairs of sunglasses, one with a broken arm.

In the second drawer there were various documents, including Clare's birth certificate, her passport, her jockey's license, and a stack of investment portfolio valuations, all of which showed that Clare had been sensibly providing for her future after riding. A future that would now never be.

At the very back of the drawer, behind the investment valuations, I found a sealed white envelope.

I opened it.

The envelope contained two thousand pounds in cash, all of it in twenty-pound notes in packs of a thousand, each pack held together with an inch-wide paper band.

I didn't immediately assume that the cash was in any way irregular or sinister. Lots of people I know keep a supply of cash in case of emergencies, although two thousand pounds was rather on the high side. However, the thing that did raise some doubts in my mind was that the bands around the cash had "Barclays Bank" printed on them, while I knew from her bank statements that Clare banked with HSBC. It was not easy to get that amount of cash from a bank where you didn't have an account.

And my suspicions were raised a further fifty or so notches by what was written on the front of the envelope in capital letters: *AS AGREED, A.*

Had Clare been paid a couple of thousand pounds for not winning? And who was "A"?

I leaned back in her chair and wondered if she had fully understood what she had become involved in. It wasn't just a game, it was full-blown criminal fraud for gain, and discovery would have resulted in not just the loss of her career but likely the loss of her freedom.

I was suddenly very angry with Clare.

How could she have been so stupid? And why had she told me it was all about power and control when, at the same time, she was accepting a couple of grand from someone? It didn't make sense. All I could think was that she hadn't thought the money important. After all, her bank balance and her investment portfolios were very healthy, and the cash had still been in a sealed envelope as if she hadn't even bothered to count it.

I wondered if there were any fingerprints on the envelope that might help identify who had given it to Clare. Or maybe DNA, if someone had licked the envelope to seal it shut. The problem was, however, that I would have to go back to the police with my suspicions in order for them to investigate and did I really want to do that? Yes I did if it was pertinent to Clare's death, but no otherwise. The difficulty was knowing which was the case.

I put the cash back in the envelope, carefully holding it by the edges, then placed the envelope in one of the cardboard boxes along with other stuff.

That left only the bottom drawer on the right, and it was full of press clippings. I looked through the lot. All but two of them were about Clare herself, stretching back over four years. I was pleasantly surprised to find that one of the other two was about me, a background piece done by a national daily a year or so previously. But it was the final clipping that was the most intriguing.

It was the two-page spread run in the *Daily Gazette* the previous May about race fixing and it had been written by Toby Woodley.

I had heard about the story at the time, but I hadn't seen the original article, so I now read through it from start to finish. There was no mention of Clare or of any of the horses she had later ridden in any of my eleven suspect races. The piece was actually more speculative than factual, as was usually the case with the *Daily Gazette*, but it did seem to firmly imply that a well-known trainer was betting to lose on his own horses.

Betting to lose was strictly against the Rules of Racing for certain individuals, in particular the owner and trainer of the horse. And not only were they banned from doing it directly, they were also banned from instructing others to do so on their behalf or from receiving any proceeds from such activity.

But Toby Woodley had stated categorically that he knew of a racehorse trainer who regularly layed his horses on the Internet and then ensured that the horses didn't win. Needless to say, he hadn't mentioned the trainer by name.

I was intrigued not so much by the article's content, which I only half believed anyway, but why Clare had chosen to keep this clipping with all the others.

Perhaps she had known it was true.

I **ARRIVED** at Tatiana's party at twenty past eight to find that I was one of the last to get there. Nowadays, it seemed, the young arrived at parties bang on time, just as soon as the caterers started pouring the drinks.

Getting ready in Clare's cottage as the day had faded into night had been very difficult. Evenings had always been the best times at Stable Cottage, with lots of parties and dinners. Even on quiet nights, there had always been open bottles of Pinot Grigio and Cabernet Sauvignon, even though Clare herself rarely had more than a single glass.

The whole place had seemed very quiet and lonely as I had showered and dressed in my tuxedo, so much so that I realized I'd made a big mistake staying there. I should have accepted one of the other offers of a bed that I'd received from Newmarket friends. I wasn't particularly relishing the thought of going back to Stable Cottage alone later, but it was too late now.

"Hello, Mark." Angela greeted me at their front door. "Coat in the dining room, then go on through. We're in a big tent in the garden. Nick's out there with Brendan."

I did as I was told, placing my overcoat on the pile in the dining room and then walking through the sitting room and out of the French doors.

I was astonished at how big the tent was. Even though I'd been here quite a few times before, I was amazed that the garden was large enough to hold such a structure.

"Incredible, isn't it?" Brendan said, standing just inside the tent with a glass of red wine in his hand. "It apparently occupies the whole place. The guylines are even secured over the fences in the neighbors' gardens."

I could see that there were flower beds down each side of the tent, and a small tree appeared to grow right through the middle of the black-and-white dance floor.

"Amazing," I agreed.

"Had any luck with finding out what happened at the hotel on the night Clare died?" Brendan asked.

"None," I said. "I can't believe the police. Someone

goes away on holiday for a week and the whole investigation comes to a complete halt. It's bloody ridiculous. Thankfully the detective is back on Monday."

"Let me know how you get on," he said, draining his glass. "I'm off to find a refill."

Brendan went over toward a waiter holding a tray just as Nicholas walked over to greet me.

"It's fabulous," I said to him. "Absolutely fabulous."

He beamed at me. "Yes, it is rather good, isn't it?"

We stood for a moment surveying the scene.

"So where's the birthday girl?" I asked.

"Over there somewhere," Nicholas said, pointing at a large crowd of youngsters propping up the bar at the far end of the tent. "She's eighteen and exercising her legal right to drink alcohol." He rolled his eyes. "Not that she hasn't been drinking alcohol for ages. I know she has. They all do. And I fear I'm going to be the villain tonight by closing the bar every so often to give them a rest. I don't want them all to get so drunk they ruin everything, not until after dinner and the speeches anyway. I've taken two bottles of vodka off a girl who I happen to know is only seventeen, and her breath smelled like she'd already drunk a third. And Brendan's boys are hitting it pretty bad behind their mother's back, and Patrick's not even fourteen until Sunday."

"At least they are their parents' responsibility, not yours."

He laughed. "Brendan and Gillian seem to be well ahead of them. They've been here since seven, as they're staying the night with us, and Brendan in particular is getting stuck in the red wine."

"I've seen," I said.

Nick waved his hand toward the group of scantily dressed girls at the bar. "But it's these other young things I'm really worried about. They seem determined to get hammered, and quickly. And they *are* my responsibility."

"Good luck," I said with a laugh.

"I'm going to need it," he said. "Especially when your mom and dad get here."

"They are coming, then?" I was surprised.

"They said so, but they aren't here yet, which is slightly ominous. They finally agreed to come only yesterday and that was thanks to you."

"Don't thank me just yet," I said with a laugh. "You know how Dad can be a nightmare."

"To tell you the truth, I was half hoping they wouldn't come, but Angie is delighted that they are, so I'm trying to be pleased too."

As if on cue, Angela came through the French doors of the sitting room into the tent with our mother and father.

"Hi, Mom," I said, giving her a kiss on the cheek. "Lovely, isn't it?"

She looked around her as if in a bit of a daze. "I wish Clare had been here to see it." I could tell that she was very close to tears.

"Yes," I said, "you're right, Mom, so do I. But tonight is Tatiana's big moment, and we have to be happy for her."

My mother smiled at me wanly. "Yes, Mark," she said. "I know. I'll be fine."

"Evening, Mark," my father said brusquely.

I had been quite forceful in telling him that Nicholas

and Angela couldn't afford to postpone Tatiana's party and that he should give his blessing for it to proceed. But I hadn't expected him actually to attend the event, and, unless he cheered up a bit, it might have been better if he hadn't.

"Evening, Dad," I said. "Doesn't it all look wonderful?"

"I suppose so," he grunted. But the tent did look wonderful, with a dozen round tables set for dinner and surrounded by white ladder-back chairs.

"Let me get you all a drink," Nicholas said, sensing the tension. He waved vigorously at one of the waiters, who brought over a tray of glasses.

I took an orange juice from the tray, and Nicholas raised his eyebrows.

"I've a speech to make," I said, "and I'm driving. I might have a glass of wine with dinner."

"You're making the toast, remember, and we have champagne for that."

"I won't forget," I assured him.

I went over to the bar to give Tatiana a kiss and wish her a happy birthday.

"You look gorgeous, darling," I said to her, although in truth I thought her skirt six inches too short and her heels four inches too high.

"Your speech is not going to be too embarrassing, is it?" she asked.

"Probably," I said.

"Oh God. It's bad enough with Mom insisting on putting these dreadful pictures on all the tables. They're so crass."

I looked at the one nearest to me. It showed Tatiana as a baby, sitting naked in the bath. I could understand how she felt uncomfortable having a picture of herself like that for all her school friends to see. But, equally, I could appreciate how Angela would have found it rather amusing.

"Don't worry," I said, "I won't be as embarrassing as that."

She smiled at me. "I'm so glad. Now, come and meet my friends."

AT DINNER, I found myself sitting between Angela and a girl called Emily Lowther. I say a girl, but she was about my age, dark-haired, slim, and beautiful. She was wearing a low-cut black dress that displayed just the right amount of bosom, and almost the first thing she told me was that she was a childless divorcée and one of Angela's best friends from the local gym.

I detected a barefaced attempt by my sister to matchmake and I told her so in a fierce whisper.

"So what?" Angela said, unabashed. "Emily needs a husband, and you need a wife. And she is gorgeous, isn't she? And frighteningly bright as well."

She certainly was gorgeous, but did I really need a wife? Was I not happy enough as a bachelor?

It was certainly true that the ending of my affair with Sarah had made me rather glum, but I'd been so depressed anyway because of Clare that a little more misery didn't seem to matter much.

And I kept telling myself that I missed Sarah only because some of the excitement had gone out of my life rather than for the loss of any undying love I might have had for her. In fact, I wondered if the possibility of being found out had been the most arousing aspect of our affair. So would I find the same thrill in a relationship that I could be open and honest about?

"What happened to her husband?" I asked Angela quietly as Emily talked to my father, who was sitting on her other side.

"Stupid man decided after four years of marriage that he preferred boys. I ask you. Left our gorgeous Emily for some French hairdresser called Pierre. The man must be a raving lunatic."

Emily put her hand on my arm. "Mark, I'm so sorry about Clare."

"Thank you," I said, turning toward her but not removing her hand. "It has been a very difficult couple of weeks."

Was it really only two weeks? How the time had dragged.

"It must have been," Emily said. She moved her hand forward and placed it on the back of mine, squeezing it a little. "Do say if there's anything I can do to help you. Anything at all."

"Thank you," I said, looking her directly in the eyes, "I will."

Was I mistaken or had I just been propositioned for sex?

13

And finally, will you all stand up and raise your glasses to join me in a toast to my favorite god-daughter—happy eighteenth birthday, Tatiana."

"Happy birthday, Tatiana," chorused the assembled guests.

We all sang "Happy birthday to you . . ." as a magnificent cake with two rows of flaming candles was brought out by Nicholas. To rapturous cheers from her school friends, Tatiana blew out the eighteen candles, cut the cake, then made a short speech of thanks to her parents, with every second word being "amazing."

"Yours was a great speech. Well done," said Emily, again squeezing my hand.

"Thanks."

"I hate speaking in public," she said. "I get so nervous."

"I do it for a living," I replied. "You get used to it."

"Yes, I know. I've seen you on television. But don't you get one of those autocue things to read?"

"Never," I said. "You only get those in a studio and I work exclusively at racetracks."

At that moment the DJ decided to turn up the volume of the music from loud to earsplitting, making further conversation difficult if not impossible. I looked at my watch. It was already almost eleven o'clock.

"Do you want to dance?" Emily shouted into my ear.

"Not really," I replied, fortissimo, in hers. "I need to go fairly soon. I've got an early start."

"I could come with you," she said, looking straight into my eyes. "If you want."

Did I want?

"I'm sorry, but not tonight," I said in her ear. "I am staying at my dead sister's cottage. I think I'd rather be there alone. But thank you."

"We could go to my place."

Was she being a tad too desperate?

"I need to be at Newmarket racetrack at seven a.m. for *The Morning Line* and it's just a mile from my sister's cottage. That's why I'm staying there."

"I'll take that as a no, then."

"Look, I'm sorry. It's not that I don't want to. It's just that . . ."

"You don't need to explain," she said quickly. "It's fine." But I could see from her expression that it wasn't really.

"I think I'd better go now." I leaned forward and gave her a brief kiss on the cheek. "It's been lovely meeting you." It was a totally inadequate thing to say, and both of us knew it.

I stood up to go but turned back to her.

"Do you have a number?" I asked. "Perhaps I could call you?"

She produced a pen from her handbag and wrote down a number on a scrap of paper, which she then handed to me.

"Call me in the morning, after the program," she said. "I'll be watching."

"OK. I will."

Was I being a fool? I'd already bemoaned to myself how lonely Clare's cottage had seemed when I'd dressed there earlier and here I was turning down the perfect opportunity not to have to spend the night there. But did I actually want to jump into bed with someone I'd only just met. Mind you, it wouldn't have been the first time, not by a long shot. But . . .

"Go on, go!" Emily shouted over the music. It was as if she knew what I was thinking. "Call me tomorrow."

I went to find Angela and Nicholas to thank them for a lovely party. Angela was in the house, where thankfully it was much quieter.

"Do you really have to go so soon?" she asked.

"I'm on *The Morning Line*," I said by way of explanation.

"But what about Emily?" she asked, looking over my shoulder.

"She's been very nice," I said.

"But isn't she going with you?"

"No," I said.

"Oh," she said, clearly disappointed.

"Nice try, sis," I said, giving her a kiss. "Enjoy the rest of the party. Where's Nick?"

"Trying to close the bar, I think. At least for a bit. Some of those girls are getting very drunk."

I personally thought they'd been very drunk for ages. Long legs, short skirts, and tipsy—some of the boys clearly thought that Christmas had come early this year, if only they themselves hadn't drunk too much to make the most of the situation. I was quite glad that none of them were my concern.

"Will you say good-bye to him for me?" I said, collecting my coat. "And to Tatiana and the rest of the family. I don't want to be a party pooper by telling them I'm going so soon. I'll call you tomorrow, but not too early."

"Early as you like," Angela said with a smile. "We've got fifty or so of Tat's friends sleeping in the tent tonight and we want them all out and gone by lunchtime."

"You must be mad," I said, opening the front door.

"Totally. But thank God she's eighteen only once."

"It'll be her twenty-first next."

"Nope," she said. "This is the only one. She had the choice."

"Well, it's a wonderful party, but I hope you have understanding neighbors."

"Both sides are here as guests. And Tatiana has been to all the houses in the street to tell them. The music will decrease in volume at one o'clock and stop completely by two."

I gave Angela another kiss. "Tatiana's a very lucky girl."

"Tell me about it." I could hear her laughing as she closed the door.

The music sounded significantly louder outside than in, and, I thought, it wasn't just this street Tatiana had needed to visit. The whole neighborhood could hear it.

I walked across and down the road to my car, which I'd parked about forty yards away.

Dammit, I thought. This was the first time for about six weeks I had been asked to be on *The Morning Line* and it would just have to be the day after I wanted to stay out and play—or even stay in and play. There was no doubt that Emily had been willing, eager even. Had I made the wrong decision?

But I knew that I had to have some decent sleep if I was to be any good in the morning. Last year I'd been out late and had a few drinks the night before I was on and I thought I'd been rubbish. Television is very unforgiving of puffy eyes and a pallid complexion. I knew of an ex-colleague who had arrived for a show slightly late and rather hungover and he had never been invited on again. There are always those like Iain Ferguson standing in the wings, waiting to take over when your star wanes, and I had no intention of giving anyone an easy ride into my seat.

I had started my old Ford and was reaching for the gearshift when something was thrown over my head and tightened around my neck. I grabbed at it, but whoever was pulling it was much too quick for me to get any fingers between the ligature and my skin.

My head was snapped back hard against the headrest. I

tried to cry out but nothing happened. I couldn't breathe, neither in nor out.

I began to panic and dig my fingers into my neck, trying to get them behind whatever was strangling me. But the harder I tried, the harder the person behind me pulled.

I reached back over my head, but I couldn't get my hands down far enough owing to the headrest.

I was dying. And I knew it.

I could feel my heart thumping extra fast, trying its best to pump blood to my ever-dulling brain. But the blood wasn't getting there. There was a blockage at the neck.

My lungs were filling with carbon dioxide, and they were bursting to breathe, but there was no way out for the poison gas and no way in for life-giving oxygen.

I thrashed around behind me with my hands, but there was nothing to grab.

This was it. I was going. Unconsciousness and death were but seconds away.

I didn't want to die.

I banged the steering wheel with my fist in anger and frustration, and I could hear the car horn sounding over the ringing in my ears.

The ignition must be on, I thought. Of course it was—I'd started the engine.

I reached forward with my left hand and, using the very tips of my fingers, I pushed the lever into first gear. Next I released the brake, then I positively stamped on the accelerator, released the clutch, and hoped the car wouldn't stall.

I couldn't see—my vision had gone completely—but I

felt the car lurch forward. I didn't know where we were going, but I didn't care either, and I kept my right foot hard down on the gas right to the floor.

It seemed an age before we hit anything, but it was probably not more than a couple of seconds. There were two almighty crashes and another loud bang inside the car as the driver's air bag deployed. Then everything went quiet, save for the music from the party.

But, best of all, the pressure on my neck eased, and I gasped in a huge gulp of night air. I leaned forward against the steering wheel, holding my throbbing neck and trying to breathe in shallow breaths to reduce the excruciating pain.

Things began to return to normal in my brain.

My sight came back suddenly with a rush, but all I could see was white. I realized my head was up against the now deflated air bag, so I lifted it and looked through the windshield.

We had bounced off another car and then hit Nicholas and Angela's stone gatepost pillar full on. The whole hood was crumpled. My dear old Ford looked to be mortally wounded, but it had clearly accelerated as well as any sports car.

I put my head back down again on the steering wheel. It was more comfortable like that, but part of my reoxygenated brain was suddenly screaming at me.

Danger! Danger!

The rest of my brain began to listen.

Someone was trying to kill me and he might still be here.

I quickly turned in the seat and looked behind me.

The back door on the driver's side was open. Whoever had been there, whoever had tried to kill me, had now fled.

My sudden turning movement had resulted in a severe bout of dizziness, so I rested my head once more on the wheel.

That was better.

In the distance, I could hear a wailing siren getting closer and closer.

"HE MUST BE DRUNK," I heard a voice say. "Look at his suit. He's been to that party."

I wasn't drunk. I'd only had a small glass of red wine with dinner and a sip of champagne for the toast. I tried to say so but nothing came out. Instead, my neck went on hurting like hell, and I was having difficulty swallowing.

I opened my eyes and lifted my head a little. A uniformed policeman was crouching in the open driver's door.

"Are you all right, sir?" he asked.

I tried to say no, I wasn't all right, but the words wouldn't form in my throat. So I just shook my head slowly from side to side.

"Sam, we need an ambulance," the policeman said.

"It's already on its way." Sam's voice, out of my vision.

"Oh my God, that's Mark's car," I heard Nicholas say. "Is he all right?" Nicholas's face appeared briefly at the car door.

"Thank you, sir," said the policeman. "Now, please stand back."

"But he's my brother-in-law," Nicholas said, disappearing from the door and climbing into the car through the open back door. "Are you all right, Mark?" he asked from somewhere near my left ear.

I started to turn my head around.

"Keep still," ordered the policeman. "You can make neck or back injuries worse if you move."

I kept still.

"Has he been at this party?" the policeman asked Nicholas.

"Yes. It's my daughter's party. Mark here made a speech."

"Has he been drinking?"

"No, I don't think so. I mean, I don't really know. I wasn't sitting with him at dinner."

Oh thanks, Nick, I thought. That's just what I need.

"Can I help?" Brendan had now climbed into the back alongside Nicholas.

The policeman looked at him. "We're trying to determine if this man has been drinking."

"Can't help you," Brendan said with a nervous laugh. "I know I have."

"I'm not drunk," I tried to say, but nothing but a croak came out.

"It's all right, sir," said the policeman, looking back at me. "You rest now, the ambulance is on its way."

I didn't want to rest. I wanted to tell them that I wasn't drunk, that someone had tried to kill me, that I'd been strangled, but my voice box and my mouth wouldn't do what my brain was asking of them.

"He must be drunk to have driven straight across the road into this gatepost at that speed," said the other policeman, Sam, the one I couldn't see. "Blind drunk, I shouldn't wonder. Is he well enough to do a breath test?"

I nodded at the policeman in the door, but he didn't immediately say anything. He just stared into my eyes. Then he shone a flashlight right in my face.

"I don't like the look of him."

I thought that was quite personal.

"In what way?" asked Nicholas.

"He's got red spots on the whites of his eyes." I didn't like the sound of that. "And there are some more on his face."

More flashing lights and another siren signaled the arrival of the ambulance, and a paramedic soon joined the policeman at the car door.

"He seems unable to speak," the policeman said to the new arrival, "and I don't like the look of his eyes."

I looked at them both as they looked at me.

"He may have had a stroke," said the paramedic.

I shook my head at them and made a gesture indicating I wanted to write something. The policeman removed a notebook from his pocket and passed it over with a pen.

I've been strangled, I wrote. *Somebody tried to kill me.* I handed the notebook back.

They both looked at what I had written and then up at my face.

I could tell from his expression that the policeman didn't believe me.

"They could be petechia," said the paramedic.

"What could?" said the policeman.

"The red spots. They could be petechia. It's the bursting of tiny blood vessels just under the skin and in the eyes. It can be brought on by asphyxia. He may well have been strangled." He gently tilted my head back and looked at my neck. "And there's definitely some bruising round the larynx. That might be why he can't speak."

"Bloody hell," said the policeman, "it's a crime scene. Sam, get everyone back. You two," he said, pointing at Nicholas and Brendan over my head, "out of the car. Now!"

IT SEEMED LIKE at least another half hour before they lifted me out of the car, by which time some semblance of my voice had returned.

One of the paramedics insisted on going behind me to attach a large plastic brace around my neck in spite of me complaining that it hurt my windpipe in front. Then they placed a board along my spine and strapped me to it. By this time the fire department had also arrived and they proceeded to remove the whole roof of the car.

Meanwhile, in little more than a croak I assured them that I was fine apart from my neck, which still hurt like hell.

"You can't be too careful," said one of the paramedics, although I believed they were being just that, a sentiment clearly shared by the plainclothes detective who had been summoned to the scene by his uniformed colleagues.

He'd already tried to talk to me twice but had been sent away on both occasions by the paramedics as they had fit me first with an oxygen mask over my nose and mouth and then with a saline drip needle in my hand.

"The extra fluid keeps your blood pressure up," one paramedic had explained, "and that helps deliver more oxygen to your brain."

Finally, they were ready, and I was lifted from the car and laid flat on a stretcher. I wouldn't have minded so much if there hadn't been such a large audience of young, scantily clad partygoers, together with most of my family, including my mother and my father, all of them standing on the sidewalk, shivering in the cool of the night.

I waved at them with my non-needled hand, much to the disapproval of the paramedic, who told me in no uncertain terms to lie perfectly still.

"I'm all right," I said very croakily through the mask. "I really think I could walk."

"No chance," he replied. "Asphyxia patients can die hours later even if they seem wide awake and well. You stay put."

I stayed put.

I was carried into the ambulance, and the detective tried to climb in with me, but the medics were having none of it.

"You can speak to him at the hospital," one of them said, "once he's stable."

"Which hospital?"

"Addenbrooke's, in Cambridge."

One of the paramedics drove while the other connected me to blood pressure and heart monitors.

"I feel fine now," I said. "It's only my throat that hurts."

"Nevertheless, it's better to get you checked out," he

said, sticking wired pads on my chest. "Don't want you dropping down dead on us, now do we?"

No, I thought, we didn't.

"You just relax and let us do the worrying."

I wasn't particularly worried, not about my health anyway. I was far more worried about who would want to kill me and why.

"SO DID YOU see who attacked you?" asked the plainclothes policeman, who had introduced himself as Detective Chief Inspector Perry.

"No," I replied in my now familiar croak.

We were in a curtained-off cubicle of the emergency room at Addenbrooke's hospital, me lying on an examination table and him sitting next to it on a chair.

"Was the car locked when you arrived at it?"

"I think so," I said, "but I suppose I don't really know. I remember the car's indicator lights flashing when I pushed the unlock button on the key, but it's an old car and does that whether it's locked or not. I know because I've left it unlocked outside my apartment before."

"But you definitely had the keys with you?"

"Yes," I said. "They were in my coat pocket."

"And was the person already in the car before you got in?"

I tried to think back.

"I would say so, yes. I don't remember hearing any of the other doors open." But, in truth, my memory of the incident was hazy in places. The hospital doctor had said it might be. Oxygen starvation, it seemed, caused funny effects in the brain. It was why he wouldn't let me go home yet.

So much for my relatively early night.

I was wide awake at two o'clock in the morning, still dressed in my party gear, minus jacket and tie, answering endless questions.

"Why do you think someone would want to kill you?"

"I have absolutely no idea," I replied. It was the question I had been asking myself for the past three hours and I hadn't yet come up with any sensible answers. Was it something to do with Clare's suicide or with Toby Woodley's murder? Or had it merely been a botched attempt to steal my car?

Somehow, I doubted that.

For a start, my Ford was very old and hardly worth stealing, and strangling the driver just to steal a car seemed rather excessive.

"Did you find a rope?" I asked.

"So it was a rope?" he said.

"I'm not sure." I felt my neck. "It may have been some sort of material. Did you find anything?"

"My men are searching the area, I haven't heard yet what they found." He wrote something in his notebook. "Do you have any enemies?" he asked, looking up at me.

"No," I said, "not really."

But I thought of Mitchell Stacey. He was an enemy. And he knew my car.

The policeman must have read something in my face.

"Yes?" he asked. "Who is it?"

"Someone did threaten me, that's all."

"In what way?"

"He told me that if I didn't stay away from his wife, he'd kill me. But I don't really believe that he meant he would actually kill me. It was just a figure of speech."

"And when was this?"

I worked it out. "Eight days ago, at Newmarket."

"And have you stayed away from his wife since then?" asked the policeman in a deadpan voice.

"Yes," I said. "Well . . . I bumped into her on Tuesday, but it was an accident. We didn't do anything, if that's what you mean. We hardly even spoke."

"And does the lady's husband know you saw her on Tuesday?"

I thought back to my encounter with Mitchell in the Stratford races parking lot. "Yes. He knows, all right. He was there."

"I'll need his name, sir."

"I'm sure he wouldn't have done it," I said. But someone had. My throat still had the bruises to prove it.

"His name?" The chief inspector persisted.

"Mitchell Stacey," I said. "He's a racehorse trainer. He and his wife live in East Ilsley, near Newbury."

I gave him the full address and he wrote it down in his notebook.

"And is he the only irate husband who has threatened you recently?"

"There's no need for irony, Chief Inspector," I said. "And, yes, he's the only one."

"I also need your full name and address. For the record."

"Mark Joseph Shillingford," I said, and I gave him the address of my apartment in Edenbridge. He wrote it down.

"Shillingford?" he said. "Unusual name. Not related to that girl that killed herself, are you?"

"She was my sister," I said. "My twin sister."

"Oh," he said. "I'm sorry."

"Do you follow horse racing at all, Chief Inspector?"

"Not really my thing," he said, shaking his head. "I'm a football man myself. Hornets fan."

"Hornets?"

"Watford," he said.

We were interrupted by a nurse, who came into the cubicle to take my pulse and my blood pressure and also look into my eyes with a flashlight.

"When can I go home?" I croaked at her.

"The doctor will do his round soon," she said. "You can ask him then."

The nurse went out again.

"Right," said the chief inspector, closing his notebook and standing up. "I'm going home to my bed."

"Is that it?" I asked, surprised.

"You'll have to give a full witness statement, of course, but that can be done in the morning. Call me round ten to fix it." He handed me a printed card with his details.

"How about Mitchell Stacey?"

"I'll interview Mr. Stacey after you've done your witness statement and after the forensic boys have examined your car. That will also take place in the morning."

"But what if he tries again?" I asked.

"Do you think he might?"

"I'm not sure it was even him," I said. "But don't I get police protection, or something, just in case?"

"I think you should be safe enough in here," he said rather dismissively.

"But how about if I go home?"

"Then I'd advise you not to get into a car without first checking the backseat."

"Oh, thanks a lot," I said sarcastically. "Why do I get the impression you're not taking me seriously?"

"I am taking you seriously, Mr. Shillingford, very seriously, but I simply don't have the resources to provide you with a personal bodyguard. Anyway, I believe that the person who tried to kill you is long gone. And I doubt that they'll try again. I've studied a few criminals in my time, and I think it's highly likely that this was a one-off attack and the perpetrator will have second thoughts before trying anything like it again."

A policeman who fancied himself as an amateur criminal psychologist was all I needed.

"No," he said, "I think you'll be perfectly safe from now on. I reckon if he'd really wanted to kill you, then you'd have been in a morgue, not a hospital."

I damn near had been.

14

I had just closed my eyes and drifted off to sleep when I was awakened again by the nurse to do her half-hourly check.

"There are two people outside in the waiting room who want to see you," the nurse said as she listed the latest results on a chart. "That policeman said we weren't to let anyone in, but they've been here for ages, and they say they absolutely won't go home without seeing you first."

"Who are they?" I asked.

"Two women," said the nurse. "One of them says she's your sister."

Clare, I immediately thought. But of course it couldn't be Clare. It had to be Angela.

"Would you please ask them to come in," I said, smiling at her. "I don't think that policeman meant to keep my family out."

"If you're sure," she said.

"Perfectly sure," I replied. "And I won't tell him if you don't."

She smiled back at me. "All right, then. I'll go and get them."

Indeed, it was Angela, and she had Emily with her, both of them looking worried and tired.

"You should both still be at Tatiana's party," I said to them in my croaky voice.

"That finished hours ago," said Angela. "In fact, it pretty much finished when you hit the gatepost."

"I'm so sorry," I croaked.

"Don't be." Angela laughed. "At least it stopped everyone drinking."

"I wasn't drunk," I said. And that was now official. I'd been Breathalyzered when I'd first arrived at the hospital and had passed with ease.

"So what happened?" asked Emily. "Nick told us something about you being strangled." I could tell from the tone of her voice that she clearly thought that Nick had been mistaken.

I wondered how much I should tell them. And how much they would believe. Attempted murders in rural Hertfordshire were hardly common, but I couldn't really lie to them, especially as I assumed the police would soon be around asking them questions.

"There was someone waiting for me in the car," I said, "in the backseat. He tried to strangle me."

The two women looked suitably shocked.

"Was he trying to rob you?" Angela asked.

"Maybe," I said. "Although it was a funny way to do it if he was. I actually think he was trying to kill me."

"But why would anyone want to do that?" Emily asked.

I decided against mentioning anything to them about Mitchell Stacey or my affair with his wife. Clare had been the only member of the Shillingford family privy to that information, and I rather hoped to keep it that way.

"I've no idea," I said. "The police are investigating. They told me they'll search my car for fingerprints."

"It was all wrapped up in blue plastic," Angela said, nodding. "And then it was taken away on a truck. It took them ages, and it didn't please the caterers, I can tell you that." She smiled. "They couldn't get their van out of the driveway. There was a flaming row between them and the police."

"So what happens now?" Emily asked. "How much longer are you going to be stuck here?"

"I don't really know. I'm waiting for the doctor to do his round."

"I'll go and find someone," Emily said, and she disappeared through the curtains.

"God, you gave us all such a fright," said Angela, taking my hand. "I couldn't bear to lose you as well." She was crying, and she wiped her eyes on the sleeve of her jacket. "I'm sorry."

"Don't be," I said.

Clare's death was still very raw for all of us. Our emotions were on knife-edge. One minute we could weep or laugh, the next minute fly into a rage.

Emily returned with the doctor. I knew from personal experience that saying no to Emily was difficult, I now fervently wished I'd said yes to her. It might have saved all this bother.

"How are you feeling?" asked the doctor.

"Fine," I answered. "Apart from a sore neck and a croaky voice."

"Your vitals are good and stable," he said, looking at the chart. He came forward and examined my neck. "You were very lucky. Your larynx is only bruised and not fractured. I see no reason why you can't go home, but you shouldn't be left alone for the next twelve hours or so. Asphyxia patients can sometimes develop cerebral edemas, and they are very dangerous."

"What's a cerebral edema?" Angela asked him.

"A fluid buildup that causes the brain to swell in the skull. It's very nasty, and often the last person to realize he has one is the patient. But I don't think you'll have a problem. I would have expected to see something by now if you did."

"We'll look after him," Emily said, holding my hand.

"Fine," said the doctor. "I'll get the discharge papers. But get him back here immediately if he starts to act strangely or slurs his words."

The doctor went out of the cubicle, and I swung my legs over the side of the table. I looked at my watch. It was a quarter past three.

"Come on," I said, "let's get out of here."

"**WHERE TO?**" Angela asked as we sat in her Volvo in the hospital parking lot. She was in front while Emily and I were sitting together in the back, and, yes, I had checked the car for potential stranglers before we'd opened the doors.

"You can't come back to our house. We're full with Brendan and Gillian and their boys. Not unless you want to sleep in the tent with Tatiana and her friends."

"We'll go to my place," Emily said decisively. "I'll look after him."

I could see Angela giggling in the rearview mirror. I suspected that this had been a rehearsed exchange.

"Where is your place?" I asked Emily.

"In Royston," she said. "About a mile from Nick and Angela."

"I need to be at Newmarket racetrack in under four hours, and Royston's in totally the wrong direction."

"But surely you're not going to do the show now," said Angela.

"Why not?" I said. "As long as my voice doesn't get any worse, I'll be fine."

"But someone has just tried to kill you."

"All the more reason for going on."

"You're crazy."

"Maybe I am," I said. "But I'll be damned if I am going to sit back and do nothing. Someone tried to kill me tonight and I'm bloody well going to find out who it was." I yawned, which I discovered was not very pleasant when one had a sore windpipe. "Please take me to Clare's cottage. I'll try and get some sleep, and I'll order a taxi to collect me in the morning. I need to change my clothes anyway. I can hardly go on *The Morning Line* wearing this."

I saw Angela look at Emily in the mirror. Their little plan was falling apart, and I could tell that they didn't particularly like it.

"Look," I said, "I am not trying to be evasive, I promise. I would more than happily go to Emily's place under different circumstances, but right now I'd like to go to Clare's cottage."

"One of us would have to stay with you," Angela said. "The doctor was pretty insistent."

"It had better be me who stays with Mark," Emily said. "Nick will be wondering where you are already." She laughed. "He's probably in the tent trying to keep those drunken, randy boys away from Tatiana."

"Don't even joke about it," Angela said. "All right, Mark, you win. Clare's cottage it is."

She started the Volvo and pointed it toward Newmarket.

IN THE END, all three of us stayed at Clare's cottage, Angela having been assured by Nicholas on the telephone that all was well, both at the house and in the tent, where Tatiana was safely cocooned amongst her girlfriends.

Angela and Emily slept together in the guest room while I settled down on the sofa in the sitting room downstairs. I suppose it would have been all right to use Clare's bed, but I sensed an air of collective relief when I had volunteered to be on the sofa.

Even though it was almost four o'clock by the time I

turned out the light, I found it difficult to sleep. My mind was racing with too many unanswered questions, the uppermost being who had tried to kill me and why?

I had told DCI Perry about Mitchell Stacey, but did I really believe he could be responsible? He had certainly shown the ugly side of his nature in the parking lots at Newmarket and at Stratford, but he was a bull in a china shop who would surely confront me man-to-man rather than sneaking up anonymously and trying to strangle me.

But what other suspects did I have?

None.

And what could anyone else gain by killing me?

Surely Iain Ferguson didn't imagine that his career would advance more quickly if I was quite literally taken out of the picture?

I MUST HAVE drifted off to sleep eventually because the next thing I knew I was wide awake and listening hard for the noise that had awakened me.

There had been a metallic clank. Or had I dreamed it?

I lay in the dark, listening. There it was again, and it was outside.

I quietly stood up from the sofa and went over to the window, my heart again pounding hard inside my chest.

I pulled back the heavy curtains to find that it was daylight and people were already up and about. Racing folk start work early, and the metallic clanks had been the sound of Geoffrey Grubb's stable staff fetching metal buckets of water for the horses.

I laughed at myself. I must be getting paranoid.

I looked at my watch. It was half past six, I'd been asleep for only about two hours. But it was high time I got myself moving if I wasn't going to be late.

I went into the kitchen and made myself a cup of instant coffee, which went some way to waking me up properly. Then I made two more cups and took them up to the guest bedroom.

Angela and Emily were both still fast asleep, and it took me about a minute of gentle prodding to wake Angela.

"Go away," she said, putting her head under the pillow.

"I need to go in ten minutes," I said. "Shall I take your car? I could be back by ten past nine."

"Do what you like," she murmured.

I collected some clothes and my electric razor from my suitcase and went into the bathroom to shave, shower, and dress. The lumps in my throat that had persisted all the previous night had finally begun to ease, and my voice seemed a little more normal. And the little reds spots in my eyes and on my face had almost faded away to nothing.

I emerged from the bathroom to find Emily standing there wrapped in a sheet, hopping from foot to foot.

"We're both coming with you," she said. "Though God knows why. Angela's said something about dropping you off and then going home."

"But I need to go right now."

"So do I. I'm bursting." She grinned, pushed past me, and closed the bathroom door.

I laughed. I decided I could get to like Emily, maybe to

like her a lot. Just as long as someone didn't succeed in killing me first.

"**WHAT DO YOU MEAN,** someone tried to murder you? That's the worst excuse I've ever heard for someone being late."

"It's not an excuse," I said. "It's true."

I could tell that Lisa, *The Morning Line*'s producer, didn't believe a word I'd said, and she clearly was not happy. I'd been only five minutes late, but there was another crisis going on with the program's main guest, who was going to be much later.

"Someone really did try to strangle me last night," I said, "and I wonder if it has anything to do with the murder of Toby Woodley at Kempton on Wednesday."

That shut her up, but only briefly.

"And does it?" she asked.

"I don't know."

"So where's the story in that?" she asked flatly. "You could at least have arrived with a smoking gun or a knife with Toby Woodley's blood on it."

"How about a bruised neck?" I asked. "And a croaky voice?"

"Not visual enough. But the voice may be a problem. We'll have to say you've got a cold."

"Why not tell the truth?"

"Too complicated," she said. "Now, have you done your homework on the two-year-olds?"

The big race at Newmarket that afternoon was the Millions Trophy, the richest contest for two-year-old horses in Europe.

"Of course I have," I replied, knowing full well that I hadn't really done enough. But I knew all the horses well from having seen them run previously.

"Good, because you might have to talk about them for much longer than planned if that bloody Austin Reynolds doesn't turn up."

"Austin Reynolds?" I said, surprised. "I thought the guest was Paul James."

"Paul had a fall last night at Wolverhampton and has cried off. Austin agreed to step in, but now he's called to say his car won't start and he'll be late."

"But he only lives in the town," I said. "Can't someone go and fetch him?"

"Seems he's coming up from London." She didn't sound pleased.

Austin Reynolds, the "nearly man" of British racing, was the trainer of Tortola Beach, one of the runners in that afternoon's big race.

Tortola Beach had been one of the definites that I'd found in the RacingTV database. Clare had purposely ridden him to lose in a race at Doncaster the previous August.

And Austin Reynolds also trained Bangkok Flyer.

"Thirty minutes to air time, everybody," shouted Matthew, the floor manager.

"I must get back to the scanner," Lisa said and hurried off.

TO THE UNTRAINED EYE, the next twenty-five or so minutes may have looked a bit chaotic, but, in fact, they were precisely choreographed.

Cameras moved from side to side, then back and forth, rehearsing, all under the control of the program director, who was sitting out in the scanner and communicating with the cameramen via their headphones.

"Fifteen minutes to on-air," Matthew shouted.

The presenters were wired up with microphones and earpieces, each of us rehearsing what we would say for sound levels and then checking with Lisa that we could all hear the talk-back and that she could also hear us.

Then we sat in our positions for final checks on camera angles while someone applied dabs of powder to those parts of our faces that were shining too much under the powerful lights.

"Five minutes to on-air."

And still there was no sign of Austin Reynolds.

"Four minutes."

I went over in my head once again what I planned to say about each of the horses in the big race.

"Three minutes."

"Mark," Lisa said into my ear, *"we'll come straight to you after the weekly roundup to discuss the fillies' race and also the Scoop6 Cup at Ascot. We'll have to hope that Austin is here by the first commercial break, and we'll do the Millions Trophy after that."*

"OK," I said, shuffling madly through my copy of the *Racing Post* to find the relevant pages.

"Two minutes."

One of the staff placed a *Morning Line*–branded cup full of coffee in front of each of the presenters.

"One minute."

There was nothing quite like live television to raise the pulse.

Nothing, that is, except being strangled.

AUSTIN REYNOLDS finally arrived on the set just before the second commercial break, by which time there was less than ten minutes left to the program. I could imagine Lisa pulling her hair out in the scanner.

"Get him in during the break," she said in all our ears.

Fortunately it was Lisa's practice always to have far more content available than we could ever have fit into the allotted time. Most weeks we ran well behind the printed schedule, and things at the end had to be either dropped or postponed until another week.

This time we were glad of it to fill in missing interview time with Austin, which had been expected to last about fifteen minutes but would now be less than five.

"Five minutes to shut-up," said the production assistant into my ear.

"So, Austin," I said, "how do you rate your chances this afternoon with Tortola Beach in the big race?"

"He should run well," Austin said, smiling. "Let's just say I'm hopeful."

"So you think he'll stay the seven-eighths-of-a-mile

trip?" I asked. "Let's have a look at his last run at Doncaster seven weeks ago. And remember, that was over only three-quarters."

"Cue VT," Lisa said on the talk-back.

The now familiar film of Tortola Beach running at Doncaster in August appeared on the screen in front of us. I continued to speak over the images. "Tortola Beach seemed certain to win from here, but he fades badly in the last two hundred yards to be third." I didn't need to watch the film again to know what happened in the race. Instead, I watched Austin's face closely for any reaction to it.

"That's true," Austin said. "But that run was inconsistent with his work at home, where he's shown good stamina even over a mile."

"Three minutes to shut-up."

The VT ended.

"Cue Mark. Camera two."

The on-air light on the camera in front of me glowed red.

"Did my sister, Clare, who was riding him there, say anything to you after the race which might have explained why he faded so badly?"

"No," Austin said. "She had no explanation for it at all. As I said, it was contrary to what he's done elsewhere. And it's not that he doesn't like to be in front. He's usually a natural front-runner. I think it must have been a one-off. Perhaps he was just having a bad day."

"Two minutes to shut-up."

"OK, Mark," Lisa said into my earpiece. *"Wind up the interview, and also close the show."*

"Well, let's hope he proves you right this afternoon," I said, smiling at Austin. "Tortola Beach is currently fourth favorite, quoted by most bookmakers at nine-to-one, and my money will certainly be on his nose to win."

"One minute to shut-up," said the voice in my ear.

"I think you'll get a good run for your money," said Austin. "And I'd like to say how sorry I am that Clare will not be riding him today. I can't believe she's gone. She's a great loss to our sport."

"Thirty seconds."

"Thank you very much, Austin," I said. "I think we all miss her. I know I certainly do."

"Twenty seconds."

"And good luck to you this afternoon with Tortola Beach."

"Ten seconds, nine, eight . . ."

I turned to face camera two as the countdown continued in my ears. "I hope you will join us this afternoon for seven races here on Channel 4 from both Newmarket and Ascot, as well as a special bonus, the Two Year Old Trophy from Redcar. And it all starts at one fifty-five. See you then. Bye, bye."

". . . two, one, shut up," said the production assistant on the talk-back just as the red light on the camera in front of me went out and the program credits appeared on the screen.

"Well done, everybody," said Lisa. *"A bit disjointed, but we had no choice. Mark, tell that bloody Austin Reynolds to get a new car."*

"Will do," I replied. "Austin, Lisa the producer says

thank you so much for coming. She's still down in the production van." And I could hear her laughing in my ear over the talk-back.

An audio technician came over and relieved me of my microphone and earpiece, and then he removed Austin's microphone as well. One should always assume a microphone was live—a lesson that some politicians never seem to learn.

Austin started to get up, but I asked him to stay with me just for a minute or two. So we sat next to each other on the sofa while the rest of the crew began dismantling the lights and packing away the cameras and other equipment around us.

"How often did Clare ride for you?" I asked.

"Oh, quite often," Austin replied. "When she was up at the northern tracks and not riding for Geoff Grubb. These days, I tend to run most of mine on the Yorkshire circuits, as many of my owners are from there. I always liked Clare to ride my horses, if she could. She rode lots of winners for me."

"Yes," I said quietly. "But how often did she *stop* them winning for you?"

15

hat did you say?" Austin Reynolds said.

"I asked how often Clare stopped horses for you."

"I don't know what you're talking about."

"Oh yes, I think you do," I said.

I had watched him intently as the VT of the race had been shown and there had been a distinct smirk of satisfaction on his face.

I was in no doubt whatsoever that Austin Reynolds had known exactly what would happen to Tortola Beach in that race at Doncaster and that he had been delighted by the outcome.

"Did you lay Tortola Beach to lose?" I asked.

"No. I told you, I don't know what you're talking about," he said, but he looked worried and sweat had appeared on his brow.

I thought back to what had been written on that white envelope in Clare's desk: *AS AGREED, A.*

Had the "A" stood for Austin?

"And did you pay Clare two thousand pounds for stopping him?"

That shocked him. I could tell from his eyes.

It had been a bit of a guess on my part but I had clearly hit the bull's-eye.

"You can't prove anything," he hissed.

"You think so, do you?" I said. "I wonder if the police can get fingerprints from twenty-pound notes. Or DNA from the envelope they were handed over in."

He went quite pale.

"And were you also sleeping with her?"

"What?"

"Were you having an affair with my sister?"

"Don't be ridiculous. Of course I wasn't."

I was tempted to believe him on this point. He had been genuinely surprised by the question, and I didn't really think that he was Clare's type in spite of the fact that she tended to fall for older men. But Austin Reynolds was very much older, some twenty-five years, and he didn't much give the impression of being a great Lothario.

"What are you going to do now?" Austin asked miserably.

"Nothing," I said. "At least nothing just yet."

"So what should I do?" he said.

"Whatever you like," I said. "Running all your horses to win might be a good start."

He looked at me with uncertainty in his eyes, mixed with a touch of hate and contempt.

"But what about the money?" he asked.

"What about it? You surely don't want it back?"

"Not that money," he said, "the other money."

"What other money?"

"Look, stop playing games with me." I thought he was close to tears. "I'm talking about the ten thousand you've asked for."

"I haven't asked you for anything," I said. "I was aware that Clare had purposely stopped Tortola Beach from winning, but I only realized that you also knew when I watched you looking at the race just now."

"Oh God," Austin said, "then who is it?"

"Who is what?" I asked.

"Who is blackmailing me?"

At that point, rather inconveniently, Lisa arrived from the scanner and walked over toward us.

"Aren't you both coming for breakfast?" she asked.

"We'll be there in a minute," I said. "Austin and I are just discussing the running of his horses."

She looked at Austin. "Did Mark tell you that I said you should get a new car?"

"I'm sorry I was late."

"Yeah, you're a bloody nuisance," Lisa said.

She had a well-earned reputation for believing that it was she who was doing the favor for the guests who agreed to come on her program rather than the other way around. And she wasn't against giving them a hard time if they didn't do as they were told.

"I said to be here by seven-thirty, not twenty to nine."

"I couldn't help it," he whined, "the battery was flat. I

had to wait for the Automobile Association. I got here as soon as I could."

I bet he was now wishing he hadn't bothered to make it here at all.

AUSTIN MANAGED to escape from my attentions by saying he was going to the gents' on our way to breakfast and then disappearing altogether.

I didn't mind too much. I knew where to find him. For a start, he would be with Tortola Beach in the parade ring before the third race later that afternoon.

"So how come you got yourself strangled?" Lisa asked as we tucked in to bacon and eggs in one of the grandstand restaurants. "Whoever did it couldn't have been much cop if you're still here to tell the tale."

"Oh, thanks a lot," I said. "I tell you, I'm damn lucky not to have been murdered."

I explained to her in detail how I had crashed my car in order to survive and how I'd spent half the night in Addenbrooke's hospital.

At last, Lisa started to take me seriously. "Have you any idea who it was?"

"None," I said. "And I've no idea why either."

I decided not to mention anything to her about Mitchell Stacey. The more I thought about it, the less likely it seemed that he had been involved. Strangulation from behind just didn't seem to be his sort of thing. But I suppose I couldn't be sure.

"Were you serious when you said it might have something to do with the murder of Toby Woodley?"

"I really don't know," I said. "Was it just coincidence that there were two 'racing' attacks only two days apart and I was present at both of them?"

"Coincidences do happen, you know," Lisa said. "And Toby Woodley was such an awful little creep that there must have been a shedload of people queuing up to kill him. Me, for one."

"He may have been an awful little creep, but his death was still horrible. And no one deserves to be stabbed in the back."

"Oh, please," she mocked, "don't make me cry. Toby Woodley deserved everything he got."

"You're a hard woman, Lisa. You might think differently if he'd died in your lap."

"Why, did he die in yours?"

"As a matter of fact he did."

She was surprised. "I'd heard a rumor that you'd helped to give him CPR, but I didn't really believe it."

"All true, I'm afraid," I said. "Guilty as charged. Not that it did him any good. He bled to death, and quickly too. Very nasty."

"Do the police have any idea who did it?"

"Not that I'm aware of," I said, "but they'd hardly tell me anyway."

"Probably someone who got fed up with his bloody sniping. I don't believe that man ever wrote a single word of truth in that rag of his."

"Do you remember that piece he did in the summer about a trainer laying his horses on the Internet and then ensuring they lost?"

"Remember it?" Lisa said with irritation. "We did a segment about it on the show. Even had Woodley on as a guest because he promised me he'd reveal who it was on the air."

"And did he?" I couldn't remember it, but I'd been abroad on holiday in late May.

"Did he, hell! It was a total waste of time. One of my worst-ever shows. Little creep just sat there grinning like the Cheshire Cat, making promises he never kept. I reckon he simply made it all up. Load of old tosh. The bastard made me look like a fool."

So that was why Lisa hated him so much.

"And, madam, what were you doing on Wednesday evening last at nine o'clock?" I mimicked a policeman holding a notebook.

"Ha, ha," she said, forcing a smile. "I was at home, Officer, watching *The Apprentice* on television, and I have witnesses to prove it."

I thought about Austin Reynolds. Had he been the trainer in the story? Had Toby Woodley in fact been much closer to the truth than Lisa, or anyone else, had imagined?

"You don't think that story had anything to do with his death, then?" I asked.

"Do you?"

I could hardly say yes without backing it up with some sort of evidence and I didn't really want to do that. Lisa had an uncanny ability for smelling out a story, and the last thing I wanted was to put her on the scent of Clare and race fixing.

"I don't know," I said tamely, "but there must have been some motive. People don't just stab someone for no reason."

"Don't they?" she said. "Haven't you watched the news recently?"

Lisa lost interest in our conversation and started talking to the show's director on her other side.

I sat there thinking about Austin Reynolds and what he had said about being blackmailed. Someone else must have known about his involvement with race fixing.

Had it been Toby Woodley? Was that why he'd been killed?

Where, I wondered, had Austin Reynolds been at nine o'clock last Wednesday evening? Could he have been in the parking lot at Kempton races, murdering Toby to save having to pay his blackmail demands?

But that didn't make any sense. Not half an hour ago when I'd confronted him, Austin had clearly thought that it must have been *me* who was blackmailing him. So why would he think that if he'd believed Toby was responsible, and to the point of murdering him?

No. There had to be a fourth party involved. At least. And that was assuming Toby's death had indeed been something to do with the race fixing story in the first place, something that was by no means certain.

———

I USED my cell phone to call Detective Chief Inspector Perry at ten o'clock, as he'd requested.

"How are you feeling?" he asked.

"Tired," I said. "I didn't get to bed until four, and I was up again at six-thirty."

"I heard from the hospital that they sent you home. Where are you now?"

"Newmarket racetrack," I said. "I'm working here, and will be for the rest of the day."

"Doing what?" he asked.

"I present racing on television. We're covering Newmarket this afternoon."

"Is that why you asked me last night if I followed racing?"

"Yes," I said. "I thought you might have seen me if you did."

"Sorry, no." He didn't sound very sorry. "Is your voice better?"

"It's a lot better now than last night, thank you." But I was glad I wasn't commentating. "Did you find any fingerprints in my car?"

"Masses of them," he said. "We now have to find out if any of them belong to our strangler. We'll do a computerized criminal records comparison first, but we may need to eliminate anyone who's recently been in the back of your car."

I thought about Nicholas and Brendan, and also the paramedic. All three of them had been in the back after the attack, to say nothing of the firemen who'd cut off the roof.

"How about the rope?"

"A search of the area revealed nothing. He must have taken it with him. Maybe it was a scarf or something."

"You said you wanted a witness statement," I said.

"Yes, please," he replied. "I'll send my sergeant over to take it now."

"How long will it take?" I asked.

"That depends, Mr. Shillingford, on how much you have to say."

"How much do you want me to say?"

"Everything that is relevant. Especially what you can remember after going out to your car."

"I have a production meeting here at eleven o'clock, and I'm going to be pretty busy after that until we go off the air at four-twenty. Can't I just write out a statement rather than have your sergeant take it down? I could do it now on my laptop and e-mail it to you."

"Could you print it out and sign it? And also have your signature witnessed? My sergeant will then collect it in about an hour."

"No problem," I said. "I'll leave it at the racetrack office."

"Right. Do that. If I need anything further, I'll leave a message at this number."

"What about my car?" I said. "What happens to that now?"

"The forensic boys are still going over it. They're apparently now looking for material fibers."

I laughed. "I don't think the inside of that car has been cleaned out since I've had it and that's about eight years.

There must be handfuls of fibers present, and dog hair, candy wrappers, and God knows what else."

"Forensics will bag everything just in case it's needed later."

"Then what?" I asked.

"I suppose it's then yours to take away, but it's rather badly bashed in at the front and it has no roof. I saw it this morning at the police compound. It would cost more to repair than a car of that age is worth, and you know what insurance companies are like, it would be better for them to write it off completely."

But not, of course, better for me. I would end up with a paltry sum from the insurers and no car. I sighed. Was it time to get a new car as well as a new house? How about a new girlfriend?

Next I called the number that Emily had given me at the party. She answered on the second ring.

"I thought you might be asleep," I said.

"I should be," she replied.

"Did you watch the show?"

"I only saw the last bit of it. I now wish I'd stayed with you instead of coming back here with Angela. But I think she was glad I did."

"And how are all the sweet young things this morning?"

"Hungover, mostly. The party may have ended prematurely, thanks to you, but if Angela thought that had stopped them drinking she was much mistaken. They must have had bottles stashed away somewhere. Half of them are still incapable of walking properly."

"That's because of their high heels."

She laughed. I liked that.

"What are you doing for the rest of the day?" I asked.

"What would you like me to do?"

"How about coming to the races?"

"Love to," she said.

I was suddenly very excited.

"Great," I said. "Can you be here at twelve-thirty? I'll meet you outside, where you drive in. Just follow the signs."

"OK, I'll be there. See you later."

"Oh, Emily?" I said.

"Yes."

"One more thing." I paused.

"Yes?" she encouraged.

"If you like," I said nervously, "you could bring an overnight bag."

"OK," she said slowly. "I would like that. Very much."

I WENT to the press room with my computer to type my witness statement for Chief Inspector Perry. Not surprisingly, with almost four hours to go until the first race, I was the only member of the press there.

It took me about forty minutes to complete the statement, reliving the horrors of the previous night and expressing them in words. But try as I might, I couldn't recall anything at all that I thought would help in identifying the strangler. I even closed my eyes and tried to evoke his smell, but there was nothing.

I could remember far better what had happened *after*

I'd sat down in my car than before. I suppose that was bound to be the case, as before had been rather mundane while after had obviously not, if one could possibly describe being propositioned by a beautiful woman for sex as mundane.

I remembered that, all right, and it made me smile in anticipation. But I decided against putting it in my witness statement, although it was perhaps the real reason I hadn't even considered my safety as I'd gone to my car. Suffice to say, my mind had been elsewhere.

I used the printer in the press room to print out the statement and was about to go in search of someone to witness my signature when Jim Metcalf walked in.

"Hi, Jim," I said. "What brings *UK Today*'s star reporter here so early?"

"Boredom," he said. "I got fed up waiting at the hotel. I stayed up here last night. I'm doing a feature on Peter Williams, and I was out on the Heath with his string at seven this morning."

"Clare reckoned his colt Reading Glass is a good prospect for next year's Guineas."

"Possibly," said Jim, "but he still needs to grow a bit behind. And Peter's got some other good young colts that will certainly shine next year as three-year-olds. He's so good at not over-racing them at two and burning them out. That's what I'll be writing about."

"I'll look forward to reading it."

"It'll be in the paper next Saturday," he said. "To coincide with Future Champions Day."

I still had my witness statement in my hand.

"Jim, could you do me a favor?" I asked. "I need some-one to witness my signature on something."

"Sure," he said. "Is it your will?"

"No," I said, laughing. "It's a witness statement for the police."

"What did you witness?" he asked.

I was suddenly not at all sure that this had been a good idea. But I'd already told Lisa, so it was hardly a secret.

"Someone tried to kill me last night," I said.

"Not Mitchell Stacey?"

I was stunned. I just stood there with my mouth hang-ing open.

"How . . ."

"Come on, Mark, I've known about you and Sarah Sta-cey for ages. Worst-kept secret in racing. You've hardly been that discreet, going out openly to pubs and restau-rants and the like. I know for a fact that you went to the theater in London together in August to see that revival of *Oklahoma!* while Mitchell was up at the sales in Doncaster. I have my contacts." He tapped the side of his nose, just as Toby Woodley had done at Stratford.

I was quite surprised that my private life should have been of such interest to him. And I didn't much like the thought that I'd clearly been watched without my knowledge.

"Did Toby Woodley also know about us?"

"I don't know, but any racing journalist worth his salt should have been able to find out."

"But Woodley never wrote anything about us in the *Gazette*."

But was that what he'd been going on about at Clare's funeral? Had he actually known about Sarah and me, but his editor had prevented the story being published in the paper so soon after Clare's death?

"Maybe he didn't know, then," said Jim, "but I'd be surprised. Most of what he wrote was rubbish and speculation, but there was usually a glimmer of truth in there somewhere, and he did have an amazing knack for sniffing out real stories."

"Yes," I said, "and how exactly did he manage that?"

"I expect he used good old-fashioned journalistic techniques like the rest of us—hiding in the undergrowth with a powerful telephoto lens, paying the police for information, and of course hacking into people's phone messages."

"Isn't hacking illegal?"

He looked at me as if I were an idiot. "Of course it is. And so is speeding on the freeway. But we all do it. At least we did before all the fuss."

"Is that how you found out about me and Sarah?" I asked.

"No. As a matter of fact, it wasn't."

"So how did you, then?" I pressed.

"You don't want to know," he said slowly.

"Yes I bloody do."

He didn't say anything.

"Come on, tell me," I said aggressively. "How did you find out?"

"Clare told me."

"Clare?" I said, surprised. "She can't have. She wouldn't have."

"Well, she did," Jim said.

"When?"

"A long time ago. I don't think she meant to tell me. It just sort of slipped out. She swore me to secrecy."

"How come she was even speaking to you in the first place? I thought she despised all journalists."

"She didn't despise me."

I wondered if Jim had been one of the string of unsuitable older men that Clare had bedded.

"Were you sleeping with her?" I asked.

"That's none of your business," he replied.

"I think it is," I said, staring him in the eye.

"OK, I was," he said. "But it was a couple of years ago now, and it only lasted a month or two." He laughed. "Only until Clare realized the error of her ways and dumped me."

So Jim Metcalf wasn't the "new man" that Clare had been so flattering about at our last dinner.

"But I still loved her enough," he went on, "to keep her confidences about you and Sarah Stacey. But it amused me to watch you both."

"Well, for your further amusement and information," I said, "Mrs. Stacey and I are no longer an item. It's over, finished. I've moved on."

"But was it Mitchell who tried to kill you? I hear through the press's grapevine that he'd found out about your affair, and I, for one, wouldn't want to be on the wrong end of that temper."

"No, you're probably very wise," I said, remembering my encounters with Mitchell in the parking lots. "I don't know if it was him, but I doubt it. Whoever it was went to great lengths to remain hidden and that doesn't smack of Mitchell's methods. He's more of a confrontational sort of guy."

"So how did this person try to kill you?"

"On the record or off?" I asked.

"Either way," he said. "You choose."

I handed him my witness statement and he read it through from start to finish.

"Blimey," he said, "it really was attempted murder."

"It sure was," I agreed.

"I never realized being a racing journalist could be so dangerous, what with that creep Woodley getting himself murdered."

"The police seem to think that might have been a robbery that went too far."

"What was stolen?" Jim asked.

"It seems his briefcase is missing."

"Ah, the famous Woodley briefcase."

"What's famous about it?" I asked.

"Don't you know? He'd always go berserk if anyone went near it in the press room. That's partly why he was so unpopular with the rest of the racing press. He treated that briefcase as if it was a bloody baby. He was obsessed by it."

"What was in it?" I asked.

"God knows," said Jim. "Probably just his sandwiches."

"Somebody must have thought it was valuable if they killed him for it."

"I can't imagine why," said Jim, laughing. "I'd have happily killed him for nothing."

"I wouldn't say that if the police can hear you." I thought back to my interview with Superintendent Cullen. I hadn't done myself any favors telling him that I hadn't liked the victim.

I looked at the clock on the wall. I was late for the production meeting.

"Jim, could you witness my signature? The police will be here soon to collect it."

I signed the paper at the bottom, and Jim added his signature alongside as witness.

"So can I use any of this?" he asked, pointing at my statement.

"Why not?" I said. "It can't do any harm."

16

I went out to meet Emily immediately after the production meeting just in case she was early.

I realized that I had no idea what type of car she drove, so I stood next to the entry road, staring intently at the driver of every vehicle that passed me, in case I might miss her. But I needn't have worried. Bang on time, at precisely twelve-thirty, she arrived flashing her lights and sounding her horn as soon as she saw me.

And I should have guessed her choice of car. She drove a metallic red Mercedes SLK sports roadster, and she had the roof down.

I was laughing as I climbed in beside her, in the sure knowledge there was no strangler lurking in a backseat because there was no backseat.

"Hello, gorgeous," I said, leaning over and giving her a brief kiss.

"Where to?" she asked, grinning broadly.

"Straight on down to the end," I said. "We'll park in the press lot, it's nearer to the entrance than the one for the public."

What was it that Jim Metcalf had said about me not being very discreet in my private life? Well, there was nothing in the slightest bit discreet about Emily's and my arrival in the Newmarket racetrack's press parking lot.

For a start, not many members of the press drive Mercedes sports cars, and even fewer arrive for a race meeting in October with the roof down. Then there was the spin of the rear wheels on the gravel by the entrance, and the slight drift of the back end on the damp grass as Emily turned sharply into the parking space.

Next came the dramatic closing of the electric roof, and, as if there were not enough of the press watching already, there was Emily's loud squeal of delight as she came around the back of the car, enveloped me in her arms, and kissed me passionately full on the mouth.

Perhaps, I thought, the public parking lot would have been better after all. But at least this might kill off any belief lingering amongst the Fourth Estate that I was still romantically involved with Sarah Stacey.

We went through the entrance to the racetrack, and I took her around to the fenced-off compound where the Channel 4 scanner and the other broadcast vehicles were parked. There was still over an hour until we went on the air, but I had to do the voice-over recordings for some of the VTs that would be shown later during the live transmission.

I also had some script notes I wanted to write out in preparation for what was likely to be a busy afternoon, with races from both Ascot and Redcar on the program, as well as three from Newmarket. The more material we had prepared and were ready to transmit at the touch of a button, the better we would be able to cope with any unexpected problems that might arise, as they surely would.

It was very much a case of the nine *P*s: *Proper prior planning prevents piss-poor program presenter performance.*

Emily sat in the scanner and watched while I recorded the voice-over for a host of video clips of previous races, highlighting the running of some of the horses that were in action again today. The whole VT would be used as part of the introduction for the afternoon.

"It's fascinating," she said when I'd finished. "It all seems so seamless when you watch on a Saturday."

"Ah, the magic of live television," I said. "Never believe anything you see on the TV. It's all done with smoke and mirrors."

"Don't tease me," she said.

"I'm not," I said. "I mean it. We will show eight races from three different racetracks hundreds of miles apart all within the span of two and a half hours, and the viewers believe that the whole thing is sequential and under our control, which it isn't. Now, that's what I call magic."

"Does it ever go wrong?" she asked.

"Often," I said. "And the real trick is to carry on regardless and make out that everything is proceeding exactly as we had expected it to, and to stop talking only when you drop down dead or the program finishes, whichever comes first."

"You're crazy." She laughed.

"Bonkers," I said, laughing back.

It was the first time I'd felt even the slightest bit happy since Clare had died. Emily was clearly good for me.

"GOOD LUCK, EVERYBODY." Neville, the producer, was speaking over the talk-back in our earpieces and headphones as the production assistant counted down to zero to the start of transmission.

The familiar theme music played, and I watched the opening sequence on the monitor in front of me.

"Cue Mark."

I took a deep breath and looked straight into the lens of the camera being held in front of my face. "Good afternoon, everyone, and welcome to *Channel 4 Racing* on the day of Europe's richest race for two-year-olds, the Millions Trophy, which is amongst the three races we're covering from here at Newmarket, as well as four from Ascot, including the Scoop6 Cup, and, as a special bonus, one of the premier northern races for the youngsters, the Two Year Old Trophy from Redcar at four o'clock."

"Cue VT," said the director, and the video clips played that I had previously voiced over.

The program was up and running.

I could almost feel the injection of adrenaline into my bloodstream that the countdown to the start had produced. And I loved it. I was an adrenaline-rush junkie and was hopelessly hooked.

I waved and smiled at Emily, who was standing about five yards away, out of picture. We were both in the New-market parade ring, close to the winner's enclosure. It is where I would stay for the duration of the program, watching all the races on the monitor set up in front of me.

The VT was coming to an end. *"Cue Mark,"* said the director into my ear.

"So let's go straight over to join Iain Ferguson for the first of our three Group races from Ascot. Good afternoon, Iain."

The red light on the camera in front of me went off to indicate I was no longer live on air. I could relax a little as the first race from Ascot was being broadcast. I went over to Emily and gave her a cuddle.

"I hope you're not too cold," I said. She had no coat and was wearing what I thought was far too thin a dress for being outdoors in October in spite of the unseasonably warm weather we had been enjoying. However, it did hug her alluring figure superbly, and that also did wonders for my adrenaline level.

"I'm absolutely fine," she said. "But aren't you meant to be saying something? I thought you told me that you mustn't stop talking."

"The presenter at Ascot is speaking now. The first race we're showing is being run there, so I reckon I've got about another eight minutes before I'm back on."

But, nevertheless, my brain would still be on the alert for the word *Mark* just in case things didn't go as planned and I had to step in. It was something you got used to: carrying on a conversation with a third party while listening for your name being spoken in your ear by the producer or director. The rest of the talk-back could float over me without really registering, but I would be brought to full awareness by the first *mmm* of Mark.

The afternoon progressed without any major problem— that is, until the third race at Ascot was badly delayed due to a horse getting loose on the way down to the start and galloping on its own right around the racetrack.

I could imagine the panic going on in the scanner as it was realized that the Ascot race would now coincide with the buildup for the big race of the afternoon at Newmarket. The pitch of the voices over the talk-back rose a notch with tension.

"If that damn nag at Ascot isn't caught soon, the two races will be run at the same time," said Neville into my ear.

It was his worst nightmare. One of the golden rules in horse race broadcasting was that no races were to be shown recorded, they had to go out live.

Once upon a time, delaying a race broadcast by a bit wouldn't have been too much of a problem, but now with Internet gambling, especially the growing popularity of betting on horses during the actual running of the race, being *live* was absolutely essential.

"Matthew," Neville called over the talk-back to the floor manager in the Newmarket parade ring, *"see if Newmarket will hold for a couple of minutes if it looks like there'll be a clash. Otherwise we'll have to use a split screen."*

I watched as Matthew ran over to the weighing room

to speak to the stewards. But delaying the race wasn't usually that simple. The meeting was also being broadcast live on the radio and any change in time, even by a couple of minutes, could badly disrupt the schedules.

"Two minutes max," said Matthew. *"On your call."*

"Great, thanks," replied Neville. *"Tell Kevin to get down to the start right now."* Kevin was the program runner, literally, and he would already be rushing down to the course to relay the producer's message to the starter should it become necessary.

"OK. Listen up, everyone," said Neville in everybody's ears. *"We continue with the big race buildup here at Newmarket, with Ascot shown, mute, picture-in-picture. We stay with Newmarket but go over to Ascot for their race live, if and when they're ready. We'll only hold the Newmarket race for the two minutes if it looks like there's going to be a clash. We might even need to take Newmarket before Ascot. If we have to use a split screen, we'll take the commentary of whichever race starts first, then switch when it finishes."*

And just when you thought things couldn't get any worse, the director reminded everyone that we had to fit in a three-minute commercial break before Newmarket's race. It was part of our contract with the broadcaster.

The loose horse was finally caught and subsequently withdrawn from the Ascot race, which started ten minutes late but just in time for the Newmarket race to go off as scheduled immediately after it. And the commercial break was somehow shoehorned in before both of them.

Heart rates all around returned to normal levels, and the talk-back profanity count reverted to more acceptable proportions. It was a running joke in broadcasting that recording the talk-back was a sackable offense.

Tortola Beach won Newmarket's big race easily by three lengths and was led triumphantly into the winner's enclosure by a beaming Austin Reynolds.

"Mark, get a quick interview with Austin—now!" Neville demanded in my ear. *"It will be a good follow-up to your conversation with him on* The Morning Line.*"*

Little did Neville know what else had been said in our conversation after *The Morning Line* had gone off the air.

The cameraman and I stepped forward boldly, me with a handheld microphone at the ready like a gun. We gave Austin Reynolds no chance to say no.

"Cue Mark."

"Congratulations, Austin Reynolds, trainer of Tortola Beach. A great run."

I pushed the microphone toward his mouth.

"Yes," he said. "Very pleasing."

"You said on *The Morning Line* earlier today that you were confident he would stay the seven-eighths-of-a-mile trip and so it has turned out. Do you think this confirms that his last run at Doncaster when he faded so badly near the finish was just a one-off anomaly?"

He looked at me with a certain degree of loathing in his eyes.

"Yes," he said. "I'm sure it was."

"So will he run in the Two Thousand Guineas next year?"

"Quoted at twelve-to-one for the Guineas by Coral's," Neville said into my ear.

"That's the plan," said Austin.

"I hear he's currently being quoted at twelve-to-one for the Guineas by Coral's," I said. "Do you think that's a fair price?"

"A bit short, I'd have said. He only started at tens today."

Yes, I thought. And I wondered if part of the reason for stopping the horse at Doncaster had been to get his starting price nice and long for this race.

"Mark, OK, wrap the interview. Link to Iain for Ascot presentations."

"Thank you, Austin," I said, turning away from him and back to the camera. "And now over to Iain Ferguson at Ascot for the presentations for their third race."

"Cue Iain," said the director, and the camera's red light in front of me went out.

I would have loved to ask Austin Reynolds right there and then who he thought might be blackmailing him and why, but I didn't particularly want everyone else in the country to overhear his answer.

I decided to have a word with him later after the transmission was over, and after my microphone had been removed.

The program went to another commercial break while the cameraman covered the Newmarket trophy presentation, which was recorded in the scanner.

"Mark," Neville said, *"on return, discuss the Two Thousand Guineas ante-post market caption, and then we'll go to the VT of our trophy presentation. Coming back to you in five, four, three, two, one . . . cue Mark."*

I looked into the lens. "Welcome back to Newmarket,

where the place is still buzzing from that spectacular win by Tortola Beach. So let us look at the ante-post market for the Two Thousand Guineas next May." The graphic appeared on the screen, and I went through the list, Tortola Beach now being quoted as joint sixth favorite. The graphic disappeared, and I looked back into the camera lens. "And now we have the Millions Trophy presentation to the connections of Tortola Beach."

"Cue VT."

The recently recorded footage of the trophy presentation was broadcast as I voiced over it live while, at the same time, I had the director and producer wittering away in my ear. *"Mark, Scoop6 update, please—after four legs, there are only twenty-six tickets still left in. Then hand over to Iain at Ascot. Back to you in picture in five, four, three, two, one . . . cue Mark."*

And so it went on, relentlessly, right through until twenty past four, when the production assistant said *"Shut up"* and we could all relax.

"Well done, everybody," said Neville. *"Good job. See you all back here next week for Future Champions Day."*

"Wow!" said Emily when I went over to her. "I had no idea." The sound engineer had wired her up and she'd been listening to the chatter on the talk-back. "It's amazing."

"It certainly is," I agreed. "Those Hollywood film stars have no idea how easy they have it, doing multiple takes until they get it right and having breaks between scenes to learn their lines. I tell you, there's nothing quite like live television to concentrate the mind."

"I could concentrate your mind," Emily said seductively.

WE WENT TO CLARE'S COTTAGE.

I didn't think Clare would have minded as she was always telling me to get a proper girlfriend. And Emily's place at Royston was simply too far away. We were both more eager than that.

I had intended seeking out Austin Reynolds to ask him more about the blackmailer, but that, too, had been postponed due to the urgency of our more basic human urges.

We hardly made it up the stairs to the guest bedroom, but, in the end, our lovemaking was gentle and tender, though not without passion and hunger.

For both of us, it was a journey of exploration, a trip into new territory, and I for one found the experience hugely satisfying.

"Wow!" Emily said again, lying back on the bed. "A day full of surprises."

"Good surprises?" I asked.

"Absolutely," she said with a smile. "Wonderful surprises." She suddenly sat up straight. "Do you have any wine? I've never been to the races before and not had a drink."

I laughed. "I'll go and see."

I picked up my shirt and boxers from where they had fallen on the landing and put them back on. Somehow it didn't seem quite right for me to be wandering around this house without any clothes on.

"Red or white?" I called.

"How about champagne?"

"I'll check."

I went downstairs and looked in Clare's fridge for some cold bubbles.

There were plenty of things that were out-of-date, and even some that were growing a nice covering of mold, but there were no bottles of champagne. I did find one, however, in her drinks cupboard in the sitting room, a nice bottle of Bolinger Special Cuvée, but it was decidedly warm.

"Do you mind if the champagne's warm?" I shouted up the stairs.

"Isn't there an ice bucket?" came the reply.

There was, a silver one, sitting on the mantelpiece along with Clare's other trophies.

I took the bucket back to the kitchen and looked in the freezer. It was one of those American-style refrigerators with an internal ice maker. The hopper was only half full, so I lifted it out and poured the contents into the bucket.

I was returning the empty hopper to the freezer when I noticed a flat plastic case stuck to the inside with some tape.

I pulled the case away and opened it.

It contained a DVD and a folded sheet of ordinary white copier paper.

I sat on a stool at Clare's breakfast bar and carefully unfolded the paper. There were three lines of printed text across the middle:

I KNOW YOU DID THIS ON PURPOSE.

A CONTRIBUTION OF JUST £200 WILL MAKE

THE STORY GO AWAY.

GET THE CASH READY. PAYMENT INSTRUCTIONS

   WILL FOLLOW.

I sat there staring at the words, turning the DVD over and over in my fingers.

So it wasn't only Austin Reynolds who had been black-mailed.

17

"Are you going to sit there all day? I'm thirsty."

I turned around to find Emily standing provocatively in the kitchen doorway, and, unlike me, she obviously had no qualms about being naked in this house.

She walked over and ran her fingers through my hair. "Are you coming back to bed or do I have to go and play with myself?"

"Sorry," I said. "I'm just coming."

"What are you looking at anyway?"

"Oh, nothing," I said, starting to fold the sheet of paper, but Emily was already reading it over my shoulder.

"Oh my God!" she screamed. "It's a blackmail note. Who sent you that?"

"No one," I said.

"And what was it that you did on purpose?"

"It wasn't sent to me," I said. "I found it in the freezer."

"In the freezer? Where?"

"In amongst the ice. It was taped to the inside of the hopper with this DVD. Clare must have hidden them in there."

"Were they sent to her?"

"I assume so."

"Who by?" Emily asked. "And what was it that she did?"

"It can't have been very much, not if two hundred pounds is all the blackmailer asked for. Perhaps the DVD will give us a clue."

"Oh yes," she said breathlessly. "How exciting."

Excitement wasn't the first thing that came to my mind, but I was intrigued nonetheless.

"There's a DVD player in the sitting room," I said. "Let's go and see."

Emily ran upstairs and then quickly reappeared wearing one of Clare's dressing gowns while I loaded the disk.

I was a bit apprehensive as I pushed the play button. Did I really want to know what Clare had been up to? And, in particular, did I want Emily to find out as well? But it was too late to stop now. I had to see, and there was no way I was going to get Emily to go back upstairs and wait for me in the bedroom while I had a quick look at the DVD on my own. She was perched on the edge of the sofa in eager anticipation, bouncing up and down gently like a child waiting for a Christmas present.

I thought it quite likely that the DVD would contain a recording of a race, but I was really surprised that it was the one at Wolverhampton the previous April when Clare had ridden Brain of Brixham into second place while mistaking the camera support pole for the winning post.

"What's so special about that?" Emily asked, obviously disappointed not to have seen some salacious footage.

"Nothing," I said.

"So what's she supposed to have done on purpose?"

"I presume it was that she didn't win."

I played the film through again and explained to Emily what had happened.

"But how can you blackmail someone for making a silly mistake?"

"That's a very good question."

I went up the stairs a little to retrieve my shoes and pants from where they had been discarded earlier.

"Where are you going?"

"I need my laptop. It's in your car."

I went out to get it, and then logged on to the *Racing Post* website to see who trained Brain of Brixham.

Why was I not surprised to discover that it was Austin Reynolds?

Time for me to go and ask him some more questions, I thought.

IN SPITE OF my protestations, Emily came with me.

"For a start," she said, "I need to drive my car. You're not insured for it."

I thought I probably was through my own insurance,

but I could see that there was no way I was going to convince her not to come.

She drove through Newmarket, then out on the Bury Road toward Austin Reynolds's training establishment, where she parked on the gravel driveway in front of his mock-Georgian mansion.

"Please wait in the car," I said to Emily firmly. "It will be difficult enough to get him to talk to me alone. He certainly won't do so with someone else listening."

Grudgingly, she agreed, and sat there rigidly holding the steering wheel while I went to ring the front doorbell.

"I don't want to talk to you," Austin said, carelessly opening the door before he saw who it was. "Leave me alone."

He tried to close the door again, but I had my foot against it.

"I only want to ask you a few questions."

"I haven't got time," he said. "We've got the Ingrams staying, and we're having a small celebration here this evening. In fact, I thought you were the caterers arriving. Come back tomorrow."

Mr. and Mrs. Joshua Ingram were the owners of Tortola Beach.

"Perhaps the Ingrams might be interested to know why their horse didn't win at Doncaster in August."

"I thought you said you weren't blackmailing me."

"I'm not," I said.

"That sounded like blackmail to me."

"It will only take a few minutes."

He thought for a moment. "Go round to my office.

Down the side." He pointed to his right. "I'll come and let you in there."

Reluctantly, I removed my foot from his door and he closed it.

"Down the side," I shouted to Emily, and she drove behind me as I crunched over the gravel.

Austin Reynolds's office was attached to the back of his house, looking out toward the stable yard beyond, and he was already standing at the door, holding it open.

"Who's in the car?" he asked.

"Just a friend." I was suddenly very glad that Emily was with me. This felt a bit like walking into the lion's den.

I followed Austin into his office. There was not a lion to be seen.

"What do you want?" he asked, sitting down behind his large oak desk.

"I want to know who is blackmailing you."

"So do I."

"But you must have some idea."

"None," he said. "All I received were notes."

I removed from my pocket the sheet of paper that I'd found in Clare's freezer and laid it out flat on the desk in front of him.

"Were they like this?" I asked.

He looked at it briefly and nodded. "Pretty much, except mine accused me of laying horses to lose."

"Did they arrive with DVDs?"

"The first one did."

"How many have you received?" I asked.

"Three."

"And what did you do about them?"

"Paid up," he said. "At least I did for the first two. Whoever it was didn't ask for very much, so I paid."

I was amazed.

"Except now," he said, "I've been asked for more and I don't like it."

"What do you mean?"

He looked at his watch and stood up. "I've got to go and get changed."

"Not yet," I said forcefully, pointing a finger at him. "Answer my questions first." He sat down again heavily. "What did you mean by being asked for more?"

"It was that bloody race at Wolverhampton," he said angrily. "I wish I'd never run the damn horse."

"Brain of Brixham?"

"Yes."

"But surely that was a genuine error on Clare's part?"

"Yes, it was."

"So why are you being blackmailed over it? Why didn't you just go to the police?"

"Clare wanted to," he said.

"So why didn't you?" I asked. He said nothing but just sat looking down at his desk. "Was it because you had indeed layed the horse to lose?"

He looked up at me. "Not a lot," he said. "I'd thought old Brainy would run really well, so I had a big bet on him to win. Too big, really. Then I started to have cold feet, especially when he seemed a bit off-color on the morning of the race."

"So you layed him on the Internet?"

"Yes," he said. "Though not using my own name, of course. And just to limit my losses if he didn't win."

Austin and I both knew that trainers laying their own horses was strictly against the Rules of Racing and would be punished by a lengthy ban from the sport.

"I didn't lay the full amount. I still stood to lose a lot if Brainy didn't win."

That probably wouldn't have made much difference to an inquiry.

"It was very stupid," he said. "I know that."

"But not as stupid as arranging with Clare to stop Tortola Beach at Doncaster."

"That was all her idea," he said. "When she found out I'd layed Brainy at Wolverhampton, she said there was a much better way of stopping a horse winning, one that nobody would ever discover."

Except me, that is.

"So did Clare pay the two hundred pounds?" I said, pointing at the note.

"I paid it for her to stop her going to the police," Austin said miserably, "along with two hundred from me. That bloody mistake of Clare's has cost me a fortune, what with the loss of prize money and my big bet, not to mention the blackmail."

"How about the second note? When did that come?"

"About six weeks ago."

"Asking for the same amount?" I asked.

"No, it was a thousand that time."

"Did Clare get another one too?"

"Yes," Austin said. "Also for a thousand."

"And did you pay that for her as well?"

"No," he said. "I told her to pay it out of the money I'd given her for losing on Tortola Beach."

She obviously hadn't done that, not if the two thousand I'd found in her desk had been the same money. I wondered if she'd paid it at all.

"But you paid?"

"Yes," he said gloomily.

"And you still didn't go to the police?"

"I couldn't, could I? Not when I'd paid up once before."

"And not when you'd also layed Tortola Beach to lose."

"That was only a bit," he said. "I couldn't do too much or it would have been suspicious."

"But why on earth would you stop a horse if you weren't making much from it?"

He looked the picture of abject misery, a stark contrast to when he had led his victorious horse into the winner's enclosure earlier that afternoon.

"Clare was adamant that we should do it. She seemed to act like it was a game. I told her not to be so bloody silly, but she said that she would give it a go anyway whether I wanted her to or not."

"So you agreed?"

"Yes."

"But why, then, did you pay her two thousand pounds if you didn't make much out of it?"

"It was like a bet between us. I told her she could have half what I made if she pulled it off without there even being a stewards' inquiry. She claimed it was easy and that she'd done it before, but I didn't believe her. I really didn't think she could do it, but, boy, did she prove me wrong. It was brilliant. I've never seen anything like it in my life."

My stupid, brilliant sister, I thought, competitive to the end. It hadn't been the money that had been important, it had been winning her bet with Austin.

"You said you've now been asked for more."

"Yes," he said. "I had another note yesterday morning demanding ten thousand." He again looked close to tears. "I can't afford that sort of money."

"Show me the note," I said.

He opened the top left-hand drawer of the desk and removed a single sheet of paper, placing it down in front of me.

TIME TO PAY A LITTLE MORE.

A PAYMENT OF JUST £10000 IS NEEDED FOR ME TO

   REMAIN SILENT.

GET THE CASH READY. PAYMENT INSTRUCTIONS

   WILL FOLLOW.

It did look remarkably like the one I'd found in Clare's freezer, but it had one very significant difference. The amount of ten thousand pounds had had the last zero added by hand. When it had been printed, it had read just one thousand. The blackmailer had obviously decided at the last minute to seriously up the stakes.

"If it had been for just a thousand like last time," Austin said, "I'd probably pay it. But ten grand is completely out of order."

I thought that even one thousand was out of order.

"When did you say this arrived?"

"Yesterday morning," he said, "in the mail."

"Where's the envelope it came in?"

He took an envelope out of the drawer and placed it on the desk. It had been addressed in the same printed small capital letters as the note, and the postmark showed that it had been mailed on Thursday even though I couldn't read from where.

"Have you had the payment instructions?" I asked.

"Not yet."

"How did you hand the money over before?"

"I was told I had to place used twenties in a brown envelope and then leave it under my car in the owners and trainers parking lot at Doncaster races, against the inside of the offside rear wheel."

"Didn't you watch to see who collected it?"

"No," he said, "I was told not to. Anyway, I had a runner in the first and had to go and saddle it."

"You could have got someone else to watch."

He stared at me in disbelief. "Oh yeah! Tell me, who was I going to get to watch the package without telling him exactly why?"

"How did you get the instructions?"

"They also came in the mail," he said. "They arrived the day before I had to leave the cash."

"Did Clare get the same instructions?"

"I don't know," he said. "The first time, I just put a note in with my payment to say that I was including hers."

Crazy, I thought.

"And was it the same drop method both times?"

"Yes," he said. "Except the second time was at York, not Doncaster."

"And you've heard nothing else?" I asked.

"Not until yesterday morning, although there were those bloody pieces in the *Gazette* this week. I nearly shit myself when I saw that headline on Tuesday."

"Why? Did you think it was written about you?"

"What would you think?" he said.

"But it didn't say anything about the horse's trainer being involved."

"It did last May when there was that piece about a trainer laying his horses on the Internet."

"Was that you?" I asked.

"I've no idea," he said. "But it was still much too close for comfort."

"Was the article printed in the paper before or after you paid the first two hundred?"

"After," he said definitely. "I remember clearly that the first note arrived on my birthday, the twenty-fifth of April. It wasn't much of a birthday present, I can tell you."

At that point a neat little woman opened the office door and put her head through the gap.

"Austin," she said in a cross tone, "will you *please* come and look after our guests."

"Just coming, dear," Austin said, standing up.

The neat little woman removed her head and closed the door.

"Please go now," he was almost pleading with me.

"OK," I said. "But let me know when you receive the payment instructions." I smiled at him. "Then we can try and catch the bastard, and without involving the police or the racing authorities."

"Why are you doing this?" he asked. "What have you got to gain?"

"I'm trying to find out why my sister died. Your secrets are safe with me as long as Clare Shillingford's good reputation remains intact."

EMILY WAS still waiting for me in her car.

"I was about to send in the cavalry," she said as I climbed in beside her. "You've been ages."

I looked at my watch. I'd actually been in Austin's office for only half an hour. Somehow it had seemed longer.

"Sorry," I said. "It was important."

"How important?" she asked. "Is that man the blackmailer?"

"No," I said, "he isn't."

"Then who is?"

I sighed. "I wish I knew."

Dammit, I thought. I'd been so busy asking Austin about the blackmail notes that I'd forgotten to ask him about the running of Bangkok Flyer at Lingfield on the day Clare had died.

That race had been the start of all of this. Would Clare have died, I wondered, if I hadn't witnessed that race and confronted her at Haxted Mill?

Why oh why hadn't I answered my telephone that night?

Emily started the car engine. "Where to now?" she said.

"I like you being my driver," I said with a forced

laugh, trying to put my guilt and self-pity back in their boxes.

"I can think of better things I'd rather be of yours."

"Good," I said, smiling genuinely. "Let's go back to Clare's cottage."

"Great idea," she said. "That champagne will be nice and cold by now."

"TELL ME ALL ABOUT IT," Emily said as we snuggled down together on Clare's sofa with the bottle of chilled champagne.

"About what?" I asked.

"About why your sister was being blackmailed and why finding that note suddenly meant we had to go and see that man."

"Austin Reynolds," I said.

"That's the one."

How much did I want to tell her? How much could I trust her? I hadn't even known her yet for twenty-four hours. But she had seen Clare's blackmail note. Was it not better to tell her something rather than have her ask other people?

"It's all nonsense, really," I said. "Clare was being blackmailed for something she hadn't even done."

"In that race?"

"Yes," I said. "All Clare did was confuse the position of the winning post. It was a genuine mistake, but someone thinks she did it on purpose."

"So what's the problem?" Emily said. " 'Publish and be

damned.' If she did nothing wrong, I can't understand how she was being blackmailed."

Nor could I, but things weren't that simple.

"And anyway," Emily said, "it surely can't matter anymore now that she's dead."

"The man I went to see is also being blackmailed and he's very much alive."

Her eyes opened wider in delight. "It's just like something on the television."

Yes, I thought, but who's writing the script.

"So what has the man done?" Emily asked eagerly. "He can't be being blackmailed for the same mistake that Clare made."

"No, he's not. But he did do something that was wrong," I said. "He's the trainer of the horse and he placed a bet that it wouldn't win that race."

"So? What's wrong with that? I thought that betting on horses was not only legal, it was almost compulsory."

"Racehorse trainers are allowed to bet that their horses will *win* a race but not that they will *lose* it. It would be too easy for them to make sure a horse didn't win by simply not training it properly or giving it too hard a gallop too close to the race."

"But surely that's not serious enough to be blackmailed over."

"The maximum penalty for a trainer betting on his own horse to lose is a ban from all racing for ten years. It is a very serious offense."

"Well, then the man's an idiot," Emily said. "And perhaps he deserves it."

There was a lot of sense in what she said, but the whole story would come out, and Clare was bound to be implicated. And, after the *Daily Gazette* articles on Tuesday and Wednesday, her memory would be tainted forever.

"Are you going to inform the racing authorities?"

"No," I said, "not if I can help it."

"Why not?"

I refilled our glasses while I thought through my answer.

"My sole aim is to discover why Clare died. Everything else is irrelevant. I couldn't care less whether Austin Reynolds loses his training license, his reputation, and his big house. He's been a fool, but I don't think he's a real crook."

I paused and sipped my champagne.

"But I really do care that Clare was driven to kill herself, and, quite possibly, the blackmailer might have been doing the driving. So I want to know who is demanding money from Austin Reynolds, and me going to the racing authorities and telling them what a naughty boy Austin's been will not help. The blackmailer would simply walk away."

"He can't be much of a blackmailer anyway," Emily said.

"Why not?" I asked.

"What blackmailer worthy of the name asks someone for two hundred pounds?" She laughed. "That's a joke amount. Two thousand at least, or maybe five. Not so much that you drive the victim to the police but enough to make it worth your while."

"I didn't know you were such an expert on blackmail," I said.

"There's lots of things you don't know about me," she

said, cuddling up and putting her hand down between my legs.

"No, hold on," I said, pushing her hand away and sitting up straight. "How come you know so much about blackmail?"

"Mark," she said, "don't be so serious. I know because I read Agatha Christie books and watch murder mysteries on the television, that's all."

I leaned back next to her.

"Blackmailers in those stories always ask for a lot. But, I suppose, that's why they usually get murdered. If they only asked for a little bit, no one would bother to murder them, they'd just pay."

Exactly as Austin Reynolds had done, I thought. Was that why the amounts had been so small?

"I saw a film once," Emily went on, "about an American high school where one of the students sends blackmail notes to every one of his graduating class demanding a single dollar or he would inform the school principal that he or she had cheated in the exams."

"What happened?" I asked.

"Nearly all of them hadn't cheated and they just threw the notes away, but four members of the class actually had and those four each gave him the dollar."

"So?"

"The blackmailer then knew which of his classmates *had* cheated and he demanded more from them. Pretty clever, eh?"

18

On Sunday, Emily drove me along the A14 from Newmarket to Huntingdon racetrack, where I was due to commentate on the six-race card.

Racing on Sundays in England was first introduced at Doncaster on July 26, 1992, although, at the start, it still was against the law to charge entry for a sporting event on a Sunday. All sorts of tricks were used, like on that first day when people were charged for listening to the Band of the Irish Guards and then given a free afternoon's racing. And the situation was further confused by the fact that cash betting was also illegal on Sundays then, but using a bookmaker's account or even a credit or a debit card was not.

Since those days, the rules have been relaxed somewhat, and Sunday is now just like any other day of the week, with at least two race meetings held on every Sunday of the year. Indeed, there are now only four days in the whole calendar when there is no racing on British racetracks: Good Friday, Christmas Day, and the two days before Christmas.

The public love the Sunday meetings, and Huntingdon racetrack was already filling nicely by the time we arrived at about one o'clock, over an hour before the first race.

Emily pulled her red Mercedes into the racetrack lot and followed the directions of the attendant to the next space at the end of the parked cars. Only when we had stopped did I notice with dismay and alarm that we had drawn up alongside Mitchell Stacey's car and that he was still sitting in it.

Bugger, I thought. And moving was now impossible as we were hemmed in by other cars parked behind us and by a tape in front. Perhaps Mitchell wouldn't notice.

"Stay in the car," I said to Emily.

"Why?"

"I really don't want to have to talk to the man in the car next to us."

Emily looked to her left, past my nose.

"Who is it?" she asked.

"A man called Mitchell Stacey."

"And why don't you want to talk to him?"

"He's a trainer," I said. "He's got runners here today. And he doesn't like me very much."

"Why not?"

I could hardly tell her that he was my ex-girlfriend's husband and I had cuckolded him or that he had threatened to kill me.

"He just doesn't."

"Kiss me, then," she said, "and he'll go away."

I leaned over and kissed her, long and passionately, as Mitchell climbed out of his car, collected his coat from the trunk, and walked away toward the enclosures. I had no idea if he'd even seen us, let alone if he had recognized me.

"He's gone," Emily said.

We watched him go through the entrance and into the track.

"I'd rather not be here when he comes back."

She must have detected something in my voice. "Are you frightened of him?"

"He has a very nasty temper," I said, "and I've been at the wrong end of it."

"What did you do?" she asked, "sleep with his wife?"

I looked at her in astonishment. "Yes, as a matter of fact, I did."

She laughed. "You men. No sense of decorum. Can't you control your little willies?"

"It wasn't all that little last night," I said with a grin.

"Don't flatter yourself," she said, giggling. "I've seen bigger."

I decided not to continue this discussion for fear of being completely humiliated.

"Come on," I said, getting out of the car, "I've got work to do."

EMILY AND I walked arm in arm into the racetrack enclosures and toward the weighing room and came face-to-face with Mitchell Stacey, who was coming out with a saddle over his arm.

We all stopped, and Mitchell stared at me. If looks could kill, I would have expired on the spot. Then he turned his eyes toward Emily.

"Whose wife are you, then?" he asked sharply.

Emily said nothing but simply smiled at him, which seemed to disturb him even more.

I, meanwhile, also said nothing, although I was tempted to ask him where he'd been at eleven o'clock on the previous Friday evening. I could still feel my sore neck.

"I've had the police round because of you." Mitchell sneered in my direction. "Keep me out of your sordid little business. Do you hear?"

I again said nothing, and suddenly he walked on, brushing past me and disappearing in the general direction of the saddling stalls.

"Not a very friendly chap," Emily said as we watched him go. "He doesn't seem to like you very much."

"No," I said. "But I don't like him very much either."

"When did you sleep with his wife?"

I said nothing.

"Recently, then, was it?"

"She's much younger than him," I said stupidly as if it mattered.

"Are you still sleeping with her?" Emily asked in a dead-pan voice, but one with multiple undertones.

"No," I said emphatically, "I am not. I've got a new girlfriend now."

"Oh really," she said, laughing. "Who's that, then?"

I squeezed her waist, but she squirmed away from me.

"Don't touch me, you . . . you . . . serial adulterer!" she cried.

"Keep your voice down," I said, looking around to see if anyone had heard. "How can I be an adulterer when I've never been married? And anyway, you told me you were divorced."

"Only decree nisi," she said. "Technically, for another week or two, I'm still a married woman."

"Come on, then, married woman, I've got things to do."

We went into the weighing room at the base of the Cromwell grandstand and then into the broadcast center.

"Hi, Jack," I said. "This is Emily."

Jack Laver wiped both his hands on his tattered green sweater and then offered his right to her.

"Lovely to meet you," Emily said, shaking it.

"Anything I should know about?" I asked Jack, making him tear his eyes away from Emily's gorgeous figure.

"Nope," he said. "Usual controls. I've already checked that your monitor's working. No problems."

"Right. Thanks, Jack. See you later."

Emily and I went out of the broadcast center and climbed the six flights of stairs to the commentary booth, which at Huntingdon was in a shedlike structure attached to the very top of the grandstand roof, almost as if it had been added as an afterthought.

The shed also contained the judge's booth and the photo-finish system as well as a position for a television camera. It afforded a great view of the course but was not ideal for anyone who didn't have a head for heights, especially when the wind blew hard, which tended to make the whole structure sway slightly.

"Wow," said Emily, moving to the open side, "it's quite high."

Not as high, I thought, as the fifteenth floor of the Hilton Hotel.

"Don't you like heights?" I asked.

"Not much," she said, hanging on tight to the rail as she looked over. "I prefer my feet firmly planted on the ground."

"You get used to it," I said. "And this is much lower than some."

I removed my binoculars from my bag and then checked the non-runners, making notes on my copy of the *Racing Post* that we had stopped to buy in Newmarket. Everything seemed in order for another day at the office.

"Fancy some lunch?" I asked.

"Have we got time?"

There was still half an hour until the first race.

"Plenty," I said.

We descended again to ground level, and I bought some smoked-salmon sandwiches, which we ate perched on barstools at a high table near the window of Hurdles Bar.

"I've been thinking about what you said yesterday— you know, about the blackmail notes and that film."

"And?" Emily said between mouthfuls of sandwich.

"You couldn't just send blackmail notes to everyone. It would be ridiculous."

"You don't have to," she said. "Suppose you only have a slight suspicion that someone has been up to no good. If you sent them a blackmail note asking for a couple of hundred quid, it would sure as hell confirm your suspicions if they then paid up."

"I wonder if that was the case with Clare. Perhaps whoever sent it to her was merely fishing and got more than just a bite when Austin paid."

"Hello, Mark," said a voice behind me. "Mind if I join you?"

I stood up and turned around. "Not at all, Harry. Pull up a stool. Harry, can I introduce Emily Lowther. Emily, this is Harry Jacobs."

Emily held out her hand, but Harry's were both full, a plate of seafood in one and an ice bucket holding a bottle of champagne in the other. He put them down on the table and shook her hand.

"Delighted to meet you, my dear," Harry said. "I'll get glasses."

"No private box today, Harry?" I said.

"No, not here. I'm on my own today anyway. No runners. I only popped along because I was bored at home. Last-minute decision and all that."

He disappeared back toward the bar.

Who is he? Emily mouthed at me.

"Racehorse owner," I said quietly in reply. "I rode a horse for him years and years ago when I was eighteen. We've been friends ever since. Nice enough chap, but a bit eccentric. He's got pots of money, but I don't know where from."

Harry returned with three champagne flutes and proceeded to pour golden bubbles into them.

"Not much for me," said Emily, "I'm driving."

"And not much for me either, thanks," I said, "I'm commentating in ten minutes."

"You're no fun," said Harry with a pained expression. Then he smiled. "But that means there's more for me. Cheers."

We raised our glasses and clinked them together. Emily and I sipped graciously while Harry downed a hefty slug before refilling his glass.

"Now then," he said, "what were you two so intent about? I waved at you, Mark, through the window, but you completely ignored me."

"I'm sorry," I said, "I didn't notice you." I laughed. "We were busily talking about sending someone a blackmail note."

The color drained out of Harry's face, and I thought for a moment he was going to drop his glass.

RATHER ANNOYINGLY, at that point I'd had to go to commentate on the first race, so I'd left Emily looking after Harry in the bar, promising to be back straight after I finished.

I later hurried down the stairs to find them sitting on the same barstools as when I'd left. The only thing that seemed to have changed was that the champagne bottle was now empty, being turned upside down in the ice bucket, and the plate of seafood had been half consumed.

Harry was intently studying the floor at his feet.

"Did you see the race?" I asked.

"On the television," said Emily, pointing to one on the wall. She smiled. "And I could hear your voice over the speakers."

"So, Harry," I said, sitting down on the third stool, "tell me."

He looked up slowly. "Tell you what?" His voice was ever so slightly slurred. I wasn't surprised after the quick consumption of nearly a whole bottle of fizz. He again looked down at the floor.

"Tell me who is blackmailing you," I said quietly but distinctly, leaning forward to speak directly into his left ear.

"No one," he said. He suddenly sat up straight and almost toppled backward off the stool.

"I tried to get him to eat something to soak up the booze," Emily said, "but he seems intent on drinking himself into oblivion. I had to restrain him from getting another bottle."

"I'm fine," he said. "I'm not drunk. I'm just a little tipsy, that's all."

"Yes, Harry," I said, "of course you are. Now, where can we take him?" I asked Emily. "Even if we could get him to tell us who's blackmailing him, he's not going to do it here, not with all these people round. How about the commentary booth?"

"Will he get up the stairs?" Emily asked.

"I should think so. I'm quite surprised a single bottle has had such a large effect on him. He's drunk me under the table before now. I'd always assumed he had hollow legs and could drink for England."

"Perhaps he started before he arrived at the races."

I stood up and put my hand under his right elbow. "Come on, Harry, let's go."

"OK," he said, standing up. "Fine by me."

He walked quite steadily out of the bar, Emily and I guiding him around to the stairs that led up to the rooftop shed. Without any hesitation, he followed Emily up quite happily, with me climbing behind him so he couldn't suddenly change his mind and retreat.

There was one chair at the back of the commentary booth, and Harry sat down on it.

"I'm fine," he said again. "Perfectly fine."

"I know you are, Harry," I said. "But just sit there for a bit while I commentate on the next race."

Hell, I thought, I hadn't been to see the horses in the parade ring or check on the colors. But the second race was a moderate two-and-a-half-mile handicap steeplechase with eight runners, and all of them had been regulars on racetracks for years. It was like seeing old friends again, and I reckoned I knew the colors already.

Handicaps are the staple of British racing, accounting for more than half of all races. They give the best chance for most owners to have a winner.

All horses in training are given an official rating in a list that is published each week by the British Horseracing Authority. With handicaps, the horses carry different weights according to their official rating: the higher the rating, the greater the weight. In this way, based on previous performance, all horses should have an equal chance of winning.

Without handicaps, the best horses would always win and there would be no real point in owning a moderate horse. And just as soccer teams are also grouped by their performances into "divisions" where they are all roughly the same standard, so horses run in races where they all have approximately the same rating.

Not only does this give every horse in the race a chance of winning, it leads to exciting close finishes because the handicapper is attempting to create a multiple dead heat with all the horses arriving at the winning post at exactly the same moment. Hence they are also great races for the betting public, who always believe they know better than the officials.

The runners for this particular handicap came out onto the track and I described them to the crowd as they made their way around to the two-and-a-half-mile start in the middle of the back stretch.

I'd seen all of these horses racing before, some of them as many as fifteen or twenty times, and I recognized them as much from the shape of their bodies and the shade of their coats as from the colors of the jockeys' silks. Nevertheless, I took a few minutes to make sure. I didn't want to be complacent and end up confusing one horse with another.

"They're off," I said into the microphone as the race began.

The handicapper should have been proud of his work.

All eight horses were still in contention as they turned into the finishing stretch for the second and last time, with just two plain fences left to jump.

Then two of them fell at the second-to-last fence, bringing down a third.

"Now, with just one to jump, it's Twickman taking up the running from Delmar Boy and Coralstone, with Vintest and Felto both making their challenge down the outside."

I smiled at Emily, who was standing next to me totally engrossed in the race.

"And, as they come to the last, it's Twickman by a length from Vintest, with Coralstone third between horses in the green."

Emily started to jump up and down with excitement.

"A great leap at the last from Vintest, who lands alongside Twickman and is quickly into his stride. Just two hundred yards to go now."

It was a long run in at Huntingdon, and plenty could change between the last fence and the winning post. And today was no exception.

"Twickman and Vintest together, but here comes the fast-finishing Felto under Paddy Dean on the outside." My voice rose in pitch with the ever-rising cheering of the crowd. "Into the last fifty yards, and it's still Twickman just from Vintest, but Felto is catching them with every stride."

I clicked off my microphone as the three horses flashed past the finish line stride for stride.

"Photograph, photograph," announced the judge.

"On the nod," I said to Emily.

"What?" she said breathlessly.

"Horses' heads nod back and forth as they run. Those three were so close that the winner will be the one whose head happened to be nodding forward just as they crossed the line. Half a stride later, one of the others would be in front. When it's that close, it's down to luck as to who wins."

"But it was so exciting," she said. "I've never really watched a race like that before—you know, concentrating on the horses. I've mostly only been to the races for the food and drink and the hospitality."

"Here is the result of the photograph," said the judge over the public address. "First, number four, Felto. Second, number seven. Third, number two. The distances were a nose and a short head."

A great cheer had gone up from the crowd as soon as the number four had been announced. Felto had started the race as favorite and lots of bets had been riding on his particular nose.

"What's the difference between a nose and a short head?" Emily asked.

"Not much," I said. "A nose is anything less than four and a half inches and a short head is between that and nine inches."

Emily made a face. "It hardly seems fair to lose by a few inches after running so far."

"A win is a win," I said. "And as the technology improves and the photographs get better, the margins get smaller and smaller. Dead heats are getting rarer."

Harry Jacobs had sat on the chair at the back of the

booth throughout the race, looking more miserable than drunk.

"So, Harry," I said, "tell us who's been blackmailing you."

He looked up at us with clear eyes. "How on earth did you know?"

"We didn't," Emily said. "We were discussing somebody else."

"Oh?" he said. "Who?"

"Two others, actually," I said. "And one of them was my sister, Clare." I felt I had to give him some information in order to establish some trust. "Someone sent her a blackmail note demanding two hundred pounds or they would tell the racing authorities she had failed on purpose to win a race."

"And did she pay?" he asked.

"Sort of," I said. "Someone else paid for her."

"And did the blackmailer then ask for more?"

"Yes," I said.

Harry nodded. "Thought so."

"Is that what happened to you?"

He pursed his lips and went on nodding. "The first demand was so small, I just paid it."

"Why?" I asked. "What had you done?"

"But that's what's so bloody stupid," he said. "I haven't really done anything."

"So what were they using to blackmail you?" I asked.

"It was an offshore bank account I had on the Isle of Man."

"What about it?"

"I opened it in a different name because I thought at one stage I might move all my assets there."

"For tax purposes?"

"Exactly," he said. "Capital gains tax, to be precise. In the end, I didn't go through with it, but I never closed the account. I'd put some money in it, and I suppose I should have paid tax on the interest it earned, but it was so small I didn't think it mattered. Also, I didn't tell my accountant or put any offshore account details on my tax return as I didn't want the tax people to think I was trying to fiddle with my taxes."

"Which you were," Emily said.

"Yeah, well . . . but not using that account."

"But you were fiddling with your taxes somewhere else?" I asked.

"Not actual fiddling," he said, slightly affronted. "I *avoid* tax, not *evade* it. There's an important difference. Avoidance is legal, evasion isn't." He smiled unconvincingly. "But I could really do without being audited by the Revenue. Let's just say it might be awkward, you know, over certain of my interpretations of the tax laws."

"Sailing close to the wind," said Emily.

"Exactly," Harry agreed. "Very close."

"So what did the blackmail note say?"

He knew it by heart. "'I know you are using an offshore bank account to evade paying tax. Just two hundred pounds will make the story go away. Get the cash together. Payment details will follow.'"

"Same blackmailer," I said. "When did you get the note?"

"Nearly two years ago. At a time when it might have been very embarrassing to have had a Revenue investigation. So I paid."

"Were you told to leave the money under your car in a racetrack parking lot?"

He nodded. "But he demanded more. About six months later I had to pay a thousand, next it was two thousand, then I got another note yesterday demanding a further twenty thousand. Now, I think that's rather too much." He sounded like someone who had just been overcharged for a meal or a hotel room.

"Have you by any chance got the note with you?" I asked.

He pulled a crumpled piece of paper out of his coat pocket. "I didn't want to leave it at home in case my wife found it."

He handed it to me and I spread it out. It was a computer printout just like the others, but as on the latest one sent to Austin Reynolds the last zero of the twenty thousand had been added by hand.

I glanced at my watch. The next race was due to be off in fifteen minutes.

"I've got to go down and see the horses in the parade ring," I said. "They're juvenile three-year-old hurdlers and some of them I haven't seen run before. I want to see them in the paddock to help me learn the colors. You two stay right here. I'll be back before you know it."

I skipped down the stairs and out toward the parade

ring. Dodging through the crowd, I ran straight into Mitchell Stacey, almost knocking him over.

"Sorry," I said automatically before I even realized who he was.

He stared at me with contempt. "Watch where you're bloody going, can't you?"

We stood facing each other for a moment.

Why, I thought, had Mitchell set up a spy camera in his bedroom to film Sarah and me? How had he known to do so?

What was it that Sarah had said to me in that last call? *I should have paid the little shit.* Paid who? Had Sarah also been a victim of blackmail?

Mitchell turned away toward the weighing room, and I went on to the parade ring to see the horses, but my brain was elsewhere. Instead of learning the colors of the jockeys' silks, I called the Stacey home on my cell phone.

"Hello," said Sarah's familiar voice after two rings.

"Sarah, it's me," I said.

"I told you that it was much better for both of us if we didn't talk again. And we had the police round here this morning asking questions about you." She sounded angry. "I'm sorry, I must go."

"No, please. Don't hang up!" I shouted quickly. "Listen. Were you being blackmailed?"

There was a long pause on the other end, and at one point I wondered if she had indeed hung up but she hadn't, I could hear her breathing.

"Did someone ask you for two hundred pounds to make the story of you and me go away?"

"Yes," she said, "but I didn't pay him. Maybe it would've been better if I had."

I should have paid the little shit.

"But you do know who it was, don't you?"

"Yes," she said. "It was that little shit of a journalist, Toby Woodley."

19

I was not at all sure how I managed to commentate on the juvenile hurdlers.

My eyes had watched the horses being mounted in the parade ring, but none of the data received had reached my conscious brain. My mind had been racing with too much other information and too many unanswered questions.

Had Toby Woodley been murdered at Kempton Park races because of the blackmail?

I didn't even properly learn the jockeys' colors as the horses circled at the start, and, suddenly, the race was under way. I had to keep glancing down to my race program to see which horse was which as they jumped the two hurdles in the stretch for the first time.

Had it been one of Toby Woodley's blackmail victims that had done us all a favor?

It was not proving to be my greatest-ever commentary. Concentrate, I told myself as the horses swept right-handedly away from the grandstands to start their second circuit. For God's sake, concentrate!

But how could Toby Woodley have sent a blackmail note to Austin Reynolds on Thursday when he'd been murdered on Wednesday night?

The horses galloped down the back of the course, and on two occasions I called one of them by the wrong name, "Woodley," when the horse was properly called "Woodmill."

Could Toby Woodley have mailed the note on Wednesday evening after the last collection so that it hadn't been date-stamped until Thursday?

The horses turned in to the finishing stretch for the second and final time, and by now even the crowd knew the colors better than I did. But thankfully I called the correct names of the leading pair as they jumped the last hurdle together side by side.

But Harry Jacobs had said that he'd received his latest note only yesterday. Could it really have taken three days to arrive?

The two horses fought out another close finish, flashing past the winning post with hardly a cigarette paper between them.

"Photograph, photograph," called the judge once more.

Or had Toby Woodley had an accomplice who was now acting on his own?

HARRY JACOBS insisted on going back to the bar after the third race.

"I need another drink," he said.

"Don't you think you've had enough, Harry?" I said. "Especially if you're driving later."

"I have a driver. I haven't got a license."

Probably lost it, I thought, from having too many boozy days at the races.

"OK," I said. "But a couple of things first. Are you sure that note arrived at your home yesterday?"

"Absolutely certain," Harry said. "It's the sort of thing you remember."

"Do you still have the envelope it came in?"

"No," he said, "I threw it away. Why?"

"I wanted to see when it was mailed and whether it was sent first or second class."

"First class, I think," he said. "But I couldn't be certain. Sorry." He stood up. "Now, where's that drink?"

All three of us went down the stairs from the grandstand shed, but while Harry peeled off toward the bar to order more champagne, Emily and I went through the betting hall to the parade ring to see the horses for the next race, a tricky handicap hurdle with eighteen runners.

"Are all your days as thrilling as this?" Emily asked as I stood silently by the paddock rail making notes on my race program.

I looked sideways at her. "Do I detect a touch of sarcasm?"

"Me?" she said, smiling broadly.

"It's not every day you come across blackmail," I said.

"No," she said, laughing, "only every other day."

"Real blackmail, I mean, not that stuff you watch on the television."

"At least that's exciting."

"How about if I told you that I knew who'd been sending the notes."

"Who?" she said, her eyes opening wider in anticipation.

"I'll tell you over dinner."

"No," she said, "tell me now."

"Over dinner," I said firmly. "I need to concentrate on the horses."

"Well, in that case I'll go and join Harry in the bar."

"I thought you said you were driving," I said.

"So?" She turned and walked away, looking back just once and waving before she disappeared into the bar.

I turned my attention back to the eighteen different silks in front of me and started to sort out which belonged to which horse.

WE STOPPED at six-thirty for an early dinner at the Three Horseshoes, a charming thatched pub in Madingley, near Cambridge.

"How lovely," Emily said as we walked in, "a romantic dinner for two. I can't remember when I last did this."

"What about last night?" I said.

"I'd hardly call takeout from the local Chinese restaurant a romantic dinner."

I smiled at her. "But if I remember correctly, it became quite romantic afterward."

She laughed. "You just got lucky."

We were shown to a quiet table by the window, over-looking the garden and the parking lot beyond it amongst the trees.

After the unwanted attentions of Harry Jacobs all afternoon, I was really looking forward to a couple of hours of uninterrupted time for just the two of us. I'd even left my phone in the car.

"Well?" said Emily eagerly after we'd ordered, "who's the blackmailer?"

"A journalist called Toby Woodley."

She seemed disappointed. "And who is he?"

"Who *was* he, you mean. He was murdered in the parking lot at Kempton Park racetrack last Wednesday evening. And I was there when he died."

Emily's interest was suddenly reawakened. "Did you kill him?"

"No, of course not," I said. "But whoever did may have been a victim of his blackmail."

"See," she said. "I told you it was just like those mysteries on the television."

"There's a problem, though," I said. "Toby Woodley was killed on Wednesday evening and Harry's blackmail note didn't arrive until Saturday. Harry thought it was sent first class, which means that in all likelihood it was mailed on Friday, or on Thursday at the earliest."

"So," said Emily, leaning forward, "who mailed it if this Woodley fellow was already dead?"

"Exactly," I said. "And I think the same person may have inserted the extra zero at the end of the amount. It seems to me that the notes had already been printed and an extra zero was added as an afterthought. It was the same with the note shown me by Austin Reynolds."

"But how do you know it was Toby Woodley who sent the first ones?"

This might be awkward, I thought.

"Well," I said, "you know the man we parked next to?"

"The one whose wife you've been sleeping with?"

"Yes, that one." It was definitely awkward. "She told me."

"When?" she squealed.

"This afternoon. I called her when you were up in the booth with Harry."

"My God! You are a sneaky bastard," Emily said with a laugh. She leaned back in her chair. "I should drive home right now and leave you here."

"I told you it was over between us." I was trying to sound honorable and trustworthy. Even though I'd met Emily only forty-eight hours ago, I suddenly realized that I absolutely didn't want to lose her.

"Anyway, what did she say?"

"She told me that she'd received a blackmail note demanding two hundred pounds to keep quiet about the affair. A note just like the others."

"But how did she know who it was from?"

I thought back to my conversation with Sarah. "She was told to leave used twenty-pound notes in a brown envelope under her car in the parking lot at Newbury races, as the others had. But instead of money, she put strips of newspaper in the envelope, and then she hid and watched to see who collected it. It was this man Toby Woodley."

"What did he do when she didn't pay?" Emily asked.

"I think he was going to write about us in his newspaper. He said something last week about being good to me. It seems his editor wouldn't let a story run because of Clare having just died. I now think the story must have been about me and Sarah Stacey. I think he then told her husband about us to get back at her for not paying."

"Nice chap," Emily said. "No wonder someone murdered him."

A waitress arrived with our starters.

"Do you fancy some wine?" I asked.

"Of course I do," Emily said, "but as you so prudently pointed out, I'm driving."

"We could always leave the car and get a taxi."

"And then how would I get to work in the morning?"

"Where is work?" I asked.

"Cambridge. I work in the university engineering department as a research assistant."

It was now my turn to say, "Wow!"

"I'm currently helping with a project to develop needleless injections. It's really interesting."

"So are you an engineer?" I asked.

"No," she said, "I'm more of a medic. But I'm not a doctor. I only did a biomedical degree."

It sounded pretty good to me.

"So I need my car in the morning to get to work."

I suppose I would need a car too. I would have to sort

that out, along with lots of other things. Thankfully, I had the day off.

"And I need to go home tonight," Emily said. "I haven't got my things for the morning."

"Do you need to collect your white coat?" I asked flippantly.

She smiled and shook her head. "No. But I do need my university pass, and I can hardly go into the lab dressed like this, so I'm going home tonight to Royston."

I wondered if I was being given the brush-off. I rather hoped not.

"You can come with me, if you like," she said, "but I'm definitely sleeping in my own bed, with or without you."

"With," I said. "But I have to go back to Clare's cottage first to collect my stuff."

Emily smiled broadly. "That's fine, then. We'll make a detour."

We ate our starters with just fizzy water as the accompaniment.

"So tell me," Emily said, "who's the second blackmailer, the one who mailed the note to Harry after this Woodley fellow was killed?"

"I wish I knew. But whoever it is, he's rather more greedy. Toby Woodley never asked anyone for very much, that's why most of them paid him."

"And do you think he asked all sorts of people for two hundred pounds?"

"Yes, I do," I said. "I reckon that's how he got some of his stories for the paper. If he had even the slightest suspicion about someone, he'd send them a blackmail demand for just two hundred pounds to make the story go away. If they paid, then he had the confirmation he needed that he was right and he would ask for more, if necessary backing up the demand with an article in the paper that proved he knew what had been going on, but of course without mentioning anyone by name."

"But enough to frighten his victims into paying up."

"Precisely," I said.

"What's it got to do with the death of your sister?"

"I don't know," I said, "maybe nothing. But she definitely was being blackmailed and that may have had something to do with it."

In truth, I felt nowhere nearer to finding out why Clare died.

"How was the journalist murdered?" Emily asked.

"He was stabbed in the back."

"And you were there?"

"Yes, I was there immediately afterward. I didn't actually see him being stabbed, but I was there when he died a few minutes later. The police thought I might have killed him because he'd written an article about Clare in that morning's paper. But they couldn't find any knife, so they let me go."

And, I thought, they also couldn't find his briefcase.

Had the notes for Austin Reynolds and Harry Jacobs been printed and ready to go in that stolen briefcase? Was the person who had mailed them not an accomplice of Toby Woodley but his killer?

———

EMILY AND I enjoyed the rest of our dinner free of further blackmail discussion, concentrating instead on learning more about each other.

"So where exactly do you live?" she asked me.

"I rent an apartment in Edenbridge, in Kent. But I'm intending to buy a house. I've even got the details on one in Oxfordshire I like the look of."

That was something else I had to deal with tomorrow, I thought, along with renting a car. I also had to contact Detective Sergeant Sharp about the Hilton Hotel CCTV footage and follow up on the guest list for the Injured Jockeys Fund dinner. Between them, I hoped they might give me some clue to the identity of the mystery visitors to Clare's room the night she died.

So much for my day off.

Both Emily and I decided against dessert and coffee, opting to go.

"We can open a bottle of wine when we get to my place," Emily said, "and have coffee there."

I looked at my watch. It was still only twenty to nine.

"Sounds good to me."

I paid the bill, and we walked out together toward Emily's car.

I was careless. Very careless.

Since the events of Friday night, I had been checking the inside of cars and avoiding all dark places, but, here and now, I had relaxed my guard.

Thinking back, I believe the fateful moment was when Emily took my hand in hers. Perhaps I was preoccupied by the thoughts of what was to come, reliving the excitement of our first lovemaking the previous afternoon. Or maybe it was just due to an overwhelming feeling of contentment that was flooding through me.

Either way, I was careless.

I didn't even notice the darkened car until it was almost upon us.

We were halfway across the gravel parking lot, and just a few yards from Emily's red Mercedes, when the roaring engine to my left finally cut through into my consciousness.

I half turned and screamed at Emily, but it was too late, much too late.

The car hit both of us, spiraling me over the hood while Emily went down under the wheels.

I remembered hitting the roof of the car, and the next thing I knew, I was lying on the gravel, panting madly, wanting to run but unable to get up.

I rolled over, trying to ignore the searing pain in my side.

The car was already out of the parking lot and on the road, traveling fast, and still it had no lights on.

Emily, I thought with panic. Where is Emily?

I gritted my teeth and rolled over again. I searched for her with my eyes, but she was nowhere to be seen.

"Emily." I tried to shout, but the sound came out as more of a croak. "Emily. Where are you? Are you all right?"

There was no reply, and I began to panic further.

I drew myself up onto my knees, and coughed.

Blood, I thought. I can taste blood in my mouth. I coughed again. This time, I knew I was coughing up blood.

Each breath was painful and difficult, and I felt sick.

"Emily," I tried to shout again.

Still nothing.

I forced myself to stand up—if doubled over and clutching my side could be considered standing up. But at least I was on my feet.

I took three small steps over and leaned on a car.

Where was she?

I staggered from car to car, wildly searching in the darkness between them.

I found her lying facedown near the exit of the parking lot. She must have been dragged there under the wheels.

I sank to my knees beside her.

"Emily," I called, touching her shoulder, but there was no reply.

Breathing was becoming very difficult, but I mustered the strength to roll her over onto her back. Her face was just a mass of blood, and I couldn't even tell if she was alive or dead.

"Oh my God!" I cried. "I'm so sorry."

Another couple came out of the pub and started to walk toward us.

"Help!" I croaked at them. "Please help me."

They stopped.

"Call an ambulance," I said, tears streaming down my face.

———————

I AGAIN ENDED UP in Addenbrooke's emergency room, just as I had the previous Friday. But this time I wasn't left alone in a cubicle to recover. I was rushed into a treatment room, where I was worked on by a whole team of medics, and they seemed to be getting more concerned as time went on.

I was placed on my left side, with my head and shoulders slightly raised, and I was wearing what the doctors had referred to as a positive flow oxygen mask strapped over my face.

But the mask didn't seem to be doing much good. My breathing was now so labored and shallow that I was hardly taking in any air at all, and I felt light-headed and close to unconsciousness.

Was this how I would die?

One of the medical staff came up toward my head and into view.

"Can you hear me?" he asked.

I nodded.

"You've broken a couple of ribs," he said. "One of them has punctured your left lung and it has collapsed. We're trying to remove the air from inside your chest cavity so that your lung can reinflate on its own."

I tried to speak, but I didn't seem to have enough breath.

"Don't talk," he said. "Concentrate on your breathing. I don't particularly want to have to put a tube down your throat as it may cause more problems. Our main concern is a rapid buildup of fluid in and round your right lung as well, but we are doing our best to remove it." He smiled a wry smile. I wasn't sure if that was encouraging or not.

One lung collapsed and a buildup of fluid in the other. No wonder it felt like I was drowning.

I desperately wanted to ask him about Emily. When I'd been carried into the ambulance, she had still been on the ground being attended to by paramedics, and I was dreadfully worried because I hadn't seen her move since I'd first found her.

The doctor resumed his attempts to remove the fluid from my lungs, and I went on breathing, albeit with increasingly rapid and shallow breaths.

I tried to take my mind off my immediate medical troubles by thinking back to what had happened in the pub parking lot.

There was no doubt in my mind that it had been a deliberate attempt to run us down. The driver of the car had made no effort to stop. In fact, quite the reverse. He had accelerated across the lot with his engine roaring and had driven off at speed.

He must have been waiting for Emily and me to come out from dinner. He hadn't put on his headlights, but there would have been enough ambient light for him to see us walking through the garden and across the parking lot.

How had he known we were there?

All I could think was that he must have followed us from the races.

But who knew I was at Huntingdon racetrack?

Anyone, I suppose, who'd listened to me either at the

track or at home on the RacingTV channel, which had covered the meeting using my commentaries.

And Mitchell Stacey had definitely known.

His car had already gone from the lot when Emily and I came out to her Mercedes, but that didn't mean he hadn't been waiting somewhere near the exit in order to follow us.

The doctor reappeared in my field of vision.

"Right. Now we need you to sit up," he said. "To help the fluid drain."

I hardly had the breath to move a single muscle and I needed the help of two burly male nurses just to swing my legs off the examination table.

I was leaned forward on a high table while the doctor inserted a tube into my back.

"There," he said. "The fluid is now draining out of your chest, and you'll soon be feeling a lot better."

As if by magic, my breathing improved dramatically over the next couple of minutes as three large bottlefuls of pinkish fluid were drained from my body.

Suddenly I began to believe that I might actually survive.

"Is that better?" asked the doctor from behind me.

I nodded. "Much," I gasped through the oxygen mask.

"Good. You were breathing for a time there with only about a tenth of one lung operational. If you'd arrived here just a couple of minutes later, you'd have been a goner."

"What about Emily?" I asked quietly, almost as if I didn't want to know.

"Eh?"

"What about Emily?" I asked him again, this time louder. "The lady I was with."

There was no answer.

"Tell me," I said.

The doctor came around to face me.

"I'm afraid she didn't make it."

20

I lay in the semidarkness of a hospital room in utter despair.

It was my fault.

I should never have placed Emily in such danger.

It was true that I'd known her for only two days, and maybe there had been something of the rebound about our coming together after my breakup with Sarah, but, even so soon, I truly felt that I'd finally met someone I would have been happy to live with, someone with whom to share the rest of my life.

And now she was gone. Snatched away in an instant.

Why?

It was *me* who should be dead, not her.

But why would anyone want me dead? There was no question that they did. Attempted strangulation on Friday and now a hit-and-run in a darkened pub parking lot on Sunday. But why?

Everything in my head came back to Mitchell Stacey.

Who else was there?

That is what Detective Chief Inspector Perry had asked me just as soon as the doctor decided I was well enough to be interviewed by him and another plainclothes policeman.

"You told me I'd be perfectly safe," I'd said to him in an accusing tone.

"I thought you would be," he had said in reply. "I'm sorry."

"How about Mitchell Stacey?" I'd asked. "What did he have to say?"

"Mr. Stacey was interviewed by officers from the Thames Valley Police early yesterday morning and he provided an alibi for his whereabouts on Friday evening. He could not have been the man who tried to strangle you."

"But he could have arranged it, and it might have been him in the pub parking lot tonight," I'd said.

"That will now be up to the Cambridgeshire force to determine." He indicated the other policeman. "DCI Coaker here is dealing with the inquiry into the murder of Mrs. Lowther. I'm assisting him only because of last Friday's incident."

I had spent the next two hours answering the two policemen's questions in increasing frustration and anger.

"Could you identify the car?"

"No."

"Could you identify the driver?"

"No."

"Do you know why anyone would want you dead?"

"No—other than Mitchell Stacey."

They asked me at least ten times about the sequence of events in the pub parking lot and each time I gave them the same answers.

I continually asked them how Emily had died and in the end they told me that her neck had been broken. She must have been rolled under the car for ten or fifteen yards. It would have been enough to break anything.

Now alone at last, I grieved for her, and also for me, and for what we might have been together.

THE MORNING brought little or no relief from my pain, or my misery, and Detective Chief Inspector Coaker came back soon after eight o'clock with more questions.

"Who knew you would be at the Three Horseshoes pub?"

"No one. Going there was a last-minute decision."

"Were you followed there from Huntingdon?"

"We must have been, but I didn't notice. Emily was driving."

Even I could tell that my answers weren't very helpful. But that didn't stop him from asking the same things over and over and over again.

"How about my phone?" I said during a lull in the questioning.

"What about it?"

"It's in Emily Lowther's car," I said. "Along with a

leather bag containing my laptop computer, a pair of binoculars, and a few other things. I need them for my job."

"I'll see what I can do," said the chief inspector.

Eventually he had to leave while a doctor came in the room to examine me, placing his stethoscope all over my chest and back while I breathed in and out.

"How are you feeling?" he asked.

"Medically or emotionally?" I replied.

"Both."

"Considering I was convinced last night that I was dying, I'm feeling pretty well on the medical front. My side is still very sore down here." I placed my hand gingerly on my left lower ribs. "But I can breathe all right."

"How about deep breaths?" he asked.

"Very painful," I said. "As is coughing."

He nodded. "But you must try to use all of your lung capacity if you can. It will help prevent complications."

I didn't like the sound of "complications," so I breathed deeply, trying my best to ignore the stabbing pain in my side.

"How long do I have to stay here?" I asked.

"There's no medical reason why you shouldn't go home. Your left lung reflated of its own accord and the function of both lungs is now good, and there has been no recurrence overnight of fluid buildup anywhere in your chest." He smiled at me. "But you must take things easy. No heavy lifting. It will take six weeks for those ribs to heal properly, and they'll give you some considerable discomfort for most of that time. I'll prescribe you something for the pain."

"Can't you strap them up to stop them hurting?"

"We don't do that anymore. Strapping the chest is no longer advised because it's constrictive and prevents you taking those necessary deep breaths. Let me tell you, a bit of pain is far preferable to pneumonia."

It certainly was, I thought. I took yet another deep breath.

"So I can go now?" I asked.

"Yes," he said. "But seek medical advice immediately if you become even the slightest bit out of breath." He paused. "How are you feeling in here?" He tapped his head.

"Pretty bloody," I said. "But staying in bed won't help that."

"No. I'm sorry."

So was I.

MY SISTER ANGELA came to collect me from the hospital around ten-thirty, and we were both in tears.

I'd called her earlier on a hospital pay phone to tell her about Emily, but she already knew, it had been reported on the radio.

"Where to?" she asked.

"Clare's cottage," I said. "I need to collect my stuff."

She drove in silence, too shocked even to ask me what had happened.

I was glad. I'd done enough answering questions for one morning. But I was sure none of my answers had been of any use to the police—or to me, for that matter. Nothing helped to make sense of Emily's death.

But I hadn't said anything to DCI Coaker about black-mail. I couldn't see how it might have been relevant.

Now I wondered if I should have. But surely that would have opened a whole new can of worms and sent the likes of Austin Reynolds and Harry Jacobs running for the hills. Then they would, of course, deny everything, and I'd be left with egg on my face. And did I really want to ex-pose my sister as a cheat and a race fixer if I didn't abso-lutely have to?

But why else did someone want me dead?

According to Chief Inspector Perry, Mitchell Stacey had had an alibi for Friday night, but he had also once threatened to have my legs broken and he would have needed some help to do that. Did he have some "heavies" he could call on for a bit of garroting to order or was I just being fanciful and maybe also guilty of confusing televi-sion drama with real life?

Oh, Emily!

How I wished this nightmare was nothing more than a fictional story line from some screenwriter's imagination.

"I NEED TO GET the key from the stable office," I said to Angela as she turned into the driveway of Clare's cottage.

But I was wrong.

The front door to the cottage was wide open, and a key hadn't been used to open it. The frame had been splin-tered all around the lock, and there were six overlapping, two-inch-wide round impressions in the door. Someone clearly had used brute force and a sledgehammer to simply smash their way in.

"Oh shit!" I said with feeling. "It's been burgled."

Angela stayed in the car while I moved forward warily to the door. I thought it unlikely that any burglar would still be in the cottage at eleven o'clock in the morning, but I didn't particularly want to disturb some crazy, knife-wielding drug addict who was searching for the where-withal for his next fix.

"Hello," I called. "Anyone there?"

I stood in the doorway listening for the sound of any movement inside or someone escaping out the back. There was nothing.

"We should call the police," Angela shouted at me through the open car window.

I'd had enough of the police for one morning.

"I'll take a look first," I shouted back.

I stepped inside, expecting to discover that the place had been completely ransacked, but I was pleasantly sur-prised to find that nothing much looked out of place. The bags of Clare's clothes were still stacked under the stairs, and the cardboard boxes I'd filled with the contents of her desk remained where I'd left them on the floor of the sit-ting room.

Indeed, the only things I could see that had been shifted were some of the papers that had been in the boxes, which were now strewn across the carpet.

However, there was something missing.

Not the fancy television set. Not even Clare's collection of silver racing trophies, which were still lined up on the mantelpiece.

It was the white envelope containing the two thousand pounds in cash that was missing—gone from the cardboard box where I'd placed it, along with the blackmail note that I had carelessly left in full view on the desk.

Austin Reynolds, I thought.

Who else would take only those items and leave the silver?

Austin Reynolds removing any evidence that could incriminate him. And this time he would have worn gloves.

I went upstairs to have a quick check around and then went back out to Angela.

"It's fine," I said. "There's no one here and nothing seems to be missing, not even Clare's trophies. Perhaps the burglar was disturbed as soon as he broke down the door."

"Maybe someone heard the noise," Angela said, "and investigated."

Possibly, I thought, but the bangs made by a sledgehammer on Clare's front door could have easily been mistaken for a horse kicking the wooden wall of his stall not ten yards away. Racehorse stables were never silent places even in the dead of night.

"Do you think we should still call the police?" Angela said.

"What for?" I asked.

"If only to get an incident number for the insurance."

"But nothing is missing."

"The front door will need replacing and that must cost

something," Angela said. "When we got burgled two years ago, we needed a police number before the insurance company would pay for anything."

"Much too complicated," I said. "The insurance will be in Geoff Grubb's name, and there'll probably be an excess on it that'd be more than the cost of the door anyway. Much easier if we just fix it ourselves without involving the police. For a start, we'd be here all day waiting for them to turn up."

Angela shrugged her shoulders. "I suppose you're right."

We went inside.

"It's really strange being here," Angela said, standing in the middle of the sitting room. "You know, without Clare."

I suppose I'd become a little used to it. I went over and gave her a hug while she sobbed gently on my shoulder.

The tears also welled in my eyes. First Clare and now Emily. Was there any limit to grief?

I SAT at Clare's desk, making some phone calls on the landline, while Angela cleared out the kitchen. I tried to tell her that she didn't need to bother, but she'd simply said that being busy would help take her mind off Emily.

I suppose she was right, but a renewed lethargy had come over me. That feeling of *What's the point?* had returned.

After a while, I pulled myself together and rang DCI Coaker.

"Any news about my phone and computer?" I asked him. "I'm desperate for them."

"They're here at police headquarters in Huntingdon."

"Can I come and collect them?" I asked.

"I'm just waiting for clearance from my superintendent," he said. "He may decide that they are evidence."

"How come?"

"Computers are routinely investigated for evidence in all crimes."

"You won't find much on mine," I said. "I only use it to access horseracing data as part of my job. And occasionally for making bets."

"Nevertheless, it will need to be checked."

"How about my phone?" I asked. "I need one of the numbers on it."

"I'll see what I can do. Call me back in twenty minutes."

I spent the time using the Yellow Pages to find a local builder who could send someone around as soon as possible to fix the broken door, and then I called a Newmarket rental company and arranged for them to deliver a car to the cottage.

I didn't know yet how I was going to replace my old Ford, but, in the meantime, I urgently needed some wheels, not least to get to Brighton races the following afternoon and Kempton Park on Wednesday and Thursday evenings, not that I really felt like going back to work.

I was completely wrung out, both physically and mentally.

"What shall I do with all the pots and pans, and the

crockery?" Angela asked, putting her head around the door. "Were they Clare's? Or did they come with the cottage?"

"I've no idea." I sighed, dragging myself reluctantly to my feet. "I'll go and ask in Geoff Grubb's office. I need to go in there anyway, and they might know."

Better than that, Geoff's secretary had a full inventory of what was in the cottage when Clare had moved in.

"Don't worry too much if it doesn't match what's in there now," she said, handing me a printed list. "It's been years since Clare moved in."

I gave the list to Angela, who eagerly disappeared with it back into the kitchen.

I checked that twenty minutes had passed and then again called DCI Coaker.

"My super says you can have all your stuff back."

"Great. How do I collect it?"

"The forensic computer guy is just finishing examining your hard drive."

I thought it was a gross invasion of my privacy and I said so.

"Sorry," he said, "but the items were in Mrs. Lowther's possession at the time of her death and therefore they have to be checked."

"So when can I collect it?"

"Where are you now?" he asked.

"Newmarket," I said.

"I'm going to Cambridge shortly. I'll take everything with me. You can collect it anytime after one o'clock from Parkside police station on the eastern ring road."

"Good. Thanks."

"And I've got your phone here for that number you need."

"Oh, thank you," I said. "I need the number for Detective Sergeant Sharp. It should be in my contacts list under *S*."

I could hear him pushing the buttons of my phone.

"Here you are." He read out the number and I wrote it down. "Can I ask why you want to speak to DS Sharp?"

"He's the Metropolitan Police officer who's investigating my sister's suicide. She fell to her death in London last month."

"Clare Shillingford," he said almost to himself. "Of course, the jockey. Now I recognize the name. I'm sorry."

"Thanks," I said. "It's not been a great couple of weeks."

"No," he agreed.

"What news of your investigation of last night?"

"None that I can give you, I'm afraid. How are you feeling?"

"Rather sore," I said, "but I'll live."

Unlike Emily.

I USED the number DCI Coaker had given me to call Detective Sergeant Sharp, but he was unavailable. I left a message on his voice mail asking him to call me back as soon as possible. "I've got some fresh evidence about my sister's death," I said, "from the hotel."

Angela brought me in a cup of coffee.

"I'm afraid we've only got powdered milk," she said.

I smiled at her. "Fine by me."

Angela sat on the arm of the sofa, the same sofa where Emily and I had snuggled down together on Saturday evening.

"Oh God!" I said, sighing again. "Life is so bloody at times."

"You really liked Emily, didn't you?"

"Yes," I said. "And I feel it was my fault she was killed."

"Why?"

"Because I didn't take enough care. I should have seen the car sooner."

"You can't blame yourself," Angela said, trying to comfort me.

"But I do."

"Have the police any idea who was driving?" Angela asked.

"Not that they'll tell me."

"Maybe it was Emily's ex-husband. From what I hear, he has a fiery temper. Perhaps he didn't like her going out with somebody else."

"She told me at Tatiana's party they were divorced," I said, "but they weren't quite. No decree absolute, apparently. Technically, she was still married to him."

"So he will still inherit her house. Now, there's a motive for murder if ever there was one."

Angela, I thought, was also guilty of watching too much television, but it made about as much sense as anything else.

"I am sure the police will have interviewed him," I said.

"Or, at least, they will have inspected his car. There must be some damage to the roof where I hit it." And some blood underneath, I thought, where Emily had gone.

"How are you getting on in the kitchen?" I asked, changing the subject.

"Done," she said, forcing a smile. "I've thrown away the food that was spoiled, and stacked up on the counter everything that wasn't on the inventory. But we need some boxes to pack it in."

"I'll get some," I said, "just as soon as the rental car arrives."

"Do you need me anymore, then?" she asked, getting to her feet.

"Not if you'd rather get off," I said, also standing up. "Thank you so much for coming to get me. It's made a huge difference."

We both hugged each other again, neither of us seemingly wanting to be the first to pull back. I felt closer to my elder sister at that point than I had ever before.

"Is everything all right in your world?" I asked, perhaps sensing something.

"Oh, yes and no," she said with a sigh. "We're just desperately short of money, like everyone else, and that was not helped by that damn party. And then the bank keeps talking about making Nick's job part-time, or even nonexistent altogether, and where would he get another job at his age?"

"But you and he are all right?"

"We seem to argue a lot more these days, mostly about money, but I think we're fine." She didn't sound too convinced. "Though I don't know how we're going to afford Tatiana's university fees next year."

It was she who was now close to tears.

"How about a student loan?" I said. "Get her to apply now."

"But it would saddle her with so much debt for the future."

"Better for her to have a debt in the future," I said, "than to have her parents split up in the present due to worries over money."

"You make everything sound so simple."

"I'd happily talk to Nick if you would like me to."

She laughed. "We always said that you couldn't arrange the proverbial piss-up in a brewery, but now you're more organized than the rest of us."

Was I? I didn't feel like it at the moment.

The telephone rang and I picked it up.

"Hello," I said.

"Mr. Shillingford?"

"Yes."

"This is Detective Sergeant Sharp."

"Oh, right. Thank you for calling back. Can you hold a second?" I put my hand over the mouthpiece. "It's the policeman dealing with Clare's death," I said to Angela.

"I'll go," she mouthed at me. "Call me later."

She gave me a peck on the cheek and left.

"Sorry about that," I said to the detective sergeant. "Someone was just leaving."

"You said in your message that you have some new evidence?"

"Yes," I said. "It would seem that one of the Hilton Hotel staff believes that there may have been a man in my sister's room when she fell from the balcony."

There was a pause on the other end of the line.

"Did you actually interview any of the hotel staff?" I asked. "It seems that my sister's arrival at the hotel caused quite a stir because she had no luggage."

I could tell from his continued silence that the answer to my question was no, he hadn't interviewed anyone at the hotel.

"But the suicide note," he said.

"I don't care about the note," I said angrily. "I want to know why my sister died."

"The inquest will establish that in due course," he said formally.

"But not if no one investigates anything first."

"It's the coroner's staff who are responsible for investigating the death," he said. "The police would be involved only if a crime had occurred."

"But I think a crime might have occurred," I said. "And anyway, the coroner's office hasn't been in touch with me. I haven't even had a copy of the report of her autopsy."

"I did discuss the cause of death with your father, as next of kin," he said somewhat defensively. "And it would not be usual for copies of an autopsy report to be issued to the family prior to the inquest. That's when the coroner will deal with any matters that might have arisen during the examination of the body."

"What sort of matters?" I asked.

"Any medical conditions that might have been present."

"And were there any medical conditions present?" I asked.

"Nothing pertinent to her death."

"Hold on a minute." I took in what he'd just said. "So there *was* something, then, but it didn't have anything to do with her death."

"There was nothing," he said, "other than her being pregnant."

21

What did you say?" I asked him in astonishment.

"I said there was nothing else, other than her being pregnant."

"Pregnant?" I almost shouted it into the phone.

"I assumed you knew," DS Sharp said. "Miss Shillingford was six or seven weeks pregnant when she died."

I was flabbergasted. I sat there staring at the wall above the desk not really knowing what to think.

"But surely you might have thought that being pregnant could have been pertinent to her death," I said.

"In what way?" he asked.

"Well, for a start it might have affected her state of mind, to say nothing of the hormone changes that must accompany pregnancy."

He said nothing.

"And," I went on, "it would have been nice to have

known at her funeral. Prayers could have been said for the unborn child."

"As I said, I assumed you knew. Your father had been informed."

Bloody hell, I thought.

Why hadn't the stupid old bastard said something? Probably because he was embarrassed by the fact that his unmarried daughter was pregnant.

God save me from my parents and their old-fashioned opinions.

"I'm sorry," DS Sharp said finally, "I should have told you."

"Yes, you should have," I said, "but at least you're telling me now. And there is something else I'd like to know."

"Fire away," he said, clearly relieved that I hadn't shouted at him more.

"Is there any CCTV footage from the hotel? Maybe for when Clare arrived and checked in? I've been to the hotel lobby, and there are cameras all over the place, and also some on the elevators. She must have been filmed by lots of them."

"Yes," he said, "I have copies of all the hotel's CCTV recordings for that evening. I suppose you want to see them?"

"You suppose correctly," I said. "Where are they?"

"At Charing Cross police station."

"Can I come and have a look?" I asked.

"I can't think that it will do any good," he said, "but I suppose so."

"Later this afternoon?"

"I'll be here until about six," he said. "Come to the main entrance on Agar Street and ask for me."

I looked at my watch. It was a quarter to one, and it would take me a good two hours to get there, especially as I had to go via Cambridge to collect my bag.

And there were a couple of other things I had to do first.

"I'll try and be there by five."

THE MAN FROM the builder's arrived soon after one o'clock, followed closely by a woman from the car rental company with a shiny new navy blue Honda Civic.

Suddenly I felt I was back in business. I could now leave the cottage secure and also get around.

I left the builder's man tut-tutting about the state of the door and how he would need to replace some of the framing, as well as the lock, which was bent beyond repair, and drove the Honda out of Newmarket along the Bury Road and into Austin Reynolds's driveway.

I didn't bother with his front door, which I assumed would be locked. Instead, I drove down the side of the house to his office, and then I simply walked in.

There was racing that Monday at Pontefract in the north and Windsor in the south, and Austin Reynolds didn't have any runners at either meeting. I'd checked in the *Racing Post* when I'd been in Geoff Grubb's stable office collecting the inventory for the cottage.

And just to make sure he was home, I'd called his house

earlier and he'd answered, although I'd hung up without speaking.

I hoped he might be in his office and I was right. He was sitting in a leather armchair, watching RacingTV's coverage from Windsor.

"What the bloody hell do you think you're doing?" he blustered, standing up. "Walking in like this without so much as a by-your-leave?"

"At least your door was unlocked," I said, "so I didn't need to use a sledgehammer."

That shut him up and he sat down again.

Austin Reynolds would have made the world's worst poker player. Every thought and emotion was readable in his face. And he was suddenly scared, shrinking back into the armchair like a small child caught with his hand in the cookie jar.

I shouted at him. "Do you think I'm an idiot or some-thing?"

He shook his head slightly, although I did think that it had been pretty stupid of me to leave the money and the blackmail note in the cottage.

"Where is it?" I asked, drawing myself up to my full six feet two inches and purposefully standing over him in a menacing manner.

"Where is what?" he asked back.

"The blackmail note you took from Clare's cottage."

"I burned it," he said with an air of triumph in his voice. "In the fireplace in the drawing room, along with the other one."

I bet he hadn't burned the money, but I did expect that the envelope had gone the same way. Without the envelope, and the words written on it, the money was meaningless.

"So what are you going to do now?" I asked him, reducing my apparent threat by moving away to his right and perching on the corner of his desk.

"What do you mean?"

"Are you going to pay?" I asked.

"Er . . . I haven't decided yet."

"Ten thousand is a lot of money," I said.

"Yes," he agreed.

"And you've just burned the things I'd hoped to use to catch the bastard."

"I have to protect myself first." He said it in a way that made me think he had rehearsed that line many times before in his head.

"By breaking in to other people's houses?"

"If necessary, yes."

"Have you received the payment instructions?"

"Not yet."

"Let me know when you do."

"Why should I?" he asked.

"Because if you don't, we won't be able to catch him, and he'll simply ask for more next time."

Austin shivered.

"And my advice would be," I said, "don't pay him this time either."

"But he could tell the authorities about me laying the horse."

"Indeed, he could," I said, "but I don't believe he has any evidence to back up his claims." I thought about Toby Woodley's stolen briefcase. "In fact, I don't really believe that the person who sent you the note last week has the faintest idea what he's blackmailing you for. I think he's just an opportunist who's taking advantage of something he found."

And, I thought, he's being far too greedy. If he'd asked Austin Reynolds and Harry Jacobs for a thousand or two, they probably would have just paid and never said anything about it to me, or to anyone else. It had been the size of the most recent demand that had been the all-consuming factor in their behavior.

"Are you certain about that?" Austin asked.

"No," I replied, "I'm not. But I am certain about something else. If you pay the ten thousand, the next demand will be for even more."

He looked absolutely miserable.

"What do you want me to do?" he asked pitifully.

"I want you to pass the payment instructions to me as soon as you get them and then do nothing."

"Nothing?" he said. "How about the money?"

"There will be no money," I said. "You're not paying."

"But . . . what if you're wrong? What if he has got the evidence?"

"What evidence could he have anyway?" I asked. "How did you lay the horse in the first place?"

"I used my wife's credit card account. It's still in her maiden name."

"But isn't her billing address the same as yours?"

He said nothing and just looked down at his feet.

How stupid could you get? I thought.

The bloody man deserved to be blackmailed.

NEXT I WENT into Newmarket, to the offices of the Injured Jockeys Fund in Victoria Way. I'd already called and spoken to Mrs. Green, the lady who had organized the dinner at the Hilton Hotel on the night that Clare had died.

"Did you have a nice holiday?" I'd asked her.

"Oh yes, wonderful, thank you," Mrs. Green replied. "The weather in Portugal was fantastic, just like high summer here."

"Good," I said, laying on the charm.

"But I was so sorry to hear about your dear sister. It was a real shock, especially as I was quite used to seeing her round the town. I live down near Mr. Grubb's stables. She was always so lovely."

"Thank you," I said to her, meaning it. "But the reason I called was that I was hoping you might be able to help me."

"Of course."

"I'm trying to obtain the guest list for your charity night at the Hilton."

"Oh." There had been a slight pause. "I suppose it would be all right to give it to you. The seating plan was on display on the night, so it can hardly be confidential, can it? One has to be so careful these days with that damn

Data Protection Act. I wouldn't be able to give you their addresses."

"Just the names will be great."

"I'd rather not e-mail it to you, if you don't mind." Mrs. Green clearly had not been completely convinced that she wasn't breaking some rule or other. "But I could print out another copy of the seating plan, if you'd like. After all, we never had them back at the end of the evening, and you could've just taken it off one of the boards in the hotel."

"Indeed, I could have," I said, playing along with her game.

I had arranged to collect it from the charity's offices and it was waiting for me at the reception desk, sealed in one of those ubiquitous white envelopes.

I sat outside in the car and opened it.

I didn't really know what I was looking for, so I wasn't too disappointed that nothing leapt out at me from the sheet of paper.

Not that I didn't recognize most of the names. I did.

They included many of the great and the good of British racing, coming together to support one of the sport's major charities.

Mr. and Mrs. Mitchell Stacey were listed, as expected, but the other guests at their table were not, at least not by name, simply denoted as "(+10)" after their hosts.

And that was true for lots of the tables, many of which had been taken by the evening's sponsors or by other companies, with only the sponsor or company name shown.

I went back inside the offices to ask Mrs. Green if she had a complete list of everyone who had attended the event.

"Sorry," she said, "the seating plan is all I have. The table hosts put their own place cards out."

I thanked her anyway and drove the Honda back to Clare's cottage to find that the man from the builder's was just finishing the repair to the front door.

"It looks great," I said, inspecting his handiwork. "Thank you."

"Where shall I send the bill?"

"Send it to Austin Reynolds." I started to give him the address, but he already knew it.

"Yeah, we do lots of work for Mr. Reynolds," he said, packing up his tools. "The firm is currently building some new stables at his yard."

I wondered whether Austin would keep his trainer's license long enough to use them.

"**WELL?**" said DS Sharp. "Do you recognize anyone?"

"Quite a few," I said.

We were in a darkened video studio at Charing Cross police station and had spent over an hour looking through the CCTV footage from the hotel lobby the night Clare had died.

"While I was driving down here," I said, "I wondered if someone had been trying to kill me in order to stop me seeing these films."

"Kill you?" he said, surprised.

"Yes. There have been two attempts on my life this last week and I've been trying to work out why."

I described the two incidents to him, including the murder of Emily, and he suddenly became more interested.

"Have you spoken to the Cambridgeshire Police about the CCTV?"

"No," I said, "nor to the Surrey lot. I only thought that it might be the reason on the way here from Newmarket this afternoon."

"So?" he said eagerly. "Is there anything on the films that was worth killing to prevent you seeing?"

"Nothing that's very obvious," I said.

It had been very strange, and somewhat emotional, to see the silent images of Clare walking into the hotel lobby and up to the reception desk. I'd seen it from about four different angles, but none of them had shown a close-up of her face or given any indication of her state of mind.

The hotel lobby had been relatively empty as she checked in, but later, as the Injured Jockeys dinner had evidently finished in the ballroom upstairs, large groups of dinner-jacketed guests could be seen making their way through to the hotel exit, and it was many of these that I recognized.

Mitchell and Sarah Stacey had been in one of the groups, obviously saying their good-byes to the owners as they all collected coats from the cloakroom.

One of the cameras even covered the area outside the hotel's front door and it had clearly shown people queuing for taxis in a rather strange, silent green-tinged world.

"That camera works on infrared after dark," DS Sharp had said, "hence the greeny pictures and the rather zombie-like eyes."

I sat, looking once more at the moving images, and thought about what had been going on exactly fifteen floors above.

"Did it capture Clare?" I asked.

We both knew what I meant. Did it capture the impact of Clare's body on the sidewalk?

"Yes, it did," he said. "But that has been cropped from this copy."

I was relieved. I didn't have to make the decision to stop watching or not.

I looked up at the clock on the wall. "I thought you were leaving at six."

"I was," he said. "But I've nothing to go home to except an empty, cold apartment, so I'm quite happy to stay here as long as you want."

I, too, had nothing to go home to but an empty, cold apartment.

An empty, cold life.

A wave of pain and grief washed over me. Hold on, I told myself sharply, this was not the time or the place. I needed to make the most of this opportunity.

"How about the cameras in the elevators?" I asked.

"They're not very good," he said.

"In what way?"

"They don't really show people's faces. It's all rather top-down."

He pushed some buttons on the machines, and, in

turn, we watched the recordings from each of the four cameras.

As he'd said, the results weren't great. The images were a bit like those filmed for a "Spot the Mystery Guest" slot on television quiz shows, giving only tantalizingly brief glimpses of people's faces, and from unusual angles.

At least we could tell which way the elevator was going as the cameras just captured the lit-up down arrows in the top corner of the images whenever the elevators were going down.

"I think this one is your sister," said DS Sharp. "The timing is right."

I watched as a young woman in jeans, pink shirt, and blue baseball cap entered the elevator and turned around, leaning up against the back wall. After a while she left the elevator. She was alone throughout.

"I timed the elevators," DS Sharp said. "It takes precisely that long to get from the lobby to the fifteenth floor."

"It certainly looked like Clare," I said, "but it's not easy to be absolutely sure with that cap."

"It's also not helped by the poor resolution of the cameras," he said. "They have such small lenses, and that tends to distort the images."

So assuming it had been Clare in the film, she had gone up to the room on her own.

"According to Carlos Luis Sanchez, one of the hotel porters, she was followed up to her room by two men, one after the other, and the first one was wearing a bow tie."

DS Sharp raised his eyebrows in my direction.

"Been busy, have we?" he said.

"I went there primarily to see where Clare died," I said. "But while I was there, I asked some questions."

"Is this Carlos Sanchez the one who says there was someone in your sister's room when she fell?"

"No," I said. "That was his friend Mario."

"Mario?" I could tell from his tone that he was somewhat skeptical.

"Yes, Mario," I said, ignoring him. "Apparently Mario is one of the night porters. According to Carlos, Mario saw the man leave the hotel after Clare had died."

While we had been talking, the CCTV footage from the elevators had continued to play on the screens, and I suddenly saw a face that I recognized.

"Stop!" I said loudly. "Can you play that again?"

He pushed some buttons on the desk in front of him, and the images went slowly backward.

"There," I said. "Stop."

There were three people in the elevator. A young man and a woman, who were too intent on fondling each other to notice anything going on around them, and a second, older man, wearing a dinner jacket and a black bow tie. This second man glanced ever so briefly up at the camera fixed above the kissing heads, allowing it to catch an image of him full face.

"Do you know that man?" DS Sharp asked.

"Yes, I do," I said, continuing to stare straight into the eyes on the screen. "It's a racehorse trainer called Austin Reynolds."

———

"**CAN YOU TELL** which floor he got out on?" I asked.

There was a time code superimposed across the top of all the video footage, and DS Sharp inched the images forward frame by frame, measuring the time between Austin entering the elevator and him leaving it.

"Assuming the elevator is going up, it is about right for the fifteenth floor, but it's impossible to say exactly. The camera position doesn't allow us to see the doors, so we can't be sure how long the elevator was actually moving."

"What time did he get in?"

He wound the video back to the exact moment.

"Twenty-two thirty-one and seventeen seconds."

Just after half past ten. Ten minutes after Clare had checked in.

Was that a coincidence? As Lisa, *The Morning Line*'s producer, had said, coincidences did happen. But was this really one of them?

"Do you have a list of those staying at the hotel that night?" I asked.

"No," he said, "I'm afraid not. But we could find out from the hotel."

"Let's check first to see if he leaves."

We went on watching the video recordings.

"Is that him?" I suddenly asked, seeing someone that resembled Austin enter the elevator. I shouted at the image, "Dammit, man, look up at the camera!"

He didn't, of course, and I wasn't very certain it had been him.

"Can you check the lobby films for that precise time?"

DS Sharp again pressed his buttons, and the wide view of the lobby reappeared on one of the screens. He wound the recording on until the time code was the same as for the shot in the elevator. He then let it run.

Austin Reynolds was clearly visible walking from the direction of the elevators to the main exit.

Without being asked, DS Sharp pulled up the shot from outside with its zombie-like eyes. Austin Reynolds had to wait about four minutes in a queue before he climbed into a taxi and was driven away.

"Twenty-two fifty-eight," DS Sharp said, reading the time on the screen. "Mr. Reynolds left the hotel more than half an hour before your sister died."

Surely no one would kill to prevent me seeing that.

"Unless he came back," I said. But even I knew that was unlikely. "Carlos said there was a second man, so let's keep looking."

We spent another twenty minutes looking at the videos from the elevators, but there was no one who I even re-motely recognized getting into any of them.

"According to Mario, the second man left the hotel during the commotion that followed Clare's fall."

DS Sharp moved the recordings forward to twenty-three thirty.

I never realized how busy hotel elevators could be. Hardly a second went past without each of the four having people in it, moving in one direction or the other, as the hotel guests came back from the theater, or diners from the high-floor restaurant and bar descended to their rooms or to the street-level exits.

But still there was no one I recognized.

At precisely twenty-three thirty-two and fifteen seconds, a man wearing a dark overcoat and a blue baseball cap entered an elevator already half full with people going down. He didn't look up at the camera—in fact, he seemed to be purposefully looking away from it, and also away from the other people.

"Is that the same baseball cap that Clare had on when she checked in?" I asked.

DS Sharp stopped and reran the film.

"It might be."

"Did you find the cap in Clare's room?" I asked. "Or was she wearing it when she fell?"

The detective sergeant didn't answer.

"Where are her things?" I asked him. "Even if she didn't have a handbag, she must have had her car keys."

"There was nothing left in the room except the note."

"How about her car? Where's that?"

No answer.

"And her phone?" I asked. "Where did that go? And did she call anyone before she died?"

Anyone other than me.

"I'll have to investigate," DS Sharp said, clearly uncomfortable.

Past time for that, I thought. Well past. He had obviously been so convinced by the note that it was straight-forward suicide that he really hadn't bothered looking for anything else.

I watched on the screen as the elevator emptied, presumably at ground level.

"OK," I said, "can you find that man in the lobby?"

He fiddled with the equipment, and a wide shot of the lobby appeared on a screen.

"There," I said, pointing.

We watched as the man walked briskly across the lobby.

Lots of other people were running toward the main doors, and some were staggering back inside with wide eyes, holding their heads or hugging one another. I didn't want to think about what they had just witnessed on the sidewalk outside.

The man appeared to be ignoring the disturbance just to his right, marching straight on toward the left-hand side of the main exit.

"Can't you zoom in?" I asked.

DS Sharp tried, but the image became very fuzzy and indistinct.

"I think he's got his collar turned up," the sergeant said. "And maybe a scarf round his face as well."

Why would anyone wear a coat with the collar turned up and a scarf when that particular September evening had been so warm? Was he trying to hide his face from the CCTV cameras?

"Try another angle," I said.

He brought up the image from the camera near the elevators. It showed the man clearly from behind as he walked away. There was no chance of seeing his face from that direction.

DS Sharp went through every camera position in turn, but there was no clear image of the man's features.

"How about the one outside?" I asked, realizing as I said it that any images from out there would also show Clare's body on the ground.

"Are you sure?" the sergeant asked. "I'll have to get the original recording rather than the copy."

"No," I said, "don't. If the man took such efforts inside the hotel not to be seen, he'd hardly let it happen once he was outside. He'd have just gone on walking with his head down."

"I can get it if you want," he said. "We only made the copy without the last bit because we didn't want some unscrupulous idiot uploading it on YouTube. The original is securely locked in my office safe."

I could feel my heart beating.

"No," I said, "I'm sure it wouldn't show anything we can't already see."

"Maybe I'll look at it later," he said, "just to be sure."

"Right." I breathed deeply and was reminded of my broken ribs by a sharp stabbing pain in my left side. But it was in my head that a bell was ringing.

"Could you please show me that shot again of the man walking away from the camera?"

DS Sharp pulled up the images onto the screen.

There was something about the way the man moved—an easy, lolloping long stride, with his head bobbing up and down slightly with each step.

Maybe I didn't need to see the man's face in order to recognize him.

22

I arrived back home at five past ten, and it was as lonely and cold as I had feared. And it was starting to rain.

Ever since leaving Newmarket I'd kept a keen eye on the Honda's rearview mirror to ensure I wasn't being followed, but nevertheless I was very wary when I parked the car on the street outside my apartment and walked quickly to the front door.

I let myself in and put my Chinese takeout in the oven to keep warm while I collected the rest of the things from the car.

Street lighting in my part of Edenbridge could hardly be described as comprehensive. There was a lamppost about twenty yards away in each direction up and down the road, but their meager glow hardly made it to my door. Consequently I was spooked by every shadow, seeing in my mind a potential murderer behind every bush.

My ribs were too painful to carry much at once, so it took me six separate damp trips to bring in the boxes of Clare's paperwork, plus other things like the racing trophies and some of the stuff that Angela had sorted in the kitchen.

With the help of one of Geoff Grubb's stable staff, Clare's clothes and shoes had been packed into my rented Honda, and I'd driven them to a charity shop in Newmarket High Street. There had been great excitement and giggling amongst the three middle-aged women who ran it when they unpacked the bag overflowing with the black lace undies.

"We normally don't resell people's underwear," one of them said, chuckling and holding up a pair, "but these are beautiful, and I think we'll make an exception. Once they've been washed, of course." She had giggled again, and I rather wished I'd just thrown them all away.

I was very glad when everything from the car was finally in the apartment and I was able to lock my front door with me safely inside. Not that I considered this particular home to be much of a castle. It had taken Austin Reynolds six mighty blows with a sledgehammer to break into Clare's cottage. Looking at the simple latch on my own front door, I thought a well-placed kick might be enough to gain entry. I'd never considered it much of an issue as I had precious little that anyone would want to steal. But was it enough to keep out a murderer while I was sleeping?

I propped one of my two kitchen chairs against the door, tucking its back under the doorknob. It probably wouldn't be enough to keep out an averagely determined child but at least it might give me a few moments' warning.

I then sat on my other kitchen chair at the table to eat chicken chop suey and egg fried rice that I'd picked up at a local Chinese restaurant in Edenbridge. It was not especially tasty, but I was hungry, as I hadn't eaten anything since my bland hospital breakfast at seven o'clock that morning.

Had that really been only this morning? So much had happened since then.

I pushed the empty plate away and leaned back in the chair.

Where did I go from here? I wondered. And I didn't mean only physically.

I cracked open the fortune cookie that Mr. Woo at the Forbidden City restaurant had kindly put in the brown bag with the fried rice and chop suey.

Use your talents wisely. That's why you have them.

I read and reread the Chinese proverb on the little strip of paper.

What particular talents did I have that I should use wisely?

I DIDN'T SLEEP very well. Partly due to the pain in my side, but mostly because of overlapping and disturbing dreams involving both Clare and Emily.

I lay awake in the darkness, trying to think what I should do.

"Can you positively identify that man?" Detective Sergeant Sharp had asked me in the Charing Cross police station's video room.

"What do you mean by 'positively identify'?" I asked him back.

"Could you stand up in a court of law and swear to his identity?"

"No," I said. "Of course I couldn't. I just think he walks a bit like someone I know."

The policeman shook his head. "I'd need much more than that to interview anyone. Lots of people walk like that. And anyway, there's no law against walking out of a hotel with your collar up and your head down, even if there is someone dead on the sidewalk outside."

"But he might have been in the room when Clare fell."

"That doesn't mean there was a crime," he said. "I'll grant you, if there was someone in the room when she fell it would almost certainly be relevant to the coroner and the inquest. The man would be able to testify as to what exactly had happened, but there is no evidence that he was involved in any criminal activity, so I can hardly arrest him. And then there's the suicide note."

"I'm not so sure it's a suicide note," I said. "It's not very specific."

"It's a good deal more specific than some others I've seen." I waited while he'd fetched a photocopy of the note from his office. He then read the last two sentences to me out loud. *"Please don't think badly of me. I am so sorry."* He put the note down on the desk in front of me. "I'm

afraid, Mr. Shillingford, that it looks very much like a suicide note to me."

Oh, Clare, how could you?

I TOSSED AND TURNED some more, albeit gingerly,
and got up to go to the bathroom just before seven with
the coming of the morning light.

I felt dreadful, and my reflection in the mirror showed
me as gray-skinned with dark circles under my eyes. I'd
probably overdone the amount of weight that I should have
attempted carrying with broken ribs.

My side was very sore, but my breathing seemed fine,
so I swallowed a couple of heavy-duty painkillers and went
back to lie on my bed until they worked.

The phone vibrated on my bedside table.

"Hello," I said, noting the Newmarket number on the
caller ID.

"This is Austin Reynolds. I've received the payment
instructions in this morning's mail."

"Yes?" I said, encouraging him to continue.

"Just as before," he said, "I have to leave the money in
a brown envelope under my car in a racetrack parking lot."

"Where?" I asked. "And when?"

"Kempton. Tomorrow night."

"What does it say exactly?" I asked.

I could hear him nervously rustling the paper. *"Put the
cash in used fifties in a brown padded envelope and leave it
up against the inside of the offside rear wheel of your car*

when you arrive at Kempton races tomorrow night. Park in the parking lot, then walk away into the racetrack. Don't look back."

"Good," I said. "Do you have anything declared for tomorrow night?"

"One," he said. "I've got a new London owner who wants his horse to run. It's in the fourth. What should I do?"

"Nothing," I said. "Just go to the races and walk away from your car. And don't leave the ten thousand."

"I haven't got that sort of cash anyway."

"What car will you be driving?"

"My dark blue BMW." He gave me the registration.

"Will it start?" I asked, remembering the previous Saturday morning.

"Yes," he said, "I've had a new battery fitted."

"Remember," I said, "just park it and then walk away."

"Shouldn't I bend down as if I were putting something by the back wheel?"

"If you like," I said. "Yes, perhaps that will be good just in case our man is watching you arrive. In fact, place a padded envelope there. It doesn't matter if it's empty."

"I'll put a few stones from my driveway in it to prevent it blowing away."

I hadn't quite worked out yet how I would keep an eye on Austin's car at Kempton the following evening, especially as I was due to be commentating there.

"I don't like it," Austin said. "I don't like it one bit. What if he goes to the racing authorities?"

"So would you rather pay him the ten thousand?" I asked.

"No," he said miserably. "I can't."

It wasn't the only thing he was going to be miserable about.

I changed the subject. "Did you enjoy the Injured Jockeys Fund event at the London Hilton?"

"What?" he asked. "But that was weeks ago."

"Less than three weeks," I said. Although it certainly felt like longer. "Why didn't you tell me you'd been up to see Clare after the dinner?"

There was silence on the other end of the line.

"Well?" I said. "Why didn't you tell me, or at least tell the police?"

"I was frightened," Austin said. "People might have thought I had something to do with her death."

"And did you?" I asked.

"No," he answered quickly. "She was alive when I left her."

"I know."

"How could you know?" he asked.

"The hotel CCTV cameras picked you up leaving half an hour before she fell."

"Oh," he said. "Good."

Even across the telephone line, I could hear the relief in his voice.

"So why did you go up to her room?" I asked, not wanting his relief to be too long-lasting. "And how did you know she was even there?"

"She texted me," he said. "It was rather embarrassing, actually. It was during the speeches. I'd forgotten to turn my phone off."

"What exactly did she text?"

"She said she had to talk to me about Bangkok Flyer's race that afternoon and that it might be a problem."

"What time was this?"

"Hold on, I'll get my phone."

I could hear him moving in the background.

"Half past nine," he said. "Nine twenty-seven, to be precise."

About ten to fifteen minutes after she'd left me at Haxted Mill.

"She said she was coming straight to see me in New-market, but I texted back to say I wasn't at home, I was at that dinner at the Hilton. She then said she'd come to the hotel."

She must have been really worried.

But she wouldn't have checked into a room just to see Austin. She could have spoken to him in the lobby or in the bar. She must have checked in to stay the night with the other man, her mystery lover.

"How did you know which room she was in?"

"She texted me again later, saying she was there, giving me the room number."

"So you went up to see her?"

"Yes," he said, "as soon as the dinner was over. But I stayed in her room only about ten or so minutes, then I left and went home. I caught the eleven-thirty train from King's Cross. My wife picked me up from Cambridge station. She doesn't really like going to those big events in London."

"What did you and Clare talk about?" I asked.

"Not much, really," he said. "I remember that most of the time I was there she was arguing with one of the hotel security men about unlocking the balcony door. What's the point, she was saying, of having a balcony room if the balcony is locked? Anyway, the man unlocked it when I was there. I'm not really sure what it was about, but Clare kept calling me 'darling' and pretending to the man that she and I were going to spend the night together and therefore the door could be opened."

The "two in a room" rule, I thought.

"So what did Clare say after the man had gone?"

"She said that someone knew about her riding Bangkok Flyer to lose. She seemed quite worried about it. I asked her who it was, but she wouldn't tell me."

"It was me," I said.

"I know that now," Austin replied curtly.

"So what was so urgent that she had needed to see you that night?" I asked. "Why couldn't it wait until morning?"

He didn't reply.

"Come on," I said, "why was it so urgent?"

"Because we had planned to do it again the next day, in the last race at Newmarket, and she knew that I would lay the horse on the Internet early on Saturday morning. But she didn't want to go through with it. In fact, she said she'd never ever do it again. From now on, she was always going to ride to win."

I sat there, holding the phone, with tears streaming down my cheeks.

"Did she say anything about killing herself?" I asked, trying to keep emotion out of my voice.

"Not at all," he said. "She seemed happy, almost as if a weight had been lifted from her shoulders. That's why I couldn't believe it when I heard on *The Morning Line* the next day that she was dead."

"Did she say anything to you about writing a suicide note?"

"No, of course not," Austin said. "I told you, I don't think she was planning to kill herself when I left her."

What on earth had happened in the subsequent half hour?

ALMOST AS SOON as I had put my phone down it rang again, and this time it was my father. What the hell did he want at this time of the morning?

"Hello, Dad," I said as enthusiastically as I could manage. "How are you?"

"What's all this bloody nonsense in the newspaper?" he replied, as always ignoring the normal niceties of polite conversation.

"Which newspaper?" I asked.

"*UK Today.*"

Jim Metcalf, I thought. "What does it say?"

"Something about you being strangled last week." I could tell from his tone that he didn't believe it.

"That's right," I said. "That was why I crashed my car into Angela and Nicholas's gatepost on Friday night."

"What nonsense," he said. "You were drunk. I heard one of those policeman say so. He said you must have been blind drunk to hit that post so hard."

"Dad, I was not drunk. Someone was trying to kill me."

"Hmph." He clearly still didn't believe me.

"And whoever it was tried to murder me again on Sunday night."

"But why would anyone want to murder you?" He said it in a manner that I felt was rather belittling, as if I wasn't worthy of being murdered.

But it was still a good question.

I'd been asking myself the same thing for almost thirty-six hours, since the disaster in the Three Horseshoes parking lot.

And I hadn't yet come up with a credible answer.

"I don't know, Dad," I said. "But I intend to find out."

"And how are *you* going to do that?" he asked, his voice again full of doubt that I could do anything. Our little moment of mutual understanding that had existed at Clare's funeral had clearly evaporated.

I decided to ignore him. He had considered my whole life a disaster from the moment I'd told him, aged seventeen, that I wasn't going to university. In his narrow opinion, not getting a degree was tantamount to failure, and the fact that I now earned at least twice what he ever had was completely immaterial.

Use your talents wisely. That's why you have them.

I did have talents and I suddenly realized how I could use them to unravel this mystery. I just hoped it was wise to do so.

I DROVE my rented Honda to Brighton races, checking frequently that I was not being followed.

I arrived early, well before the racing was due to start, as there were people I needed to see.

"No problem," said Derek, the RacingTV producer, when I asked him about my plans for the following evening at Kempton. "Night racing is always less frenetic than the afternoons because there's only a single meeting, so we'll have a full half an hour between races. Masses of time."

"Dead easy," said Jack Laver, the technician who ran the racetrack broadcast center.

More of the *easy*, I thought, and less of the *dead*.

I always liked racing at Brighton. It is one of the more unusual of the British racetracks in that, like Epsom and Newmarket, it is not a complete loop but a long, curving mile-and-a-half horseshoe-shaped track that runs along the undulating ridge of Race Hill, part of the South Downs range of chalk hills, two miles to the east of the city center.

The view from the top of the grandstand on that particular October Tuesday was magnificent. The Indian summer of the past weeks had been swept away by a series of Atlantic weather fronts that had finally cleared through overnight, leaving cool, crisp conditions with spectacular visibility.

Away to my right, the bright sunlight reflected with a million flashes off the surface of the sea, and in the far distance I could see a line of freighters making their way eastward toward the Strait of Dover.

To my left, I looked out across the roofs of houses in the valley below toward where the gate was being towed into position at the one-mile start, ready for the first race.

It was a truly beautiful day, the light azure sky contrasting with the lush dark green of the turf and the deep blues of the English Channel.

I sat on the chair in the commentary booth and badly missed Clare. She used to ride frequently at Brighton, often staying the night before or after with our parents at Oxted. She had last been here for the festival in August, and I could still remember her delight in riding three winners on opening day while I'd been commentating.

I smiled at the memory.

There had been nothing strange or unusual about her riding on that occasion, just magnificent judgment and timing, as she had swept up the hill to win the Brighton Mile Challenge Trophy, the big race of the day, by the shortest of short heads.

Commentators were expected to be unbiased and objective, but there had been nothing impartial and balanced about my words that day as I had cheered with delight as she had pulled off the last-gasp victory.

Now it seemed such a long time ago, and I grieved for the loss of any more such joyous days.

————

I WENT DOWN to the press room to find myself a bite to eat and a cup of coffee.

Jim Metcalf was there ahead of me, and he'd already eaten all the ham-and-mustard sandwiches from the selection provided.

"Did you see my piece today about you?" he asked.

"No," I replied. "But I've heard about it from my father. He says it's a load of rubbish."

Jim tossed a copy of it to me across the room. "It's only what was in that statement of yours."

"Yeah, but *UK Today* must be desperately short of news to have run that today when it happened last Friday," I said. "And anyway, you've completely missed the real story."

"What real story?" he asked, slightly concerned.

"Whoever it was trying to kill me had another go on Sunday night, and they killed a friend of mine instead."

He stared at me. "Are you serious?"

"Absolutely," I said.

"Which friend?"

"Someone called Emily Lowther."

He was already typing her name into his laptop.

"The Three Horseshoes, Madingley," he said, reading from the screen.

"Very impressive," I said. "How do you do that?"

"Coroners' database of reports for the Department of Justice. It records every case referred to a coroner in England and Wales. If this Emily Lowther was killed in Madingley on Sunday night, then the coroner for the area would have been informed of her death, probably yesterday, or this morning at the very latest. Either way, it's now been entered on the database."

"Is it legal for you to have access to it?"

"Probably not," he said, "so I don't ask." He read the details on his screen. "This entry doesn't say anything about you."

"That's probably because I didn't die," I said. "Not quite."

"So who was Emily Lowther?" he asked.

"Just a friend."

"Was she that flash bird I saw you with at Newmarket last Saturday?"

"Do you spy on me all the time?" I asked.

"No, not always, but it was a bit difficult not to notice." He laughed. "Not the way you were pawing each other all afternoon."

"Yeah, well." I sighed deeply, trying hard not to lose my composure. "It was her who was killed, but I think it was really me who was the target."

"Why do you think that?" he said.

"I just do." Although I remembered what Angela had said about Emily's husband having a motive to kill—to inherit her house.

"How was she killed?" Jim asked.

"Run down by a car with no lights on in the pub parking lot. I went over the top, she went under the wheels. I lived, she died."

"Do you want me to write about this as well?"

"Not really," I said.

"Then why are you telling me?"

"I don't know," I said with another heavy sigh, "I just needed to tell someone. I seem to be living a nightmare at the moment. First Clare and now Emily, and the police don't seem to be getting anywhere. They're even suggesting that it might have been a hit-and-run in the pub lot when I'm quite sure it was premeditated murder. And I've got the broken ribs to prove it."

"I'm sorry," he said. "Let me know if there's anything I can do."

I deduced from Jim's tone of voice that he also must believe that the car hitting us was probably an accident. The alternative just seemed too far-fetched.

"Jim," I said, "can I tell you something off the record?"

"Not if it's a news story," he said.

"It's about Toby Woodley."

"What about him?"

"You know you said he had an uncanny knack of sniffing out real stories amongst all the gossip. Well, I think I know how he did it."

"Tell all," Jim said, his journalistic antennae starting to quiver madly.

"I'm not certain but I think that if Toby Woodley had even the slightest inkling that someone had been up to no good, he would send them a blackmail note asking for a paltry sum, like two hundred pounds, or he would go to the authorities."

"So?" said Jim.

"If they paid, then he knew he'd been right."

"Bloody hell!" Jim suddenly shouted. "The bastard did it to me."

"You're kidding?"

"No I'm not," he said. "I got this note last year from someone saying that they knew I'd used phone hacking to get a certain story and that if I didn't pay them two hundred quid they would go to the press-complaints people and report me."

"What did you do?"

"Well, as it happens I hadn't used hacking to get that particular story, so I ignored it. But I remember being really worried. I *had* used some information obtained from hacking to get another story round the same time, so I very nearly paid just to shut him up."

"But you didn't?"

"No," he said. "I was even told where and when to leave the money, but in the end I decided not to pay, and I never heard another thing. I'd all but forgotten about it."

"I think Woodley did it to everyone, and when someone took the bait he then demanded more, writing a story in his paper that was close to the truth but without mentioning anyone by name. I believe the stories were solely designed to give his victims the incentive to pay him the new, larger amounts."

"And do you think that's what got him murdered?"

"Yes," I said, "I do."

"The little creep," Jim said with feeling. "Got what he deserved, if you ask me."

"But there's someone else," I said.

"Someone else what?" he asked.

"Toby Woodley was murdered last Wednesday evening at Kempton, and I know of two people who have received blackmail demands that must have been mailed after he died."

"Who?" he asked eagerly.

"Ah, no," I said, "I'm not telling you that, on the record or off it. Suffice to say, they are both reliable sources."

"So who is this someone else?" Jim asked.

"I don't know, but I think it must be someone who was also being blackmailed because he seems to know Toby Woodley's payment method, and I reckon it must be the same person who killed him."

"Why couldn't it simply be an accomplice who's taken over?"

"Partly because I don't think Toby was the sort of man to have an accomplice, and also because of the missing briefcase."

"The famous Woodley briefcase."

"*Infamous*, more like," I said. "I'll bet that far from containing just his sandwiches, that briefcase held his blackmail notes and the details of all his victims. That's why he was always so protective of it. And now someone else is using what was found to go on with the blackmail."

"So what are you going to do about it?" Jim asked. "Go to the police?"

"Maybe," I said. "But that would almost definitely involve breaking confidences." I laughed. "Perhaps I'll just catch the murdering bastard myself."

"Oh yeah?" said Jim sarcastically. "You and whose army?"

23

I hadn't imagined there would be so many policemen.
They stood in groups of two or three inside each of
the racetrack entrances, with clipboards, asking everyone who came in if they had been there the previous
Wednesday, the day of Toby Woodley's murder.

I had arrived at Kempton really early in order to help set
up the equipment, but now I wasn't at all sure if the whole
thing hadn't been a waste of time.

With all these coppers around, surely only a fool would
attempt to collect blackmail money. But the blackmailer
had been the one to specify the time and place, and you
couldn't actually see the police from the parking lot.

I'd telephoned Austin Reynolds earlier just to check that
he wasn't getting cold feet, and also to finalize when and

where he was to park his car. I had to take a chance that the blackmailer wouldn't be made suspicious by Austin's parking close to where the RacingTV scanner would be.

"Park close to the big blue television broadcast vehicles that are at the far side of the parking lot, near the fence behind the saddling stalls."

"How can I do that?" Austin had asked. "Don't I have to go where I'm told by the parking lot attendants?"

"There won't be any attendants," I'd said. "They don't have them for the night meetings because parking is free and the crowds are small. People park where they like, mostly as close as they can to the enclosure entrances. There are always plenty of spaces. Arrive at precisely half past four and enter by the racetrack main gate on Staines Road. Drive round toward the television vehicles and try to choose a space with an unoccupied one alongside its right. I promise you the parking lot will not be busy, especially more than an hour before the first race."

"All right." He hadn't sounded very confident.

"Austin," I'd said. "This is all you have to do, so do it right."

I wasn't at all sure that he would even turn up at Kempton, but he did, and at precisely the right time, turning his large blue BMW through the main gate at exactly four-thirty.

I had been waiting for him out on Staines Road in the rented Honda Civic, and I now pulled out into traffic and followed him into the racetrack parking lot and around to the TV trucks.

Austin parked in a free space just three away from the scanner, and I pulled the Honda into the space immediately alongside him on his right. Perfect, I thought. I couldn't have positioned the two cars better if I'd painted white crosses on the blacktop.

I climbed out of the Honda and walked directly to the scanner without looking once at Austin or his car. One never knew who was watching.

"Ideal," said Gareth, one of the bright young RacingTV technicians who had been as keen as mustard to help out. "Anything for some bleedin' excitement."

Gareth had spent the morning and afternoon setting up all the camera equipment around the racetrack, and he would take it all down again later after the racing had finished. He was only there in between times in case any part of the system broke down, then his job was to fix it. He always joked that he was the only member of the broadcast team who actively wanted something to go wrong in order to alleviate the mind-numbing boredom of the actual program.

Gareth didn't really like racing, but he absolutely loved television cameras.

"Can it be done?" I'd asked him.

"'Course it can, me old sugar," he'd replied in his strong London accent. "I can do bloody anything when it comes to cameras. Mr. Bleedin' Magic, I am."

And he was.

He hadn't even wanted to know why I needed a particular car to be kept under constant observation. To him, it was clearly just a game and the reasons for it didn't matter. "Ask no bleedin' questions," he'd said, "and I'll be told no bleedin' lies."

He'd set up one of the small handheld cameras in the back of the Honda so that it pointed out the side window behind the rear door, and he'd shown me how to park the car for maximum coverage. We now sat together in the scanner looking at a monitor that showed the images received from the camera through a link Gareth had established between the roof of the Honda and the signal-relay vehicle.

"Bleedin' marvelous," Gareth exclaimed, staring closely at the monitor. "Crackin' good picture, too, considerin' it only uses a normal Internet wireless link."

The wide-angle lens on the camera meant we could see all the way down the far side of Austin Reynolds's car right down to the ground, with a particularly good shot of the offside rear wheel, behind which I could already see the corner of a brown envelope sticking out.

"Can you run that back?" I asked Gareth.

"Sure," he said, and the image jerked slightly on the screen as he put the recording into reverse. Even when the tape was played backward, it was clear for us both to see Austin Reynolds as he'd climbed out of his car, opened the back door, removed his coat from the backseat, closed the door, put on the coat, and then leaned down to place a brown padded envelope behind the rear wheel before walking off toward the entrance to the enclosures.

"What's in the envelope?" Gareth asked, his inquisitiveness getting the better of him for a moment.

"Just some stones," I said.

"Diamonds?" Gareth was suddenly quite interested.

"No such luck," I said, laughing. "Just a few pieces of ordinary gravel to stop it from blowing away."

Gareth didn't ask me why Austin was placing a worthless envelope behind his rear offside wheel, which I was then going to such trouble to watch—*Ask no bleedin' questions and I'll be told no bleedin' lies.*

"How about the other camera?" I asked.

"No problem," he said, looking at another image on his monitor. "I'll just go and make a small adjustment."

He disappeared outside, and I watched the monitor as the camera moved slightly to the left and Austin's car came clearly into view, with the racetrack entrance beyond. This second camera was attached to the side of one of the receiving-dome frameworks on the roof of the signal-relay vehicle that was parked alongside the scanner.

Gareth returned and seemed satisfied with his handiwork.

"Right," he said. "That should do it. Good thing we've got no girls tonight or we'd be needin' that camera."

"Girls," in this instance, did not refer necessarily to womankind. It was the nickname for any presenters, male or female, who sat in the glass-fronted booth overlooking the parade ring and described the horses before a race. Someone once stated that the presenters had chatted away with each other like a pair of schoolgirls, and the nickname had stuck.

The use of such paddock booths was once routine, but now they are seen mostly at the big meetings only, where one of the small cameras is employed to briefly show the girls, mostly men, usually sitting side by side and wearing headphones.

No girls tonight.

Oh God! Don't remind me.

THE BLACKMAILER took the envelope at seven thirty-five just as the seven runners for the fourth race were being mounted in the parade ring and at the precise moment when Austin Reynolds was giving his jockey a leg up into the saddle.

By that time it was dark, and just like the CCTV camera at the Hilton Hotel, Gareth's two small ones had automatically switched to infrared, both assisted by an infrared lamp positioned on the signal-relay vehicle that bathed the area in radiation that was invisible to humans but clear as daylight to the cameras.

I nearly fell off my stool in the commentary booth, from which I hadn't moved since well before the first race. It was good that it didn't happen during a race commentary, I thought, or I would have completely lost the plot.

Jack Laver had worked his magic and installed not one but three monitors in the commentary booth, the extra two showing images from Gareth's hidden cameras.

And there was the blackmailer, bold as brass, walking over to Austin's car, bending down, removing the envelope, and stuffing it in his coat without stopping to open it and count his money—not that he'd find any.

And just for good measure, as he bent down he looked straight into the camera hidden in the Honda from a distance of just a couple of feet. His image may have been monochrome green and he may have had zombie-like eyes, but his features were clear and distinct.

Almost before anyone would have had a chance to react, our man was up and gone, visible now only via the second camera, walking briskly back toward the racetrack entrance, once more to mingle with, and become anonymous amongst, the other racegoers and the attendant policemen.

The man's head bobbed up and down slightly with each step, and I had seen that easy, lolloping long stride before in the video room at Charing Cross police station.

The man who picked up Austin Reynolds's envelope, with its filling of gravel, was the same man who had exited the Hilton Hotel just minutes after Clare had fallen to her death.

But this time I'd seen his face. And in spite of the greenness and the zombie eyes, I was certain I knew him.

I knew him very well indeed.

"GOT 'IM," Gareth said excitedly, bursting into the commentary booth. "Did you see? Bleedin' marvelous."

To him it was still only a game, but, to be fair, that's all that I'd implied it was.

"Yes," I said almost equally excited, "I did see."

I was thinking fast.

"Take this." I dug into my leather bag and gave him an unmarked DVD. "I need you to do a bit of editing," I said, and I explained what I wanted him to do.

"No prob," he said, taking the DVD. "Give me about ten to fifteen mins." He left as quickly as he'd arrived.

The horses were coming out onto the course for the fourth race, a three-quarter-mile maiden stakes for two-year-olds with seven runners, one of whom, Spitfire Boy, had run at Lingfield in the race when Clare had stopped Bangkok Flyer. That race had been about a mile, and Spitfire Boy had faded badly in the last two hundred yards. Perhaps this shorter trip would suit him better.

I described the colors of the jockeys' silks as the horses made their way to the start on the back stretch, taking particular note of Ground Pepper, the young colt trained by Austin Reynolds.

I tried to concentrate on the horses but my heart was pounding.

If I was right, the man who had collected the envelope had murdered Toby Woodley. I should tell the police straightaway.

Concentrate, I told myself. For God's sake, concentrate on the racing!

Try as I might to learn the colors, visions of the man's face with his zombie eyes kept crowding my consciousness.

"They're loading," I said into my microphone as the horses began to be inserted into the starting gate by the team of handlers.

I flicked my main monitor over to the current betting odds and gave the meager crowd an update.

"Spitfire Boy is the favorite at three-to-one, Ground Pepper at fours, eleven-to-two bar those."

I switched the monitor back to show the horses at the start.

"Mark, coming to you in ten seconds," said Derek into my headphones, *"nine, eight, seven . . ."*

"Just three to go in now," I said over the public address.

". . . six, five, four . . ."

"Ground Pepper will be the last to load."

". . . three, two, one . . ."

As always, I paused fractionally as the satellite viewers came online.

"That's it," I said, "they're all in. Ready." The gate swung open. "They're off, and racing."

I thought I did pretty well, considering the minimal amount of time I had devoted to learning the colors.

I was helped by Spitfire Boy, who was a determined front-runner, taking the lead in the first few strides and setting a strong pace that spread the field around the far end of the course, making their identification easier.

As always, the horses bunched together more as they turned into the stretch, and, on this occasion, their jockeys' faces didn't remind me of Clare. This time they all appeared to have green faces and zombie eyes full of murderous intent.

Spitfire Boy held on to win by a neck, with Ground Pepper fading to finish fourth of the seven.

As soon as the last horse crossed the line I grabbed my cell phone and called the number of Superintendent Cullen's sergeant. There was no answer. I tried it again. Still no answer, so I left a message asking him or his boss to call me back urgently.

What should I do now?

There were police downstairs by the entrances. Should I go down to one of them or should I call 999?

Gareth's voice came over my headphones. *"Mark, I've done the edit. It runs for just thirty-eight seconds. I'll send it through to your monitor."*

"What the hell are you doing on the talk-back?" I said. "Where's Derek?"

"They've all gone on a bathroom break. We've got commercials for the next"—he paused while he checked—*"three mins and twenty. Do you want to see this or not?"*

"Yes, of course," I said. "Put it on."

I watched as his handiwork came up on my main monitor.

The unmarked DVD that I had given to Gareth was a copy that Detective Sergeant Sharp had given to me of the Hilton Hotel CCTV footage of the man with the baseball cap and turned-up collar coming down in the elevator and then walking across the hotel lobby, including the view from behind.

Just as I had asked, Gareth had edited the CCTV footage together with that from the cameras tonight so that the images appeared side by side on a split screen, first with the close-up of the man's face alongside the shot of him in the elevator, then the two views of him walking away from the camera, one in the hotel, the other in the Kempton parking lot.

And it was those final fifteen or twenty seconds of walking that left no doubt whatsoever that the two men in the films were one and the same person.

I glanced out of the commentary booth toward brightly lit bookmakers' boards and the dark racetrack beyond and was horrified by what I saw.

Gareth may have been Mr. Bleedin' Magic when it came to cameras, but he was Mr. Blitherin' Idiot when it came to acting as a producer.

The edited films were not just playing on my monitor but playing on the huge television screen set up in front of the grandstands.

"For God's sake, Gareth," I shouted through the talkback, "it's on the big screen."

"Bugger me. So it is. It's bleedin' everywhere."

He thought it was funny.

Derek didn't. In fact, he was furious.

"Was this your doing?" he demanded loudly. *"I go to the bloody toilet and the next thing I know we're broadcasting God knows what to all the television sets right round the racetrack."*

"I'm sorry," I said. "It was only meant to come to mine."

"Bloody amateurs."

I heard him click off his microphone. No doubt young Gareth was getting his earful directly without the aid of technology. I hope it didn't result in either of us losing our jobs.

But Derek's reprimand was not my main worry.

Had the blackmailer seen the film? And did he know it was me that had initiated it?

I'd find out soon enough.

I STAYED in the commentary booth for the rest of the evening, hiding myself away.

Twice more I tried to call Superintendent Cullen or his sergeant, but to no avail. I even tried DS Sharp at Charing Cross, but his phone, too, went to voice mail. Policing was obviously mostly a nine-to-five occupation.

The last two races seemed to go by in a blur, but I must have been all right as Derek, at least, didn't complain about my commentary. He did complain about almost everything else, though, and was even talking about having a bucket installed under the desk in the scanner so that he'd never have to go out to the bathroom again.

"You seem to have caused a bit of a stir!" he shouted into my ears. *"The racetrack chairman has been only one of those we've had down here demanding to know what the bloody hell is going on."*

"What did you tell them?" I asked.

"I told them they'd better speak to you."

Oh thanks, I thought.

I hoped that one of his visitors hadn't been the man with the zombie eyes.

I hung around in the commentary booth for quite a while after the last race, hoping that everyone would go before I made my way down. For one thing, I didn't want to have to explain myself to the racetrack chairman.

The door of the booth opened and I jumped.

"Bye, Mark," said Terence Feynman, the judge, putting his head through the gap. "Will I see you here tomorrow night?"

"Yes, Terence," I said, "that's the plan. Bye, now."

Terence withdrew his head from the gap and closed the door.

Damn, I thought a few moments later. I should have gone down to my car with him. Safety in numbers and all that.

I quickly packed my computer, my binoculars, and my colored pens into my black leather bag and went out into the long corridor after him, turning right toward the exit.

Terence had already disappeared, but another man came around the corner into view, walking briskly toward me, his head bobbing up and down slightly due to his easy lolloping stride.

I stopped.

"Hello, Mark," the man called down the corridor.

That heart of mine was thumping once more in my chest.

He was just fifteen or so yards away and closing in rapidly.

"Hello, Brendan," I said.

My cousin, Brendan Shillingford, smiled at me, but the smile didn't reach his eyes—his zombie eyes.

24

Run, my body told me, flooding adrenaline into my bloodstream, ready for flight. But where to? The only way out was past Brendan.

Or was it? I dragged some fragment of memory back into my mind.

Fire escape.

Hadn't I once been told that there was a way out over the roof in case of a fire?

I turned and ran the other way, away from him, sprinting down to the far end of the corridor and up the metal staircase toward the photo-finish booth and the door to the roof, rummaging madly to get my cell phone out of my pocket.

I could hear Brendan coming after me.

I wondered if he'd have a knife. I didn't want to look.

I fumbled with the door and finally turned the lock, tripped over the step, and fell out onto the grandstand roof, dropping my phone in the process. I searched madly for it with my hands, but it had fallen through the metal grille floor of the walkway and my fingers couldn't reach it.

I could now hear Brendan on the stairs, so I moved quickly away from the door, down the walkway and toward the back of the roof, from where I had watched the horses the previous week. I looked down at the now deserted parade ring. Where was a policeman when you needed him most?

The sky above was pitch-black, but there was enough spillage from the racetrack floodlights for me to see across the roof quite well.

There was a junction in the walkway, and I had to make a decision. Which way was the fire escape?

Surely, I thought, there should have been a sign.

I went right but quickly learned that was wrong. The walkway came to an abrupt end after about fifteen yards, next to an electrical junction box.

I turned around and came face-to-face with Brendan.

He was standing about ten or so paces away and looking pretty pleased with himself. Something flashed in his right hand.

"Is that the same knife you used to kill Toby Woodley?" I had to shout over the continuous whirr of the air conditioners.

If he was surprised by the question, he didn't show it.

He took a step toward me.

"And did you murder Clare too?" I shouted.

He took another step forward.

I threw my black leather bag at him, then ducked under the walkway's railing and ran over the corrugated-steel roof.

Brendan followed.

The grandstand roof wasn't flat, and I don't mean just the corrugations.

It sloped up at the front like a giant ramp. And there was a gantry, an enormous structure extending some twenty feet out and up from the front of the roof, that held several banks of floodlights.

I clambered through the main supporting spar that ran right across the middle of the roof. I was trying to double back to the fire escape or return to the door, but Brendan cut me off and drove me on toward the front of the grandstand, toward the sloping part of the roof.

Twice he got so close that I could feel him grabbing for the collar of my coat, but each time I managed to pull myself away.

I was thirty-one and Brendan was nearly ten years older, but I was hampered by my broken ribs, which made scrambling over the large steel pipes of the support spars exceedingly painful. He, meanwhile, seemed to skip over them with ease.

I reached one of the walkways, rolled myself through the railing, stood up, and ran.

But still it wasn't the right way for the fire escape.

The walkway ended next to another junction box.

Dammit.

I turned around, kicking something loose on the floor. I looked down. There were several poles, like ones used for scaffolding but smaller in diameter. They appeared to be the same as that used to make the railings of the walkways, probably left behind after construction.

I quickly bent down and picked up one that was about six feet in length.

Brendan was facing me on the walkway.

I jabbed the end of the pole toward him and he stepped back a stride, so I did it again.

We stood like that for what seemed an age, but it was probably only a few seconds.

It was a standoff—me with the pole and him with the knife.

I advanced a stride, jabbing the pole forward. He retreated slightly.

"What are you doing?" I shouted at him. "I'm your cousin."

He didn't reply. He just stared at me with no emotion visible on his face.

"Did you kill Toby Woodley?"

No reply.

"How about Clare?" I shouted. "Did you kill her too?"

"I loved Clare," Brendan said. "And she loved me."

The mystery boyfriend, I thought. The wonderful lover who had made her happy.

Her own cousin.

My cousin.

My married cousin with two teenage children.

"What happened in that hotel room?" I shouted at him.

He said nothing.

"Did you push her off the balcony?"

He continued to stare at me, but in spite of the dim light I thought I could read some pain in his eyes.

"Did you know she was pregnant?" I shouted.

He went on staring at me.

"She was six or seven weeks pregnant."

Still nothing. He had known.

"Was it yours?"

It had to be, but he went on saying nothing.

"Was that why you killed her? Did she want an abortion?"

His head came up a bit. "Shut up."

"So was that it?" I said. "You wanted the child and she didn't?"

He slowly shook his head. "It was the other way round." He spoke quietly, and I had to strain to hear him. "She did it on purpose, to trap me."

It was not an excuse. There can be no excuse for murder.

I thought I could see tears on his face. Crocodile tears.

"It's no good crying now," I shouted at him. "You shouldn't have killed her."

"It was an accident," he shouted back.

"Oh yeah?" I said, mocking him. "Just like it was an accident in the pub parking lot on Sunday? You killed Clare, just like you killed Emily. And you nearly killed me, twice. Why don't you admit it, you bastard?"

"I told you," he screamed at me, "it was an accident! I just pushed her away, and she . . ." He trailed off. "She tripped. I didn't mean for her to fall."

He was mad with anger, and with grief.

That made two of us.

"Did you make her write the note?" I shouted.

"What note?"

"The suicide note."

"There was no note. I told you, it was a bloody accident."

"And was sticking a knife into Toby Woodley's back also a bloody accident?"

"He deserved it," Brendan said with real menace in his voice. "The bastard was blackmailing me."

"He was blackmailing everyone," I said, "but no one else killed him."

"He knew about Clare and me. He said he'd put it in the paper."

I wondered whether Toby had really known or had just been guessing. Perhaps a blackmail note had given him the true answer. It had certainly condemned him to death.

"But you blackmailed people too," I said. I thought back to the handwritten zeros added to the amounts. "And you were much greedier than Toby."

"It seemed like an opportunity not to be missed." He was suddenly smiling as if pleased with himself. I couldn't think why. To continue the blackmail had been stupid and far too risky, and it had finally given him away.

"And what about me?" I said. "Why did you try to kill me?"

"You said at the funeral that you were going to see the video from the hotel."

"And you thought I'd recognize you?"

He nodded.

He'd almost been right.

He suddenly lunged forward and grabbed the end of the pole with his left hand, pulling it sharply toward him, and me along with it.

He slashed at my hands with the knife, and I had to let go or else I'd have lost my fingers.

Now the tables were turned, and he jabbed the end of the pole toward my face, forcing me to duck wildly sideways.

This really isn't funny, I thought, and maybe for the first time I was scared, very scared.

I tried to reach down to pick up another of the poles, but Brendan swung the one he had in a great arc, bringing it down heavily on my back between the shoulder blades. It would have landed on my head and killed me if I hadn't seen it at the last second and ducked.

Even so, the blow was bad enough, driving the air out of my lungs and causing me to drop to my knees. My broken ribs didn't like it much either.

I sensed, rather than saw, the pole being lifted again for another blow. This time, I thought, it will be fatal.

I rolled to my left, out through the railings of the walkway and onto the roof proper, as the pole smacked down where I had just been.

I was not going to bloody die, I told myself. Not here. Not now.

I stood up, dragged some air into my aching and injured lungs, and ran.

I ran on the corrugated steel toward the front of the grandstand and I could hear Brendan running behind me. I didn't have time to look back, but I was sure he'd have the pole in his hands, ready to strike me down as soon as he got within range.

I ran up the slope of the roof and didn't stop when I got to the brink. I didn't even pause, running like a tightrope walker, straight out from the roof on one of the cylindrical spars of the lighting gantry.

Desperate situations necessitate desperate measures, and running as fast as I could along a metal spar eight inches in diameter with nothing but air beneath for more than a hundred feet was desperate indeed.

And the spar wasn't horizontal. It sloped up at an ever-increasing angle as I moved away from the edge of the roof toward the floodlights. I was tightrope-walking uphill, and my only stability came from movement.

As the slope caused me to slow, I began to wobble.

I went down on my hands and knees, clutching with my fingers at the metal, trying to dig my nails into the smooth, hard paint.

Nevertheless, I began to slide backward, down the spar, back toward the edge of the grandstand roof, and back toward Brendan and his pole.

It wouldn't take much for him to push me off with it.

All there was below me was hard, unforgiving, deserted concrete, a hundred and twenty feet straight down. The fifteenth floor of the Hilton Hotel or the roof of the Kempton Park grandstands—different distances, maybe, but the outcome would be much the same.

I could imagine what would be said: *It's such a shame— Mark never came to terms with his twin sister's suicide, nor the loss of another close friend and the breakup of a long-term relationship. But he found a way out of his pain.*

I managed to turn myself over so that I was now sitting on the spar, with my ankles locked together beneath it and my hands down in front of me on its cold metal.

But still I slid down, inch by inch.

Brendan was standing just short of the edge of the grandstand roof proper, holding the pole in both hands and watching me intently as I moved ever so slowly but inexorably toward him.

He stepped forward and swung the pole at me.

I had time to see it coming, and keeping my legs tight around the spar, I leaned back flat against it as the pole whizzed past harmlessly just inches from my eyes.

But the sudden movement meant that I slid still farther down.

Next time I'd easily be in range. I knew it and so did Brendan.

I tried my best to climb away from him, but for all my efforts I only managed to slide even closer.

Brendan was smiling again. He was sure he had me now.

Not if I could help it.

As he swung the metal pole at me I purposely leaned forward into it, taking a heavy blow on my left wrist, which made my whole left arm go numb.

However, at the same time, I grabbed the pole firmly with my right hand and pulled hard.

Just as it had done with me earlier, it caught Brendan unawares.

He should have let go.

Even so, he would probably have been all right if the grandstand roof had been flat at the front, allowing him to have a steady stance. But it wasn't. The slope meant that he was leaning forward slightly, and now my sharp tug on the pole had him reeling over the abyss.

I could see the horror on his face as he pitched forward, grasping desperately for the wire stays that crisscrossed the framework to give it added rigidity.

But he didn't fall.

The bulk of his body had gone over the edge of the roof, but he was still supported by the pole that was underneath him, held up at one end by a wire stay.

The other end of the pole was still in my right hand, and Brendan's weight was beginning to rotate me alarmingly around the spar.

I looked across at him and he stared back at me, terror deeply etched in his features, a dreadful realization apparent in his eyes—his zombie eyes.

I thought of my darling sister Clare, and also of the lovely Emily, and what might have been.

Maybe I could have saved him if I'd wanted to, or maybe I couldn't.

I'd never know.

I let the pole slip through my fingers and decided to look upward at the black sky rather than downward at the concrete.

I had no wish to witness another of Brendan's "accidents."

EPILOGUE

Two months later, on a bright cold morning just two days before Christmas, a thanksgiving service was held for Clare in Ely Cathedral, and this time I organized everything myself.

The original plan had been to hold it at St. Mary's parish church in Newmarket, but such had been the demand for tickets that somewhere larger had to be found, and the cathedral, just half an hour up the road, was perfect.

There is something very grand about our great churches, and Ely Cathedral is certainly no exception, sitting as it does on a small mound surrounded by the flatlands of the Fens.

The service matched the surroundings, and, unlike at her funeral, there was lots of live music, with the cathedral choir adding to the splendor.

Geoff Grubb read a lesson, as did James and Stephen, while Angela and I both gave eulogies.

Indeed, the Shillingford family had turned out in force.

Even Joshua, Brendan's younger brother, was present, although Gillian, Brendan's widow, and their boys were not.

Life for them had been far from easy.

Not only had their father died that night at Kempton but he had been shown to be a murderer, and the press had not been kind to him.

Toby Woodley may not have been the most popular member of the press but he still was one of their brotherhood, and they had devoured his killer like a pack of hungry dogs.

"You can't libel the dead," Toby had said to me at Stratford races.

So right he was.

Jim Metcalf and his fellow journalists had taken full advantage of that fact, dismantling any semblance of good reputation that Brendan had built up over his years as a trainer.

It had even been widely reported by some that Brendan had been the trainer who had layed his horses to lose, the trainer about whom Toby Woodley had written in the *Daily Gazette* the previous May.

That, I was sure, had come as a great relief to Austin Reynolds, although both he and I knew it wasn't true.

The service concluded with a five-minute film tribute to Clare that was shown on big screens set up on either side of the altar and also on a number of screens placed along the nave.

The previous week I had spent a whole day in RacingTV's editing suite in Oxford putting the film together. It started with a montage of photographs of Clare from throughout her life together with some home movies of her riding her pony as a child. Then there was footage of her career, including big-race victories intercut with snippets of interviews and celebrations. And for the soundtrack I had chosen, appropriately, the song "The Winner Takes It All" by ABBA.

When I had first played the finished film through for myself, it had made me cry, and now as the music echoed around the arches and vaulted ceiling of the Norman cathedral, there were many more tears all around me.

But the film wasn't all doom and gloom. Quite the contrary.

There was laughter, too, and spontaneous applause when it finished with a still image of Clare, standing high in her stirrups, all smiles and happiness, punching the air, having just won a race at Royal Ascot.

I STOOD under the West Tower, shaking hands, as the huge congregation spilled out past me through the West Door onto Palace Green.

I suppose I initially had chosen a day when there was no racing in the hope that enough people would come to fill St. Mary's Church in Newmarket. Now it seemed that ab-

solutely everyone I knew in racing, and many more that I
didn't, had turned up at Ely Cathedral, and soon my right
hand was aching from so much shaking.

It was a good thing that it wasn't my left hand.

That was only just out of a cast after eight weeks.

Brendan had fractured my wrist in six places when he'd
hit me with the pole, and it had been almost more than I
could manage to get myself off the floodlight gantry and
back onto the grandstand roof without going the same
way he had.

Detective Sergeant Sharp and Detective Chief Inspector Coaker came out of the cathedral together.

"Lovely service," they both said in unison. "Very
moving."

"Thank you," I replied. "Any news?"

"Mr. Brendan Shillingford's car has now been confirmed as the one that hit you and Mrs. Lowther at the
pub in Madingley," DCI Coaker said. "It had been re-
paired by a garage in Bury St. Edmunds. Mr. Shillingford
apparently told them that he'd hit a deer in Thetford For-
est. But we've been able to extract a sample of Mrs.
Lowther's DNA from blood found on the underside of the
vehicle."

I suppose I was pleased.

"How about the knife?" I asked.

"According to Superintendent Cullen at Surrey, the
knife found on Mr. Shillingford was consistent with that
used to kill Mr. Woodley, although they were unable to
find any trace of his blood on it."

"Will there be a trial?" I asked.

"Only the remaining inquests," he said, shaking his head. "There'd be no point in a criminal trial."

"Will the inquests name Brendan as the murderer?"

"That doesn't happen anymore. I expect the coroners to record verdicts of unlawful killing in the case of Toby Woodley and Emily Lowther, but there will be little doubt about who was responsible. Mr. Shillingford's verdict will probably be misadventure."

Brendan's misadventure.

The policemen moved away through the door and outside into the pale December sunshine.

I turned to see who was next in the line.

"Hello, Mark," said Sarah Stacey.

I anxiously looked around behind her.

"Mitchell's not here," she said. "I've left him."

I stared at her. "When?"

"About six weeks ago."

"Why didn't you call me?" I asked.

"Because I didn't leave Mitchell for you," she said with determination. "I just left him. Time will tell what happens from now on."

"But where are you living?"

"With my sister," she said.

I hadn't even known she'd had a sister. "What about the prenup?" I asked.

"My lawyer says it's not enforceable. Not after fourteen years of marriage."

"I hope he's right."

"Call me sometime," she said, and then she turned and walked away, out of the cathedral. Was it also out of my life?

I watched her go. Maybe I would call her or maybe I wouldn't. As she had said, time would tell.

Harry Jacobs came bounding up to me.

"A fitting tribute," he said. "Well done. Clare would have been proud of you."

"Thanks, Harry," I said, shaking his hand.

He smiled at me warmly and moved away. Nothing more needed to be said, not today.

In November, I had visited Harry's impressive country mansion near Stratford-upon-Avon to give him the good news that both of his blackmailers were dead and that his guilty secret had died with them.

I certainly wasn't going to say anything to anyone about any blackmail.

We had sat in his conservatory, looking out over the rolling Warwickshire countryside, and his relief had been almost palpable.

"I want to close that offshore bank account," he had said, "but there's more than twenty-five thousand pounds in it, and I can hardly bring that back into my regular accounts without my accountant or tax lawyer asking where it came from."

"Then give it to charity," I told him. "Send it anonymously to the Injured Jockeys Fund."

And that was precisely what he did, right there and then, using his computer and Internet banking.

"Tell me, Harry," I asked him as I was leaving, "where does all your money come from?"

"Don't you know?" he asked, slightly amused. "When I was young and extremely foolish, I managed to borrow an obscene amount of money from a bank to buy fifty acres of industrial wasteland. It was contaminated with all sorts of toxins and heavy metals. Dreadful place. I almost cried when I saw it after I'd bought it."

"Surely you saw it beforehand?"

"I went to the auction to buy something else, but it sold for far too much. The next lot was the fifty acres and the price seemed too good to be true. So I bought it, completely unseen. I'd thought I must be on a winner whatever it was like."

"And were you?"

"I didn't think so just then. I tried to sell it immediately for less than I'd paid for it, but there were no takers."

"So where was the land?" I asked him.

"Somewhere called the West India Docks," he replied, beaming broadly. "East London. It's now part of Canary Wharf, and there's over two million square feet of offices on my land alone." He laughed. "The bank I originally borrowed the money from now pays me a fortune each year in rent for their headquarters building. Money for old rope."

One of the other advantages of having the service on a non–race day was that all my colleagues from RacingTV were able to attend. More than that, Gareth had set up his cameras in the cathedral to record everything for posterity, and I'd even seen Iain Ferguson doing a piece for the camera outside as everyone had arrived.

That should have been my job.

"Hi, Mark," Nicholas said, walking over and shaking me warmly by the hand. "Lovely service."

"Thanks, Nick," I said, meaning it. "And Angela was great too."

"Yes, she was rather good." His tone almost implied surprise.

"How are things?" I asked.

"Pretty good, at the moment," he said. "The bank has realized they can't do without me. Thank God." He smiled broadly. "It seems there was almost a riot amongst the senior management when it was suggested by the chairman that I should be let go. I'd never realized how much I was appreciated. Perhaps I'll ask for a raise next." He laughed. "How about you?"

"I'm finally moving house," I said. "I've bought a place in Oxfordshire, and I move in after the New Year."

"Congratulations," he said. "Although I think it's a bit extreme to go to all that trouble just to get away from your dad."

We both laughed.

"He's not been so bad recently," I said. "Almost human."

I looked across to where my father was standing with my mother on the other side of the West Door, also talking to people as they left the cathedral. As I was watching, he glanced in my direction and smiled at me, a genuine smile that reached all the way to his eyes.

I smiled back. "I think he's been better since the conclusion of Clare's inquest."

Not that the verdict had been quite the one we would have wanted.

The coroner had recorded an open verdict in spite of my assurances that Brendan had as good as admitted to me that he'd been responsible for her death—accident or otherwise. Not that I'd been able to properly get my head around the fact that Brendan and Clare had been lovers and that she had been pregnant with his child.

But at least the verdict wasn't suicide, even though the coroner had still placed great emphasis on the existence of the note addressed to me.

I had tried to explain that I believed it was a letter Clare had been writing to me, after our row at dinner, because she couldn't reach me on the telephone. It was nothing to do with her death, and it had probably been half written, as found, when Brendan had first arrived in her room.

But the coroner had not been convinced and stubbornly maintained that the note, in fact, was strong evidence of her suicide, although, as he'd said, no one could be sure of what had happened in the hotel room that night.

But I knew.

I was certain of it and that was enough.

Whatever anyone else might think was irrelevant.

FROM *NEW YORK TIMES* BESTSELLING AUTHORS

DICK FRANCIS
AND
FELIX FRANCIS

Silks

Geoffrey Mason isn't terribly disappointed when his client Julian Trent is found guilty. Despite being paid handsomely as Trent's defense counsel, he believes Trent needs to be locked up for a good long time. He only wishes it had happened more quickly—if the trial had ended just a bit earlier, Mason could have made it to the Foxhunter Steeplechase and fulfilled a long-standing dream as an amateur jockey.

Soon afterward, Trent is set free when witnesses and jurors start recanting—due to intimidation, Mason suspects. Remembering Trent's threats at the time of his conviction, Mason is none too happy. Things get even worse when one of Mason's fellow jockeys is found dead. The suspect, another rider, wants Mason's help, but Mason is reluctant to take it on. Then a note arrives:

TAKE THE STEVE MITCHELL CASE—AND LOSE IT.

DO AS YOU ARE TOLD. NEXT TIME,

SOMEONE WILL GET BADLY HURT. . . .

penguin.com

GHOST
LIGHT

Clare McNally

BANTAM BOOKS
TORONTO · NEW YORK · LONDON · SYDNEY

GHOST LIGHT

A Bantam Book / December 1982

ISBN 0-553-22520-0

Published simultaneously in the United States and Canada

Bantam Books are published by Bantam Books, Inc. Its trademark, consisting of the words "Bantam Books" and the por-
trayal of a rooster, is Registered in U.S. Patent and Trademark
Office and in other countries. Marca Registrada. Bantam
Books, Inc., 666 Fifth Avenue, New York, New York 10103.

PRINTED IN THE UNITED STATES OF AMERICA

H   0 9 8 7 6 5 4 3 2 1

Special thanks for their expert advice and support to Denise Marcil, Marc Tantillo, Linda Price, and Michael Pastore.

GHOST LIGHT

PROLOGUE
December 12, 1921

She was such a darling child. Bonnie Jackson was the little girl everyone wanted—bright, pretty, talented. At the tender age of five she'd already made a name for herself on Broadway, charming both audiences and critics with her incredible voice range and talent for acting. Even other actors, who saw kids and animals as proverbial menaces, enjoyed working with this cheerful, appealing child.

Sometimes, though, Bonnie wasn't very cheerful. On a particularly gloomy day in late autumn she sat in her dressing room and stared solemnly at the reflection in her vanity as her mother tied a frothy white bow in the child's shoulder-length black hair.

Bonnie was sad because her parents had just had an argument, one that left Mommy's mouth set hard and Daddy searching the room for a flask of bootleg whiskey. Bonnie's pink lips turned down in a pout, and her round cheeks flushed as she fought her tears. She hated it when her parents fought.

"Why the hell does that guy have to follow us to every theater?" Philip Jackson wanted to know.

"He's a friend, Phil," his wife answered. "Just a friend."

"I'm not an idiot, Margaret," Phil said. "I know what Aaron Milland means to you."

Bonnie looked up at her mother and in her desire to understand this argument dared to interrupt with a question.

"Do you like Aaron Milland, Mommy?"

Margaret glared at the reflection of her daughter's eyes, growing wider by the moment as Bonnie waited to be reprimanded. Sometimes Mommy became very angry with her. Sometimes, she even hurt her.

This time, however, she didn't say a word. Instead, she turned back to Phil.

"What does it matter, how Aaron and I feel about each other?" she demanded.

1

"Look," Phil said, "Bonnie shouldn't be hearing this. We can talk later in private."

Margaret sighed.

"All right, we'll talk later," she said. "Let's just concentrate on getting Bonnie ready for her debut."

As if by magic the stern look on her face fell away, replaced by a smile. Bonnie wished her mother would smile more often.

"Imagine," Margaret said, "our baby in the Winston Theater!"

"Only The Palace is bigger, Bonnie," Phil told his daughter.

Bonnie grinned at her father, her perfect white teeth glistening. He grinned back, caught a strand of his hair, and pushed it over his ear. It was plastered down with spice-smelling hair cream, parted in the middle and shining like the fender of a new Hudson Phaeton. Bonnie thought her daddy was very handsome. She loved him more than anyone, maybe even more than Mommy. Daddy never hit her, or yelled at her, or put her in dark places.

But she wouldn't think about the dark places. She'd think only of the songs she'd be singing tonight on the bright stage of the Winston Theater.

"Stand up now, darling," Margaret ordered.

Bonnie did as she was told, and modeled the new dress her father had ordered from Paris. Its hem was just fingertip length, and when she twirled around, rows and rows of lace ruffles fluttered like wispy clouds. Her parents admired her from head to toe, taking in her white bow, dress, stockings, and finally a pair of white Mary Janes with pearl buttons. It was when Margaret's eyes reached the shoes that her smile disappeared again.

Bonnie stopped dancing and stared at her mother with eyes that silently asked what she had done now. She was glad Daddy was here. Daddy wouldn't let her be hurt. He never did.

"My God, Phil!" Margaret cried. "Her shoes are scuffed, and she's on in five minutes!"

Bonnie looked down at the offending shoes and noticed that a few black streaks ran over the very tips of her toes.

"For crying out loud, Margaret," Phil said. "They're coming to hear her sing, not look at her shoes!"

"She has to be perfect," Margaret said. "I have to make her perfect."

She lifted Bonnie up and sat her on top of a black costume-trunk, quickly unbuckling the Mary Janes.

"Do you have any lighter fluid?"

Phil took out his silver flask of whiskey and joked, "This stuff'll set 'em on fire."

Bonnie giggled, and Margaret snapped, "I'm not amused!" And the little girl frowned again.

"Damn it," Phil said, reaching into the pocket of his pants. "Here, here's some lighter fluid. Jeez!"

Margaret went to work on the scuff marks. By the time she was done, Bonnie was being called on stage. Phil and Margaret took seats in the second row to watch her perform. The audience loved her here at the Winston Theater as had audiences everywhere else—they applauded and smiled and cheered the tiny performer. Some of the women and men even felt tears in their eyes.

But they didn't know the melancholy sweetness in her voice was not part of an act. All the while she was singing, Bonnie couldn't help thinking of the fight her parents had had. When she was finished, she met them in the wings, and holding Margaret's hand, she hurried back to her dressing room.

"You were terrific," Phil said. "Which you would have been with or without the scuff marks."

Margaret shot a look at him and pushed open the door to Bonnie's dressing room.

"As a matter of fact," Phil said, "a performance like that deserves a reward."

"I don't think that's necessary," Margaret said.

"Sure it is," Phil answered. "I'm going to head over to F.A.O. Schwartz and buy a new doll for you, Bonnie."

"Oh, Daddy!" the child squealed with delight. She ran to him and hugged him around the knees.

"I love you so much, Daddy," she said.

"And Daddy sure loves you," Phil replied.

Margaret stared icily at them, but said nothing. Phil took his trenchcoat down from its brass hook.

"I shouldn't be too long," he said. He reconsidered that

and glanced at his pocket watch. "Well, I guess the Christmas rush might delay me. Give me an hour."

"Phil, I think you're being foolish," Margaret commented.

But Phil only winked at Bonnie and left the room. Margaret began to see red, hating the fact that Bonnie was being rewarded simply for doing her job. What about Margaret? Why didn't Phil reward *her* for all the years she slaved to get the kid where she was? My God, she hadn't even wanted a baby! And look what sacrifices she'd made!

Her thoughts were cut off by a knock at the door. Bonnie watched her mother's face change once again from angry to cheerful as Aaron Milland walked into the room. The little girl shrank away from him, hating his gaunt cheeks and dark eyes. He reminded her of a skull. Ignoring Bonnie, Aaron pulled Margaret to him and kissed her neck.

"Mmm," she said. "Not here. Not here!"

She giggled and pushed him away.

Finally, Aaron noticed Bonnie. Bonnie didn't like Aaron Milland. He'd met her mommy last year during a preview run in Philadelphia, where he'd been stage manager. Now he followed them to every theater, always coming to see her mommy when her daddy wasn't around. Bonnie could sense there was something wrong with that.

"You kissed my mommy like my daddy used to," she said. "Why?"

Margaret gasped and put a hand to the low V-neck of her silky dress.

"How dare you ask such a question!" she cried. "Oh, Aaron, I'm so sorry. Sometimes she gets too big for her britches. It's this business, you know."

"That's okay," Aaron said. "No harm done. She's just a kid, Margaret."

"Nevertheless, I'd like you to excuse us," Margaret said.

Bonnie, though she didn't like Aaron, wished he wouldn't leave the room. What would her mother do to her? But he did, and now Margaret grabbed her by the arms, crushing the delicate organza of her puffed sleeves. Her long string of beads swayed forward, tapping the child's face lightly.

"You are rude, mean, and nasty," she hissed. "Aaron is my friend, and will be your daddy someday!"

"No!" Bonnie cried. "I only want my *real* daddy!"

Margaret slapped her little round cheek. Bonnie burst into tears and tried to pull away.

"You are a bad, bad girl," Margaret went on. "For being rude to Aaron, you'll stay in the closet until I come get you out!"

Bonnie kicked and protested with all her might as her mother pulled her toward the dark little closet. Why didn't anyone hear her? she wondered frantically. Why didn't one of the other performers come in and help, or even that Aaron? Bonnie decided then that she hated everyone in this theater. They didn't care what happened to her. They only cared if she made money for them.

Her mother shoved her into the closet. Bonnie's head struck the back wall, and she sat momentarily stunned as the door slammed shut and the lock clicked.

"Mommy, no!" Bonnie screamed. "No, please! I hate the dark! Please take the dark away!"

But the only reply was the sound of retreating footsteps and another door closing. Then laughter. Her mother was laughing, and so was Aaron! Bonnie recognized the deep voice of her mother's "friend."

"I hate you," she whispered, sniffling. "I hate you!"

She sat back and pulled her knees up to her chin, crying softly, rocking herself back and forth. Her daddy said he'd be right back. Maybe if she made herself small, if she closed her eyes, the monsters who hid in the closet wouldn't get her. Daddy would rescue her. Daddy always rescued her.

Cold and sick with fright, she collapsed into a deep sleep.

When her eyes opened again, it was darker in the closet than it had been earlier. Bonnie realized there was no light coming in from the room outside anymore. Had someone come and turned it off, not realizing she was in here? She crawled over to the door and tried to open it. Still locked.

"MOMMY!" she cried, pounding on the door. "MOMMY? PLEASE LET ME OUT!"

She would be good. She'd be a good girl if Mommy let her out. It was cold in here! And dark, so dark . . .

"I DON'T LIKE THE DARK, MOMMY!"

A door opened, there were footsteps, and suddenly Bonnie heard a key jangling in the closet lock. The door opened, but it was just as dark outside. She couldn't see who was there.

Strong arms lifted her, and Bonnie started to struggle. Who was it? Who was going to hurt her now?

"Hey, it's me!" a man's voice cried. "It's your daddy!"

Bonnie relaxed, as her small hands found the familiar comedy/tragedy pin he always wore on his coat.

"Oh, Daddy!" She buried her face in his shoulder and sobbed.

"Did your mother do this?"

Bonnie nodded. "She said I was rude to Aaron," Bonnie answered.

"Aaron?" Phil echoed. "Aaron was here?"

Again, the child nodded. "Daddy, why is it so dark?"

"We've lost all the lights. Must be a fuse, honey," Phil said. "Here, I'll light a candle."

Bonnie felt herself being placed on a velveteen loveseat. Her father kissed the top of her head, then went groping across the room to a chest of drawers. After a lot of rummaging noise, he found a candle and lit it. A soft glow illuminated the room, and Bonnie immediately felt better. Her daddy had brought the light.

"You wait here," he said. "Daddy's got a few words to say to Mommy."

"Daddy, where is everyone?" Bonnie asked. "Why didn't anyone hear me?"

"Everyone's gone home, darling," Phil said. He stopped and thought. "Didn't you know?"

"No, Daddy," Bonnie said. "I fell asleep."

Phil rubbed his eyes.

"You've been in that closet for three hours," he growled. "God, I'm sorry about that! I called your mother—she said everything was okay."

And all that time she was screwing Aaron . . .

"You just wait here," Phil said. "I'll be right back."

He opened a drawer in a tall cabinet, reached way into the back and pulled out a gun, grasping it firmly in a white-knuckled fist.

And then he left. Bonnie sat staring at the candle flame, waiting for him. But soon the candle burned out, and still her daddy hadn't returned. Terrified to be alone in the dark, Bonnie slid off the loveseat and decided she'd try to find him. She shuffled her way toward the door and opened it, entering the long hallway outside her dressing room. She could see nothing in either direction, but she could hear voices. Yelling voices—two men and a woman.

"If I follow them," she said out loud to reassure herself, "I'll find Daddy."

But it was so hard to tell where they were coming from in the theater's maze of pitch black hallways. Bonnie walked slowly, listening, turning when the sounds seemed to grow louder. But none of the doors she opened led to Daddy.

All of a sudden she heard the sound of running footsteps. And then her mother's voice crying, "That child is more trouble than she's worth! You keep her! I hate her!"

Bonnie's eyes filled with tears. Her mother really did hate her, didn't she?

And her mother was going to hurt her now. That's why she was running. To catch Bonnie. To hurt her.

Terrified, the child pulled open the nearest door. At first, when she felt some hanging sandbags and lengths of coiled rope, she thought it might be the stage. But no, this couldn't be the stage. There was no light here. Daddy told her that all stages had a "ghost light," a single bulb that always burned at the apron so that no one would walk off it in the dark. This had to be a storage room.

"BONNIE JACKSON, HOW DARE YOU RAT ON ME?"

Margaret's shriek resounded throughout the building. And then Phil's angry voice boomed out of the darkness.

"DON'T YOU HURT HER! I'll kill you if you touch my baby."

Bonnie prayed her daddy would come get her. She poked a thumb in her mouth (Mommy would smack her if she saw her) and started backing away from the door, afraid her mother would enter.

Suddenly, from some faraway part of the theater, came a loud, cracking noise. The sound of a gunshot startled Bonnie so that she lost her footing and tumbled backwards into a dark void. She screamed, realizing too late that the blackout had also claimed the ghost light. She crashed to the floor of the orchestra pit, her head striking a metal chair. Blackness came, and all the life and sweetness of the little girl who had charmed Broadway drained away—as easily as blood flows.

ONE

Music was playing, tinny as an old gramophone recording. And on a vast stage stood a beautiful, dark-haired child, singing sweetly to an invisible audience. To either side of her, gold and white curtains reached up toward colored lights. A man stood in the wings, feeling happy inside to hear her sweet voice. It was good, so very good.

And then the music stopped, abruptly, and darkness enshrouded the stage. The air grew hot and thick. The man felt his lungs tighten as he desperately sought to breathe. It was growing hotter by the moment, painfully hot. The little girl turned to him now with eyes that were huge with fear.

"Take the dark away! Please!" she screamed.

The man reached out, but he could not move. Flames illuminated the stage, racing around the man and teasing his pant legs. There was no escape. The child screamed and backed away from the fire. Suddenly he saw her small body disappear into the blackness of the orchestra pit.

"NNNNOOOO!!!"

The man broke free of the invisible force that held him and raced toward the apron of the stage, his arms outstretched. And then he, too, tripped down into the blackness, down and down, staring in horror as the fire claimed the gold and white curtains. He thrashed, feeling cloth entangle him. The curtains had torn from their rod, and he was entangled in them . . .

. . . in the comforter of a huge brass bed.

Nate Dysart sat up abruptly, a questioning noise escaping from between his chattering teeth. Confused, he looked around, trying to remember where he was. This wasn't his California apartment! This bed wasn't his! His room was never this dark before . . .

Trembling, he twisted the satin sheets and fought to calm himself. The room slowly began to look familiar. There was a tall armoire; there between two French windows stood a bookshelf. As his eyes adjusted to the light he saw a gold-

framed painting on one wall. It was just a bedroom. The stage
and the fire had been a dream.

But in his thirty-one years Nate had never been so un-
nerved by a nightmare. On the rare occasions he had them
he was usually able to forget them and fall right back asleep
again. But not tonight. He breathed heavily. He could hear
his heart pound. He was soaked with sweat. Suddenly he
realized where he was—in a bedroom of the Connecticut
estate where he'd grown up. He'd arrived two days ago to
attend his father's funeral.

But why would that make him dream about a little girl in a
burning theater?

Groggily, needing to clear his head, Nate got out of bed
and groped through the darkness to his bathroom. When the
light went on, a pale and unshaven face stared at him from
the mirror over the black marble sink. Nate groaned at his
reflection and turned on the cold water faucet.

Like a slap driven to the face of an hysterical man, the icy
liquid shocked him into complete wakefulness. Again and
again he brought up his cupped palms, soaking himself until
he had finally driven away much of the anxiety. With his eyes
squeezed shut, he reached out to find a towel.

It seemed to come to him from midair, and as he took it
Nate's hand brushed cool flesh.

"What the hell?!

He stumbled against the shower, grabbing for the curtains
to steady himself as a familiar voice said, "I'm terribly sorry,
sir. I didn't mean to startle you."

He rubbed his eyes and looked up at his father's butler, an
old man named Carl. Sitting down on the edge of the tub,
Nate said, "I must look like an idiot."

"Certainly not, sir," Carl said. He took the towel, folded it,
and returned it to its brass rod. "I shouldn't have entered
unannounced. But your father always insisted we servants
remain silent unless spoken to."

"You know I'm not like my father, Carl," Nate said, standing up again. He was dressed only in his briefs, and the
full-length bathroom mirror reflected a well-tanned, if slightly
underweight, physique. Nate rejected the satin robe Carl was
holding open for him. "I'm going right back to bed. What are
you doing up, anyway?"

"I heard you cry out, sir," Carl said. "Did you have a nightmare?"

Nate's head nodded, a strand of hair falling over his forehead. Pushing it back, he said, "One of the worst in my life. It was so real. But I'll be okay."

Carl followed him into the bedroom, switching off the bathroom light.

"Under the circumstances," he said, turning on a lamp and readjusting the twisted covers of Nate's bed, "I'm not surprised. You must be terribly exhausted after traveling all the way from California, and then attending your father's wake."

"I'd rather not think about it," Nate said, sitting on the edge of the bed. "I'm here because my father's financial adviser talked me into it, not because I want to be. You know how I felt about my father, Carl."

"Yes, sir," Carl said softly, reading bitter hatred in the younger man's eyes. "Sir, the funeral is in just a few hours. I suggest you try to sleep again."

Nodding, Nate lay back and closed his eyes. He wished he would not have to attend the funeral, but knew he had no choice. Not when a sizable inheritance was at stake.

Nathaniel Dysart Jr. had spent the first twenty-six years of his life living under the same roof as his multimillionaire father, and yet in all that time he had never grown close to the man. How could he, when Nathaniel Sr. had nothing but contempt for him? The beautiful Sandra Dysart had died giving birth to Nate, and his father held the innocent child responsible. But he had promised Sandra, the only woman he'd ever loved, that he'd always see to the boy's welfare. And so Nate was kept in the big, opulent mansion—a poor little rich boy, as the cliché goes. He often wondered, as he looked back on a lonely childhood filled with days of ridicule and abuse, if he might have been better off with strangers. His father was no more to him. A stranger who refused him love.

Yet here he was, dressed in a dark suit, standing in a cemetery as the local minister read a eulogy to the old man. He stared, expressionless, at an ivory-inlaid coffin. My father is in there, he thought. Dead at age sixty-seven of a stroke, and soon to be buried. Nate wished they would hurry. He wanted to get back to California, to forget all this.

"... a pillar of our community..."

The minister's nasal twang cut through the chilly November air. Of the three dozen people who had gathered for the funeral, not a single one had really cared for the old man. The senior Mr. Dysart had long ago alienated anyone he might have called "friend," with his miserly, temperamental ways.

No, they were all here to make an impression on Nate. And as far as the young man was concerned, they could all drop dead with his father. Including the pompous minister, who insisted upon telling them all how wonderful the old man had been. Maybe he hoped his church had been mentioned in the old man's will.

Lies, all lies, Nate thought.

He felt a hand on his shoulder and turned his head slightly to Jim Orland, his best friend. Without speaking, the stocky, curly-haired man was able to tell Nate he knew how hard it was to be here. He and Nate had been friends since early childhood, and Jim had often witnessed the cruel way Nate had been treated by his father. But he knew Nate was only here because his father's financial adviser had suggested it. As one of the few members left in the Dysart clan, he stood to inherit a great deal.

"That's a laugh," Nate had said to Jim at the wake. "If he left me anything, it'll be a few sticks of broken furniture or worthless stock."

"Then why'd you bother coming?"

Nate had shrugged. "I don't know. Maybe, after all that's happened, I'm still a hopeful kid. I'd still like to think my father had some affection for me, and any inheritance will make me believe that."

Here at the funeral there were others who had more than just a passing interest in Nathaniel Dysart Sr.'s will. The head of a major shipping company thought of the promise Dysart had made him for a considerable amount of money to bail him out of financial difficulties, and wondered if provisions had been made. Several people who had made large investments in Dysart Enterprises were so busy praying the old man's death wouldn't cause a dip in stock values that they didn't take time to pray for the deceased himself. And Nathaniel Sr.'s secretary, Lisa Bateson, was certain she would be fondly

remembered after thirty years of loyal service to the old
bastard.

Besides Nate, the only other relatives left behind were
Pearl and Vance Dysart. Because he was Nathaniel's only
nephew, forty-five-year-old Vance expected to take in a good
cut of the Dysart fortune. As far as he was concerned, he
deserved it more than Nate—who had been nothing but
trouble for his father from day one of his life. Now Vance
tilted his head back a little and stared across the coffin at his
cousin.

Look at him, he thought. Not a tear in his eye. He's glad
the old man is dead!

Nate caught him staring and held his eyes for a few
moments. Then he blinked and watched as the minister
splashed holy water on the ivory coffin. A faint aroma of
incense filled the air, followed by the jangling of bells.
Mesmerized by the minister's droning, Nate began to sway a
little. Suddenly, he was no longer looking at a white coffin.

In its place sat a simple pine casket, its only decoration a
gold cross. It was the coffin that had held his wife Meg five
years ago. He'd left for California right after that funeral.
Nate blinked, and the ivory casket was there again.

His mind wandered, carrying him back to the time when
Meg was alive. She had been so beautiful then, so happy.
Nate, Meg, and Jim had owned a tiny theater company
off-off-Broadway. But one day, there had been a terrible
accident, one that made Meg an invalid until her tragic death
several months later. He had wanted his own life to end, too.

Nate shook memories of that time from his head, letting a
cool gust of November air bring his senses back to him. He
watched grimly as four husky men, cemetery employees, took
the ends of the ropes that ran under the coffin. Carefully,
they lifted it up. The minister took Nate's hand and led him
to the grave's edge. Suddenly, Nate was reminded of the
orchestra pit in his dream, but the thought was lost when he
felt something cold in his hand. A shovel. He was expected to
throw in the first mound of dirt.

All of a sudden, a startled cry broke the solemnity of the
service, as one of the four men slipped on a slick patch of wet
grass. The rope flew from his hand, and the minister grabbed
desperately for it. But it was too late. The coffin fell off

balance and smashed to the ground below. It hit so hard on impact that the top half fell open, and the old man's head and arm flopped out.

Nate felt anger tighten his muscles as he looked into the pit at the thin old face. He hadn't wanted to see his father again, ever! In a moment of fury, he turned the shovel over and let dirt drop on the cadaver. For a second, he thought he saw the old man's lips curl into a sneer.

He's going to start yelling at me . . .

It was an unbidden thought, one that Nate had had many times during his childhood. Hearing it, he felt a chill rush through him as he realized he was still fearful of the old man—even in death. As the cemetery workers tried to organize themselves again Nate squinted and backed away from the site.

Please, God, make this day end quickly!

He wrapped his arms around himself as if to control his fears and stared at his shoes for the rest of the ceremony.

Despite the fears he'd experienced at the funeral, Nate was going to be all right. About thirty-million-dollars' worth of all-right, according to the family lawyer, and that was after taxes. To his shock, he learned that he hadn't inherited only those broken pieces of furniture and worthless stocks. Every piece of furniture, every stock and bond, every inch of property was his—as soon as the will was out of probate.

Strangely, no one else had been included in the will—not Lisa Bates, not his cousins, or anyone else. Nate decided he'd give Lisa something in gratitude for her years of service. And he'd make certain all his father's debts were paid off. But, as far as his cousins Vance and Pearl were concerned, Nate didn't care what happened to them. He and his only cousin had never been close.

Nate spent hours each day going over his father's papers, trying to understand the wealth and responsibility that was now his, and making plans for the future. A few weeks after the funeral, he met Jim for lunch. Nate had a letter his father had written to him just before his death and felt Jim was the only one he could trust to read it.

"He's going to get a dig at me any way he can," Nate said.

"Don't worry about him anymore," Jim said. "He's dead. Dead and gone."

"Just listen to this, anyway," Nate said. He held the letter toward the window for better light. A bus, advertising a new brand of liquor along its side, moved past his line of vision. "'Though I detest you, and though I never called you "son," I am leaving my fortune to you. Long ago, your mother made me promise all this would be yours. Because of my intense love for her, I will respect her wishes.'"

"You can almost read 'choke on it,' in that," Jim commented.

Nate refolded the letter and shoved it into the pocket of his western-style shirt.

"I can't imagine my father feeling intense love for anyone," he said.

Jim reached across the table and punched him lightly on the chin.

"Hey, forget it," he said. "You shouldn't let the old man bother you so much anymore. What do you care about him, anyway? You've made a name for yourself as a director in California, and all without a cent of his money."

"Yeah," Nate sighed. "Five years in California, directing theater productions, living in two-room apartments. And now I've got a mansion with more rooms than I can count."

"Do you intend to stay here in the East?"

Nate shook his head. "I don't know. There's no reason for me to leave, now that my father's gone and everything is taken care of back in California. I resigned from my job and managed to get out of the lease for my apartment."

He lifted his coffee cup and drained it, then rubbed his eyes.

Jim watched him, seeing weariness in his friend's expression, and he said, "There's been a lot on your mind, hasn't there? You look like you haven't slept since you came here."

"I've slept," Nate said as a waitress came to refill his cup. "But not too well. I keep having this weird nightmare."

"What about?"

"I'm standing in the wings of a theater," he said, "watching this little girl sing."

"Who is she?"

Nate shrugged. "Beats me. In the dream, I know her. But I don't recall her face when I wake up. Anyway, the theater suddenly goes black, and catches fire. She falls into the orchestra pit, and I fall in after her."

"I think you're just overexerted these days. Once your father's will is out of probate, you'll be living so easy that you won't worry about a thing anymore."

Nate still looked worried.

"Hey, eat already," Jim said. "Forget about the dreams. You're old enough to know there ain't no boogey man. Now what are you going to do with all that money?"

Nate laughed and started eating again. With his free hand, he opened a copy of *Variety* that sat on the table.

"I've got an ad running in here today," he said. He found the page and turned it toward Jim. "See what you think."

Jim read the quarter-page ad, calling for people to back an original production to be presented by Nathaniel Dysart Jr. He nodded, approving.

"With all your money," he said, "you could almost back the thing yourself. But that would be financially disastrous, of course. Even if you are the best director-producer I know."

"Flattery won't get you any further than you are," Nate said. "You're already my best friend. And, I hope, you'll be my assistant when I open the theater."

"You can bet on it," Jim said. "Got any ideas where you'll rent?"

Nate shook his head. "I looked around a bit this morning, but nothing impressed me. Anyway, there's time."

"This is gonna be like old times," Jim said. "The way it was before you took off to California."

"You know why I left, Jim," Nate said. "I couldn't stand being in New York. Everything I looked at reminded me of Meg."

Jim could see Nate falling into a depression and quickly changed the subject. Nate was too melancholy these days, Jim thought. He would have to see to it that his friend cheered up a bit.

"Remember the first company we tried to start?" he asked. "I think we were about eighteen."

"It was in the basement of our church," Nate said, "and the Seriant twins were our stars."

"So tell me," Jim said, laughing. "Did we spend more hours working, or making out with those two?"

"I couldn't guess," Nate said. "We must have done some work, because we managed to put on a play. God, we've come a long way since then."

Jim nodded in agreement.

"It's hard to believe you're going to open your own Broadway company," he said. "Even if you did make a name for yourself in California theater. By the way, have you thought about the play itself?"

"I want to do an original production of a comedy called *Making Good*. I read the script before I left California. It's great," Nate said. "And I'm going to get Sander Bernaux as the lead."

Jim laughed and cuffed his chin again. "Are you kidding?" he said. "Sander Bernaux is the biggest star on Broadway!"

"And you know how I've dreamed of working with him," Nate said. "My father used to say I'd never get to work with him, that I was too untalented."

"Your father said a lot of things, Nate," Jim said.

"Yeah, well, I'm going to prove my talent," Nate replied. "I'm going to get Sander Bernaux, no matter what. The part is perfect for him."

In truth, Jim wondered if Nate could handle a man like Bernaux. Sure, Nate was talented, dedicated, and hard-working. When they'd had the off-off-Broadway production company a few years ago, the critics were already noticing him. But Sander Bernaux was mean-tempered and pathologically suspicious of everyone. Jim hoped Nate could cope with him. But why not? He had coped with his father's temperament for most of his life. Bernaux couldn't be much worse.

"Hey," he said finally, "I'll bet he begs to work with you." He looked at his watch. "Speaking of work, I should remember I still belong to another production company. I've got to get back to the theater, Nate."

"Need a ride?" Nate asked, standing. "I came to New York in style today, you'll notice."

As he moved away from the table Jim looked out the window to see an antique Rolls-Royce waiting at the curb. Others had noticed it, too, for almost every passer-by on the crowded street stopped to gape at it.

"Really getting into this money thing, aren't you?" he teased as they walked towards the cashier.

"Oh, hell," Nate said. "You know I still prefer my jeans."

Jim laughed, knowing this was true. He couldn't really picture Nate as a member of the elite upper class, though his friend had been brought up surrounded by luxury. That luxury had never been shared between father and son.

They said good-bye outside the restaurant and walked in opposite directions. Nate climbed into the back of the Rolls and ordered George, his chauffeur, to head directly home. There was to be a meeting with his father's lawyers that afternoon, and Nate wanted to be ready for it. George nodded and turned on the ignition, easing the car into the street. Nate ignored the traffic, more interested in reading his copy of *Variety*. Suddenly, he felt a cold rush of wind and heard a voice say:

"I'm waiting for you!"

He looked up.

"What was that, George?"

"I didn't say anything, sir," George replied.

Nate let the matter drop, thinking it must have been one of the pedestrians crossing the street who had spoken. He turned a page of his trade paper and found the next one virtually blank, except for a small, two-line ad in its center. It gave an address, claiming this property was for sale.

"What a waste of space," Nate said. "They must be desperate to sell the place to take out an ad like this."

Still, the location was nearby, and he was intrigued. He ordered George to turn around and find it. The street was home for several theaters, office buildings, and restaurants. But there was no such number as the one given in the ad.

"Perhaps it's that empty lot we passed," George suggested.

"Let's take a look," Nate said.

After George had managed to find a parking space around the corner, Nate left the car and made his way back to the site. It was located between a restaurant and hotel, a dead spot on an otherwise lively street. Cinder blocks were scattered over its unkempt grass, a resting place for cigarette butts, tattered newspapers, and rusted cans. But there were no signs indicating the property was for sale.

Nate's eyes were drawn to a cloud of white smoke that hovered over the grass, then disappeared. He heard a small voice.

"We'll be together, soon."

It was a childish voice with a faint southwestern accent.

But when Nate looked around, he saw he was alone. None of the people walking by even looked at him.

"Funny," he said out loud, his words making clouds in the chilly air, "that's the second time I thought I heard voices."

But he wasn't going to worry about it. Like the dreams, it was probably caused by having so much on his mind. He knew what stress could do to you. Like after Meg died. . . .

Suddenly, he felt someone touch his arm. He turned quickly to see a dirty, ragged old man gazing at him through filmy eyes that might once have been bright blue. But years of drinking had taken their toll, and Nate could smell the pungent aroma of stale wine when the man spoke.

"Bad t'ings happen at dis place," he said, his mouth toothless and slack.

He belched loudly, the sickening odor of his breath making Nate turn away with a grimace. The old man shook his head and shuffled off down the street, scratching the seat of his pants with fingers that poked through torn knit gloves.

"Crazy old man," Nate growled.

Well, he thought, weirdos like that came with the territory. They were all part of the ingredients that made New York interesting. If he built a theater right on this spot, it would just add to the fascination. And why shouldn't he do just that, he thought? He certainly had the money for it. He'd call the realtor this afternoon. Imagine, not only his own company, but his own theater, built to his own specifications, a building to last into the next century and to bear his name.

Nate climbed into the back of the Rolls and lifted his copy of *Variety* from the floor. He flipped through it, trying to find the ad. But it wasn't there anymore. Finally, after going over each page twice, he dropped it to the floor again. The page had probably fallen out when he'd opened the car door.

The address, though, had stuck in his mind. When he arrived home, he had his father's secretary call several dozen realtors until she finally located someone who claimed the property. It was for sale, they told Nate. But they were surprised to learn where he'd heard of it. No one at their office had put any ads in *Variety*.

TWO

The next weeks were the most hectic Nate had ever known. There were papers to be read and signed, contracts to be drawn up regarding purchase of the property, and contracting companies to be negotiated with to make the best deal possible for building his theater. But he didn't mind the fast pace. It left him so exhausted at night that only twice had he experienced that strange nightmare.

Finally, after the will came out of probate and he had signed the last paper necessary to make him owner of the vacant lot, Nate hired the best architect in New York to work with him on the theater's design. He sat with Fred Johnson now in his midtown Manhattan office, going over sketches laid out on a drafting table.

"I see you've incorporated the Art Nouveau theme I wanted," Nate said.

"What made you choose something so decorative?" Fred wanted to know. "These days, most of my clients want the Bauhaus style—steel and glass, that is."

"It's just something I've always liked," Nate said.

During a dark and ugly childhood he had developed a taste for beautiful things, but he did not discuss this with Fred.

The architect rummaged through the papers on his drafting table and pulled out a watercolor sketch.

"Look at this," he said, "it's my initial idea for the building's facade. I thought stone ivy would look good encircling the doors."

"Fine," Nate said. He clapped his hands together once, then slid off his three-legged stool. "Well! Since I want construction to begin as soon as possible, I'll leave you alone with your work. You're on the right track."

"I'll call you with a progress report in a few days," Fred said.

Nate left the office, feeling elated. Soon he would have his own theater. As he stood waiting for the elevator he hummed a tune. It almost masked the sound of a light voice calling out to him.

"I'm waiting for you!"

Nate looked behind and around himself, but the hallway was empty. Reasoning it must have come from one of the half-dozen offices along the hall, he was about to enter the elevator when he heard it again.

"Take the dark away, please! Please take the dark away!"

Nate shuddered and hurried onto the elevator. As the doors closed he tried to turn his thoughts elsewhere. But one fact kept haunting him. In the dream the little girl had said almost the same thing as that voice he'd just heard. It hadn't come from behind one of those office doors, but from his own mind. The dream was following him in daylight now.

"When the hell is this going to stop?" he asked the flashing elevator numerals.

In the lobby, he hurried out to the street and waited for George to arrive with the car. He would keep even busier than he'd been, he thought. That way, he would have no time for tricks of the mind.

Upstairs in the hallway outside Fred Johnson's office, a little girl walked, unseen by the two gossiping secretaries. She didn't like this big building, with its cold beige walls. But she had to be here. There were things to be done. She moved towards the door to Fred Johnson's office.

Fred put down his mechanical pencil and went to open the door. It was suddenly very stuffy in the room, and he thought he might get some cross-ventilation from the hallway. He should complain about the thermostat. They weren't supposed to let it get this hot in here anyway, were they? Energy conservation and all.

He rubbed his eyes and yawned.

"Don't know why I feel so tired," he said out loud, heading back to his drafting table.

For a moment he couldn't see the table or anything in front of him. It was as if a black curtain had been drawn down over his eyes. He swayed a little; his head felt very light. From somewhere deep in his mind he heard voices, voices that commanded him to return to work. In less than a minute Fred was sitting at the table again. He had no memory of his dizzy spell or even of getting up and opening his door. The temperature was normal again, and in Fred's mind it had never changed. He picked up his pencil and went to work again, so busy over the next hours that he did not stop to question why, when Nate had agreed the original designs were just fine, he was completely changing everything he'd drawn so far.

Nate could not stop thinking about the voice he'd heard. He was certain it had come from his mind, and yet it seemed external, as if someone unseen were following him around. He knew, though, that this was ridiculous. It was tension, just like everyone said it was. And now to ease some of it, he was lying in a room in his father's house (he wondered when he'd begin to think of all this as his) under the care of a masseuse.

Lulled by the kneading of his muscles, he soon fell into a deep sleep. But it was not a restful one. The dream came again. The little girl began to sing, surrounded by the gold and white curtains. And then the darkness came, and the heat and the fire and the falling...

"Wake up, Mr. Dysart!"

The masseuse was patting his cheek when Nate opened his eyes.

"You were dreaming again," she said. "You're really very tense, sir. Do you want me to set up the whirlpool?"

Nate rubbed his eyes and sat up, feeling weakened by the dream. When would they stop? He felt as if he were being maneuvered towards something, as if the dreams were trying to control him.

"No, I'll just take a shower," he mumbled as the masseuse helped him to his feet. Feeling like a helpless old man, he tried to put strength in his voice when he said, "Don't worry about me."

Everyone *was* worrying about him since his return East.

"Swimming in January," Jim said with wonder as he pulled himself up a steel ladder leading from Dysart Manor's enclosed pool. "This place never fails to amaze me."

Nate rubbed himself briskly with a towel.

"It's good for what ails you, anyway," he said. "I might consider keeping the housing up all year round."

"It's better to let the sun shine down unobstructed in the summer," Jim said.

The pool was just outside the mansion, and because of the cold weather, it had been covered by a movable glass and steel frame. There were dressing rooms at one end of it, and the two men headed to these. They spoke through a natural-wood divider as they dressed.

"Think you'll ever get used to calling this place your own?"

"I lived here for twenty-six years," Nate said. "I could live here another twenty-five, and still refer to everything as 'my father's.' I'm more at home in a theater, Jim."

He pulled a velour sweatshirt over his head and tucked it into his jeans, then walked barefoot from the cubicle, carrying his shoes. Jim was already sitting on a bench, tying his own.

"How's this theater of yours coming?" Jim asked.

"I've spoken to Fred Johnson a few times since our first meeting three weeks ago," Nate said. "He's really brilliant and dedicated to his work. He changed everything around from the originals because he thought he'd found a more effective design."

"Good for him," Jim said. He looked at his friend. "Did you like what he did?"

Nate shrugged. "Blueprints mean nothing to me. I'm waiting for him to do some drawings."

Jim stood up and started to roll his wet towel and bathing suit, but Nate stopped him.

"I've got maids to handle that sort of thing," he said. "Just leave it there."

"Big shot," Jim said, cuffing Nate's chin.

In the library Nate fixed drinks. Settling down in a huge leather rocking chair, Jim swiveled back and forth and looked around at the safari trophies on the walls.

"The idea of killing a wild animal disgusts me," he said. "When I was a kid, my favorite show was *Wild Kingdom*. It breaks my heart to see life destroyed just to decorate a wall."

Nate looked up at a bear's head.

"My father didn't sympathize with anything," he said, feeling the bitterness rise in him again. As if to wash it away, he took a long sip of his drink.

"Hey, easy with that stuff," Jim said. "That's good scotch you've got there."

"I just had a thought about my father," Nate said.

Jim lifted his glass.

"Then drink up," he said, "I thought I told you to forget about that old bastard. Exorcise his ghost. Why do you even think about him?"

"I don't know," Nate said. "It's hard to put it out of my mind. You know the funeral was barely two months ago and I've gotten a few nasty letters from people who thought they belonged in my father's will. They keep reminding me of him."

"They're crazy. Just think about your theater," Jim said. "That should be your only concern."

"Right," Nate said, finishing his drink.

The theater alone, he thought. No nightmares, no visions of his father. Just the theater.

Later that night, while going over papers in his father's study, Nate was interrupted by the jangling of the telephone. Still working as he said "hello," he did not hear the name mentioned at the other end.

"Pardon?" he asked, clicking his pen shut.

"Your cousin, Vance, Nate," a man's voice said. "Callin' to ask about your daddy's will."

"It's none of your business," Nate said.

"It sure as hell is!" Vance cried. "I figure it must be out of—of—what's that word? Predate?"

"Probate," Nate said.

"Well?" Vance drawled. Nate did not answer him directly, and so he went on. "Now, you listen. You know I was very close to dear Uncle Nathaniel. I've got to be one of his heirs!"

You hated his guts just like everyone else, Nate thought.

"I'm sorry," he said, "but you weren't included in the will."

Nate heard a sharp noise, like a fist striking a tabletop. He sighed and looked up at the elk's head over the door. Thank God he only had one relative!

"Some of that money is rightfully mine!" Vance yelled. "I was better to your father than you ever were! You couldn't have gotten all his money."

Impatiently, Nate slammed down the receiver. He was

too busy to bother with an idiot like Vance Dysart, a man who carried a perpetual chip on his shoulder.

Fred Johnson had been working on his sketches for Nate's theater for nearly three weeks when he finally decided he was satisfied with the finished product. He held a watercolor rendering at arm's distance and scrutinized it. It was perfect, right down to the gold filigree on the wainscotting, and about as opulent as Louis XIV's palace.

"I'm usually better at Bauhaus designs," he said. "God knows where I got the inspiration for this thing."

The room grew cold suddenly, as if an icy wind had found its way through the vents. Fred buttoned his sweater, unaware that he was being watched. When the cold snap passed, Fred went back to work, adding a few finishing touches here and there.

That afternoon, he met with Nate. The young producer rolled open the blueprints on the drafting table and held either end with his palms to keep them from snapping closed.

"That's an outer hallway," Fred said, pointing. "It should keep things flowing smoothly during performances."

"Good idea," Nate said.

The next blueprint was a cross-section.

"Why so much space between the first floor and basement?" he asked.

"Those are air passages," Fred explained, "for air conditioning and heating equipment."

Nate made a grunting comment and rerolled the papers. Fred Johnson was working for him because he was the best money could buy, and obviously he knew what he was talking about.

"Have you got any sketches of the finished theater?" he asked.

"There on my desk," Fred answered. "In the black portfolio."

Plastic pages slid to either side of metal rings as Nate opened the leather folder. He flipped back to the first page and studied the series of watercolor renderings Fred had done. The color that dominated all the pictures was gold. The seats were gold, the wainscotting, the trim along the balcony. A painting of the stage showed that its curtains were to be done in gold, too, with white designs woven through them.

"Very nice," Nate commented, turning the page.

But a second later, he turned back again. He studied the picture of the stage for a few moments. The dream. In the dream, the curtains were gold and white.

"Why did you choose this color scheme?" he asked, abruptly.

"You wanted it to be opulent," Fred answered. "What's more elegant than gold?"

"Crimson is regal-looking," Nate snapped.

"But I think gold works better," Fred pressed. He did not know why, but it seemed important not to change any details of his work.

"Forget it," Nate said. "Gold is fine."

He felt a little idiotic, having reacted so strongly to a simple color scheme. The fact that these curtains were gold and white was coincidental, of course!

"It's all very beautiful," he said, a little more calmly. "How soon will it be complete?"

"There are a few minor details left," Fred said. "But I should be through by the end of the week."

Nate pulled one of Jim Orland's business cards from his pocket and handed it to the architect.

"My stage manager will be handling this," he said. "You can have the finished drafts sent to his place."

With that, Nate left the studio and waited in the hallway for the elevator. To his relief, there were no voices to haunt him. When he left the building, he walked a few blocks to the nearest bus stop. It amused him that people would stand in the middle of the street watching for a bus, as if that would make it come faster. But after standing for five minutes, he understood their impatience. He wished he had brought the car today, but George had been sick and he had taken the train.

Finally, the bus arrived, very crowded. Though it was a cool March day, the bus was uncomfortably hot and Nate was glad when he reached his destination.

Whenever he came into New York, he liked to stop at the property he'd bought and imagine his theater there. He had been approached by quite a number of people willing to back his production. As Nate walked toward the lot he smiled to think some of those backers were acquaintances and contacts of his father's. The old man had had a great deal of disdain for the theater and would be turning over in his grave if he knew

how his business associates were fawning over the son he
hated.

It amused Nate to imagine how those stuffy old men would
cringe at the sight of the broken, gum-encrusted, littered
sidewalk that ran in front of the property their money had
helped buy. He stepped aside to let a bag lady get by, her
small brown eyes staring down at the toes of her pink
bedroom slippers. Suddenly, she looked up at the lot and
shook her head sadly, her thin lips forming a string of silent
words. Then she continued on her way, as if anxious to get
away, teetering back and forth between the loaded shopping
bags she held in either hand.

The chain-link fence was surrounded by tall planks of
wood, which were already covered with graffiti and posters.
Nate, who loved children, though it might be a nice gesture
to the city to allow some school kids to paint over it. Just as
this idea occurred to him he noticed a little girl watching
him, half-hidden in the doorway of the adjacent building.
Nate smiled at her.

"Hi," he said. "What're you doing there?"

The child whimpered and pulled herself further into the
doorway. Funny, one didn't usually see small children left
alone on the city streets. Sensing she might need help, Nate
approached her.

But the doorway was empty. Nate reached for the handle of
the door and tried to pull it open. It was locked.

"She must have gone inside," he rationalized. "I don't
know how kids move so fast."

But it wasn't his problem. He returned to the lot and
unlocked the gate, aware that curious passers-by were looking
at him, probably wondering what new building would be
erected there. Nate opened it and walked onto a stretch of
smooth dirt. At his orders, the place had been cleaned up
after its purchase. The dead grass had been plowed under,
the bottles and cinder blocks and litter had been hauled away.
Nate leaned back against the fence and shoved his hands into
his pockets, the words "Dysart Theater" coming to mind. He
smiled.

"Pretty soon," he said.

He left the site and locked the gate behind himself, then
headed over to Broadway to take a taxi to Grand Central

Station. A thousand people saw him, but no one would recall his face. No one but a little girl who stood on the sidewalk with her arms outstretched, watching him fade into the distance.

After Fred Johnson finished his work, Nate went over the plans with Jim and then sent them to the contracting company he'd hired. In the meantime, he began interviewing people to man his stage.

"I'm glad that's over with," Nate said after the final employee had been hired. "God, do you realize it's April already? I've never interviewed so many people in my life!"

"Hey, look," Jim said, "it keeps you off the streets. And you'd better get used to seeing people. You're a big producer now, Nate. We do things on a bigger scale here on Broadway than you did in California."

Nate squinted.

"Off-Broadway was never like this," he said.

There was a knock at the door, and Jim got up to answer it. Virginia Atwell, an older woman whom Nate had hired as casting director, entered the room.

"How's the deal with Sander Bernaux?" he asked.

"I've spoken to his agent half a dozen times," Virginia replied. "We're still negotiating his contract. He's tough."

"Give him whatever he wants," Nate said.

Jim folded his arms and said, "Nate, that kind of talk could get you into a lot of trouble."

"What do you mean?"

"I mean," Jim said, "if Bernaux sees you're desperate he'll milk you for everything he can get."

Virginia looked from Jim to Nate. "I agree," she said. "I've worked with him several times, and I know how ruthless he can be."

Nate turned to gaze out the window for a few moments before replying. Across the street, he could see a garment factory, where several dozen women were hunched over gray sewing machines.

"You also know how much it means to me to work with one of Broadway's greatest actors," he said, still watching the factory. "I've got to prove to my father that..."

"Nate, your father is dead," Jim interrupted. He waved a

hand at Virginia, dismissing her so that they could talk privately.

"Why do you have to prove something to a dead man?" he asked.

Nate finally met his eyes. "Maybe I'm trying to prove it to myself, then," he said.

"Prove what?" Jim demanded. "That you're good enough to work with a guy like Bernaux? You already know that's true."

"You know what my father used to say to me?" Nate said in reply. "Whenever he heard Meg and me talking about someday working with a star like Sander Bernaux, he'd start in with that crazy laugh of his and he'd say, 'Sander Bernaux wouldn't spit on you, let alone work with an untalented amateur!' And then he'd ask how I dared hope I'd ever be a success."

"Nate, your father was a jackass," Jim said, straightening. "Forget him, will you?"

"I can't," Nate insisted. "It's something embedded too deeply in me."

For a few moments, both men were silent. Jim watched Nate's expression, reading bitterness in his eyes. Nate would probably never get over the pain of his childhood, Jim thought. And those strange nightmares. What were they about? A little girl in a burning theater. Very symbolic. He was beginning to have an idea of what they meant.

"I've just figured something out," he said.

"What's that?"

"Maybe those dreams of yours have something to do with this obsession you have," he said. "Maybe that little girl isn't really a little girl at all, but represents something. The burning stage, too, and the orchestra pit."

Nate shook his head.

"I don't go for that supernatural stuff," he said.

"Listen to me," Jim pressed. He held up a hand and started pressing back his fingers with the other. "First, let's look at the kid. Could she be your career, begging to be started again? Second, the burning theater. Maybe that represents your fear that you might not be successful. It would make sense, considering how your father criticized you all the time."

"Sounds interesting," Nate said. He liked the idea that there might be a simple explanation to the nightmares and encouraged Jim to go on.

"Finally, there's the orchestra pit you fall into," Jim said. He cocked his hand back and forth, making a comparison. "Falling—plunging. You're plunging into a career no matter what the consequences. And I think that means, Nate, that you're going to do all right."

Nate grinned.

"You sound more like a psychiatrist than a stage manager," he said.

"But doesn't it make sense?" Jim asked.

"Yeah, I guess so," Nate shrugged.

But it made perfect sense. And Nate decided he would hold on to Jim's simple explanation. It was better than believing he was being tormented by some uncontrollable force.

THREE

Nate often visited the site where his new theater was being built, watching its progress with a feeling of excitement and pride. He ached for the day it would bear his name and decided to keep a record of the building stages so that he could look back on them one day and remember this happy time. He bought himself a camera and took pictures of the men digging the foundation, pouring the concrete, erecting the steel girders. The roll was completed about the same time as the building's frame, and Nate mailed it to a local developing studio. It was Jim who brought him the return package one morning, along with a pile of other mail.

"We've got an article in the *Times* today," he said, putting the pile on Nate's desk. "And another in *Architect's Digest*. That one has a four-color shot."

"Great," Nate said, removing the red-and-white photo envelope. "I'll take a look at it in a minute. First I want to see how my own pictures came out."

He slid them out, being careful not to drop the negatives, and started thumbing through them. The first few were good shots, taking in details such as a worker's hands on a drill or the date etched into the foundation's corner. Nate handed them up to Jim one at a time but stopped when he found a picture with a flaw, a white blur that hovered just above one of the girders. Further inspection showed that all of the other pictures were marked in the same way, though the blurs were in different places and varied in size.

"I'd better stick to directing," Nate joked. "I didn't do very well with my new camera."

"These pictures are fine," Jim said, holding up the first few. "What's wrong with those?"

He came around to Nate's side and looked at the remaining photos.

"Kind of looks like a person," he said. "See those two sticks coming out of the bottom? They could be legs."

"Hovering in midair?" Nate asked. "Hey, knock off the spooky stuff. You'll make me have those nightmares again."

Jim put the photos down on the desk.

"How long has it been since the last one?" he asked thoughtfully.

"A couple of months," Nate said, smiling. "Ever since you gave me that crazy explanation of yours."

"See what I told you?" Jim asked. "It was just your subconscious trying to relay a message to you. Now that the theater is going up, you don't need those dreams anymore."

"I *have* relaxed a great deal since the funeral," Nate agreed. "In spite of the annoying phone calls I keep getting from my cousin Vance. He doesn't really bother me, though. And I suppose the fact that Virginia's finally reached an agreement with Sander Bernaux's agent has something to do with it."

"When are you meeting with him?"

"After the preliminary auditions," Nate said. "I wish it could be sooner, but a man like Bernaux always has other commitments. But, since we have to wait for the theater to be completed anyway, it doesn't really matter."

Jim nodded. "So long as someone doesn't come along and steal him from us."

"Don't say that," Nate ordered. "I've got Sander Bernaux under contract, and that's that."

In the autumn of 1981 the finishing touches were put on the Dysart Theater, and at last Nate's lifelong dream became a reality. A small gathering of press people joined the employees of Nate's company, taking pictures and scribbling notes as they all watched the theater's name being chiseled into the stone above the doors.

"It's finally real," Nate whispered to Jim. "I can't believe it!"

"It's yours, all right," Jim said. "You've got your name up there to prove it."

"This theater is going to be the most famous on Broadway," Nate promised himself, out loud. "In a year's time, everyone will know its name."

"Good luck with it, Nate," Jim said.

Just then, as the last letter was carved, everyone burst into applause. Nate grinned, turning up his collar against the cold September air.

Nearby, an elderly wino took a swig from a bottle hidden in a paper bag. They'll be sorry, he thought. This was a bad place, an unlucky place. A lot had happened here.

But Nate and the others were too elated to think anything but good thoughts. The wino shook his head and staggered away, a piece of discarded newspaper rolling in the wind and catching his ankles. He bent down to pick it up and stuffed it into a torn pocket of his jacket. He felt a cold chill as he did so, but thought it was only another gust of wind.

"Dennis Richmond," a woman with a southern accent said loudly to the young boy seated beside her on the subway train, "why must you always carry that silly basketball?"

"It isn't silly," her eleven-year-old son replied. "Daddy sent it to me, and I like it."

"Don't sass me," Georgia Richmond scolded. "I'll tell you what's silly and what isn't. A boy your age couldn't possibly know."

Denny shifted on the hard plastic seat and looked up at his mother.

"I do so know," he said. "I know going to five auditions in two weeks is stupid. None of those TV guys wanted me—I'm sure. Same thing with that theater we went to.

"You just have to be patient, Denny," Georgia said, kissing the brown hair that hung loosely over his ears and forehead. "There hasn't been a chance for anyone to give us a call-back. Someone will hire you, of course. Remember how everyone praised your acting down home?"

"South Carolina isn't the same as New York City," Denny protested.

That was for certain, he thought, looking around at the unintelligible graffiti that completely covered the walls. Above a row of seats crammed with sour-faced passengers, someone had drawn private body parts on a woman clad in a bikini who was grinning out from a poster written in Spanish. If someone did that in his hometown, Denny thought, he'd spend a week in jail!

As the train came to a halt at the Forty-second Street station Georgia stood up and took Denny by the hand. People jostled them back and forth in a mad rush to the stairs. Georgia yelped as she felt someone pinch her backside. She pulled Denny close to her and quickened her pace. She held him tightly, afraid he'd come in contact with the walls, which were covered with filth sprayed from thousands of trains. As another train rumbled into the station, they reached a flight of stairs and hurried up them. Traffic was as insane as ever in busy Times Square, and Georgia was tempted to hang on to Denny to protect him from the taxi drivers who screeched around corners without looking.

"Button your jacket," Georgia ordered. "It's cold out here and I don't want you sniffling during your audition."

Denny shifted his basketball to his other arm, then buttoned his corduroy jacket, weaving in and out of the crowds as he did so. He thought it was funny that you could rarely walk a straight line in New York City.

"I sure hope we don't have to wait for two hours," he said, "like the last audition!"

"A good actor never gives up," Georgia said, taking his hand once more to cross the busy street.

At last they reached their destination. Georgia stopped momentarily to admire the facade of the theater, praying that her son might someday work inside it. Elaborate curvilinear motifs swirled around the glass doors which were trimmed in highly-polished wood. Georgia pushed through them and found a sign directing her to the auditions. Denny opened one of the vestibule's etched glass doors for her and together they entered a crowded lobby.

"My goodness," Georgia drawled. "I didn't expect it would be like this!"

The other auditions had been crowded, but the lobby of the Dysart Theater was so full of hopefuls that Georgia could hardly make her way to the line at the sign-in table. Determined, though, she pushed Denny ahead of her and took a place behind a red-haired woman. She tapped her on the shoulder and said, "Is this where we give our name?"

The young woman smiled.

"Yes, it is," she said. She looked at Denny. "Hi, I'm Adrian St. John. And I suppose you're trying out for the part of Jimmy Bertrand?"

"He sure is," Georgia said before Denny could speak. She kissed his freckled cheek, making him squirm a little. "My little Denny is going to make them forget every other kid here today."

Adrian laughed, seeing the way Denny rolled his eyes. She understood how embarrassed a kid his age could be by his mother, having several younger brothers of her own. Georgia, she thought, was like a character in her own comedy, with bleached-blonde hair and a bright multicolored dress. Adrian was glad to see Denny had worn a white shirt and dark slacks. Appearances meant a lot when you were competing with so many others.

"I'm trying out for the part of Jimmy's mother," she said, moving forward with the line. "Daisy Bertrand, that is."

"You're really calm," Denny said, in a southern accent not quite as thick as his mother's. "You must go to a lot of auditions."

Adrian held up a small hand to show him the trembling there.

"I could do this every day," she said, "and never get used to it."

"But you must have experience?" Georgia asked.

"A few heads off-Broadway," Adrian said. "And I had a minor role in Horace Rightwood's last production here on Broadway. But it was all comedy, so that gives me an edge here."

Adrian gave her name and address to the woman seated at the sign-in table and noticed there were quite a few other names listed under "Daisy". That meant she would have a little time to go out for some fresh air and calm down.

"Good luck," Georgia said as she moved off the line.

"You mean, 'break a leg,'" Adrian said with a smile. "Thanks. Maybe we'll work together, huh, Denny?"

The little boy nodded, then took his place in front of the table.

"Full name, please," the woman said, her pencil held over a yellow pad.

"Dennis Randall Richmond," Georgia said. "He's eleven years old, and..."

The woman looked up at her.

"I'd like the boy to speak for himself," she said. "Now, Dennis, where are you currently living?"

Denny told her, and the woman recorded the information. Then she pulled another pad in front of herself and wrote his name. Denny watched his name go under the subtitle "Jimmy" and saw the number fifty-eight go before it. The woman waved her pencil at him and said, "You can find a place to sit until we call you. And be sure to leave that basketball with your mother."

Before leaving, Georgia asked if there was a bathroom open.

"Upstairs," the woman said.

"I want you to try to go," Georgia said as she and Denny moved back into the clusters of waiting actors.

"Mom," Denny gasped. "Don't talk like that with so many people around!"

"I don't care," Georgia said, though she lowered her voice. "I want us to be right here when they start calling names. What will I say if you're off in the little boys' room then?"

"I'll be okay," Denny said. "For crying out loud, Mom. I'm not in diapers anymore!"

Georgia pointed toward the vast staircase and, with her expression, ordered obedience. Shaking his head, Denny handed her the basketball and headed toward the stairs, leaving her to talk to a young man. As soon as he started up the stairs, Denny forgot his embarrassment. He'd never seen stairs so huge in his entire life or a banister so polished.

"If I get hired, I'm going to slide down this thing," he promised himself.

He stopped at the top landing and folded his arms over the railing. From here, he could take in details of the crowded lobby. There was a huge concession stand at one end, trimmed with gold that swirled in a flowery pattern. Two bronze statues of Greek goddesses stood on either side of the etched glass doors leading into the auditorium. Denny's eyes moved to take in the bar, empty now, with three small chandeliers that hung from the ceiling, and a door at the far end marked No Admittance.

Then he saw his mother looking up at him and hurried away. But when he was certain she could no longer see him, he opened one of the doors leading into the mezzanine. It was chilly and dark inside, and Denny had to wait a moment for his eyes to adjust to the tiny lights that dotted the rows of seats. Holding out his arms to balance himself, he walked down toward the railing. What he saw there made him gasp with awe.

The stage was the biggest he'd ever seen in his life, draped with gold and white curtains that seemed to glitter like stars. A huge chandelier, which Denny was certain contained a few thousand pieces of crystal, swayed almost imperceptibly overhead. He raised his eyes further and saw a ceiling painted to resemble a sky. At each corner there was a painting that depicted one of the four seasons. Old man Winter blew clouds that whirled all around, Spring was wrapped in curling flowers, and Summer and Autumn carried on the same flowing theme.

"Gosh," Denny whispered.

Wondering what else there was to see, he turned toward the doors again. But as he did so, someone appeared in front of him in the dark. With a cry, Denny stumbled backward, landing hard on his rump.

From the stage down below, someone called, "Who's up there?"

Denny looked up to see a little girl. Realizing he was in no danger, except of getting in trouble for being there, he ignored the man on the stage and raced toward the door. When he got out in the hallway, he was surprised to see the little girl already there.

"Whatja go sneaking up on me like that for?" he demanded.

She did not reply. Denny sat on one of the velveteen chairs lining a wall and sighed. The child stood in front of him, staring at him with dark eyes. She was wearing a white dress layered with rows of frilly ruffles, and her dark hair was drawn to one side with a frothy white bow. Denny guessed she was in costume.

"What part are you trying out for?" he asked. "I don't remember seeing any other little girls in the lobby."

She shook her head.

"I'm all alone," she said. "This is my theater."

"Oh, I get it,". Denny said. "Your Daddy owns the place."

His mother had told him that Nate Dysart was very rich. In his hometown in South Carolina the rich people always put their little girls in fussy dresses like the one this kid was wearing. He didn't like those rich, snobby kids. And he had already decided he didn't like this little girl. Why did she have to stare that way?

"Don't you have some place to go?" he asked.

"This is my place," she replied. "I'm always here."

Denny stood up and headed for the men's room, figuring she wouldn't follow him in there. But she did, and she leaned against a marble urinal as he unzipped his pants. He quickly closed them again and cried, "Will you get lost?"

"No," she said. "This is my theater, and you can't tell me what to do!"

"Boy, what a brat!" Denny said. "I'm going downstairs. Why don't you try to find your mother?"

His words upset the child so much that she started screaming, a high-pitched wail that made Denny cover his ears.

"Cut it out!" he ordered.

She glared at him.

"Don't want to see Mommy," she hissed. "Mommy made it dark and the dark hurt me!"

Denny watched her for a moment, then decided she was crazy and ran out of the bathroom. He did not look back as he bounded down the stairway, hoping he'd gotten rid of her. He decided then he was glad he didn't have any little sisters.

An hour and a half passed before Adrian's name was called. She said good-bye to Denny and entered the auditorium with several others, behind Virginia Atwell. Once on stage, she was handed a script and positioned up center. Adrian could see about a dozen people in the seats below, all holding black notebooks. They ranged in age from thirteen to eighty, representing a cross-section of people who might be found in any given audience. Adrian knew the "casting committee" had been selected so that the director could get an idea how an actor related to different audience types.

Now a handsome, blond-haired man in a plaid shirt spoke up, telling one of the other women to read the part of Daisy, and assigning the part of Jimmy to a young boy. The others, including Adrian, were given peripheral roles.

"You can start any time," Nate said, biting the end of his pencil.

Adrian was surprised to see he was such a young man, hardly older than her twenty-eight years. But he dismissed and replaced the people on stage with so little emotion that she knew he was completely professional. Still, it was his first Broadway production. When her turn came to read the part of Daisy, she put her all into it. She liked the idea of working with someone who was up-and-coming in the business.

"Why, if it hadn't been for this blessed crucifix," she said, picking up where the actress before her had left off," my little son Jimmy might well have died!"

She brought it to her lips and kissed it, a gesture not in the script but that came naturally to a woman who had attended twelve years of Catholic school. As she did this several of the people watching her took notes, and Nate said, "Nice touch, Miss, uh . . ." he looked at his list. "Miss St. John."

She paused, expecting to be dismissed.

"Go ahead, dear," Virginia said from the wings.

As Adrian continued her monologue Nate forgot the pad in

his hand and leaned forward to take in every moment of her acting. She was the most talented woman he'd seen so far, and she worked easily with everyone who came on stage. Not only that, she was very attractive. Her wavy hair was a lovely strawberry blonde, framing a fair, childish face that spoke of Irish descent. Her green eyes sparkled under the stage lights. She was small in stature, almost childlike, but her voice was filled with flirtatious sensuality.

"I like the way she works," Virginia whispered. "She could even con me into buying one of those phony crosses."

"Put her down for a call-back," Nate answered.

By the time Adrian was dismissed from the stage, everyone in the casting committee agreed she should be considered for the part. But Adrian didn't know what they were thinking, and when she entered the lobby again her stomach knotted. She thought of a dozen little things she should or shouldn't have done and wished she could go back in and try again.

"Wow, they must have really liked you," Denny said. "You were in there a long time!"

"I don't know," Adrian said. "I think I'm just going to go home and wallow in self-pity."

"I'm sure you did just fine," Georgia insisted.

Outside it had started raining slightly, and of course she did not have an umbrella. But maybe that was a good sign, a portent that she'd done all right after all.

A smile spread over her face at the thought, and she stood in front of the theater deciding which way to go. She noticed a little girl huddled next to the row of doors, staring at her with something like hatred in her eyes. But Adrian only smiled at her, determined to think positively.

The wet, musty smell of fallen leaves rose thickly from the ground as Jim Orland jogged through the park that sat just a block away from his Connecticut home. He'd spent the previous few weeks in Manhattan, renting a small apartment so that he could easily get to the theater. After the hectic pace of auditions, the tranquillity of this park seemed almost surrealistic. Alone in this atmosphere, he was better able to think about the way things were going for him. As far as Jim was concerned, things couldn't have been more perfect. It was great to work with Nate again after so many years. Funny how sometimes the friendships that you formed as a kid were the best ones of your life. During his other jobs in the theater, Jim had been sort of an underdog, always careful not to step on toes. But as Nate's right-hand-man, he held a position of some authority—and if the play was a success, he could make a name for himself. Jim looked forward to this new production with the same delighted anticipation he felt whenever he began a new job.

His mind elsewhere, Jim nearly tripped over the dog who suddenly cut across his path. His sneakers made a sharp slap on the pavement as he brought himself to a halt, stretching his arms out from his sides to balance himself.

"Ho, Sport," he said.

The dog, a Heinz-57-Varieties type, picked up a stick with its huge jaws and gazed at Jim imploringly. Jim hopped back and forth, full of adrenaline from his run. He took the stick and flung it, sending the mutt bounding into a clump of bushes.

He began to run again. The dog kept pace with him, cutting back and forth across the path, its curly tail wagging. Jim, still running, took the stick and threw it again.

"Red!"

Suddenly, the dog stopped, perked up its ears. Hearing its name again, it dropped the stick and gave one bark. In a moment Jim saw a woman hurrying across the grass, her canvas jacket flying open and the dog's leash dangling from her hand.

"Red, what's the big idea?"

She crouched down and clicked the leash onto Red's collar. Jim watched in wonder, unable to find even a single red hair in the mongrel's coat. Finally, the woman looked up and smiled at him.

"Red was making a pest of himself, I guess," she said, apologizing.

"Not really," Jim replied. "It helps break the monotony of jogging, anyway."

The woman, young and blonde and pretty, stood up. The smile on her face widened.

"Wait a sec," she said. "I know who you are!"

"You do?" Jim asked, unable to recognize the woman.

"You work with the fellow who just inherited all that money," she said. "Uh—sorry if I get your name wrong. Is it Jim Orville?"

Jim laughed. "Orland. How'd you know?"

"Read it in the paper a few Sundays back," she said. "I'm Debbi Natanson."

"Glad to meet you," Jim said. "And flattered too. This is the first time I've ever been recognized."

For the next half hour Jim strolled through the park with Debbi, happy to talk about his job and the new play. He promised her a ticket for opening night, but he knew he wouldn't want to wait that long to see her again. Reunited with his best friend, working in a terrific job, and having a beautiful woman in his future, Jim believed that things could not have been more perfect.

FOUR

Both Denny and Adrian were called back to the final auditions, but when two weeks went by without a word from Virginia Atwell, Denny assumed he hadn't gotten the part. His mother waited by the phone as much as possible, but Denny had too much energy in him for that. So today, on a cool September afternoon, he was outside playing with his friends.

"Watch this," he said, aiming his basketball at the hoop they'd set up on a telephone pole. The street was their court, marked with yellow chalk to indicate boundaries. Denny let the ball fly and executed a perfect shot.

"You gonna try out for the basketball team at school?" Mikey Smith wanted to know.

"That's gonna be hard," Paul Kasson said. "He's got all this actor stuff going on. How could he have time for sports?"

Denny bounced the basketball a few times and then threw it to Mikey.

"I didn't get a part yet," he said. "I guess I might try out. Might as well, since I don't seem to have much luck as an actor."

"My mother says your mother is nuts for dragging you to Manhattan so much," Mikey said. "She says you'll probably miss too much school."

The little boy felt his collar tighten as Denny grabbed him and pulled him close.

"You tell your mom that she's got no right to talk like that," he said. "I'm gonna get a private tutor, and I bet I learn more than any of you."

He let go of Mikey and took his ball away. Paul knocked it away, laughed, and in a moment the three boys were playing happily again. A few minutes later the sound of a window scraping open alerted them to Denny's building. Normally, they wouldn't even pay attention, but it was too chilly a September day for anyone to open a window. Denny looked up to see his mother waving at him.

"Denny!" Georgia Richmond cried. "They called! You got the part! You're in Nate Dysart's play."

Denny's mouth dropped open in shock. He felt one of the other boys slap his back and barely heard Paul say, "Whoa, a big shot actor!"

Denny grinned and ran to the apartment building, where his mother greeted him with a big hug and kiss.

"Let's go out and celebrate," she said. "Here, put on your good shirt."

Denny changed into it, mumbling "I don't believe it" over and over. During the auditions, he hadn't dared hope he might be in the play. But it was true!

Across town Adrian St. John hung up her own telephone and went to the refrigerator to find a bottle of champagne. She'd been saving it for this moment, to celebrate her first leading role on Broadway. Pouring it into a crystal glass, she carried it over to a mirror and toasted her reflection.

"Way to go, lady," she said.

News like this was too good to keep to herself. Yet Adrian didn't have many friends here in New York. She spent so much time pursuing her career as an actress that her social life was rather quiet. Still, she was bursting with elation. She had to call her family in Ohio. They had been so worried when she came to New York, thinking she would only be disappointed. Yet she was about to play the female lead in a major Broadway production!

She was so jittery that she had to hang up and dial twice before getting the number right. She could hear faint sounds through the telephone wire, disembodied voices of thousands of people sharing the line. Then finally, there was a click, and then a series of faint-sounding rings. When her mother answered the phone, Adrian was surprised at how clear she sounded.

"Hi, it's your famous daughter!" she cried delightedly.

"Adrian!" Martha St. John replied. "It's so good to hear from you."

Adrian heard her telling someone who it was on the line.

"Your father wants to know when you're coming home," Martha said.

"Maybe never," Adrian said with a laugh. "Don't worry, Mom. I'm all right. In fact, I'm terrific. Guess what?"

Martha made some hesitant noises into the phone, and Adrian could imagine her waving a wooden spoon. More voices filled the background, youthful and excited.

"Is everyone there?" Adrian asked.

"Bill and Pat are in town," Martha said, referring to Adrian's oldest brothers. "But the other seven boys are right here sharing dinner with us. Sure wish you could be here, Adrian."

Adrian grinned. "Mom, wait till you hear what happened! I auditioned for a new play that's going to be right on Broadway. And I got the part!"

"Adrian!" Martha cried with delight.

Someone in the background asked what happened, and Martha told the family her daughter's news.

"Wait, there's more," Adrian said. "I'm the female lead— and I'm playing opposite Sander Bernaux!"

"Sander who?"

Martha's confusion made Adrian laugh again. "The most important actor on Broadway. Working with him is going to make me famous, and really help my career."

"Well, darling, that's wonderful," Martha said. "Wait, your father wants to talk to you."

Tom St. John sounded very serious over the phone, but Adrian knew that he was bursting with pride.

"How much are they paying you?" he asked.

"Lots," Adrian said. When she told her father the terms of contract, he whistled shrilly. "So you see, you don't have to worry about me."

There was a long pause, and then Tom said carefully, "You'll be real busy, huh?"

"Oh, yes," Adrian said. "Rehearsals start soon."

"Too busy to visit home?"

"Dad, why don't you and Mom come to New York?" Adrian suggested. "You could let Bill and Pat watch the little ones, and be here for my opening night in December."

"That sounds like a great idea," Tom said. "We'll talk about it, your mother and me."

Adrian finished the conversation off with a few trivial bits of news, then hung up the phone. She poured herself another little glass of champagne and laughed out loud.

"Small-town kid makes good," she said, grinning broadly.

In the Dysart Theater, Jim Orland was setting up for a little party to celebrate the fact that they were finally through with auditions.

Jim and Virginia were moving two metal tables onto the stage, working along with the others in the casting committee. Nate was busy in his office, doing a telephone interview for a national magazine.

"I always feel a great burden has been lifted when auditions are over," Virginia said, setting up a row of plastic utensils.

"Imagine how hard it is for the actors," Jim replied. He shrugged. "But it's the price you pay."

As they worked, the theater's mascot, a Siamese cat, who had rather mysteriously arrived, the day the theater opened, walked delicately around the orchestra pit railing. Suddenly, her ears lay back flat against her head, and her back hunched up. Jim and Virginia looked at each other, then turned to the cat. Cartier seemed to be staring at something in the orchestra pit.

"Don't tell me our brand-new theater has mice already," Virginia said.

Jim walked to the apron and looked down.

"There's nothing there," he said. He waved a hand at the cat. "Get lost, pest!"

Instead, Cartier turned and stared down the center aisle with saucer eyes that seemed to be watching something neither Virginia nor Jim could see. Just then, the door at the end of the middle aisle opened a little. Jim saw a small child's silhouette and started to ask Virginia about her. But the casting director had turned back to arranging the tables. At first, Jim thought the little girl must belong to someone working here. But she stood apart from the group for so long that he wondered if she might need help. Finally, he left the stage to ask her what was wrong.

A long hallway running alongside the auditorium led him to the lobby, where he found the little girl. Approaching her with a smile, he said, "Hi, honey. Where's your mom?"

She stepped back a little.

"Mommy's gone," she said.

"You don't have to be afraid of me," Jim told her. "I won't hurt you. Want to wait for your mommy inside? We've got some nice soda you can have."

The little girl shook her head and moved backward to the winding staircase. Then, suddenly, she turned and raced up them. Jim followed closely, trying to catch her. He didn't want a small child alone upstairs. They didn't want any unfortunate accidents when everything was going so well.

"Wait up!" he cried. "God, how can you move so fast?"

She ducked into a closet and slammed the door. Jim, losing his patience, tugged it open and reached to pull her out.

The closet was empty.

"Wait a minute," he said, opening and closing his eyes. "I'm sure I saw her go inside!"

He looked around and found the child standing clear across the lobby, twisting the front of her ruffled white dress with tiny fists.

"Hey, you can't be playing up here," Jim said. "Come on and I'll take you downstairs."

"*No!*" the child cried.

Jim pointed a finger at her.

"Listen, I'm pretty patient with kids," he said. "But you're cruising for a bruising. Either you come with me, or I'll tell your mother you were up here."

He grabbed hold of her and lifted her into his arms. She was very light, almost weightless, and he thought he would have no more trouble from her.

"I'm sure your mommy is looking all over for you," he said.

Suddenly, she began to whimper.

"Don't want to see Mommy," she said.

"You have to, I'm afraid," Jim answered firmly.

"NNNNOOOO!!!!"

Her scream was so ear-piercing that Jim nearly dropped her. But she grabbed hold of his head and clung to him, her hands squeezing his temples. Now it was Jim's turn to scream, for a pain was seizing him, a burning pain more horrible than any he had ever known.

"I won't go to mommy!" the child cried. "I won't! I won't let the dark come again!"

Jim's mouth snapped open, and a gutteral choking sound came out as he collapsed to the floor. Hideous pain crept over his body, making his legs and arms quake involuntarily at his sides. The child straddled him, staring into his wide eyes with an eternity of hatred in her expression.

"You tried to hurt me," she hissed. "You want the dark to come again. Terrible man!"

Jim tried to speak, but a strange clicking noise was the only sound that escaped his throat. His body jerking, he watched the child rise above him like a demon, floating towards the carved ceiling. And then she was gone.

The pain stopped. Jim's eyes fluttered, and he lost consciousness.

Nate was smiling when he walked on stage. Someone insisted that he, as the head of the Dysart Theater, should do the honors of opening the champagne. Nate obliged, and in a moment the liquid was flowing into paper cups. Nate raised his own cup.

"To surviving three crazy weeks," he said. "And to a great group of people. Jim, want to come up here where I can see you?"

He scanned the group but did not see his friend.

"Where did he go?" he asked Virginia.

"I don't really know," she said. She had been so busy setting up for the party that she hadn't seen the stage manager leave.

Nate waved the back of his hand at the table.

"Go ahead everybody and drink," he said. "I'll try to find him."

As he was heading toward the down-right exit a strange

groaning noise filled the auditorium. Nate looked up and saw Jim at the edge of the mezzanine, holding out his arms. Jim seemed to be swaying unsteadily at the edge, but Nate couldn't be sure because of the dim lights. He walked down to the floor and called up to him.

"What's the matter?" he asked. "What are you doing up there?"

But Jim did not reply. The pain that had made him pass out a moment ago had returned, burning him, crawling over his flesh. When he'd woken up, he had come in here to call for help. But somehow, he had no voice. He reached out into the air as if to grab his best friend, as if Nate could take the pain away. Nate came closer and saw Jim more clearly. His face was red, and sweat poured profusely over his skin, staining the blue chambray shirt he wore and plastering his curly hair. But his eyes were what made Nate break into a run to get upstairs. They were wild eyes, filled with terror.

Nate took the steps two at a time and moved like lightning into the mezzanine. Once inside, he caught hold of his friend's arm, pulled him away from the edge, and tried to sit him down. Instead, Jim backed further away and screamed.

"What the hell is wrong with you?" Nate demanded, panicking. His friend had always been so easygoing, yet now every muscle in his body was contracted in fear. "Jim, can't you talk to me?"

Jim wanted to talk to his friend but couldn't. The pain wouldn't let him. With a cry, he sank to the steps and closed his eyes, tears spilling uncontrollably.

"Dear God," Nate whispered. He called to the people on the stage below. "Virginia, get a doctor!"

He sat down next to Jim and carefully put an arm around his shoulder. This time, Jim did not shrink away. He was breathing heavily, and his sweat was pouring even more profusely.

"God, I wish you could tell me what's wrong," Nate said. "I'm your best friend, and I can't even help you!"

A few seconds later Virginia rushed through the mezzanine door and down to them.

"I sent for an ambulance," she said. She looked into Jim's dilated eyes. "Has he been able to say what's wrong?"

"He can't talk," Nate answered, frustrated at being unable to help.

They both looked at their friend again. Jim seemed to be staring at the stage below, his fixed pupils reflecting the light from the chandelier. But Jim didn't see the stagehands and assistants who stood near the tables that had been set up on stage. They were gone, the tables were gone, and in their place stood several groupings of actors in costume. The men wore loose-fitting suits, and the women wore flapper dresses, long fringe tickling their knees, and cloche hats encircled their heads. They moved about slowly, their lips parted as if in laughter, and yet no sound came out.

Jim moved his gaze down to the audience, so enthralled by the illusion that for the moment he did not feel his pain. It was as if his spirit had risen from his body, leaving pain in the empty shell. The audience was filled with people dressed in evening clothes. There were people in the mezzanine, too. Jim looked into the blue eyes of the girl next to him, seeing not Virginia, but a young woman dressed in a satin gown that showed off every curve of her figure. She smiled at him, then turned her eyes back to the stage below. She started to applaud, her small white hands coming together and yet making no sound. Jim, too, looked down at the stage. There was a child there, standing at its apron, dressed in white ruffles . . .

"Jim?"

Nate's voice traveled to him from far away, breaking the spell that had held Jim captive. The pain returned again, and with it a feeling of dread even greater than before. How could he have seen a theater filled with people dressed in 1920s styles?

"Jim, can't you tell us what happened to you?" Nate pleaded.

The little girl, Jim thought. *It was a little girl.*

But he could not tell them this. Virginia, he saw, had a paper cup full of water in her hand. She held it out to him, but instead of drinking it he poured it over his burning head. For a brief moment, the pain on his face subsided. But then it returned as horrible as ever. Jim looked at Nate with pleading eyes, then passed out once again.

The room grew cold suddenly, and the crystal chandelier

jangled melodically, as if unseen hands had pushed it. Behind Nate and Virginia, the door leading into the mezzanine slammed shut.

"Oh, my God," Nate whispered, a cold chill rushing over him. With a trembling hand he took hold of Jim's wrist.

"I can't find a pulse!" he cried. "There's no pulse!"

"Get him on the floor!" Virginia ordered. "We'll do heart massage on him."

Quickly, Nate and Virginia straightened out Jim's body, opening his shirt. They took turns pressing down on his chest, praying they were not too late.

"Come on, you big jackass," Nate said, frustrated and terrified. "Come on and breathe, damn you!"

"Nate, let me try," Virginia said. With her strong arms she pulled the director aside, then straddled Jim's body. From somewhere downstairs, they heard the sound of shouting. Nate went to the balcony and yelled.

"Up here! Hurry!"

Seconds later, two paramedics appeared. They ordered Nate and Virginia away and went to work on Jim. But all the modern means they had of reviving the man were useless. Finally, one of the men looked up at Nate and shook his head.

"I'm sorry," he said. "He's gone. I can't do anything more for him."

Nate gritted his teeth.

"What the hell do you mean?" he demanded. "Jim's my best friend! He's like my brother! How can he be dead? You made a mistake!"

"No, I'm sorry," he said quietly. "We'll contact the coroner's..."

"Try again," Nate ordered, forced calm in his voice. "Try the heart massage thing again."

The paramedic was about to protest, but saw the look in Virginia's eyes and with a sigh made a new effort. Nothing happened. He looked up at the other paramedic.

"Get a stretcher."

Nate brought his hands up to his head and tugged at fistfuls of hair, wanting to scream at this injustice. How could Jim Orland possibly be dead? He had been Nate's strength all these years, the brother he had never had, the man who had loved him for himself, not because he was rich or famous or talented. The only other person in Nate's life who had felt the same way had been Meg, but she'd died, too. Now there was no one left, no true friends.

"I don't want to be alone," Nate whispered.

"Shh," Virginia said, taking his arm as the paramedics carried Jim's body away. "Come downstairs. I'll get your chauffeur and have him take you home."

She led Nate out of the mezzanine and downstairs. As he had at his father's funeral, Nate descended into a dazed state too horrified to believe what had just happened. Virginia called George, and the chauffeur helped Nate into the back of the Rolls.

"See to it that he rests well tonight," Virginia said.

Nate looked out his window with bloodshot eyes as George switched on the ignition. Suddenly, a little girl came through the doors and stood beside Virginia and the others who'd come outside the theater. Nate knew she wasn't part of the company. What had she been doing in the theater?

"Hey!" Nate cried.

He leaned toward the window and gestured at the child. Everyone turned to find out what he was pointing at but saw nothing. A few passersby gazed at the man who tapped on the car window, wondering if he was yet another city weirdo. And then Nate, too, realized there was no one there. He slunk down into his seat and buried his face in his hands.

It had been his imagination. There was no little girl.

Nate went back to his theater the very next day, too frightened of his thoughts to stay at home alone. It had been like that after Meg's death—so bad. He tried to keep himself busy with paperwork but could only think of Jim and the crazed look that had been in his eyes before his death. It seemed so unreal now, just a day later. But Nate was forced to accept the truth when the phone rang and someone from the city coroner's office asked to speak to him.

"You'll have to come down to the office," she said. "There are some questions the medical examiner would like to ask you."

Nate sighed, knowing he had to face this sooner or later.

"I'll be there in half an hour," he said.

When he arrived, he was taken into a sterile-looking office

with metal furniture and glass walls. He sat in a metal chair and asked the coroner, "What exactly happened to my friend?"

The coroner shook his head.

"I'm afraid we don't know yet," he said. "His mother only consented this morning to an autopsy. But, since you were the last person to see Mr. Orland alive, I want to hear whatever you can tell me."

Nate swallowed and began his story.

"I was in my office doing a phone interview," he said, "while my crew was setting up for a little party. We were celebrating the end of auditions, which is a rather grueling job. When I came back to the stage, I noticed Jim wasn't there."

"Where had he gone?"

"I didn't know, at first," Nate said. "I asked about him, but everyone had been too busy to notice when he'd left. Anyway, I was about to go look for him when I heard him up at the edge of the mezzanine. I asked him what he was doing up there, but he couldn't answer me."

Nate shifted a little as the chair grew more uncomfortable.

"What do you suppose was wrong with him?" he asked. "I never saw him behave in such a way"

"What way, Mr. Dysart?"

"His face was red and covered with sweat," Nate said, waving his hand around his own face. "And all his muscles were jerking. I tried to help him, but he couldn't even tell me what was wrong. All I know is that he was in terrible, terrible pain."

"About how long did this last?"

"Four, five minutes," Nate said. "I'm not sure, exactly. And I don't know how long he'd been like that before I found him."

The coroner made some notes, then said, "Tell me what he had to eat yesterday."

"How the hell should I know?" Nate asked, not seeing the relevance of the question.

"Please cooperate with me, Mr. Dysart," the coroner said. "It's possible your friend ate something that poisoned him."

Nate thought a moment, then said, "I don't know. We didn't share lunch yesterday."

More notes went into the coroner's book.

"All right then," he said. "If anything is to be found, we'll see it in the autopsy."

He stood up and offered Nate his hand in thanks. Nate shook it, then opened the glass door.

"I suggest, Mr. Dysart," the coroner said, "that you rest for a few days. You look terribly worn out."

Nate laughed a little, without humor.

"Jim used to accuse me of the same thing," he said. "But don't ask me to rest. The only way I'll keep my sanity now is by working harder."

After speaking to the coroner, Nate returned to the theater. He walked upstairs to the mezzanine and looked around. Work would not officially begin on the production until after the funeral. The theater was deserted. Except for the glow of the ghost light, everything was dark.

It was so silent, so lonely, that Nate was unable to stop a sudden flow of emotion. He leaned forward and put his arms on the railing, covering his face as he sobbed in anger. It felt good to cry, with no one around to criticize him. As a child, he was never allowed to shed a tear, no matter how much the beatings he received hurt.

He looked down at the ghost light, his chin resting on his forearms, blinking away the last of his tears.

Something was there, something like a human figure.

Nate straightened up and stared at it for a long time, his head aching. It was a white blur, like the ones in the pictures he'd taken.

"Who's there?" he called, standing.

The white light rose about a foot, then vanished. Nate rubbed his eyes and moaned.

"God, now I'm seeing things."

A small voice with a southwestern accent answered him.

"That man was bad! He hurt me! He wanted the darkness to come!"

Nate was on his feet in a flash, looking around. The mezzanine seemed empty, but could someone be hiding in its shadows?

"Who the hell *are* you?" he cried.

No answer came. Infuriated, Nate ran through the mezzanine, demanding the stranger come out to the open. The little lights along the rows of seats seemed to wink at him, teasing him, telling him he was acting like a madman.

"I'm not crazy," Nate said out loud. "I know I heard someone!"

Finally, he was forced to admit he was all alone. That voice had only been his imagination. His mind was playing tricks on him again, as it had after his father's death. That was all it was. Imagination.

Nate shuffled wearily into his office and, burying his head in his arms at his desk, wished to God he could be sure.

According to the coroner's report, Jim Orland had died of a heart attack. When Nate protested that the man never showed any signs of a weak heart, the coroner told him these things sometimes happened without warning. And so Nate attended his second funeral in a year, comforting Jim's parents as the man was put into the ground of the same cemetery as Nate's wife, Meg, and Nate's father. A numbness held him fast all the time he mourned his friend, and he knew he would never get over this loss.

More than ever, he was determined to make his production a success. He doubled his working hours and dedicated his efforts to both Jim and Meg. With these two in mind, he contacted Sander Bernaux a few days after the funeral. He had wanted Jim to be here when the interview was held. But now he was alone, and Nate knew he had to get along without Jim's help.

Sander Bernaux entered his office in the company of his agent. Nate had one of his assistants serve coffee to everyone, then dismissed her from the office. He watched Sander take a seat on the leather couch, unable to determine by his expression what kind of mood he was in. Sander was about forty-five years old, with thick dark hair just turning gray at the temples. His tanned face was more carved than molded, with light green eyes set far behind prominent cheekbones. He had the kind of mysterious good looks that made women in the audiences squeal with delight when he came on stage. It surprised Nate that he had never tried making the transition to the screen.

"Have you read the contract?" Nate asked finally.

"Of course," Tom Selton, Sander's agent, said. "And we're quite satisfied with it."

Nate felt a wave of relief wash over him, relaxing the tension in his muscles he was feeling in the presence of this great star. But he almost lost his calmness when Tom said, "However..."

"However," Sander interrupted, "while the contract is most tempting, I'm not certain I can afford to risk working with an unknown like yourself."

"I assure you I'm well-qualified," Nate said.

Sander leaned back on the couch with his coffee cup nested between his two hands. He was wearing a diamond and gold ring fashioned in the comedy/tragedy mask design, a gift Nate knew he'd received from one of his girlfriends.

"First of all," Sander said, "what experience do you have? I understand you're able to afford this opulent palace because of your inheritance. But that doesn't qualify you as a producer/director."

"I've done a good deal of work in little theater since I was a teenager," Nate said. "In 1975 I had started my own production company, and the few performances we put on were met with excellent reviews. I can show you my scrapbook, if you'd like."

"What do you mean, 'the few performances we put on?'" Tom wanted to know. "Why did you stop?"

Nate lowered his eyes, hoping he would not be asked too many questions about Meg. Then he looked up and said quietly, "My wife died then. I decided to leave for a while, and went to California."

"What did you do there?" Sander asked.

"Started another production company," Nate said. "In fact, I'm pretty well known around the L.A. area. I would have stayed out there, but my father's funeral brought me east again. And when my inheritance came through, I knew I had the means, as well as the talent, to start my own company right here on Broadway."

Sander leaned forward and placed his coffee cup on the table before him.

"All right," he said.

Nate shook his head. "All right?"

"I'll work with you," Sander replied. "Because I can sense

when a person is sincere, and I sense that in you. But just remember, I must have star billing for this production. No other actor can be put before me."

Nate bit his lip to suppress a silly grin of joy.

"Of course," he said, extending his hand.

Sander's grip was tight when he shook it. Now Tom brought out the contract, and the three signed the last page.

When Sander had left, Nate could not help whispering to his father's spirit.

"You never thought I'd get him, did you?"

But he had gotten Sander Bernaux, and he had his company and his theater. And in about two month's time, he was going to give Broadway something to be proud of. He only wished Meg were here to share this with him.

1975

Nathaniel Dysart Sr. bumped a thin knee against the foot of Nate and Meg's four-poster bed, shaking the mattress so that Meg would wake up from her nap. He grinned with evil delight, readying himself for another confrontation with Nate's wife. Never, ever, would he call her his daughter-in-law.

Startled from a deep sleep, Meg sat up with a gasp and stared at the old man. Fear crept over her pretty face. As if it were a protective wall, she pulled up her blanket and clenched it with trembling fists.

"Are you ever going to get out of that bed, lazy bitch?" Nathaniel Sr demanded "Your accident happened a long time ago!"

"It's only been a few weeks," Meg said. "My doctor says I need rest. Please, stop tormenting me like this!"

"Why should I?" Nathaniel Sr. asked, his long nose wrinkling in a sneer. "This is my house that you live in. As long as your husband is too lazy to make a living of his own . . ."

"He isn't lazy!" Meg cried. "Nate works so hard—hours and hours at our theater! We'll make a name for ourselves one day!"

The old man threw back his head and let out a high-pitched laugh. Meg cringed and fought tears. How could a man be so cruel, she wondered? How could he delight so in hurting her?

"A name for yourselves?" Nathaniel Sr. said. "You're nothing but a pair of failures—in every way!"

Now it was Meg's turn to scream. She would not be comforted until Nate came home and took her in his arms to protect her from his monstrous father.

FIVE

After Sander left, Nate decided to get through some paperwork. His publicity department had put together a flyer on the progress of the theater, to be mailed to all the backers, and wanted his okay on it. Nate read it carefully, making the necessary corrections. Then he picked through the accompanying black-and-white photographs. Nate was to indicate which, in his opinion, was the best one. As he went over them, he recalled his own photographs. None of these had the strange white flaw; it must have been caused by his camera.

Still, he could not help thinking about the strange light he'd seen on the stage the other day, while standing alone on the darkened mezzanine. It had looked so much like something human, very similar to the shadow in his pictures. He laughed quietly.

"Jim thought it looked like a person himself," he said out loud.

But it really wasn't funny, and he bit his lip in anger to think of his friend. He opened his left top drawer and pulled out the red-and-white envelope of his snapshots. The glossies were lined up on his desk, and below them Nate placed his own photos. The comparison proved nothing.

He punched a button on his telephone and rang the office of the man he'd hired as his new stage manager.

"Do me a favor, Don," he said. "Find out if the design crew has a magnifying glass I can borrow."

After obtaining the magnifying glass, Nate chose one photo and began to study it. The white cloud became more discernible now, but it still did not look like anything more than a mistake made by an amateur. Most of the other pictures were the same, and Nate was almost ready to think he was imagining things. After all, none of the professional photos showed this blur. But as he neared the end of the pile, he saw something not visible in any of the other pictures.

There were dark spots at the top of the blur.

Dark spots that looked something like the features of a face.

"Oh, God," Nate said. "What are you thinking?"

There had to be a logical explanation for all this, but Nate couldn't begin to think what it might be. He decided he'd have the picture enlarged. If there was something to be seen, it would show up better then. He pushed back his chair and lifted the photographs' envelope from his desk, carefully removing the negatives. After finding the correct one, he wrote the number on the package and slid it into the back pocket of his jeans.

In the hallway outside his office he could hear the loud banging of the hammers and the buzz of saws as the building crew worked downstairs on the sets. He knocked on a door, and his chauffeur George came out of a tiny office.

"Get the car," Nate said. "I've got an errand to run."

George nodded his head once and headed for the back door. After Nate let Don know he'd be gone for a while, he headed to the back door. But just as he was about to pull it open, he heard a voice.

"Don't leave me in the dark!"

It was a childish voice with a southwestern accent. Nate's fist turned white as it clenched the doorknob. He refused to acknowledge what he was hearing.

"Please take the dark away!"

Nate jerked open the door and ran out into the chilly October rain. He slumped into the backseat of the car and gave George a destination.

What had made him hear that voice? he wondered. Was his mind playing tricks on him again? Was it brought on by the fact that he'd been going over the photographs, imagining he saw a human figure? *Was* it just in his mind?

Or was it something external, something he could not control?

When George stopped for a red light, Nate gazed at the passers-by, amused as he usually was that they all took a look at his funny car. But one face in particular caught his attention, and a moment later he had his window rolled down, calling to a red-haired woman carrying a flowered umbrella.

"Miss St. John!" he called. "Adrian!"

Adrian, who had just come out of a boutique, turned at the sound of her name and looked around in confusion. When she noticed somone waving to her from the fancy car, she took a step forward and squinted. Then, recognizing her new director, she smiled and walked over.

"Well, hello, Mr. Dysart," she said. The idea of calling a man so young "Mister" struck her as funny. But after all, he *was* her director and deserved respect. "How are you?"

"Wet," Nate replied simply. He clicked open the door and slid over.

"Come on," he said. "I'll give you a ride."

Adrian wasn't about to pass up such an offer in that nasty weather, and so she stretched over the flooded gutter and climbed in beside him. Shaking her umbrella outside before closing her door, she said, "Great day for ducks."

Nate laughed, his blue eyes brightening. Adrian felt a surge of infatuation and looked down at her lap to drive it away. She was old enough to know "love at first sight" was an impossibility.

"I shouldn't be making jokes," she said, serious now. "Not after what happened to Mr. Orland."

"Well..." Nate sighed, shrugging. He did not want to discuss Jim right now.

She looked at him, her green eyes rounding.

"It must have been horrible for you, Mr. Dysart," she said. "I read in the papers that you were with him when he died."

Her director nodded.

"Did you get the flowers I sent?" Adrian asked. "I would have attended the funeral, but I didn't have any way of getting there."

Nate smiled a little.

"The flowers were beautiful," he said. "That was very thoughtful of you. And don't worry about missing the funeral."

The rain hummed on the car roof as they rode across town.

"He was your best friend, wasn't he?" Adrian asked softly.

"Yes, he was," Nate said.

Impulsively, Adrian leaned across the seat and kissed Nate's cheek. When she pulled away, she ran her fingers through her wavy red hair, embarrassed, and said, "I hope you didn't mind."

"Why did you do that?" Nate asked, touching his cheek. It had been a long time since anyone had kissed him that way.

"You look like you need it," Adrian said. "Hey, don't worry. I'm not coming on to you. I'm not like that."

"I didn't think you were," Nate assured her. "You just— well, it kind of surprised me."

"I come from a very big family in the Midwest," Adrian said. "We're all very affectionate, and whenever anyone's down we give him a big kiss."

Nate smiled again, trying to imagine what such a home life would be like. There would be no beatings, no yelling, and no accusing and belittling. His own father had never even shook his hand.

"What part of the Midwest do you come from?" he asked, shutting off thoughts of his father.

"A little town in Ohio," Adrian said. "My parents and my nine brothers live there."

Nate whistled.

"Are you kidding?" he said with a laugh. "Nine brothers? How old are they?"

"The youngest is twelve," Adrian said, "and the oldest is two years my senior—thirty."

"Are any of them here in New York?"

Adrian shook her head.

"I was the only St. John with stars in her eyes," she said. "My parents fought like crazy to keep me home, but I was determined to come to New York and make a name for myself. And look at me, Mr. Dysart. I'm going to play the leading role in your production!"

"I think you'll be great as Daisy," Nate said.

"I can't wait until rehearsals start Monday," Adrian said. "I'll get a better feel for Daisy on the stage."

Their conversation was interrupted when George pulled the car into a side street to park.

"I just want to drop these negatives off," Nate said. "I'll have George drop you off wherever you want to go."

The man in the photographers' shop told Nate the print could not be ready for a week, but when the producer pressed a bill into his hand, he changed his tune.

"Monday," he said.

Nate walked out to the car again, where Adrian was having a discussion with George. She smiled at him when he got in.

"Your driver was telling me this car is forty years old," she said. "How do you keep it so new looking?"

"George sees to that," Nate said.

The car could not be in any other condition, he thought, considering that in most of those forty years only his father had been a passenger. Nate was never permitted in the precious vehicle.

"So, where to?" he asked Adrian.

"Macy's," Adrian said. "If it's not too far out of your way."

Nate insisted it wasn't. As they drove downtown he asked about her family and about her career and what she wanted to do in the future. By the time they reached Thirty-fourth Street, he was thinking that he hadn't met a woman so intelligent and charming and warm in a long, long time.

Rehearsals began the following Monday morning and everyone was very excited. The stage held only a few pieces of scenery, but conveyed enough of the idea for the actors to work well. While the new stage manager, Don Benson, took charge backstage, Nate found a seat in the front row. On his lap were a copy of the script and some rough sketches of the way the scenes would look with the actors in their proper groupings. He began by giving the actors an account of the first scene and what the set would look like when completed. Then he reminded them that the play would be tried out in a Connecticut theater before its Broadway opening, and ordered them to begin rehearsal. A few moments went by before he interrupted the action on stage.

"Okay, wait a minute," he said, waving his pen at the actors. "Let's see how it would look if Adrian and Denny moved left center."

The two actors shifted positions, and Nate made a note in his book. The woman beside him, his assistant stage manager, did the same. Now Nate gave orders for the action to begin again, and Adrian started to talk to Denny. Don watched from the wings, ready to cue the actors who would be walking on next. He held Cartier, the theater's mascot cat, in his arms.

"Now, Jimmy," Adrian, as Daisy, was saying to Denny,

"when your daddy points his finger at you, start moaning like you got the devil himself in your blood."

As Denny was answering her Don felt someone come to stand beside him. He turned and looked at Georgia Richmond, watching her son with a smile of pride on her face. Her bleached blonde wig seemed to glow in the shadows, and her makeup was gaudy.

"Excuse me," Don whispered as two actresses moved by him, "but you really aren't allowed back here."

Georgia turned to him, still smiling.

"Oh, I know," she said. "But it's the first time Denny's performed on Broadway, and I'm so terribly proud!"

"Well, I suppose it's okay for just this one time," Don consented.

"Thank you," Georgia replied.

A few moments later, she was brushed aside by an actor hurrying on stage. It was Sander Bernaux, and, according to his script, he climbed on top of a chair and started calling to the people on stage. Sander was playing the role of a hell-fire preacher, in reality a con artist. His speech was loud and forceful, but suddenly it was cut short. Sander fixed his eyes on one of the extras and said, "You're wearing green!"

The actor looked down at his clothes and pressed his hands on the front of his green Lacoste shirt. Then he looked up at Sander with innocent eyes.

"Don't you know what an unlucky color green is?" Sander asked.

Nate stood up and walked toward the stage, resting his hands on the railing of the orchestra pit.

"I'm sure Mr. Smith was not aware of that particular superstition," he said.

"How can I work with such amateurs?" Sander demanded. "Young man, don't you know that color is reserved for the fairies?"

Smith doubled his fists.

"Who're you callin' a fairy?"

Nate tried to explain to the confused young man what had upset Sander, though, in his mind, the actor was making a big deal out of nothing. Nate did not share the beliefs that some superstitious actors held.

"People used to believe the fairies would get jealous if they saw an actor wearing green," he said. "It was supposedly *their* official color, and reserved for their use alone."

Sander clicked his tongue.

"It isn't as unimportant as you make it sound," he said.

"Well, have a sense of humor about it," Nate said. "After all, this is a comedy we're doing."

Smith looked over at Nate, who nodded his head.

"I guess I could take it off," he said.

"Have the wardrobe mistress give you something else to wear," Nate said.

The actor hurried off the stage, cursing temperamental Sander under his breath. Now Denny walked up to the famous actor and said, "If the color green is so unlucky, Mr. Bernaux, then why do we call the place where we rest between scenes the greenroom? That's a place where it's happy!"

"Impudent brat," Sander snarled, for lack of a better answer.

They rehearsed for another two hours. When lunchtime came, everyone started talking about the morning's work, and friendships started to form. Adrian met Nate as he came up the staircase next to the stage and said, "We seemed to do all right."

"There's a lot of room for improvement," Nate said. "But yes, you did fine for a first rehearsal."

They walked along the hall together.

"I liked the faces you were making during Sander's speech," Nate went on. "You're wonderfully expressive, Adrian."

"Oh, did you think I should have exaggerated that look on my face when I drank that cheap wine?"

"You might even spit the stuff out at your husband," Nate suggested.

Adrian laughed.

"I'll bet Sander wouldn't appreciate *that* scene!"

Halfway down the hallway, they parted company—Adrian heading for her dressing room and Nate for his office. He planned to go back to that photographers' shop today. So far, this first day of rehearsals had been uneventful. Nate wondered if he might be inviting trouble if he started thinking about the pictures again.

But he had to find out if there was anything there.

As he was walking toward the front door he bumped into an attractive young woman who was dressed in coveralls and had her arms filled with lighting equipment and drooping extension cords. They both began to apologize and then started to laugh.

"This is a very pretty theater, Mr. Dysart," she said. "It makes me think of the Palace of Versailles in France!"

"Thanks," Nate said. He brought a hand to his mouth. "Miss, uh . . ."

She smiled.

"It's Mrs. Warner," she said. "Barbara Warner. I work on the lighting crew."

"Oh, yes," Nate said, recalling her name now. "I hope you like it here."

"Oh, I love everything about the theater," Barbara said, her eyes lighting up.

Nate turned and walked to his car. He was happy to be working with such good people. If only his father could see him now!

After visiting the photographer's shop, Nate did not wait until he got back to the theater to look at the enlargement. Holding it toward the car window for better light, he studied it slowly. A chill rushed over him as he realized it *was* a human figure in the picture! In this larger print he could see the eyes and mouth, though these were only faint, and the suggestion of short, dark hair.

But this seemed an impossible photograph, for the figure was faded even though everything around it was perfectly clear. Someone was playing a trick on him. That had to be it. But why? Who would do such a thing to him? Nate thought he had no enemies in the world, yet he knew there were some unscrupulous people in the business. There was a lot of money tied up in the theatrical world, not to mention a lot of temperamental, sometimes unstable people. Was someone trying to drive him crazy?

All sorts of explanations ran through Nate's head. Someone had paid to have the development of the photos tampered with, of course. Someone who wanted to see Nate fail. Maybe, just maybe, this was also the explanation behind the voices he'd been hearing. There were plenty of places in the Dysart Theater where someone could hide a tape recorder.

It wasn't difficult to imagine he might have enemies now. His father had been associated with many people, and yet had left his entire fortune to Nate. What about his cousin Vance? Nate got at least one angry phone call from him every week. The man seemed to get more irrational all the time. Nate almost felt sympathy for his cousin, who had been a loser all his life. Or could one of his father's business associates be responsible? Someone who had wanted a cut of the Dysart fortune and was getting his revenge by trying to bring Nate to ruin?

"I don't understand this," Nate whispered. "But I know one thing. My show is going to be a hit, and nothing is going to stop me!"

Angrily, he tore up the photograph and threw it on the floor of the car. He promised himself he would completely ignore the voices next time he heard them.

He would not let himself think that no one else could possibly know what the little girl in his dreams said to him.

Barbara Warner picked up her two-year-old son Alec and gave him a big bear hug. The child squealed, then wriggled out of her arms and ran back to the wooden blocks he'd piled up under the dining room table. She smiled to see him toddling about. He was such a happy, healthy, well-behaved child. Never gave them a moment's worry.

"Why're you so happy today, Mom?" her eight-year-old, Bobby, wanted to know. He stood in the doorway to the kitchen, armed with a can of soda and a handful of pretzels. She resisted the impulse to tell him not to spoil his appetite for supper.

"Your mother's always happy, Bobby," his father said. Joel Warner winked in his wife's direction, then put aside the newspaper column he was writing.

"I take it you're still enjoying this new job of yours?" he asked, putting his arms around her.

She accepted his kiss, then laughed again as Bobby made a face at their affectionate display and retreated into the kitchen. Give him a few years, Barbara thought, and he'd understand about hugging and kissing.

"I met my boss today," she said. "He's such a nice man, Joel! He doesn't keep his nose in the air like some of the producers I've worked with."

"He's a pretty young guy, isn't he?" Joel asked.

"Oh, about thirty or so and very handsome," Barbara said. She studied her husband's eyes through the wire-frame glasses he wore. "Say, you aren't jealous, are you?"

"Of course not," Joel said, hugging her close. "I know you love me."

Barbara kissed him.

"More than anything in the world," she said.

Barbara Warner, secure with a loving husband and family, thought that life would always be this wonderful.

SIX

Many actors have a mascot, some little trinket that they believe will bring them good luck. Because her son had carried his basketball to all the auditions, Georgia decided this was an appropriate amulet for him. She didn't stop to think it would have been more effective if he'd chosen it himself. To Georgia, her son was too young to make a decision like that.

Denny, on the other hand, did not believe in such things. He carried the basketball around because it was a concrete reminder of a father who had left a year ago to live in Arizona. His parents were divorced, and Denny knew there was no way they'd get back together. But still he wished they could have made up for just one day, for his birthday several months earlier. That way, his father could have given the basketball to him in person, instead of through the mail.

During the first week of rehearsals, he played with it in his dressing room, tossing it at his trash can or into an open drawer. But the room soon became too confining, and he decided the hallway would be a great place to fool around. He was dribbling it along the tile floor, back from lunch only a few minutes, when his mother came up to him and said, "Don't disturb the other actors, Denny."

"It's okay, Mom," Denny said, lifting the ball up to twirl it on his finger. "No one asked me to stop."

Georgia watched the ball go around. "My, you really do well with that, don't you?"

Denny let it drop.

"Yep," he said simply. He saw she had her purse in her hand. "Where are you going?"

"I thought I'd do some shopping," Georgia said. "And don't you be asking me to come. I may get stuck on a long line, and I don't want you to be late for this afternoon's rehearsals."

"Sure," Denny said. "Have a good time."

Georgia kissed him and left. As Denny was working around the hallway, he noticed the back door, and decided he'd check and see if there was room to play outside. The yard beyond the blue metal door was littered with wood and metal scraps left over from the theater's construction. But concrete had been poured on one corner of the yard, a place where trash cans were kept. Denny decided this would be a suitable basketball court. He kicked away the debris and moved the cans to a far corner.

Denny crouched down and dribbled the ball, bending and twisting his way around the makeshift court. Suddenly, he slammed into something he knew had not been there before. He let the ball drop and turned to see a little girl standing near him, watching him with big brown eyes. She looked vaguely familiar, yet he couldn't place her. He clicked his tongue and said, "Do you have to stand so close? I could have knocked you down!"

"You couldn't knock me down," the child said, matter-of-factly.

"Are you kidding?" Denny asked. "I'm twice as big as you."

He looked at her for a moment.

"I remember you now," he said. "You're that weird kid from the preliminaries. What're you doing back here now?"

"I want to play with you," she said. "Where did you get that orange ball?"

"My dad gave it to me," Denny said. "He lives in Arizona."

The child's eyes rounded.

"Arizona is forever away," she said. "Why isn't your daddy here with you?"

"He and my mom are divorced," Denny said, bouncing the basketball again.

"Divorced?" the girl said, lisping the word. "Did a man come and steal your mommy away from your daddy?"

Denny frowned at her. Sure, a man came. Lots of men came. That was what broke up Georgia and Randall Richmond—Georgia's steady stream of boyfriends. But Denny did not like to think about that.

"You didn't answer me."

"I don't have to," Denny replied. He started dribbling the basketball again, hoping she'd lose interest and go away, but the little girl skipped after him, easily keeping up with his pace.

"Hey, you might fall," Denny cautioned. "Then you'll mess up that pretty white dress of yours."

Wouldn't hurt you to get a new one, anyway, he thought. That thing looks like it's a thousand years old!

The child smacked the basketball from his hands, sending it flying into a pile of crates.

"I like my dress," she snapped. "It's from Paris, and my daddy bought it for me!"

Denny's mouth dropped open. How did she know what he was thinking? Unable to figure it out, he moved off the concrete to retrieve his basketball.

"I've got to go back inside," he said, watching the child's glaring eyes as he moved towards the back door. "I'm due on stage soon."

"No!" the child cried, racing toward him. "Stay here and be my friend!"

"I can't," Denny said, wishing she'd go away. All he needed was a little kid following him around. "I've got to rehearse. Uhm—uhm, maybe I'll see you next time I come out."

With that, he slipped into the building and shut the door. As he was heading toward his dressing room, he heard the door open and close again. But when he turned around, there was no one behind him in the hallway.

Nate was surprised to find himself a little jealous as Sander and Adrian rehearsed a love scene. He had known Adrian only a few weeks, but he had enjoyed their few conversations, and realized he was beginning to think of Adrian as more than just an employee. She had already shown genuine concern for him, the way a true friend would.

He interrupted the action on stage.

"Sander," he said, "let's see a little less tenderness in that kiss. Remember, Nigel Bertrand looks at Daisy as 'just another broad.' He doesn't have any true affection for her."

"I'm well aware of my character, Mr. Dysart," Sander said coldly.

"Fine," Nate replied, undaunted. "Okay, go on with it."

He smiled slightly when Sander eased up on the kiss and made a note in his book even as the assistant stage manager did the same. On cue, Denny walked on stage. For the next half hour, Nate watched the action, interrupting with suggestions and recording them in his book. Finally, he called an end to the rehearsal.

"Adrian, Sander, take a break," he said. "Denny, you've got another scene coming up, so stick around."

"Sure," Denny said. He thought about asking Mr. Dysart if he knew that strange little girl, but decided it didn't matter. Besides, his mother wouldn't like him bothering a busy important man like Mr. Dysart with such a silly question.

As Sander and Adrian walked toward the dressing rooms Sander turned to her.

"You did very well this time. I find it easy to work with someone as professional as you."

Adrian smiled, though she felt confident enough to do without Sander's condescending praise.

"Thank you," she said. "But I'm afraid Daisy came on a little too strong."

"Not at all," Sander told her. "She's an exaggerated character as it is, Ms. St. John."

Adrian thanked him for the encouragement, then headed for her dressing room. She thought of how excited she'd been at first to learn she'd be working with Sander Bernaux. Most actresses would give their right arm for such an opportunity. And yet, somehow, she wasn't all that impressed by him. Of course he was a fine actor. And he was handsome in a classical way, with his chiseled features and gray-tinted hair. But he wasn't her type.

"Now, that director of mine," she said to her reflection as she took her hair down to brush it. "He's a real doll. Mmm—those gorgeous blue eyes!"

She laughed at her infatuation, thinking she sounded like a teenager, and leaned over to pick up her hairbrush. As she did so, she caught the reflection of a little girl sitting in the brown armchair across the room. Adrian turned abruptly.

"Who are you?" she asked. "How did you get in here?"

The child stared at her without speaking. Adrian started brushing her hair, smiling at the little girl. With eight younger brothers, she was used to the ways of children. The child was obviously very shy.

"I don't remember you from the cast," she said. "Do you belong to someone in the crew?"

The little girl shook her head.

Adrian put her brush down and found some hairpins to roll up her red tresses. She decided to give the child a few moments to speak to her. But all the while the little girl simply stared, until Adrian finally became so bothered that she moved her chair so that she couldn't see the child's reflection.

"Well," she said, when the last hairpin was in. "I'm going to the greenroom to get some coffee. Would you like to come with me?"

She turned to the little girl.

The chair was empty.

"Hello?" Adrian called. She stood up. "Are you hiding somewhere?"

Crouching, she looked underneath the furniture, then stood up and walked over to the trunk and checked behind it. The child was not there. Nor was she in the small closet.

"Strange," Adrian said. "She must have sneaked out when I had my back turned.

Adrian passed several people on her way to the greenroom. No one saw the little girl who walked at her side.

Fishing in her pocket for change, she punched the vending machine for a cup of coffee. As she watched the liquid pour into a paper cup, she heard someone say, *"You can't have him!"*

She turned around and saw that no one was near her. Deciding it was not meant for her ears, she carried her drink over to a couch, where two women sat talking. They smiled up at her and said, "Taking a break, Adrian?"

"Just for a few minutes," Adrian told Barbara Warner and Judy Terrel. "How are things on the lighting crew?"

"We're putting up more fixtures in the building room," Judy

said. "The light's so damned poor in there the workers could go blind."

"Judy, don't talk that way," Barbara said, looking down at her lap.

Judy laughed. "I only said 'damn,' for crying out loud."

She said to Adrian, "Barbara's father was a minister. She doesn't like anyone to swear."

"Oh, I'm not such a prude," Barbara insisted, a bit embarrassed. She changed the subject. "How do you like working with Sander Bernaux?"

"The same way I like working with every other actor," Adrian said, sipping her coffee. "He doesn't impress me."

"Really?" Judy said. "But he's the biggest star on Broadway! I'd die if he even said 'boo' to me!"

Barbara and Adrian laughed at this. Barbara explained that she was only impressed by her husband and asked if Adrian had someone.

"If I'm not being too nosy," she added quickly.

"Not at all," Adrian said. "There was somebody a while ago, but it just didn't work out." Conscious that she sounded sad, she brightened her voice. "There isn't anyone in my life right now. I've been too busy lately."

"What kind of guy do you go for?" Judy asked, leaning forward.

Adrian thought a moment.

"Blond hair, blue eyes," she said. "A good build and not too tall. And he has to be intelligent with a gentle disposition."

Judy nudged Barbara with her elbow.

"She just described Nate Dysart perfectly," she said. "Now *there's* a good-looking man!"

"Isn't it a romantic idea?" Barbara sighed. "The director and his leading lady."

Adrian blushed a little to think they were reading her thoughts.

"How about your husband, Barbara? What does he look like?"

"You'd know if you read the papers," Barbara said. "I'm married to Joel Warner."

"Oh, yes!" Adrian said, recognizing the name. "I read his articles all the time."

Joel Warner was an investigative reporter who freelanced

for all the city's papers. Adrian considered Barbara to be lucky to have such a man for a husband. A picture of herself with Nate came unbidden to her mind, and Adrian smiled. She wondered if there was a chance for her and Nate.

Suddenly, she felt a sharp, burning pain on her arm. She dropped her paper cup, fortunately empty of coffee now.

"What happened?"

"I don't know," Adrian said, taking off her jacket. "It feels like something burned me."

But when she looked, there was no mark at all on her arm.

"That's strange," she said. "I really felt *something*."

"Maybe it was a bug-bite," Barbara suggested.

"In the middle of autumn?" Adrian wanted to know. "There must be a wire sticking out of this couch somewhere, or a pin."

"Say," Judy said with a laugh, "maybe this theater is haunted."

"Oh, that's childish!" Barbara said. "It was just an accident."

"You're probably right," Adrian said. "It's no big deal."

She stood up, moving very close to the little girl who stood unseen next to the couch.

She forgot completely about the stinging pain as soon as rehearsals began. When the day was over, she went to her dressing room and got ready to leave. The theater was still bustling with activity as others did the same. As she left, she noticed the lights were still on, and wondered if anyone was rehearsing.

When she walked on stage, Nate was busy reading his script, going over notes he'd recorded that day. Adrian's shoes clicked along the wooden floor, but he didn't hear her. For a moment, she stood admiring him, thinking how handsome he looked under the stage lights. Finally, she spoke up.

"Hi, there," she said.

Nate nearly dropped the script, and he turned quickly to look up at her.

"Adrian," he said, feeling like a fool. He had thought it was the voices again. "You startled me."

Adrian took a seat next to him on the edge of the stage and put her purse down at her side.

"You must have been working really hard," she said. "I guess you didn't hear me come in."

"I guess not," Nate said. He showed her the script. "I'm trying to decipher my notes while I still can. By this time tomorrow these scribblings will turn into a foreign language."

"You could compare with your assistants," Adrian suggested. "Why don't you take a break? You've been working nonstop since lunchtime."

"I've got a lot to do," Nate said.

In truth, he wanted to keep busy so that he would not think about the strange things that had happened in the last months. Nate was certain that the cure for the voices he had heard was hard work, total dedication to his production.

"Oh, really," Adrian said. "The work will keep! Aren't you even going to break for dinner?"

Nate's eyes widened.

"Are you inviting me out?"

"Oh, no!" Adrian cried with a laugh. "I didn't mean it that way. I guess it's the country girl in me talking again. Don't want you to miss a meal."

Nate closed his script and smacked his knees lightly with it.

"You know you're right," he said. "I could use a good dinner right now. How does seafood sound to you?"

Adrian shook her head. "Fine, I guess. But I was going home in a few minutes. I have some chicken I made the day before yesterday, and . . ."

"Forget the chicken," Nate said, standing. He offered Adrian his hand and helped her to her feet. "Let me take you out to dinner."

For a few moments, he did not let go of her hand. She gazed into his blue eyes, so caught up in them for a moment that she did not see her purse sliding into the orchestra pit.

"That would be nice," she said.

Then she realized what she was doing and pulled her hand from Nate's. She wanted him, but not this way. If she was going to have a serious relationship with the good-looking blond man, she would go about it slowly and let it develop in its own time.

"But I'll have to go home right after," she said. "I mean, I want to read the script for tomorrow's rehearsal."

"I'll have my chauffeur take you home," Nate said.

They walked off the stage together, and in the wings Nate

switched off all the lights, except for the ghost light. When he closed the doors, a small child suddenly appeared on the floor of the orchestra pit, holding Adrian's quilted purse in her hands. She unzipped it and turned it upside down to spill its contents. She did not like what that red-haired lady was doing. She would teach her a lesson.

Lipstick, a purply color. Daddy didn't like makeup. He said women looked prettier when they were natural. She had promised her daddy she would never, ever wear makeup. Not even when she was old enough to date boys. She didn't want to date boys, anyway. She just wanted to be with her daddy, for ever and ever.

And now someone was trying to spoil her plans. Her anger grew, engulfing her tiny frame and making her pretty face turn ugly. She took the lipstick and started scribbling on the polished floor. Then she threw down the empty tube.

A memory came back to her suddenly, a memory many times older than the mortal part of herself that had died so long ago. She was in a dressing room, playing with her mommy's lipstick.

"How dare you touch my things?" Mommy had yelled, smacking her hands. "A brand-new lipstick! You'll have to be punished for this, young lady."

And then her mommy had put her in a small, dark place. Was it a trunk or a closet? It didn't matter, it was frightening all the same.

The child looked around, hating the blackness that hovered just outside the beam of the ghost light, waiting to gobble her up. Mommy had brought the dark. Mommy had hurt her. But Daddy—Daddy would make it light again. He would help his little girl.

She bowed her small head.

"I want my daddy," she whimpered, like the innocent child she had once been.

After Nate had put his papers away, he and Adrian started for the car, where George was waiting to take them to dinner. But just before reaching the back door, Adrian winced and said, "Oh, I went and left my purse on the stage."

"Let's go get it, then," Nate said. "We've got plenty of time."

He and Adrian walked back to the stage, where Nate turned on the overhead lights again.

Adrian said, "I'm not usually so absentminded. I left it right over . . ."

She went to the place where Nate and she had been sitting, but the purse was not there. Nate came to help her look for it, and in a few moments they found it down in the orchestra pit, its contents strewn all over.

"It must have dropped down there," Adrian said. "I guess I left it open."

"Let me get it for you," Nate offered, crouching to jump into the pit.

"Oh, it's all right," Adrian said. "I can manage."

But Nate was already putting everything back into the small quilt bag. He handed it up to Adrian and started to hoist himself onto the stage again.

"Thanks," Adrian said. She looked over the contents of the purse, then said, "Oh, wait a minute. My lipstick is missing."

Nate put his feet back on the floor.

"I don't see anything else down here," he said, turning around with his eyes to the floor.

"But I know I had it," Adrian said. "I just bought it today. Oh, let it go! I'm sure I'll find it tomorrow."

Nate waved a hand at her.

"Let me look for it while I'm down here," he said.

Adrian was still making apologies when Nate found the missing lipstick. He lifted the now-empty tube from the shadows cast by the front of the stage.

"I thought this was brand-new," he said, handing it up to her.

"Maybe it broke," Adrian said. She sighed. "Well, that's a few dollars down the drain!"

"I'll buy you a new lipstick," Nate told her. "But let me find where the broken piece went before I have purple goop ruining my floor here."

He found the rest of the lipstick, smeared all over the floor at his feet. But it wasn't just a smear mark that he saw. It was something more definite than that. The smudge marks looked like letters.

"Maybe you should let the janitor do that," Adrian suggested.

Nate did not reply. He knelt down and examined the smudge marks closer. There was a message scrawled on the floor.

I AM WAITING

Quickly, he rose to his feet again. This was a trick again, just like the photography and the voices. He would not fall into their trap.

"You're right," he told Adrian. "That's what I pay him for."

He climbed back up onto the stage, and together he and Adrian left the theater. On the way to the restaurant Nate could not stop thinking of the strange words he'd seen on the floor.

SEVEN

It didn't dawn on Nate until he was at the door of Bailey's Seafood House on Manhattan's fashionable East Side that this was his first "social" outing since his arrival from California. He couldn't call it a date, really, since it was a spur-of-the-moment decision to join Adrian for dinner. He was just enjoying a night out with a woman who was already proving to be a new friend. Certainly it would not go beyond that, he thought as he held the door open for her.

They both ordered sautéed bay scallops and talked of trivial things, the way people do when they don't really know each other. But Nate's smile was a forced one; he could not get that strange message off his mind. "I AM WAITING," scrawled in lipstick. What could that mean? *Who* was waiting? And why?

"Hey, those scallops taste better hot," Adrian said, tilting her head a little so that her silver hair-clips caught the lights.

Nate shook his head abruptly and found her watching him with smiling eyes.

"Sorry, I was thinking," he said, starting on his food again.

"About what?"

He waved a hand at her.

"Oh, nothing that you need bother about," he said. "Something about the theater."

Adrian took on a mock-serious expression.

"Well, then, I certainly will worry about it," she said. "Anything to do with that affects all of us.

Nate shook his head, thinking, *It doesn't affect you at all. You don't have nightmares or hear voices.*

"Come on," Adrian pressed. "It seems to really be bothering you. Don't you think you'd feel better getting it off your chest?"

Nate chewed his mouthful of scallops and thought about that. Yes, it would feel better. Each time he'd discussed his problems with Jim, it was as if a little of his burden was lifted. But why should he discuss them with Adrian? He didn't know her very well—as yet, not even as a colleague. She'd probably think he was crazy. But he did need to talk to someone, and Adrian was so willing to listen...

He decided to start with the least of his problems.

"Adrian," he asked, "do you know anything about photography?"

"Photography?" she echoed, not understanding. "Well, very little. One of my brothers took a summer-school course in it, so I might know something by osmosis. Try me, anyway."

"Okay, imagine this," Nate said, holding up both hands. "You take a picture—say of a building. And there are no people in the scene. Yet when the picture is developed, someone is there—or rather, what *seems* to be a person."

"Maybe he ducked into the shot at the last minute, and you didn't notice," Adrian suggested.

"No, it's not like that," Nate said. "This figure is floating in midair. Above a girder of the theater's frame."

Adrian rubbed her lower lip with the rim of her wineglass, thinking about this. She didn't have the slightest idea what Nate was leading up to, but could tell by the tone of his voice and the serious expression on his face that it really bothered him.

"Eat some of that food," she said finally, for lack of a better response.

Nate laughed for the first time in ten minutes.

"Country girl," he said. "Did your mother equate food with comfort?"

"I suppose," Adrian said, smiling slightly. She sounded

more like an older sister now. She tried to cover herself by turning back to the photograph issue.

"This figure you're talking about," she said, "you aren't one hundred percent sure it *is* a person?"

"How can I be?" Nate said. "It's very blurry, and like I said, it's floating in midair."

"Well," Adrian said, "unless Casper the Friendly Ghost got in on the picture, it must not be a person. Probably a flaw in the film."

But, Nate thought, a flaw would not be exactly the same in almost an entire roll of film. Still, it was a possibility, considering how little he knew of photography.

"Nate, why are you asking me all this?" Adrian wanted to know.

"Oh, well," Nate said, not sure how much more to tell her, "it's just that something like that happened to a roll of film I took. I can't explain it, and it really bugs me."

Adrian finished her plate of food and pushed it away.

"Why don't you take another set of pictures, and see what happens? If it's the film, there should be nothing wrong with this roll. But if there is, I suggest you go out and buy a new camera."

"You think it might be as simple as that?" Nate asked.

There was a worried yet hopeful look in his eyes that made Adrian think something more was bothering him.

"Try and see," she said. Impulsively, as she did many things, she took his hand. "Nate, is something else on your mind? I hardly think the mistakes of an amateur photographer should make you so intense."

Nate shook his head, deciding he'd told her enough. He would not frighten this lovely woman with talk of voices and nightmares, though it seemed Adrian was not the type who was easily frightened.

"Please," she said softly, "if there's anything you want to talk about, I'm willing to listen. And I can keep a secret."

Nate smiled at her.

"I'm okay," he insisted, squeezing her hand. "I guess I'm just tired. Sorry I'm not a better dinner partner."

Adrian pulled her hand out of his, patted his wrist, then picked up her wineglass.

"No wonder you're tired," she said. "You work so hard, and such long hours!"

She wondered, though, if that was all that was bothering him. Though he *did* work hard, he seemed to enjoy himself while doing so. Was it just fatigue she was seeing right now? Or something more?

Adrian decided then that she would watch Nate closely. If he needed someone, she would be there.

When he arrived home, it was to receive yet another phone call from Vance. Nate slammed the receiver down in his usual angry way, but his cousin had upset him so much that he was unable to fall asleep that night. His mind was a boiling cauldron of thoughts and memories. The dinner with Adrian had been purely platonic—Nate hadn't even kissed her good night. But it stirred up memories of another woman, his wife, Meg, that were so clear he could almost imagine her next to him in the big brass bed. Nate rolled over onto his stomach and threw out his arm as if to embrace her, a chill running through him when he felt only the cold satin sheets.

It was all right to want to get close to someone again, wasn't it? In the six years since Meg had died, Nate had dated on occasion, but had never felt anything like he did tonight. Adrian was something special. Someone caring and warm who was willing to listen to his problems. And he so needed to talk.

"Adrian," he whispered aloud to the full moon hanging just outside the room's balcony.

He gave up trying to fall asleep and crawled out of bed, groping in the dark room for his bathrobe. It was a warm, summery night, and sitting by the pool might be relaxing. Quietly, Nate walked along the darkened hallway toward the back staircase. He passed ancient portraits of family members, staring at him with cold eyes. Nate could not help stopping at the portrait of his father that hung just outside one of the mansion's countless bedrooms.

"I spent nearly eighty dollars on dinner tonight," he whispered. "It was all your money, too."

Nathaniel Dysart Sr., dressed in a black suit with a white handkerchief in his pocket (hand-rolled, Nate was sure), simply watched his son without response. Nate thought it seemed strange not to hear his father yelling at him. Even though the old man had been dead nearly a year, Nate had yet to get used to the blissful silence in the big house.

1975

Nate found his wife standing outside their room one night, holding on to the marble railing of the balcony and staring at the moon. He came up behind her and kissed her softly on the neck, putting his arms around her. She didn't turn around, but sighed and sniffed back a tear.

"Meg, you're crying," Nate said. "Again. What happened?"

She turned and buried her face in the soft folds of his velvet robe.

"Your father," she choked.

"I might have known," Nate said. "What did he do this time?"

"It's always the same thing, Nate," Meg said. "He says I was a clumsy fool. He says the accident was all my fault!"

Nate squeezed her and kissed her hair.

"Meg." He sighed. "My father is a cruel, vicious man. Don't even listen to him."

"I can't help it!" Meg said. "He harps at me all day long!"

She burst into tears, and choked, "He says I killed her! He says I killed our . . ."

"Meg, no," Nate said. "Don't ever talk like that! It wasn't your fault and you know it!"

He turned her around and led her from the chilly balcony to their bedroom. A soft light was burning next to the four-poster bed, and Nate switched it off after he had climbed under the covers with his wife. He put his arms around her and closed his eyes to fall asleep.

There were footsteps outside the door, thumping angrily over the old carpeting. They stopped suddenly, and as they did so Nate felt Meg stiffen a little.

"Clumsy bitch!"

Meg covered her ears to shut out the words she had heard so often as Nate held her close.

"Ignore him," he whispered. "Just ignore him."

But Nate knew better than anyone that this was impossible.

Adrian met Nate just outside his office as she walked to her dressing room the next morning. She shifted her handbag to her other shoulder and smiled at him.

"Thanks again for dinner," she said. "It was wonderful."

"I enjoyed it," Nate said. "Maybe—maybe we'll go out again soon."

"I sure hope so," Adrian answered, grinning.

She stood there until Nate had entered his office and closed the door, then whispered to herself, "Way to go, lady."

She smiled all the way to her dressing room. Adrian was completely infatuated by Nate. He was so vulnerably sweet, she thought. And yet beneath those sad eyes and that soft voice was a strong, highly professional head of a theater company already noticed by the critics. Whatever problems Nate had, he did not let them get in the way of his production. Adrian admired him for that.

EIGHT

The next week passed uneventfully, innocent of strange voices and nightmares for Nate. He was in a particularly good mood one October morning when he met Georgia and Denny in a hallway. Georgia, noticing his good mood, seized the opportunity.

"Mr. Dysart," she said, fingering a string of colored beads around her neck, "I've been wanting to ask you a favor. May I?"

Nate lifted his hands a little and dropped them.

"Sure," he said. "What can I do for you, Mrs. Richmond?"

"Well, I was thinking," Georgia said. "Do you mind if I watch Denny from the wings? Your new stage manager said I have to wait in Denny's dressing room. But it's so boring in there, and I really want to see how my son is progressing."

Nate didn't like the idea of working with stage mothers, yet despite her rather strident appearance and behavior, Georgia had never butted in. He decided he might give her a chance.

"What do you think, Denny?"

The boy's lips curled.

"I have to do whatever she wants," he said. "She's my mom."

Nate laughed and gave his consent.

Georgia stood out of the way in the wings and kept her eyes fixed on her son, who went through a dialogue now with Sander. On stage, Denny lost his faint southern accent and replaced it with a New York one so perfect no one would have guessed he was from South Carolina.

Don carried the Siamese cat, Cartier, around with him as he gave instructions to the waiting actors. He stroked the animal's head, and soon she began to purr so loudly that Sander turned to look at her. He interrupted the action on stage to say, "Be certain that animal doesn't come out here on stage."

"Would that bring more bad luck, Mr. Bernaux?" Denny asked, looking up at the tall actor.

"It certainly would," Sander replied. "A cat watching from the wings is good fortune, but he must never run onto the stage."

"All right," Nate said from his seat in the front row. "Enough about the cat. We've got a play to rehearse, remember."

As the actors continued their scene, with extras walking on or off stage as Don cued them, Cartier continued to purr. But all of a sudden, she was silent. Her eyes fixed on the floor at Don and Georgia's feet, growing so wide that the stage lights were reflected in her golden irises. She stiffened a little, her ears laid flat against the sides of her head.

Suddenly, she let out a horrible shriek and jumped from Don's arms, clawing him in her frenzy. She tore onto the stage, climbing up the nearest tall thing she could find—Sander's leg. The actor cried out as her claws dug into him and kicked her across the floor.

"Don't!" Denny cried, hurrying after the cat.

"What's wrong with that beast?" Sander roared, rubbing his leg. "Get it off the stage!"

Nate stood up and walked to the apron of the stage, telling Denny to be careful as the boy attempted to coax the animal from her hiding place behind the curtains. Finally, after she'd calmed down, she let Denny lift her into his arms.

"Poor kitty," Denny said.

"Bad luck," Sander mumbled. "It means bad luck."

"It'll be all right," Nate soothed. He looked at Georgia and Don.

"What do you suppose happened?"

"It's as if she was spooked," one of the extras said.

Georgia took the cat from Denny.

"We'll never know," she said. "But I'll take the poor thing back to the wardrobe mistress's room, to her bed and food. She'll calm down. Sometimes it's hard to understand cats; they do the darnedest things. Why, back home we had a cat..."

Nate signaled the actors on stage back into position, cutting her off.

"All right," he said, "the excitement's over. Sander, I'm sorry that happened. But let's get back to work. Previews start in Connecticut on November twenty-third, and we don't have time to waste."

Sander's jaw stiffened, but he joined in like the professional that he was. Nate returned to his seat in the first row, wishing all his problems were as minor as a cat. He tried not to imagine what might have frightened the usually well-adjusted animal.

Cartier would never be able to tell him of the strange little girl who burned him with her tiny hands.

Nate and Adrian sometimes shared lunch, but two days after the cat incident Nate backed out by saying he had an interview with someone at the *Times*. Adrian planned to eat in the greenroom and was looking forward to a leisurely hour after a busy morning. She pulled the brown paper bag containing her lunch from the drawer of her vanity, checked her purse for small change, then turned to leave the room.

A little girl was blocking the way.

"Oh!" Adrian gasped. "You startled me!" She brought a small hand up to her neck and laughed nervously.

"Who are you?" Adrian asked.

"You're a bad woman," she said. "I've seen you with him. Don't think I haven't! But you can't have him!"

"Who?" Adrian asked.

"The dark is going to come," the little girl said in reply. "The dark and the fire."

Adrian, beginning to lose patience, took her by the arm.

"Come on," she said. "I'll take you to your mommy. You can't just run around the theater by yourself."

The little girl pulled away and began to scream. Adrian

covered her ears, demanding that she stop. The child did and glared at her.

"Don't want to go to Mommy," she hissed. "Mommy makes it dark! I hate the dark! The dark hurts!"

"I don't find you amusing," Adrian said sternly. "I think you're a temperamental brat, and when I locate your mother I'm going to tell her you need a good spanking!"

With that, she reached for the doorknob. But the child grabbed her arm. Adrian gasped as a burning pain shot over her skin.

"Don't you say that to me," the child warned in a low voice.

Adrian pulled her arm away, suddenly afraid. The pain—it was like that sting she'd felt the other day in the greenroom! And yet, there was nothing on her arm.

"What is this?" she demanded.

"You can't have him," the child said. "If you try to take him away, I'll kill you."

Adrian suddenly lost her power to speak, and stared for a long time into the deep, dark eyes. And then, the sound of someone laughing in the hallway brought her to her senses. She pushed the child aside.

"Stay out of my dressing room," she said. Then, before she realized how ridiculous it sounded to speak this way to a child, she added, "And stay away from me!"

She jerked open the door and hurried to the safety of the greenroom. The little girl stared after her, angered. She would have to get rid of that woman.

Denny and Georgia were discussing Georgia's plans for the lunch hour. She wanted to do some shopping and didn't want Denny to come along. He guessed she was starting her Christmas shopping and promised to behave himself while she was gone.

Denny liked the idea of being left alone. It was unusually warm and sunny for October, so he'd play in the backyard. He hardly ever went back there. During all his breaks, his mother insisted he study his lines, and then there were the hours spent doing schoolwork with his tutor. But this was lunchtime, and his mother was gone. He was on his own—free!

"Free!" he cried, running around the cement and bouncing the ball vigorously. "No one's gonna bother me!"

Suddenly he noticed the little girl in the white dress. She was standing a few yards away, watching him with those spooky black eyes of hers. Where had she been hiding?

"Not you again," he whined. "Get lost, will you?"

But she walked right up to him and took the ball from his hands.

"I want to play with you," she said, her voice commanding. "I want you to be my friend."

"Look, why . . ."

Denny cut himself off. He wouldn't let this nutty little kid ruin his fun. He decided to go along with her, hoping she wouldn't come and pester him next time.

"I don't suppose you can play basketball," he said. "You're too little."

"I can do anything," the child said.

"Sure," Denny drawled. "Well, let's play catch, anyway. I don't want to stand around talking."

They started to toss the ball back and forth. To Denny's surprise, she caught it easily, never missing. He was about to ask her where she'd learned such coordination (Denny was proud to know a big word like "coordination") but didn't. He wouldn't show any interest in her. Then, maybe, she'd leave him alone.

"Your name is Dennis Richmond," the little girl said.

"How'd you know that?" Denny asked. "I never told you my name!"

"I know so many things," the child said. "I know because I wait and listen."

"Well, go wait and listen someplace else!"

Like many boys his age, Denny didn't like playing with little kids, boys or girls. And this child in particular was annoying to him with her fussy rich-girl's dress.

"You're not my friend," the child shouted, throwing the ball so hard at him that he stepped back a few paces with it.

She walked over to him and wrenched the ball from his grip, tossing it aside.

"Cut it out," Denny said. "Boy, what a brat!"

She didn't respond. Instead, her hands reached up to touch his face. But it wasn't a caress. Denny felt something hot against his skin, like an iron that had once burned him. But this pain was ten times worse.

"Cut it out!" he yelled.

"You have to be my friend," the child said. "You have to help me!"

The pain stopped, but Denny could not move. His mind was no longer in his control, but completely in the power of the small girl standing before him. She continued to speak in a monotone, drawing him further and further into her spell.

"You will do everything I tell you," she said. "You will help me and be my friend."

"I don't want to be your friend..." Denny's voice was pathetic and weak.

But then the horrible burning pain came back again when she touched him, and he was forced to relent.

"I'll be your friend!" he whimpered. "Stop hurting me! Please stop hurting me!"

"Just remember what I can do to you," the little girl said.

All of a sudden, Denny was standing alone in the backyard, feeling strangely dizzy. He saw his basketball over by the trash cans and wondered how it had gotten there. What had happened?

"I don't feel so good," he said softly.

His head pounding, he rubbed his eyes and went to retrieve the basketball. As he brought his thin arms up, he happened to see his watch. All the weariness of a moment ago vanished, replaced by panic. Somehow, his lunch hour was over, and he was due on stage right now!

Panicking, he raced into the theater, slamming into his mother on his way to the stage. He winced.

"Dennis Randall Richmond," Georgia hissed. "If you are ever late for another rehearsal, I'll find a hickory switch somewhere in this big city and tan your hide!"

Denny hurried onto the stage, still holding his basketball.

"Not only is he late," Sander sneered, "but he brings his toys with him!"

Denny apologized to Nate for losing track of the time.

Nate smiled at the boy, but as a producer, his words were stern.

"I'm sure it won't happen again," he said. "Give the ball to

Don and let's get started. Remember, we're opening in Connecticut in just three weeks."

Georgia stood in the wings watching, feeling sorry for yelling at him, but reasoning that he would have to learn some self-discipline if he was to make it in this tough business. She did not know that Denny's mind was preoccupied during the entire rehearsal, wondering who the little girl could be, and hoping she wouldn't come back.

After rehearsals were through, Nate took Denny aside to talk with him. He put an arm over the boy's shoulders and walked out of earshot of Georgia and the others.

"Denny, what was wrong today?" he asked gently. "Your timing was off completely and you kept forgetting to use that terrific New York accent."

Denny shrugged.

"I don't know," he said. "I—I sort of didn't feel well."

He thought about the little girl but decided not to mention her. His mother might be angry to know he'd been playing with a stranger. She'd warned him about talking to strangers in the city.

"You do look tired," Nate said. "Maybe you should stay home tomorrow. I don't want you coming down with something, and missing our premiere."

"Oh, I would never do that," Denny said, looking up at Nate. "I want to come to work tomorrow, really. I'm okay now. I promise I won't goof up again."

"Hey," Nate said, giving him a friendly hug. "We all have bad days."

"You're not mad anymore?"

Nate shook his head.

For the first time in several hours, Denny grinned. But there was one watching them who did not feel happy. She watched Nate ruffle Denny's hair, and clenched her small fists in anger. Denny was getting in the way. He'd have to be dealt with, the child thought.

With something akin to jealousy stirring in her, she decided how she would use Denny in her plans.

"Denny wasn't his usual self today," Adrian commented to Nate as they walked towards their rooms.

"He did look a little tired," Nate said. "But I think it was frustration. His mother told me he'd been playing in the back yard and I guess he got carried away with it. She was pretty upset. It isn't a pleasant thing to have a parent angry with you."

He bit his lip to think of his father, who's anger had caused him a lot of grief. Nate could almost feel the sting of the old man's cane on his shoulders.

"What's the matter, Nate?" Adrian asked.

"Nothing," Nate insisted.

She knew this wasn't true, for in the past few weeks she had gotten to know his moods fairly well. But she also knew that Nate didn't like discussing his personal affairs. She decided to let him tell her, if he wanted to, in his own time.

"Are you doing anything for dinner tonight?" Nate asked.

Adrian smiled. "I'm meeting a girl friend. But I think I can get out of it."

"Great," Nate said. "I'll get us reservations at Lutece, and . . ."

"Nate!" Adrian gasped. "We can't go there! They don't even have prices on the menu!"

"So?"

"You don't have to spend so much money," she told him.

"I'm trying to impress you," Nate said.

Adrian looked into his blue eyes and sighed. "Nathaniel Dysart, you already have."

There was a moment of silence as the two gazed at each other, suddenly lost in their own world. All the sounds of the crew and cast members faded out, the pictures on the wall did not exist, there were no doors along the hallway. There was just the two of them.

Nate pulled Adrian close to him and kissed her warmly, at first in a gentle way. But her body was comforting to him, and he found himself tightening his embrace until it seemed she'd break. He wanted her so much. And with her sighs, Adrian showed she wanted him too.

It was an impulsive kiss, exchanged because imagination would no longer suffice. But there was one who did not share their ecstasy. Nearby, a little girl watched them, her fists clenched tightly at the sides of her ruffled dress.

Suddenly, a loud cry interrupted the two lovers. Adrian

pulled away from Nate as the two of them looked around, startled.

"It's coming from the basement," Nate said, breaking into a run.

Adrian, close at his heels, followed him down the stone steps. They were halfway across the basement when they smelled smoke, coming from the building room. Nate crashed through the door and found the room in total chaos as the crew members rushed around trying to put out a fire and save what they could from the flames.

"It's one of the sets!" a carpenter shouted at Nate.

Nate grabbed a fire extinguisher. A scream rang out. One of the men had been burned. He was holding his hand up, roaring in pain.

Nate turned back to the fire, squinting against the heavy smoke. Suddenly, he saw a vision in the flames that made him drop the extinguisher in fear. It was a body. The body of a child ...

"Hey, that isn't empty yet!" one of the crew shouted at Nate, pointing to the extinguisher.

When Nate didn't pick it up again, the man retrieved it and blasted at the fire. Nate continued to stare at the figure near his feet. It was curling up, blackening. And he couldn't move to save it.

"Take the dark away!" a child's voice screamed. *"Please take the dark away! It hurts!"*

Slowly, Nate crouched down, his arms reaching out toward the blackened little body. But all of a sudden he was wrenched back, as the carpenter roared, "Are you *nuts?!*"

And the little child became a piece of wood. Just a piece of wood.

"We can't save anything here," the carpenter said. "Let's get the fire out before it spreads to the other sets!"

Nate had to get away from the fire. His mind was playing tricks on him again.

I'm going to lose my theater, his thoughts said. *It's going to burn up again like it did ...*

Nate shook his head. His theater had never burned! Why had he thought that?

Finally the flames were doused and only a few wisps of smoke remained.

"Thank God it only damaged one set," someone said.

"All that hard work ruined, and you're thanking God?"

"How did this happen?" Nate asked.

"I don't really know," the carpenter said. "We were packing things in for the night when I thought I smelled smoke. Before we could stop it, the whole damned thing went up."

Nate snapped out of the daze that had held him a moment ago and became the efficient company head that he was.

"Open some windows to air this place out," he said. "When the smoke clears, I want someone to check through that pile. God help you if I find evidence this fire was caused by carelessness."

Upstairs in the greenroom, Adrian was sitting with the crewman who'd gotten burned. He had his hand in a bowl full of ice water.

"Oh, Nate," Adrian said, looking up. "Is the fire out?"

"Yeah, it's out," Nate said. "How do you feel, Ronnie?"

"It doesn't hurt when I keep it in the water," Ronnie said.

Nate looked into the bowl. What he saw was not a man's hand, but something out of an old horror movie, like those drive-in flicks where a man is deformed after having acid thrown at him.

"Maybe you should go to a doctor," he said. "Those blisters look pretty ugly. How exactly did it happen?"

"It was kinda weird," Ronnie said. "I was running toward the extinguishers when someone grabbed me by the hand, and I felt this awful pain. But when I looked around, no one was there!"

"You might have accidently touched something heated up by the fire," Adrian suggested.

"Yeah, I guess that was it," Ronnie replied. "It was an accident, of course."

"Of course," Nate said, though he couldn't be sure.

NINE

Because the fire had delayed them, Nate and Adrian settled for a small Italian restaurant on a street near the theater, and now they sat in silence, each lost in thought. Adrian worried about Nate, watching him poke at his food without eating it. He, in turn, was trying to understand what had happened. Why had he been so frightened by a fire? And what in heaven's name had made him think that piece of wood was a child?

He put down his fork. Maybe all this wasn't rigged. Maybe he really was hearing voices and seeing things that weren't there.

Maybe the pressure of this business really was too much for him, and he was going to be a failure, like his father always insisted.

"Nate, it's going to be okay," Adrian said softly. "They'll rebuild the set in no time, you watch and see."

He managed a smile for her, but it was a false one, and she knew it. She took his hand and squeezed it.

"Nate, what's really wrong?" she asked.

"Nothing," he said.

Adrian clicked her tongue. "Damn it, I know something's bugging you. Will you please tell me about it?"

All of a sudden, Nate was blurting out everything that had happened since his arrival from California. Adrian listened quietly as he told her of the strange dream, of the voices, of the idea he'd had that someone might be trying to break him.

"The first suspect is my cousin, Vance Dysart," Nate said. "Even though he was my father's only other blood relative, he wasn't included in the will. He's damned pissed about that."

"Enough to want to hurt you?"

Nate nodded. "But he really doesn't have the brains to mastermind any of this." He sighed. "I don't know—maybe I'm just paranoid. I *did* see something in that fire, but if it had been set up, someone else would have seen it too. Maybe it *is* in my head."

"Oh, Nate," Adrian said. "I don't know what to tell you, except that I think you might be working too hard."

Nate shook his head.

"It isn't that," he said. "I worked steadily for five years in California, and for several years here in New York before that. I enjoy my work."

"Maybe it's finally caught up with you," Adrian said.

"Look, all those things you told me are tricks of an exhausted mind. Why don't you take a vacation?"

"With a show opening in New York in December?" Nate asked.

"Only for a few days," Adrian said. "Don Benson is qualified to take over."

"We've only been rehearsing for two weeks," Nate said. "I can't leave now. Well, I might have been able to if Jim were here..."

He shook his head.

"Nate, you've been through so much in the past year," Adrian said. "With your father dying, and then your best friend. Any man would be weakened by such experiences."

"I'm not weak," Nate insisted, almost hearing his father in her voice. "I'm a damned good director."

"And a terrific producer," Adrian agreed. "I've never worked with a better one. But all this that's on your mind is bound to affect your work sooner or later. I really think the best thing for you to do is take a few days off."

Nate knew she was right, but still he shook his head. He would keep on working, for it was only when he was busy that he wasn't haunted by morbid thoughts.

"I wouldn't be able to relax, knowing my theater was out of my hands," he said.

"Don't be so stubborn," Adrian said.

He waved a hand at her.

"I can't help it," he said. "I'm only happy when I'm working. I'm trying to achieve a goal, Adrian. Six years ago, when I had my own production company, my father used to make fun of me. He said I'd never amount to anything and would be a total failure. I have to prove him wrong."

"You already have," Adrian said, wondering why he cared what a dead man thought. "The box office has already sold out tickets for the first week of *Making Good*. Now, that doesn't sound like failure to me!"

"I won't be satisfied," Nate said, "until I see how the preview audiences react. And then I'll still worry about our Broadway opening!"

Adrian gazed over the light of a candle set in a wine bottle, wanting to throw her arms around him and kiss the sadness away from his face.

"Nate, I love you," she said softly.

It was so abrupt a statement that it took Nate by surprise, in spite of the passionate kiss they'd shared just a while earlier. Before he could respond, she reached up and brushed her fingers along the side of his face.

"I want to help you forget everything," she said. "I want to make you happy."

He caught her hand and kissed it.

"Come back to the theater with me," he said. "No one will be there but the night watchman, and we won't be disturbed."

Without a word, Adrian nodded her head in consent.

They walked onto the stage half an hour later, holding hands. Nate found the control board in the wings and switched on the overheads, beams of light washing the huge stage.

"Are you sure the guard won't bother us?" Adrian asked.

"If you're having doubts," Nate said, "it's okay."

"Oh, Nate," Adrian said, "I've never been so sure of anything."

Nate took her head in his hands and kissed her again.

"I just want to be with you tonight," he said. "I just want to hold on to you."

He turned back to the control board, dimmed the lights, and pulled the curtain across the stage, cutting them off from the theater and creating their own private cocoon.

"I could have gotten a room at the Pierre or the Plaza," he said, "but that didn't seem right, somehow." He paused to kiss her again. "I don't even need lights, the way you shine on this stage."

"I hope the critics are as flattering as you in a few weeks," Adrian said, laughing quietly.

But the smile disappeared when Nate pulled her close, kissing her. She smelled of lavender soap, so fresh and real. He wanted her so much. He loved her as he never thought he'd love a woman again.

Silently, he pulled her onto the sofa that was part of the set for the living room. Only the ghost light was left shining through the slightly parted curtain. Adrian looked like an angel in the soft light, her arms reaching up to him. She was so beautiful...

When they had given themselves to each other, Adrian laid her head on Nate's bare chest and fell asleep. For a little while, Nate rubbed her back lazily. And then, lulled by the steady rhythm of her breathing, he dozed off himself, smiling.

In the orchestra pit, a little girl watched the two of them, her feelings tottering between hurt and anger. Why were they always together? Why did they always smile when it was so dark and lonely in here?

"Daddy, please take the dark away," she whispered.

If only she could get rid of that woman somehow things would be right again.

Nate stirred a little as a cold breeze washed over him, and opened his eyes. It was dark, except for the glow of the ghost light. He squinted and tried to read his watch by it, but looked back up again when he saw something white and filmy moving across the stage. It hovered just outside the range of the ghost light, then vanished.

"Damn it!" he cried, jumping to his feet so quickly that Adrian was jerked awake.

"What?!" she yelped. She looked around in confusion, then saw Nate hurrying towards the wings. Seconds later, the stage was brightly illuminated and the curtain opened.

"What's wrong, Nate?" she asked, covering her eyes against the blinding light.

"I saw something," Nate said, walking towards the apron. He looked down into the orchestra pit, then surveyed the shadowy room before him. It was deadly still.

"What do you mean, you saw something?" Adrian asked, standing up.

Nate walked across the stage, looking all around himself. He pointed towards the ghost light.

"It was a white figure," he said. "Like the one in those photographs."

Adrian crossed the stage to him.

"Maybe you were just dreaming," she said. "I don't see anything."

Nate was looking at the curtains covering the exits on either side of the orchestra section. Could someone have slipped through them?

"Whoever it was," Adrian said, playing along with him although she had her doubts, "he's gone now. Forget about it for tonight, darling."

Nate turned to her, ready to burst out that he could not

forget about it. But somehow, instead, these were the words that came out, "Adrian hold me? I need you."

She moved closer to him and put her arms around his shoulders, wishing she could say something to calm him down. His fears were so genuine—could they also be justified? Was there really someone spying on him? Nate seemed rational at other times, and he was, as she'd said, a completely professional director-producer.

"Nate, I have an idea," she said finally. She hadn't come to terms with the idea of someone trying to destroy Nate, but she would not deny it completely. "Why don't you spend the night at my apartment?"

"I'd like that," Nate said. Now he pulled away and threw his arms up in the air. "No I won't. Look at me! I'm acting paranoid."

Adrian took both his hands.

"Don't say that," she said. "You have every right to be frightened. This is a tough business we're in, and I'm sure there *are* people who'd like to see you fail. Jealous people. But if I were you, Nate, I wouldn't give them the satisfaction of seeing me cringe."

Nate looked into her eyes.

"When I got the enlargement of that photograph," he said, "I thought someone had paid the person who developed it to tamper with it. And then I thought the voices I'd heard were coming from a tape recorder someone had placed in the theater."

"You see?" Adrian said. "That's probably what it is. A vicious, childish prank."

"And I vowed I wouldn't let it get to me," Nate went on. He bent down and picked up his shirt.

"Could Vance have done this?"

"I don't think so," Nate said. "He couldn't have known I took the pictures, anyway. Much as I dislike the guy, I can't blame him for this. Some of my father's business partners would be smart enough to pull it off, but would it be worth all this effort?"

"Nate," Adrian said, "just keep telling yourself the only thing that matters is your play. This culprit will get tired and will eventually leave you alone."

Nate put his arms around her. He prayed she was right. In

a moment, the embrace changed to a long, warm kiss. Nate could easily forget his problems in Adrian's arms. He could forget there was anyone else in the world.

But they were not alone. The little girl who'd watched them sleeping a moment ago, her heart filled with anger, stood nearby and clenched her fists. She would get rid of that red-haired woman. She would make certain Adrian didn't interfere.

First, however, she'd let them think nothing more was going to happen. When they were least expecting it, she'd strike again.

As she turned her key in the lock on her apartment door Adrian heard the phone start to ring. Who would be calling her at this hour of the night? It had to be Nate, of course. She hoped he wasn't in trouble...

"Adrian, it's your mother."

"Mom, hi!" Adrian gasped. She hooked the receiver between her shoulder and jaw and wriggled out of her coat. "Why are you calling so late? Is something wrong?"

She thought about her father, who had had a heart attack several years earlier. A quick switch to her other ear allowed her to finish taking off her coat, but cut off her mother's first words.

"...at all," Martha was saying. "We're fine. But I've been trying to call you all night. We got our airline tickets to New York this afternoon!"

Adrian smiled. "Really? When are you coming?"

"Do you have to ask?" Martha said. "We'll be there the tenth of December, and we're staying about a week. Might as well make a trip of it, you know."

"That sounds great," Adrian said. "So you'll be here for my debut."

"Wouldn't miss it for the world," Martha said. "Oh, I've been *busting* all night to tell you. Where've you been?"

Adrian bit her lip and shifted a little, embarrassed. Then she laughed at herself. Imagine, acting coy at her age! And with her parents living five hundred miles away!

"I went out with Nate Dysart tonight," she said. "We had a lovely dinner in the city."

And an even better dessert, despite unpleasant surprises, she thought.

"That's nice," Martha said. "I'm glad to hear you get along so well with your director."

"I can't wait until you meet Nate, Mom," Adrian said. "He's really a good guy."

"Do I hear wedding bells?"

Adrian clicked her tongue.

"I'm too busy with my career right now, Mom," she said. "And speaking of that, I don't mean to cut you short, but I'm really tired."

"I understand," Martha said. "You need your rest. Call me again soon, okay?"

"Sure will, Mom," Adrian said. "See you the tenth!"

How nice it would be for her parents to see her Broadway debut, she thought as she hung up. Adrian just hoped that whoever was tormenting Nate would be long gone before her parents arrived.

"You must have been right," Nate said to Adrian, as they headed out to lunch together. "I've been too busy to worry about those voices, and nothing's happened."

"See?" Adrian said. "You're showing whoever it was that nothing will keep you from opening. They've probably given up."

Nate shook his head.

"I don't know," he said. "I've seen stretches of peace before, and then something always happens. I hope you're right this time."

Adrian put her arm through his.

"I bought a roll of film for your camera," she said, "and I want to take pictures of the theater again. I'll find out how that white flaw could be put on the negatives. It might help us locate the culprit. Any clue we get is worth the effort."

"I thought you didn't want to pay attention to this guy," Nate said.

"That doesn't mean I don't want to catch him!"

Nate was glad to have someone on his side, a confidante who didn't think this was all his imagination.

When they returned to the theater after lunch, Adrian hurried to her dressing room to get ready for the afternoon's rehearsals, and Nate headed for his office. He passed Georgia and Denny in the hallway. Denny's eyes refused to meet Nate's, as if he were embarrassed to be caught carrying his basketball again.

"I promise I won't be late this time," he said.

"You have about a half-hour," Nate told him.

Georgia nodded vigorously.

"Don't you worry, Mr. Dysart," she said. "I'll see to it that he's early."

"I'm sure he will be," Nate said, ruffling Denny's hair. "Right, kid?"

Denny nodded even as an unseen little girl clenched her fists and let out a silent scream of jealousy. She wanted to feel someone touch her hair, she wanted someone to smile at her. She wanted to see *him* smile at her.

The time had come, she decided, to get rid of Denny.

The three parted company, Georgia walking Denny to the backyard. When Nate reached his office, the phone was ringing. To his anger, the voice at the other end belonged to his cousin.

"Don't hang up," Vance ordered.

"How the hell did you get this number?"

"Well," Vance said, "a big-shot producer like yourself can't expect to hide away forever. I called Information. Decided I haven't been getting across to you."

Nate rubbed his forehead and said impatiently, "Look, let's get this over with once-and-for-all. What exactly do you want from me?"

"Only my fair share of the estate," Vance said. "I think thirty percent isn't asking too much."

"You're insane," Nate accused. "If you want help financially, just ask for it. But cut out these games, otherwise!"

"You cheat! You damned cheat!" Vance bellowed. With an exaggerated groan, Nate slammed down the receiver. By the time he headed to the stage, he had pushed the call from his mind.

When Georgia and Denny entered the backyard, the air was thick with the smells from a nearby restaurant. From one of the nearby streets, the sound of a jackhammer reached their ears, mingling with car horns and a long police siren. Georgia frowned in disgust to see the litter covering the ground and pulled Denny close as if afraid he'd touch it.

"Why on earth do you want to play here?" Georgia asked. "Lord only knows what diseases you could catch in this filth!"

Denny started dribbling his ball on the cement ground.

"Aw, Mom," he said. "There's no food or anything back here to attract germs. Just a few bottles and some crates."

"Don't sass me, young man," Georgia said. "I know what big cities are like! Those boxes could be hiding rats!"

"I haven't seen any," Denny said, gravely. Mothers could be funny sometimes.

Georgia shook her head and found a crate to sit on, kicking it over first to be sure there were no bugs or vermin under it. Satisfied, she settled down and watched her son. What she didn't know was that a small girl was also watching him, making plans. Denny had promised to help her. He wouldn't dare break that promise, and now the child was coming to collect. First Denny could help her get rid of that woman named Adrian, she thought.

A moment later, she was inside the theater, moving down a long hallway. There were so many hallways here, so many twists and turns. But they no longer frightened her as they did so long ago. She knew exactly where she was going.

One of the crew members was returning from his lunch shift and was heading toward the cellar. He didn't see the little girl but felt a sudden dizziness and stopped walking. Rubbing his eyes, he stood still for a few moments. Then, as if remembering something, he went to the back door and pulled it open.

"Mrs. Richmond?" he called. "Nate wants to see you."

"Me?" Georgia asked. "Not Denny?"

"No, just you," the stagehand said.

Georgia looked at her son.

"Now, what do you suppose this is about?" she asked. "Well, I'd better go see. Now, I may not be able to get back out here to remind you, so you'd better know what time it is."

"I promise I won't be late again," Denny said.

His mother left him and went inside the building. A moment later, he noticed the little girl standing at the edge of the yard. He was about to make a nasty comment to her but felt a sudden wave of fear creep over him and forced a smile.

"Hi," he said.

"Hello," the child replied, coming toward him. "I want you to help me today."

Denny nodded, somehow knowing it would be dangerous to refuse. Softly, uncertainly, he said, "I never learned what your name is."

Maybe, if she thought he liked her, she wouldn't hurt him.

"My name's Bonnie," the child said. She turned and looked at the door through which Georgia had just entered the theater. "There's someone in there that I don't like. You'll help me get rid of her."

"Who's that?"

But the child named Bonnie would not tell him. She took his hand, her tiny one feeling like a cube of ice. Denny wanted to pull away but couldn't. He let her take him back inside the building, keeping his eyes on her. What was she going to do to him?

They passed several stagehands in the hallway. They all greeted Denny, but none of them acknowledged the little girl at his side. She took him to the basement stairs, pointing down.

"They'll think she hurt you," Bonnie said.

Denny did not understand, but was too frightened not to follow her as she descended the stone steps. He couldn't understand why he should be afraid of this little kid, a girl wearing a sissy dress. In the distance, he could hear the building crew at work and wanted to cry out to them for help. As if reading his mind, the child turned and glared at him with wide black eyes. Denny looked at her, feeling sick in his stomach.

"Once when I was bad," she said, "my mommy put me in a dark place. And when my daddy found me, he was really angry. He told my mommy she was *wicked*. Now, you'll go in a dark place too. And everyone will be mad at *her*."

"What dark place?" Denny asked, his voice barely a whisper. It was deserted at this end of the basement, and he began to look around for a way out. But he knew Bonnie would never let him escape. She'd hurt him again, make him fall or burn his skin. Or something worse...

They entered the boiler room; it was small and stuffy. Though the theater was new, this room had already taken on the heavy, dusty odor of an ancient cellar. Denny rubbed his arms nervously and watched as the little girl walked across the room.

There was a steel grating on the wall, an entrance to the passages of the theater's air ductwork. The little girl lifted it out easily, as if it were weightless. Denny backed away, frightened by her strength. She set the cover on the floor and turned to him.

"Get in there," she said, pointing.

"I—I can't," Denny protested. "There's no room, with all those pipes and things!"

"I said 'get in there,'" Bonnie pressed, her tone grim. "You have to stay in there until they find you, and then they'll be mad at that woman and make her go away!"

"M-make who go away?"

"DON'T ASK QUESTIONS!"

Denny covered his ears at the sound of her scream as the floor suddenly opened up beneath him. He was falling, falling down into a big black pit! He was going to die! He was going to die!

"*Sssttoooppp!!!*" he screamed, his voice stretched out and sounded far away.

The floor was back again.

"If you don't do as I say," the child threatened, "I'll make you fall into the darkness forever!"

Fighting tears, Denny nodded. Scared as he was, he didn't want a girl to see him cry. Yet whoever, whatever this child named Bonnie was, he could not fight her. She made him crawl into the opening in the wall. Denny cringed back in the darkness, feeling a cold metal pipe against his lower back, and sat silently as Bonnie replaced the grating. She stared through it at him for a long time, ancient memories stirring up in her mind. Mommy had done this to her, too. And Daddy had been mad. Maybe he would get mad again to see this child hurt. And then he would get rid of that new lady . . .

"Who did this to you?" she asked finally.

"Y-you did," Denny choked.

The ringing of metal grated his ears as she slammed a little fist against the cover.

"No!" she cried. "Adrian did this to you! That woman named Adrian. Tell them Adrian did it, or I'll . . ."

"Adrian," Denny whispered, too weakened by her powers to argue.

TEN

Georgia Richmond fingered her plastic beads, trying to hide her embarrassment. Imagine, interrupting one of Mr. Dysart's rehearsals because some silly stagehand said Nate wanted to see her! Georgia decided she'd find the stagehand later and give him a piece of her mind. But right now she had to retrieve Denny, who was due on stage any minute.

She knocked softly on the dressing room door and entered. But it was dark and deserted, with no signs that Denny had been there at all. He always left the lights on, despite her scoldings. Putting her hands on her hips, Georgia said, "If I am shamed again today because that boy missed another rehearsal, I really will tan his hide!"

Angry, she marched toward the back exit and pushed it open. But the yard, too, was empty. Georgia felt a wave of guilt; what if he were already on stage even as she had thought about punishing him. She closed the back door and walked toward the stage. Don met her in the wings.

"Where the hell is Denny?" he asked. "He's late!"

"You mean he isn't here?"

"No," Don whispered, "and he's due on in a few minutes."

The guilt of a moment ago vanished.

"Let me look for him," Georgia said. "I promise I'll be right back!"

She checked the dressing room once again, then went to the greenroom, where she found Adrian chatting with Barbara.

"Oh, Adrian!" Georgia called. "Have you seen Denny anywhere?"

Adrian shook her head. "No, I haven't. Is he outside again?"

"I checked there," Georgia said. "And he isn't in his dressing room."

Barbara looked at both women and said, "Maybe he's in the—the—"

"Little boys' room?" Georgia said. "That's a good idea. I'll certainly check there."

"Don't worry," Adrian said. "I'm sure you'll find him."

Georgia left the room and located a lavatory in one of the hallways. Lord, this was a complicated building! Denny could be anywhere! She stood outside the door for a few minutes until someone came out, then asked, "Did you see a little boy in there?"

The stagehand shook his head and told her the men's room was empty. Now Don Benson came up to Georgia, as her fingers reached up to fidget with the beads she wore.

"Oh, dear," she said. "I can't find him!"

"Well, we've called his understudy, Johnny Hemlock," Don said. "You really should do something about your boy, Mrs. Richmond."

Georgia nodded slowly.

"Oh, I will," she said. "Believe me, when I find him, I'll take care of him!"

"Any ideas where he might be?"

"I looked everywhere I can think," Georgia said.

"The backyard?"

"Yes, and he wasn't there," Georgia replied.

"Let's check again," he said. "It's possible he accidentally threw his ball over the fence and went to get it."

Hoping he was right, Georgia followed the stage manager. Denny was not in the yard, but Don wouldn't give up. He leaned over the back fence and noticed a dead-drunk wino sleeping in the narrow strip that ran between the garage and the building behind it, but no sign of Denny. There were no footprints in the mud, indicating that he hadn't even climbed the fence.

"Then he's got to be inside," Don reasoned.

When he turned back to the yard, he noticed something orange hidden behind one of the crates. It was Denny's basketball.

"Oh, my Lord!" Georgia cried as Don went to pick it up. "Something's happened to my baby! He would never go anywhere without that thing! There are so many awful types in this area. Someone's taken him!"

"Take it easy," Don said. "He probably realized he was late for rehearsal and dropped it when he ran inside."

"Oh, dear," Georgia said. "I hope so!"

Don put his arm around her shoulder.

"Let's check the stage again," he suggested.

With a mixture of anger and worry stirring in her, Georgia followed him back inside.

Denny sucked at his knuckles, trying to drive away the pain he felt from banging so hard on the grating. He couldn't understand why someone didn't hear him. He had shouted and banged and kicked with all his might.

And then he realized something. He was in the back end of the cellar, and the building crew was making too much noise! No one could possibly hear him over it!

Was he going to be stuck in here forever?

Until he died?

Somehow, the strong boy he had always been took over for the moment. He looked around. The passageway he'd been forced into was about three feet high, big enough for him to crawl through. He'd have to snake his way around the twisting pipes, but if there was a grating here, there might be another one nearer to people. He had to take that chance, if he was going to get out of here.

Trying not to think what might be hidden in the darkness ahead, Denny got on his hands and knees and started crawling forward.

Georgia's eyes were bloodshot from crying when she and Don walked up to the front row, where Nate sat. Don leaned down and whispered into his ear, "Sorry to interrupt, but we've got a problem."

"What's that?"

"Denny's missing," Georgia said. Her tears began to flow again. "Oh, my Lord! My little boy is missing!"

Adrian hurried to the apron and looked down at Nate worriedly. She could tell by his expression that he was trying not to think something bad might have happened to the boy.

"Did you check the backyard?" Nate asked.

"Yes," Georgia said weakly.

"And his dressing room and the greenroom?"

"Yes! Yes!" Georgia cried, her voice shrill. "I looked every-where. I can't *find* him!"

"He doesn't seem to be anywhere in this theater," Don said. "And I found his basketball in the yard. Georgia says he never goes anywhere without it."

Adrian brought a hand to her lips and saw Nate open and close his eyes briefly—an expression so subtle that only she noticed it. In seconds, Nate's voice took on the sound of authority.

"We'll postpone rehearsals until he's found," he said. "Adrian, you and I will check the lobby and balcony. Don and Geor-gia, the basement is yours. The rest of you check the dressing rooms. We'll find him."

"Of course we will, Georgia," Adrian assured her.

With Sander protesting that the boy was probably just hiding to avoid punishment for being late again, all the actors and crew went their separate ways.

Something light and airy brushed over Denny's face, and he backed up a little, his ankles skimming under a low length of pipe. Cobwebs. He grimaced and had to remind himself he wasn't afraid of bugs. But he was afraid of everything right at that moment, and his muscles were tensed as if in anticipa-tion of—something. There might be roaches down here or black widows or . . .

"I'm not gonna think about that," Denny said out loud, his voice sounding hollow in the long tunnel.

Holding his hand in front of himself to brush away the cobwebs, he moved onward. Sometimes, it was necessary to flatten out and slither under pipes like a snake or to pull himself up over them. But for the skinny boy, the going wasn't that rough. It was the dark that weakened him. The dark and the close, thick air.

He had been crawling for a few minutes and guessed he should be near the building room. Surely, there would be another grating there, and one of the crew members would get him out. Encouraged by the idea, he kept moving, though his back ached and his breathing became more difficult.

And then he saw a patch of light, just a few yards away. Denny could hear the increasing volume of hammers and saws, and knew he was about to get out of here. He was so elated that the terror he'd felt a moment ago vanished completely.

"Hey, somebody!" he shouted. "Help! Help!"

No one came to investigate his cries. Denny sighed, realizing his voice could not be heard over the din of the workers. He would have to get right up to the grating.

Suddenly, the patch of light disappeared. Denny blinked, but still it did not return. What had happened to the light? And there were no sounds either. It was as if everyone else had vanished. Denny, confused and exhausted, stretched out and rested his head on a pipe, one of his legs thrown up over another pipe that ran along the wall. With his heart pounding so hard that it hurt his chest, he fell asleep.

"Let's try the hallway that runs alongside the auditorium," Adrian suggested as she and Nate descended the twisting lobby staircase.

"You do that," Nate said. "I'm going to take a look at the stage. We might cover more territory if we split up."

Adrian agreed, but before she turned toward one of the doors leading off the lobby, she took Nate's hand and said, "Nate, it's okay. Nothing's happened."

He tightened his fingers around her hand.

"Let's just find Denny," he said.

He did not know what to make of this incident. Was it just the mischievous act of a little boy? Nate hadn't heard the voices yet. There had been no visions. And yet he couldn't help feeling that something *would* happen. The theater was just too silent. The calm before the storm.

He walked slowly down the slanting floor that led to the stage, looking left and right between the rows of golden chairs. No one was there. The orchestra pit was empty, and so was the stage. Nate walked through a door and climbed a few steps, checking first the hallway to the left of the stage, then crossing it and investigating the right hallway. Empty.

"Denny?" he called. "Hey, kid, are you there?"

He listened carefully, praying for an answer. But there was only silence.

Someone was calling his name. Denny's eyes fluttered open, and for a moment he did not know where he was. He pulled his head away from the pipe it had rested on, crying out as he looked around in the darkness. Then he realized that he was still caught in the air passage. The air was so thick in here. The boy coughed for a few moments, rubbing his tearing eyes.

He heard his name again, and recognized Nate's voice from somewhere far away. Then another voice called to him—Adrian's. No! He wouldn't answer her! *She* had done this! She had hurt him and now she wanted to hurt him again!

He had to get out of here. He had to get out before she caught him.

"Mommmm," he groaned. "I want my mom!"

Nate and Adrian met the others near Nate's office and gave their reports. Georgia's face was red, and she clung fast to Don's arm. He shook his head to see Nate's questioning eyes.

"We didn't see him anywhere," he said. "And no one we asked saw him, either."

"I can assure you the boy is in none of the dressing rooms," Sander volunteered.

"And he's not in the lobby or balcony," Nate said. "Or anywhere else we looked."

Georgia choked on a sob and said, "Maybe he's been kidnapped!"

"Of course he hasn't," Adrian said quickly, though in her mind she was anticipating something far worse. To push aside her own fears, she said, "We'll find him, for sure."

For sure, Nate thought.

Denny didn't remember ever being so frightened. He tried to make a game of this, pretending he was a soldier like his dad had been in Vietnam, crawling along the ground to avoid enemy fire. He was an international spy, a space explorer, a . . .

It didn't work. The illusions would last only a moment, and then he would remember where he was. Trapped. Trapped in a dark, stuffy tunnel. And it was Adrian who had done it.

His head bumped something. He reached forward and felt the pipes with his hands, finding that they made a right angle here into a tunnel too small even for his skinny body. Panicking, Denny tried to turn around and go back, but couldn't. Ready to burst into tears of fright, he backed against the wall and sat up a little. His head did not touch the ceiling. Carefully, Denny reached up and put his hand through an opening overhead.

"Hey," he whispered.

It was a shaft leading to the next floor, where only a thin pipe ran! Could this be a means of escape? Denny wriggled his head and shoulders up into it, then scuffed his heels along the floor until he was halfway into the shaft. With his elbows pressed together in front of him, he reached forward and felt the bottom of another passageway. He pushed his chest against it and heaved himself up, bracing his feet along the thin length of pipe behind him. Finally and only because he was a thin, limber boy, he managed to get into the upper tunnel. He collapsed on its floor and tried to catch his breath, finding it somehow easier to breathe here than down below. The air was fresher and cooler.

"DENNY?"

He picked up his head. That was his mother's voice! His mother could help him!

"DENNY, BABY, WHERE ARE YOU?"

"MOM? MOM, HELP ME!"

He crawled forward, pulling himself along a pipeline.

Not too far away, Nate and the others stopped and listened.

"Where's that coming from?" Adrian asked. "It sounds muffled."

"He's locked up somewhere," Georgia said. "I know it!"

Nate held up a hand.

"Wait," he said, "there it is again."

Denny's voice reached them from somewhere far off, but in the complicated structure of the building it was hard to tell where it was coming from.

"Denny!?" Adrian cried. "Keep calling, and we'll find you!"

At the sound of her voice, Denny clamped his mouth shut. He couldn't let her get at him again! Trembling with fear, he scurried ahead, refusing to call out even though he heard them shouting his name.

There was another light up ahead. But Denny did not hurry to it, certain it would disappear.

But it didn't. It grew wide and the space around him

opened out. Denny was able to stretch both arms from his sides. He moved toward the light, his heart beating wildly.

He was under the stage. Blissful fresh air hit his face as he crawled out over the orchestra pit.

There were people out there, sitting in the audience. Why was that? This wasn't a performance! Denny squinted and gazed out over the crowd. Something's wrong, he thought. Those people don't look right...

They were wearing funny clothes, not at all like the styles he saw out on the street every day. The women were wearing hats that fit close to their heads, and most of them had ear-length haircuts. Their dresses were either fringed or beaded, and some of them had feather fans. The men all wore suits that were cut in a funny way, not the tailored look Denny was used to seeing. A memory came to him, a thought of a movie he'd once seen that took place in the early nineteen-twenties. These people were dressed just like that!

"What...?"

He could say no more. The weakness in his muscles overcame him, and as he crashed to the floor the illusion of the audience dissolved.

In the hallway with the others, Adrian took Nate's hand as she heard the thud.

"That came from the stage," she said.

"Let's look there," Nate said, breaking into a run.

They found Denny lying on the floor of the orchestra pit, his hair mussed up and his clothes covered with dust. Nate jumped down into the pit and turned the boy over, taking his small wrist in his hand.

"There's a pulse," he said, looking up at Georgia.

"Oh, praise God!" Georgia cried.

"He's barely breathing," Nate said. "Don, call an ambulance."

The stage manager hurried to the nearest phone. Georgia pulled Denny's head onto her lap and brushed back his sweaty hair, rocking him as tears flowed from her eyes. Denny's cheeks were flushed, and his hair and clothes were thick with dust. Nate stared at her in silence, his fists clenched, waiting for the voices.

"Look," Adrian said. "He's coming to."

Denny opened his eyes once, closed them again, then opened them and looked up at his mother.

"Mom," he whispered. "I can't breathe..."

Georgia hugged him close.

"My baby," she said. "My baby. Mommy's here. You're safe now!"

"Mom, she—she—" Denny stopped to cough, then spat out, "She made me do it."

Nate knelt at his side, putting a hand on the boy's arm. Someone had made him crawl under the floor. Someone had tried to kill him...

"Who, Denny?" he pressed. "Who made you do this?"

Denny blinked at him, then looked over his shoulder. Nate followed his gaze, which seemed to rest on Adrian. The actress shook her head, confused. Abruptly, Denny turned and hid his face in his mother's arms.

"Adrian," he said weakly. "Adrian made me do it."

"Denny!" Adrian cried. "What are you talking about? I'd never do such a thing!"

"Denny, tell us who really made you crawl in there," Nate said.

Memories of a little girl came to the child's exhausted mind, but he could not form the words to describe her. It did not matter, though. It was Adrian who was guilty.

"Mom, she hurt me," Denny whimpered. "Adrian hurt me!"

Georgia kissed him, then turned to glare at Adrian.

"You monster," she hissed. "How *could* you?"

Nate stood up and put his arm around Adrian's waist.

"I didn't do a thing!" she cried.

"Georgia, the boy is hysterical," Nate said. "He doesn't know what he's saying."

"My son doesn't lie," Georgia snapped.

"Adrian..." Denny said before succumbing to another coughing fit.

"Where is that ambulance?" Georgia demanded.

At that moment Don returned to say the ambulance was on its way. Adrian closed her eyes and rested her head on Nate's shoulder, grateful the child had been found. But why, she wondered, had he said *she* had tried to hurt him?

ELEVEN

"Get her out of here!" Georgia screeched as Adrian and Nate entered the hospital emergency waiting room.

"Georgia," Nate said firmly, "Adrian and I have come as friends. We're very worried about Denny."

"You ought to be," Georgia said, staring at Adrian, "after what you did!"

"I didn't do anything," Adrian insisted. "I told you that earlier! Please believe me!"

Georgia seemed ready to cry out again, but instead her expression softened.

"I'm sorry," she said. "Of course I shouldn't blame anyone until the entire story is heard. It's just that I'm terribly upset."

Adrian put a hand on her arm.

"I understand," she said.

A doctor came out at that moment to tell Georgia her son had been moved to an upstairs room. He was conscious and could see his mother.

"I'd like to speak to him too," Nate requested.

"That's impossible," the doctor said. "Denny can have no outside visitors for the rest of the day. He's still quite weak."

"Is he going to be okay?" Adrian asked.

The doctor did not reply, but took Georgia's arm and led her towards the elevators. Adrian, watching them go, said, "I won't be able to rest until I learn what my connection to this is."

"You have *nothing* to do with it," Nate said. "I know something is going on at the theater, and I'm sure it involves what happened to Denny."

Adrian held up a hand.

"Maybe Denny will be able to give us a clue," she said. "I shouldn't say such a cruel thing, but maybe his ordeal is a blessing in disguise."

"You mean that it might help solve this mystery," Nate

109

said. He sighed. "Maybe he can give us a name. God, I hope so."

Adrian put her arms around him and together they walked to a waiting area. Finding a place to sit in the crowded room, they waited in silence for Georgia to return.

"He's a little tired," Georgia told them when she came back half an hour later. "But other than that, he seems fine. Of course, I can't be too sure. We have to wait for the test results."

Georgia seemed better herself. Her eyes were no longer bloodshot, and she had stopped twisting her necklace. Somewhere between Denny's room and here she had found a mirror, and her hair was neatly combed again.

"Did he tell you anything more?" Adrian asked.

"I'm afraid not," Georgia said. "I didn't press the poor darling for details. I think it would be too much for him right now."

"Sure," Nate said, obviously disappointed. But Georgia's next words made him feel better.

"I'd like to say how sorry I am for my earlier behavior," she told Adrian. "I should never have acted that way."

"It's no problem," Adrian said, smiling a little.

"I'm sure you're not to blame," Georgia went on, though Adrian could hear doubt in her tone. "Denny's told me on several occasions that you've always been very nice to him."

"Do you have any idea who might really have done this?" Nate asked.

Georgia thought a moment.

"No," she said. "Everyone on the cast and crew liked Denny, I believe." A slender hand found her beads again.

"Although," she said, "that Sander Bernaux was abrupt several times."

"Sander's abrupt with everyone," Adrian said. "Besides, he was on stage when Denny disappeared."

"You weren't, though," Georgia said to Adrian. The accusation filled her eyes again. "Where were you at the time, Adrian?"

The actress looked at Nate, then back at Georgia.

"In the greenroom," she said. "On my break."

Georgia's eyes thinned as the doubts of a moment ago came back.

"Can you prove that?"

"Of course I can," Adrian said. "There were other people in there!"

Georgia did not say anything, but Nate and Adrian could tell she was wondering again about Adrian. Finally, she said, "I'm dreadfully tired. I'm going home to rest so that I can be here early tomorrow."

"Don't worry," Nate said. "We'll find the culprit."

"We'll leave that to the police," Georgia said, eyeing Adrian.

After she'd left, Adrian said, "She still thinks I'm behind all this."

"Forget about her," Nate said. "You and I both know you're innocent. Come on, let's go home ourselves. We can talk in the car."

A few minutes later they were seated in the back of the Rolls-Royce.

"I still can't figure out how Denny fell off the stage like that," Adrian said.

"Neither can . . ." Nate cut himself off. "Oh, God."

"What is it?"

"I just realized something," Nate told her. "He didn't fall *off* the stage, he fell from *under* it. The theater is built with air passages running through it. He must have been crawling in them."

"That poor kid," Adrian said. "No wonder he was delirious."

"Someone must have forced him inside," Nate said.

Adrian clicked her tongue.

"And Georgia thinks that someone was me," she replied. She turned to Nate. "But I'd never do such a thing."

"No you wouldn't," Nate said.

"It all comes back to those voices you heard," Adrian said. "And your idea that someone is doing this to torment you."

She took his hand.

"You once said you thought it might be your cousin," she said.

"It's possible," Nate said. "But I still don't think Vance could pull off something like this. For one thing, he lives and works up in Connecticut. It would be hard for him to get down here that often."

"Did your father ever cheat anyone?" Adrian asked.

"Probably," Nate said. "Although I heard nothing about it.

I made certain that all his debts were paid off once the will was out of probate."

"But is there still a possibility of one of *them* doing this?"

"I have little association with my father's people," Nate said. "I let others run his businesses, and they report to me only on occasion."

"There's obviously someone who's trying to cause trouble," Adrian said. She scoffed at that. "Trying! More like succeeding!"

"I won't give in to it," Nate said defiantly.

"Good for you," Adrian said.

She rested her head on his shoulder and closed her eyes. Nate kissed her soft hair.

"Come home with me tonight?" he asked.

Adrian's curls tickled his neck as she shook her head.

"You've had a tiring day, Nate," she said. "I think we'd be better off going our separate ways."

"I wish . . ."

"Shh," Adrian said, touching his lips. "I want you to go home and rest, if we're going to get up early to see Denny in the morning."

"You're right," Nate sighed.

But he could not rest that night. Though his body was tired and the satin sheets were comforting, Nate could not relax. Sleep was not a panacea to him but poison that unlocked the horrors in his mind. When he closed his eyes, he heard a shrill laugh.

"She killed the child!" someone shouted. "She killed it!"

"Denny's alive," Nate protested. "Adrian didn't . . ."

But he was not in his bedroom anymore. He was in another room in the house, in a carved wooden bed. And his father was standing at the foot, pointing at him and yelling.

"She killed the child!" he shouted again. "You made a weak child together, and *she* killed it."

Nate felt something press against him and found Meg at his side. Her eyes were bloodshot as she stared up at him, clinging to him with trembling arms.

"Make him stop, Nate," she begged. "Please make him stop!"

Nate jumped to his feet with a cry of his own.

"You bastard!" he shouted. "You bastard! I won't listen to

you anymore! I'm going to kill you for what you did to my wife!"

He ran after the old man, but somehow Nathaniel Sr. kept ahead of him and slammed the bedroom door in his face. Nate opened it, but didn't walk into a hallway. He was on a stage again, watching the little girl singing. The nightmare of the theater repeated itself once more, coming to an abrupt end when Nate forced himself awake.

"Damn," he whispered. No matter how many times this happened, he could not get used to it. He sat up and brought his knees under his chin. He had been reliving a day when he'd finally stood up to his father, sick of the old man's ridicule. Nathaniel Sr. had tormented Meg endlessly, even invading their privacy by entering their bedroom.

Anger still tensed Nate's muscles, and he could not stop himself from getting out of bed and hurrying down to the kitchen. He found a butcher knife hanging over a counter and tore it from the wall.

Like a madman, he raced back upstairs to his father's hallway portrait.

"Bastard!" he screamed, slashing at it. "You bastard! You killed my wife!"

There were running footsteps, and suddenly Carl was wrenching the knife from him.

"Nathaniel!" he cried. "Stop this at once!"

Nate stood back and looked at the ribbons that had once been a portrait of his father. He felt satisfied at first, and then frightened. Why had he done this? Was he really going mad?

"Come back to bed, sir," Carl said. "You must have been having another nightmare."

"No," Nate said slowly. "No, it was real."

"Perhaps you should discuss this with a doctor," Carl said as he led Nate back down the hall, carefully holding the machete down at his side.

"I don't need a doctor," Nate insisted. "I'm *not* crazy!"

But after tonight, he was no longer sure of that.

When Nate met Adrian in the hallway the next morning, he crushed her to him and held her for a long time. Feeling the tension in his muscles, Adrian rubbed his arms and said, "Did something else happen?"

"Last night," Nate said. "I had the worst nightmare, ever."

"It's no wonder," Adrian said, thinking of what had happened to Denny. She took Nate's hand. "Come on, let's go inside your office and you can tell me about it."

She called to one of the director's assistants and ordered two cups of coffee, then followed Nate into his room. He sank down onto the leather couch, holding an arm out to take her and pull her close to him.

"I'm glad it's daylight," he said. "Isn't that sick? Thirty-two years old, and I'm glad it's daylight."

"What kind of dream did you have?" Adrian asked. "The little girl in the burning theater again?"

Nate nodded yes.

"But it started differently," he said. "I was in my bed—in the bed I used to sleep in when my father was alive. And he was standing at the foot of the bed, pointing his finger, yelling something about . . ."

He rubbed his eyes, unable to remember all the details. Adrian watched him, feeling anger grow inside herself to see this dear, loving man hurt so much. Why did he have to suffer? Wasn't the work he did at the theater demanding enough?

Now more than ever Adrian thought that she'd always be there to help him.

"I—I don't remember very much," Nate said. He wouldn't tell her about Meg. He couldn't do that. "Uhm, I remember jumping from the bed and running after him."

He breathed deeply.

"Next thing I knew, the butler was yelling at me," he went on. "I'd gotten hold of a knife, and I was slashing up my father's portrait." His hands clenched into fists. "God, I was acting like a maniac!"

"Oh, Nate!" Adrian cried, throwing her arms around him. "Don't say that! Never say that!"

"Adrian, I hear voices, I see things that aren't there," Nate said, running his fingers through his hair. "Why else would that be happening?"

"You thought someone was causing it," Adrian reminded. "Someone who doesn't want to see you succeed."

"But how could they control my dreams?" Nate asked. "That's the one aspect of all this that I have no explanation for whatsoever."

"I don't know, Nate," Adrian said.

There was silence for a moment while Adrian sat staring at the calendar, circled in red on November twenty-third, the date of the previews, and Nate tried desperately to understand what was happening to him. All of a sudden, he pulled away from Adrian and leaned forward, burying his head in his arms.

"Damn it," he growled. "I am *scared*. And I don't know what it is that frightens me!"

"Nate," Adrian said, "you've been through so much. I think..."

He sat up and looked at her, his eyes glassy.

"Don't suggest seeing a psychiatrist," he said. "My butler suggested the same last night. But I *know* I'm not crazy. And nothing will make me leave this production."

He slammed his fist on the coffee table, sending a rattling vibration throughout the room.

"This is my life," he said forcefully, "and no one can take it from me!"

"Of course not," Adrian said. She took his hand. "Everything's going to be all right, Nate. Denny's going to be out of the hospital before we know it, and..."

But Nate, unable to stop himself, had turned away from her with tears in his eyes. They were tears of frustration, of a man who wondered what he had done to deserve such torment.

Of a man who felt himself being driven to the brink of madness with no outlet in sight.

"Help me, Adrian," he pleaded.

She took his shoulders and rested her head on his back.

"Nate, my love," she said, "I will help you in any way I can. I won't let anyone hurt you."

He turned again to look at her and she kissed him softly.

"I promise," she whispered.

Nate was his usual professional self at rehearsals and even felt a little ashamed of the scene in his office. He knew Adrian would never ridicule him. But if his father were alive...

Someone tapped him on the shoulder, and his father's image vanished into the darkness of the auditorium.

"There's a policeman in your office," Don Benson whispered. "He says Georgia Richmond sent him here."

Nate didn't like the interruption but knew it was inevitable he'd be questioned. He ordered those on stage to take five, then left for his office. He found the cop sitting on the leather sofa and was greeted with a firm handshake and the presentation of an ID.

"Sounds like you had some trouble here yesterday," the policeman said. "The boy's mother requested that I ask you some questions."

"I'd be glad to help," Nate said, taking a seat behind his desk.

"According to Mrs. Richmond," the cop began, "Denny was last seen playing in the backyard of this theater."

"He likes it out there," Nate said.

"But when she went to look for him," the cop went on, "he was gone. And he didn't seem to be anywhere you looked. I understand you formed a search party."

"Yes, I did," Nate said. "And we combed every inch of the theater. I suppose Georgia told you he'd somehow gotten into the air passages?"

The policeman nodded.

"But I don't get it," he said, "how could he move so freely if the building is run through with pipes and such?"

"Have you seen Denny?" Nate asked. "He's a skinny little kid. You know how limber they are at that age."

"That's true," was the reply. "Now, Mrs. Richmond also said a woman named Adrian may be involved with this. Can I talk to her?"

"Adrian has nothing to do with it," Nate insisted, wishing he did not have to drag her into this mess. But Adrian had vowed to share this all with him, and she did have a right to defend herself. He punched a button on his phone and asked an assistant to locate her. After he'd hung up, he said, "Denny did accuse her of forcing him into those air passages, but I know Adrian would do no such thing."

When Adrian opened the door, she frowned momentarily on seeing the cop.

"Georgia sent him," Nate explained as she sat down.

"What can I tell you?" Adrian asked.

The cop opened his small notebook and readied his pencil. "Everything you were doing yesterday afternoon," he said.

For the most part, Adrian's story coincided with Nate's and Georgia's, but there was one opening the cop didn't like.

"You took your break the same time as Denny disappeared," he said.

"Yes, I suppose I did." Adrian sighed. "But I have witnesses to prove I was nowhere near Denny in that time."

"Can you get someone to come in here?" Nate asked

Adrian turned to him.

"Barbara Warner was with me," she said. "I was with her in the greenroom the entire time."

Again, Nate punched a button on his telephone and sent word that he wanted to see Barbara. She entered the office a few minutes later, dressed in coveralls and adjusting the ribbon that held back her long hair. She could sense there was something wrong and, embarrassed, slowly lowered her hands.

"Sit down over there, Babs," Adrian said. "The police officer just wants to talk to you."

"You were with Ms. St. John yesterday, weren't you?"

"For about a half hour," Barbara said. "We took our breaks yesterday after she came off the stage."

"And what time was this?"

Barbara shrugged, then finally recalled the hour. The cop put this down in his notebook.

"You say others can prove you were in this—what did you call it?"

"Greenroom," Nate said. "It's the place where actors take their breaks."

"Greenroom, yes," the cop replied.

"I can prove I was there," Adrian said.

Barbara's eyes grew wide.

"Why does she have to prove anything?" she demanded. "Are you accusing Adrian of hurting Denny?"

"I just want . . ."

Barbara interrupted the cop.

"This is awful," she said. "I know Adrian, and I can tell you she'd never hurt anyone!"

Across the room, a small statue suddenly crashed to the floor. Everyone in the room turned abruptly to see the shattered pieces.

"Vibrations from the building crew," Adrian said quickly, seeing Nate's eyes glaze over. He blinked and looked at her.

"I'll have it cleaned up later," he said quietly.

Bonnie stared at the woman named Barbara and thought that now there were *two* to be gotten rid of. Two women who interfered.

They would both pay.

TWELVE

Denny was in such good spirits when Nate and Adrian entered his hospital room that it seemed the terror of the previous day had never happened. There were no frightened looks in Adrian's direction, no accusations. He was sitting up in a sterile-looking bed reading a copy of *Sports Illustrated*. There was a tube connected to him that seemed hardly bigger than his thin arm. He smiled and pointed to the suspended bottle over his shoulder.

"That's an IV," he said. "It means I'm being fed inter-inter—*in-tra-venously*. In my veins."

"That's great," Nate said, relieved to see Denny was his old self again.

He offered a chair next to Denny's bed to Adrian, then took one himself.

"How do you feel, kid?" he asked.

"Kinda tired," Denny said. "My neck aches, and so do my legs. The doctor says it's cause I was stuck in that air passage."

Adrian leaned forward and got to the point of the visit.

"Denny," she asked, "what do you remember about that?"

"I crawled through an opening in the wall near the boiler," Denny said.

"But why would you do such a dangerous thing?"

Denny looked at her, then at Nate. He lowered his head and started to fidget with his plastic ID tag, his lips turning down. From somewhere out in the hall, he could hear the squeaking of a metal cart. Someone else was ringing for a nurse.

"I didn't want to do it," he said softly. "She made me."

The voice was pained, not the cheerful one of a moment ago.

"Who did?" Nate asked.

Denny's expression went blank, and he said in monotone, "Adrian made me."

"Denny," Adrian said calmly. "I was with several other people when you disappeared. Please tell us the truth."

Denny wriggled a bit and whined, "It is the truth! Why is everyone mad at me?"

Nate patted his leg. "No one's mad at you. We just want to know the truth so we can help you."

"She did it!" Denny cried loudly, the brown of his eyes wavering behind tears. "She did! She made me do it!"

He was pointing at Adrian, who in turn was watching Nate with worry and confusion in her eyes.

"Easy, Denny," Nate said. "We don't have to talk about this now if . . ."

Denny's lips curled and his eyes thinned as if to squeeze out his tears, but for the moment he had calmed down. He refused to look at Nate, afraid of the hurt in the director's eyes. Something was wrong here, Denny sensed. He wasn't saying the right thing. Adrian didn't . . .

"Denny," Nate said in a gentle tone, "I know you're scared. But Adrian and I are your friends."

"Adrian . . ."

"Shh," Nate said. "Listen to me. I think someone else made you climb into the air passages. Someone who frightened you so terribly that you are afraid now to tell us who it was. Denny, did someone tell you to use Adrian's name?"

Silence. Denny continued to twist his ID bracelet. He wanted to tell the truth, but he didn't know what the truth was! A memory was trying to emerge, something about another child. Denny closed his eyes tightly and tried to bring it into focus.

"Bonnie," he whispered.

"I didn't hear you, Denny," Nate said. "What was that?"

But the word wouldn't come out again. Denny's lips would not form to say it. He was frozen, his hands opened stiffly on his lap, his head hung. And then the trembling began.

Suddenly, he began to feel hotter and hotter. From some-where far away he heard Adrian's voice.

"Pull his covers up, Nate. He's cold."

Not cold. Hot. Terribly hot.

Denny's two legs began to kick spasmodically, and all sensation of the bed beneath him was gone. There was no bed, no floor, no ground. He was falling! Falling into the darkness!

"MMMMMAAAA!!!!"

"Denny?!"

Falling! Falling!

"Adrian, get a nurse!"

"MMMMMMMAAAA!!!!"

There was darkness everywhere. His bones had no sub-stance, his arms and legs refused to hold him. He was going to go splat all over the ground! He was going to die!

Someone was touching his shoulders.

"Denny, snap out of it!"

Adrian was back with a doctor and a nurse.

Falling! Gonna smash up like a water balloon!

"Denny, wake up!"

A face came into view, floating in the darkness above him as he fell. A woman's face. Adrian. She had hurt him.

"NNNOOOO!!!"

Denny's arm lashed out and caught her across the bridge of her nose. He screamed with such terror that tears came to Adrian's eyes as she brought the back of her hand to her bleeding nose.

The nurse ordered them from the room as the doctor readied a needle. Nate took Adrian's arm and walked out into the hall. They held each other and listened as Denny's pitiful screams filled the air. Then, after a few long minutes, silence.

"The sedative's taken effect," Nate said.

"My God, Nate," Adrian said, dabbing with a tissue at her bloody nose. "What was going on in there?"

Nate shook his head.

"I don't know," he whispered. "It's like everything else. I just don't know."

The door to Denny's room swung open and both the doctor and nurse came out. The doctor, a sad-eyed Indian, looked at Adrian and asked.

"Are you the boy's mother?"

"No, I work with him in Nate's—in Mr. Dysart's production company," she said nodding her head toward Nate.

"You're Nate Dysart?" he asked, recognizing the name.

"Yes, I am," Nate said. "Can you tell us what's wrong with Denny?"

"That's one terrified little boy," the doctor replied. "But since he's a minor I can only discuss his condition with his parents."

Nate waved a hand.

"Then maybe you can answer a nonmedical question," he said. "Did he mention any names? Did he accuse anyone of hurting him?"

"He said 'Adrian,' once." The doctor paused, as if considering. "There was one other name. I couldn't quite make it out, but it sounded like Tommy, or Bonnie, or . . ."

He gestured to indicate the array of similar-sounding names. Nate felt his heart jump as the name Bonnie conjured up some sort of elusive memory.

"Bonnie?" he repeated.

"Does that name mean something to you?" Adrian asked.

"No," he said. "I thought it sounded familiar, but I guess it doesn't."

"If you'll excuse me," the doctor said, "I have other patients to see."

Nate thanked him for his time, then put his arm around Adrian's shoulder. Together they walked from the hospital. There was nothing more they could do here today.

The afternoon's rehearsal went smoothly. John Hemlock, Denny's understudy worked well, pleased to be on stage. At the end of the day Adrian and Nate were approached by Judy and Barbara.

"How's Denny?" Barbara wanted to know.

Nate assured her the boy was doing fine. He deliberately didn't mention Denny's outburst.

"You know what this one did?" Barbara asked, pointing to Judy.

"What's that?" Nate asked.

Barbara looked away, as if embarrassed.

"On our lunch hour," Judy said, "she got everyone who was in the greenroom with Adrian the other day to come with her to the police station. And she insisted the sergeant there take a statement from each one."

"I thought it might help Adrian," Barbara said. "Georgia Richmond insists you hurt Denny, but we all know better."

Adrian threw her arms around Barbara.

"What a sweet thing to do!"

It made her happy to know she had such good friends.

The police were finally convinced of Adrian's innocence after comparing all the statements. Adrian had ample witnesses to prove she was nowhere near Denny at the time of his disappearance. And when Georgia returned to the theater a few days later, she was also made to see the truth.

"I refuse to believe Denny did it on his own," she insisted, however. "He's mischievous, yes. But not malicious! He wouldn't tell lies!"

"We think someone made him give Adrian's name," Nate said. "Georgia, do you know anyone named Bonnie?"

The southern woman shook her head.

"Not a soul," she said. "Why?"

"Just asking."

"Did someone named Bonnie hurt my son?"

"I don't know," Nate said. "Possibly. He mentioned the name when we visited him the other day."

"Well, whoever it is," Adrian said, "we're going to find him or her."

"And when you do," Georgia drawled, "I'd like to see him tarred and feathered!"

THIRTEEN

The boy's accident became the primary topic at the theater, even edging out the fast-approaching previews in Connecticut. Everyone was glad to hear Denny had been released from the hospital and was planning to return to work as soon as possible. Nonetheless, they all wanted to see his tormentor found. Everyone liked Denny and couldn't understand how anyone could be so cruel. No one said much, but they all wondered, if someone among them was a traitor, some kind of psychopath who could lash out at any moment.

"Just look at Son of Sam," Judy told Barbara as they returned from lunch together. "Everyone thought he was a nice guy, and he turned out to be a murderer."

Barbara shuddered, thinking of her own kids. "I hate to think someone like that is in this theater, right now."

"I just hope they find the bastard," Judy said.

"Judy!"

Barbara's best friend widened her eyes in amusement.

"You are such a little girl!" she cried. "I only said 'bastard,' and that's exactly what he is!"

"I still don't like to hear swear words," Barbara said.

It grew suddenly cold in the hallway, and just then the lights began to flicker. Judy laughed and patted Barbara's arm.

"I guess you're right," she said. "That must be a sign from above."

"Don't make fun of me," Barbara said, though she laughed herself.

When the lights came on again, the two stopped their giggling, and found themselves looking at a small child. She stood in the middle of the hallway, staring up at them with solemn black eyes, her hands clenched into tiny fists at the sides of her ruffled dress.

"Where'd you come from?" Judy asked.

The child said nothing. Barbara, comfortable with children because she had two of her own, asked, "Are you waiting for someone, honey?"

"I'm waiting for you," the child said. Her pretty face was expressionless.

Barbara held out a hand.

"Come on," she said. "I'll take you to your mommy."

"NO!" the child snapped.

Barbara felt something twist inside of her to see the pretty child's eyes grow cold. She took a step toward her but was suddenly pushed aside when the little girl broke into a run and sped past the two women. Before Barbara could move, Judy had her by the arm.

"Let her go," Judy said. "She isn't your worry."

But Barbara could not stop thinking about the child. After what had happened to Denny, a little kid shouldn't be allowed to wander alone in that big theater. She could be the next victim! Barbara decided to find the child's mother, whoever she was, and warn her.

Judy headed straight for the stage, where the lighting crew would be working this afternoon, but Barbara went downstairs to the basement lockers to drop off her jacket. At the other end of the huge basement, the sounds of the building crew started up again, and Barbara wondered what the new scenery would look like. In all her years as a lighting technician, she had never tired of the magic of the theater. Next to her beautiful family, it was the best part of her life.

She opened her locker. It had been empty earlier, but now something small and yellow sat in it: a stuffed dog, one of those autograph hounds from years back. Barbara took it out and examined it, wondering if Judy might have put it in here. And yet Barbara had a feeling Judy *hadn't* done this. Something was wrong. A yellow dog meant something, but what?

Suddenly, Barbara dropped the toy as if it had burned her. She knew what a yellow dog meant! There was an old theatrical superstition that said a yellow dog found in the theater meant someone was going to die!

"Oh, no," she whispered.

Could the maniac who had hurt Denny have left this here? Was she going to be his next victim? She looked around. She was completely alone. Anything or anyone could be hiding behind the long rows of lockers. Nervously, she tried to unzip her jacket, but the zipper stuck.

"Damn!" she hissed, hardly noticing the curse word.

She fumbled with it; her hands began to tremble. Was someone watching her now, waiting?

It was no use. She decided to pull the jacket off over her head. It had an elastic waist, and she crossed her arms to pull it up. Suddenly, she was tangled up inside the thing. She couldn't see. Struggling to escape, she felt something touch her knee.

Barbara's startled cry was muffled by the sound of a buzz saw from the far end of the basement. She jerked the jacket back down and found herself staring at the little girl.

"You scared me," she said, suddenly relieved and ashamed of her fear.

No reply.

"Can you help me get out of this thing?" Barbara asked. "I don't want to wear it under the hot stage lights, but I can't seem to get it off."

The child made no move.

"It gets so hot on that stage," Barbara said.

"Terribly hot," the child agreed, walking slowly toward her.

Without warning, she pushed at Barbara with all her might, slamming the woman's body against the metal lockers. A resounding bang echoed down the row as Barbara's eyes widened in shock.

"Hey!" she cried. "Don't..."

But the little girl had her by the front of her jacket, pulling her down to the floor. Barbara struggled to resist, not understanding the child's incredible strength. Her hand felt the yellow dog. *Someone in the company was going to die ...*

"What do you want?" She choked out the words.

"To punish you," the child said. "You are a *bad* lady."

Barbara shook her head and tried to break away from the child's grip. Instead, she was slammed back against the locker. The child pressed close to her, bringing her hands up to Barbara's face. The woman froze, wanting to cry out in pain but unable. A horrible burning sensation filled her entire head, a pain worse than any she had ever known. When she looked into the little girl's eyes, she could see the reflection of flames.

"You have to suffer the way I did." The child's voice had a demonic tone to it, hollow and unemotional. Barbara stared at the flames in her eyes, until suddenly the darkness came. It was not the darkness of a fusebox giving in to the strain of power drills and chain saws, but the dark that comes when evil overtakes the mind.

Barbara began to fall, tumbling head over heels, like Alice down the rabbit hole. Now she was in an unfamiliar hallway, with rows of glass-knobbed doors and a black-and-white tile floor. At the far end stood an enormous door, larger than any of the others, beckoning her like a gateway to safety. By the light of some unseen bulb that flickered nearby, Barbara tried to read the white letters painted on it. But the door was edged in shadow and too far away. Shadows and light wavered like apparitions, giving the hallway a pulsating life of its own. Barbara tried to open her mouth to cry out, but could not make a sound.

"*You have to pay!*"

She looked around at the sound of the child's voice. Her head moved slowly and felt terribly light; her joints were numb. And the hallway was empty.

Someone in the company was going to die . . .

She broke into a run, heading toward that big door. But there was no door at the hallway's end. Barbara slammed into a solid wall that teasingly said FIRE EXIT. But there was no exit. No way out.

Something crashed behind her, sending vibrations up from the floor and through her body. Barbara turned with a gasp and saw that one of the ceiling beams had fallen to the floor. All around her, flames were shooting along the walls and ceiling like so many red and orange party streamers. A two-by-four fell and barely missed her head. Barbara tried to scream, but all that escaped was a pathetic mouse-like squeak.

"*You have to pay for bringing the dark!*"

The little girl was standing before her, screaming. The ruffles of her fancy dress glowed orange and yellow, changing colors as the flames waxed and waned. She tilted her head to one side, her black tresses brushing over a small shoulder.

"*It's too late,*" she said. "*You ruined my plans, and you're going to die!*"

As the child stepped forward Barbara stiffened, anticipating the horrible pain she'd feel at the touch of those small hands.

But there was no pain. The fire disappeared, the little girl faded away, and suddenly Barbara was standing before her locker, her head pounding. A few moments passed before she was fully conscious. Everything was ominously silent. Barbara's eyes darted around her like those of a frightened animal. She knew she had to get out of the basement, and it terrified her that she didn't know why.

Leaving her jacket on, Barbara quickly locked her locker and ran for the stairs. Each time her foot struck the ground, a pain swelled up inside her head. By the time she reached the stage she was ready to scream.

But she didn't scream. She held her fears inside, afraid the others would think she was hysterical. After all, nothing had happened—nothing she could recall. She just had a sense that time had passed in the cellar, time that was lost to her.

"I must have had a dizzy spell," she rationalized to herself. "Maybe I ate something that disagreed with me." Vaguely she wondered if she could perhaps be pregnant. She remembered the dizzy spells she'd suffered before her youngest was born. No, that wasn't likely, still ...

As she walked onto the stage Judy Terrel came over and looked at her with concern. Any other time, Barbara would have assured her that everything was fine. But now, somehow, she only wanted to poke out Judy's pretty blue eyes.

"God," Judy said, "you look awful. Maybe you ought to take the day off—you look like you've seen a ghost!"

"I'm okay," Barbara insisted.

"Your face is pale," Judy pointed out. "And why are you still wearing that jacket? It's warm in here! Babs, you really should ..."

"I said I was okay," Barbara snapped. "What the fuck do you care what I look like, anyway?"

"Well, aren't you the bitch?" Judy shot back. "And where did you learn to swear, minister's daughter?"

Barbara ignored the remark and walked over to Mike Woodson, the chief electrician. "I want the mediums put up over the striplights today," Mike was saying as Barbara joined the group. "Three of you have to get up on the scaffolding."

Several hands went up. Mike picked two of the men and was about to choose a third when he noticed Barbara's hand. She had experience at this type of work, so Mike chose her. She picked up a toolbox and climbed the steel ladder that led up to the scaffolding.

"Mike," Judy said softly, "I don't think she belongs up there."

"And why not?" Mike said, looking over a lighting plan that was rolled open like a scroll between his hands.

"She's not ... Oh, heck, I don't know. But I think ..."

"There's a lot of work to do, Miss Terrel," Mike said, abruptly.

Judy turned away and went to her own work, looking up at Barbara. She wanted to call to her, to apologize for the senseless words, but Barbara was too far away and probably wouldn't hear her, anyway. She sighed and walked away.

Up above, Barbara was reading a diagram that told her in what order to place the mediums—colored pieces of glass in metal frames. "RED, BLUE, AMBER, RED..." She picked up a red piece and started for the first light. Her hands trembled as she worked, and her head ached. But this was the job she loved, and maybe if she concentrated on it, the uneasy feelings she had would go away.

Still, she couldn't help looking over her shoulder every once in a while.

Barbara moved along the scaffolding, fitting the lights with color frames in the right sequence. Unconsciously she chewed her lips to fight the headache that pounded at her brain. Maybe she should have listened to Judy. Maybe she really shouldn't be working this afternoon.

But she was afraid to stop, to leave here. As long as she was with the other stagehands, she felt safe. From what, though, she didn't know.

Barbara noticed that a lamp in front of her was cracked and decided to replace it. She unscrewed it, but her hands were shaking so that it slipped from her grip and crashed to the floor some thirty feet below. Barbara froze. A sensation of falling came over her, and her knees locked as if to prevent her own body from tumbling off the scaffolding. Mike Woodson's voice carried up to her a moment later, breaking the spell.

"Careful!" he yelled. "That's a helluva drop!"

"It—it slipped," Barbara called back.

Judy turned away from her work to look up at Barbara. She noticed the windbreaker Barbara still wore, and wondered about it. But her friend did not seem as upset as before, and Judy returned to the panel she was wiring.

While waiting for a new bulb to be sent up, Barbara continued to work down the line. The next color was amber, wasn't it? No, red. Barbara rechecked her diagram and confirmed the latter. She had never lost track like this before. But it was the headache, of course.

Suddenly she heard a hissing noise very close to her ear. She looked around for steam escaping a pipe but could find none. It was growing terribly hot there, though, and she wished she could take off her jacket. She was about to ask one of the

men to help her with the zipper when she felt something
burn her skin. She jumped, gasping.

"Hey, hold still," one of the men working with her called as
the lightweight platform shook.

But Barbara didn't even hear him. She was looking down
from the scaffolding, out into the theater. It was filled with
people, but not the actors, actresses, and stagehands she had
been working with. These were women dressed in fringed
and beaded shifts and satin gowns, and men with slicked
down hair and straight-cut evening jackets! Hundreds of
them. They were running toward the doors, pushing and
screaming in panic, and yet there were no sounds coming
from their lips. Just as suddenly as it had come, the illusion
disappeared, and once again the theater was empty.

"Hey, you look like you've seen a ghost," the man down
the platform called.

Barbara didn't answer him. She was staring at something
he could not see—the little girl in a white dress. The child
was frowning at her in such a way that Barbara's blood ran
cold despite the intense heat she felt.

"You shouldn't have interfered," the child was saying. "You
have to pay now. You have to *die*."

Barbara shook her head, backing away as the child advanced slowly upon her. Down the scaffolding, her partner
noticed her wild eyes and perspiring skin and called, "Hey,
Babs, are you okay?"

"You have to die," the little girl said again, her voice
audible only to Barbara.

Suddenly, she lunged forward, pushing the woman with all
her might. All those who were watching thought Barbara had
somehow lost her balance. Her thoughts filled with visions of
fire and crashing timber, she tried desperately to grab for
something, but there was nothing within her reach. Barbara
Warner hit the floor so hard on impact that she never felt a
thing.

"*Barbara!*"

Judy's scream broke the silence.

The two men above leaned over the railing and looked
down in horror. Someone shouted orders to get a doctor, and
someone else ran to find Nate. He was in his office, holding a

cast meeting with Adrian and the others. Without a word, he hurried to the stage.

"What happened?" he demanded.

"She—she f-fell from the scaffolding," Judy stammered. "I don't know how, but she fell!"

Nate knelt down beside Barbara and gently touched her. Then he looked up at Adrian, something souring in the pit of his stomach.

"Her neck is broken," he told her in a whisper.

"Oh, my God," Adrian replied, bringing a hand to her mouth. She looked around at the people on the stage. "Did someone call an ambulance?"

"I did," Mike Woodson said.

No sooner had they spoken when they heard sirens. Someone ran to let the paramedics in, and they immediately went to work. But after a futile effort to revive Barbara, one man shook his head sadly.

"No need to rush with this one," he said.

No one else spoke. They all backed away, standing en masse and watching in silence as the paramedics lifted Barbara onto a stretcher. Two of the women were crying. Judy stood expressionless, too stunned to cry.

Nate held on to Adrian's hand, squeezing it until she was certain he'd break her fingers. She winced, and he loosened his grip. But Adrian understood. He was thinking about Jim Orland. Two people in his company had died. Two innocent people. Now Adrian saw Nate's eyes widen, but she did not hear the voice that came to his ears alone.

"She had to be punished!" a child cried. *"She ruined everything and she had to pay!"*

Nate turned to the groups of crew members, his eyes weary.

"Who said that?" he asked softly.

"No one said anything, Mr. Dysart," Mike told him.

"Damn it, I know I heard someone!" Nate cried.

He waved a hand angrily, realizing the voices had returned. In a fury, he rushed off the stage, Adrian close at his heels. He stormed into his office and sat down at his desk, weaving his fingers through his hair.

"What's happening here?" he demanded. "What the hell is happening?"

"Nate, it was an accident," Adrian said, standing behind him so that she could massage his shoulders. "All those people saw Barbara fall."

"No, no," Nate said. "It was meant to happen."

Adrian kissed the top of his head.

"Nate, I understand why you'd think that," she said, "but this time, it's obvious there's nothing sinister involved. Too many people are witnesses!"

Nate heard tension in her voice and knew she was frightened too. He wanted to tell her about the voice he'd heard but instead backed up his chair and stood up.

"I have to go back on stage," he said. "I'm in charge here. I should take responsibility."

"They expect it of you," Adrian said.

Together, they returned. The paramedics were gone, and the place was thick with stunned silence. Nate sucked in his breath, forcing himself to remain calm. Another outburst and he'd lose the respect of his cast and crew.

"Where's Judy?" he asked, noticing the woman wasn't here.

"She went to contact Joel Warner," Mike said. "Barbara's husband."

Adrian mumbled something to hear the name. Joel Warner was an investigative reporter—would he try to learn what exactly had happened to Barbara? She decided not to think about it. Instead, she moved closer to Nate.

"Look, God only knows why this happened. It shouldn't have. Barbara Warner was a wonderful human being. She shouldn't have . . ."

Mike cut Nate off.

"That scaffolding was checked earlier today," he said.

"But still Barbara fell," Nate said. "And damn it, I want to know why!"

Judy returned now, walking onto the stage with red rims around her eyes. She looked at Nate and said softly, "I've told Joel."

"Thank you," Nate said.

Judy came closer to the group on stage.

"Barbara had two little boys," she said. "Alec and Bobby. Alec is just two years old."

Her lips curled now, and she began to sob.

"They're just babies," she choked, covering her face.

Adrian hurried over to her and put her arms around the woman. Nate watched the scene with anger growing in him. Someone would pay for this.

"Go home, everyone," he said. "Take tomorrow off. I'll let you know about Barbara's . . ."

He waved a hand to dismiss them. He did not want to think he was about to attend his third funeral in one year.

1975

Nate stood out in the rain, watching red lights of an ambulance whirl around, coloring the portico of Dysart Manor. Behind him, his father stood in the doorway, openly cursing the attendants as they carried out a stretcher.

"Damned blockheads!" he cried. "What's taking so blasted long? I want that maniacal bitch out of my house!"

Nate heard a weak voice call out his name. His hands, shoved into his pockets, balled into fists. Didn't his father have even a drop of pity for a sick person?

Slowly, he turned around. He saw Meg lying on the stretcher, strapped down like some unruly animal. That had been his father's doing. Nate felt a lump in his throat to recall what had happened just half an hour earlier. Meg, fed up with Nathaniel Sr.'s constant torment, had flown at the old man in a rage. It didn't seem possible that the pale, tiny woman on that stretcher could have been capable of such fury.

Nate glanced back at his father again, who waved an impatient hand and closed the door. Then he stopped the attendants and knelt down to take Meg's hand.

"I don't want to go, Nate," Meg whimpered.

Nate kissed her.

"It's only for a few days," he said. "You know you haven't been getting better since the accident, and the doctors want to do some tests."

"I didn't mean it," Meg said softly. "I didn't mean to hurt our . . ."

Nate hushed her with a gentle kiss, stopping the words he did not want to hear.

FOURTEEN

Adrian turned over in the brass bed and ran the back of her hand along Nate's face, enjoying the feel of the roughness of razor stubble. He sighed and moved closer to her, burying his face in her neck. She was here tonight because he hadn't wanted to be alone. Like some little kid, he was afraid of what his dreams might be.

Two people were dead at the theater. Two deaths that on the surface did not seem to involve foul play. But Jim Orland had died of a heart attack, in horrible pain, though he had never had a heart condition and was strong as an ox. Barbara Warner had fallen from a scaffolding—with ten years of experience at that kind of work behind her and no record of carelessness. What had happened that had caused her to lose her balance and fall?

Had she lost her balance?

Nate pulled away from Adrian and lay on his back, staring up through the darkness. His hand found hers, and she squeezed his fingers.

"Thanks," he said.

"For what?"

"For coming here tonight."

Adrian propped herself up on an elbow and leaned down to kiss Nate in the darkness. He put his arms around her and held her until they both fell asleep. For Adrian, it was a sleep edged with worries about Nate. But for Nate, it was something far, far worse.

The nightmares came back again.

He opened his eyes, and saw a dark-haired woman beside him. She turned over and smiled—Meg's smile. The bed was no longer brass, but wood, and the sheets were cotton, not satin. Nate smiled back at Meg. But soon her expression changed, her eyes growing big with fear. Silent tears dripped over her cheeks.

"I didn't kill her," she whispered. *"I didn't kill our . . ."*

"Meg, don't!" Nate cried, pulling her close to him. *"Don't!"*

133

There was laughter from somewhere. High-pitched, insane laughter. And suddenly Nate's father was at the foot of the bed, invading their privacy, mocking them as they held fast to each other.

"Failures! Failures! Couldn't even keep a baby!"

Nate broke away from Meg and leaped from the bed, running after the old man. But when he pushed through the door, it was not to enter the hallway. He was in the wings of that stage again. The stage where the little girl was singing. The stage of fire and darkness and falling...

"NNNNNOOOOO!!!"

Someone was shaking him as he fell into the darkness of the orchestra pit.

"NNNOOOO!!!"

"Nate, honey!" Adrian said. "Wake up! You're dreaming!"

His eyes snapped open and he stared at her, but what he saw was his wife.

"Oh, Meg," he groaned, throwing his arms around her.

Adrian stiffened. Meg? Who was Meg? She hugged Nate, feeling his body heave as his breathing slowed. He looked so terribly vulnerable then that she could not help lifting a hand to rub his back. There was certainly an explanation for the name he'd called her.

Finally, he moved away and settled down on his pillow.

"God," he said.

"Another nightmare?"

He nodded.

"I don't know when they'll stop," he said.

A few moments passed, and then Adrian said quietly, "You called me Meg."

"I..."

Nate cut himself off.

"Meg was my wife," he told her.

"I didn't know you were married."

She heard his hair brush the pillow as he shook his head.

"She died a few years ago," he said. "I—I guess I was dreaming about her."

"Tell me about her, Nate."

Nate was silent. He at first did not want to talk about Meg, but the encouraging feeling of Adrian's arms as they went around him shattered his inhibitions. For years, he had kept the truth bottled up inside, yet now he was telling the new woman in his life everything he could.

"We had a little production company," he said. "Jim, Meg, and I. Jim used to say it was so far off Broadway that it might fall into the East River."

He sighed to remember how they'd laughed at that little joke.

"Meg was always helping out," Nate said. "She did more work than any of us, even though she was very frail and should never have tried to strain herself. But she had a hell of a mind. She was terrific at scenic design and costuming. When you don't have a lot of money, you double up on your jobs."

"But I thought you were very wealthy," Adrian protested.

"My father was," Nate said. "But he didn't share that wealth with anyone. Whatever we put into that company, we did on our own. My father thought the theater was a waste of time. He used to say we were overgrown children playing make-believe."

Adrian began to rub his stomach.

"Tell me about Meg."

"Well, she always did more than her share of work," Nate continued. "One day, she was up on a scaffolding. She—she slipped and fell from it. When I saw Barbara lying on the stage, I could only think of Meg."

"Oh, Nate," Adrian said.

Nate paused to deal with the wave of anger that was rushing over him. When he had calmed again, he went on with his story.

"It turned out Meg was several months pregnant," he said. "I didn't know it. She didn't tell me yet. I guess it was because we were so busy with the theater. She lost the baby—a little girl."

He bit his lip.

"But she was more ill than we realized," he said. "She should have survived that miscarriage. She should have lived to have a family with me."

"What happened to her afterward?"

Nate shook his head.

"She died," he said simply. He turned away. "I don't want to talk about it anymore."

There was still a part of the story he could not discuss. A memory so terrible that Nate had not thought of it in all the years since Meg's death.

1975

Meg Dysart stroked the hair of the doll in her arms and rocked herself back and forth on a cushioned floor. She knew she was supposed to be in her bed, but she didn't like that bed. It was so cold, with its metal fixtures and white sheets. She wanted the big wooden four-poster again. She wanted to be home again, with Nate.

There was a vague memory of leaving home in her mind. She knew she had become very, very angered at someone. She had started screaming and had gone completely hysterical— so hysterical that an ambulance was brought to the big house. It took her to this hospital, where she was told she would be able to relax. A nice woman had given her this doll when Meg had said how she loved babies.

She wished this dolly was a real baby.

She wished Nate were here with her.

"I want to go home," she whispered.

But she couldn't go home until she remembered why she had come to this hospital in the first place.

That Thursday, just four days before the Connecticut previews were scheduled, everyone from the Dysart Theater company attended Barbara's funeral. The old church was beautiful, thick with the scent of incense and illuminated only by wooden chandeliers. Nate could see Judy Terrel at the front, holding on to the hands of two little boys.

When the service was over, Nate made his way to Joel Warner and offered his condolences. He didn't know quite what to say—everything sounded clichéd.

"If there's anything I can do . . ."

"You can't bring Barbara back again," Joel said. "She shouldn't have died, Mr. Dysart."

Nate shook his head and stared at the doors to the church.

"I want to ask you some questions," Joel said. "When the time is right. But at the moment my children need me."

With that he hurried toward the car that waited to take him

home. Nate felt Adrian's hand reach for his, and together they walked to the car.

"He suspects something," Nate said as George opened Adrian's door.

"He's just upset, I'm sure," Adrian said.

"But he has a right to be," Nate answered. "Barbara shouldn't have died. There shouldn't have been an accident."

"That's just what it was too," Adrian said. "An accident, no matter how awful. And no matter what else had gone on in that theater!"

The engine started and the car rolled onto the street, bumping over a pothole. Nate looked out the window at the group in front of the church, some of whom were staring after the huge Rolls-Royce. Then he said, without turning, "I heard voices on the stage."

"When?" Adrian asked, her tone concerned.

"After we found Barbara," Nate replied. "I heard someone say she deserved to die."

Adrian took his hand. "But darling," she said, "no one else heard anything."

She kissed him.

"I believe you heard something, though," she said quickly, soothing him. "When we go back to work tomorrow, we can ask if anyone else remembers something."

Most of the crew who'd been on stage that afternoon hadn't paid attention to Barbara until they heard her scream. Mike Woodson did remember that he had thought it was strange that she wore a jacket, but since she didn't complain about being ill, he didn't give the matter much thought. Only Judy Terrel had more to say.

"After lunch Barbara went down to her locker by herself to hang up her jacket," she said. "But she was still wearing it when she came back upstairs. I asked her about it and she snapped at me."

Judy looked down at her hands.

"She said 'fuck,' Nate," she went on. "That was from a woman who blushed at the sound of 'darn.'"

"What happened during lunch?" Nate asked. "Anything that might have upset her?"

"Not really," Judy said. "Well, she did seem to be preoccupied. But Barbara tells me everything that's on her mind, so since she didn't say anything, I assumed she was okay."

"Then it's possible something happened to her in the cellar," Adrian said.

Nate looked at her.

"Yes, it is," he said. "Judy, can you tell us anything more?"

"No," Judy said apologetically. "She was in a foul mood when she came back to work. And I've never heard her swear in my life."

She stood up.

"Do you mind if I clean out her locker?" she asked. "There might be something in there Joel should have."

"Please do," Nate said. "And when you see Mr. Warner, tell him I want to help in any way I can."

Judy headed down to the cellar. Barbara's locker was next to her own. It was locked and except for a stuffed yellow dog, it was empty. Judy pulled the toy out, guessing it was a Christmas present for Bobby or Alec.

As she was coming up the stairs a thought occurred to her. Something seemed familiar about the yellow dog. But before she could figure out what it was, she bumped into Sander Bernaux.

"Where did you get that thing?" he demanded, something like panic in his voice.

"It was in Barbara's locker," Judy said. "I guess she bought it for one of the children."

Sander breathed in deeply through his long nose to calm himself.

"Ah, yes, Barbara," he said. "It was a shame what happened to her."

The yellow dog had already brought bad luck, the superstitious actor thought. It had already killed one member of the company. And if it were removed from the premises quickly, all would be well again.

"You say that as if you were talking about an animal hit by a car," Judy said. "Barbara was a dear, sweet woman who shouldn't have died."

"I'm sure it could have been prevented," Sander replied. "Dysart may be a good producer, but he isn't worth much when it comes to fine details, is he?"

"What do you mean?"

Sander shrugged.

"Oh well, there have been a number of tragedies here, haven't there?"

"That isn't Nate's fault."

"I would say it is," Sander told her, tilting his head back a little. "He's responsible for everything that goes on in this theater. And if you ask me, the man is incompetent and..."

"That's nonsense," Judy retorted. "Nate had nothing to do with Barbara's accident. Mike Woodson himself checked the scaffolding! Nate can't be everywhere at once!"

Sander sniffed haughtily, thinking of the emotional way Nate had reacted when he saw Barbara's prone form on the stage. A weakling!

"If you'll excuse me," Judy said, "I'd like to go home. It's been a difficult time for some of us."

She sidled past the actor and hurried down the hall. Sander watched her, chilled. A yellow dog in the theater! Someone in this company was going to die...

But then, someone *had* died. Sander couldn't help a smug grin, thinking how often people made fun of his superstitions. This time, he was right.

In spite of tragedy, "the show must go on," and that old adage applied to Nate's production. The following Monday, the twenty-third of November, he brought his entire company up to a theater in Connecticut, where they put on the previews of *Making Good*. The first showings of a play were always done outside New York. It gave the director a chance to see where more corrections could be made, so that it would be perfect for his Broadway opening. Nate sat in the back row of the audience and kept notes. He watched the audiences' reactions and felt happier than he had in a long time. They applauded and laughed and cheered—they seemed to love *Making Good*.

And it was the same every night—the theater was even packed on Thursday, Thanksgiving Day. To Nate's surprise, his cousin Vance showed up at the last performance. Nate tried to ignore Vance when he came backstage, but his cousin persisted, until Nate finally threatened to take his head off if he so much as mentioned the will.

"Did I say anything about the will?" Vance asked innocently.

"I just came back here to tell you you've got a fine show. Maybe not Broadway material, but . . ."

"Thanks," Nate said, cutting him off. One of the extras walked by him, smiling. "You did great, Mike."

"Thanks, Mr. Dysart."

Nate walked along the small hallway, reading his notes. To his dismay, Vance kept at his heels.

"I've got something else to tell you," he said. "Pearl and I are heading out to Montana next week. You know, I've got sabbatical coming up."

Nate stopped and looked at him.

"Why?"

"Pearl wants to visit her folks," Vance said, dismissing it with a shrug. "We'll be gone for a few months so you can have a little vacation from me—if you know what I mean."

"I'm very busy, Vance," Nate said.

He hurried away from Vance, dwelling on his cousin's words for only a moment before the elated mood of his company brought a smile to his face again.

It was obvious Nate had a hit. When the company returned to New York the following Monday, for two weeks of rehearsals before the Broadway opening, everyone was elated. Even Nate, who smiled at everyone who walked on stage for rehearsal.

"I'm so proud of all of you," he said, not for the first time. "Have you seen the reviews? Here's one that says, 'Broadway's got a treat coming up!' And the *Times* is overflowing with praise."

On stage the actors applauded happily. Only Sander remained still. It was bad luck to get too sure of one's self. And he knew that New York critics were tougher than anyone.

But this did not matter to Nate. In spite of all that had happened, he hadn't been destroyed. People would know now what a good director he was. And maybe, somehow, his doubting father would know it too.

"All right," he said. "You were terrific in Connecticut, but there's room for improvement before we're good enough for Broadway. Places, everyone!"

The morning passed quickly. Everyone worked well. Good feelings were in the air. Then just before lunchtime, Joel Warner walked onto the stage. The cast all watched in stunned, embarrassed silence.

"Take five, everyone," Nate said.

Adrian wanted to stay, but something in Joel's eyes told her she was not welcome.

"What can I do for you?" Nate asked. It was a stupid question, and Nate wished he could retract it. But the sandy-haired, mustached reporter seemed not to hear him. He was staring at the scaffolding overhead, the colored lights making little stars on his wire-rimmed glasses.

"It's a long way down from there, isn't it?" he asked.

"About thirty feet," Nate said, following the man's gaze upward.

Joel took a few steps, his shoes making echoing sounds on the wood floor. He studied the ropes, pulleys, and lead weights at either side of the stage. The gold curtains sparkled, and rainbows shot out from the crystal chandelier. Joel found it was wrong that the sight of his wife's death should be so opulent.

"Was that thing checked before work began?" he asked.

"It's checked every morning," Nate said, "at my insistence. And it was checked again after Bar—after the accident. My insurance people told me there was nothing wrong with it."

Joel stopped pacing and turned to Nate.

"Barbara worked on lighting crews for ten years," he said. "I can't bring myself to believe she slipped and fell thirty feet by her own carelessness."

Nate wanted to say that he did not believe it, either, but he kept silent. He would not involve this man, an outsider, in the tragedies befalling his theater. He would let Joel think it was an accident.

"I don't know what you want me to tell you," he said finally.

"What really happened."

"Barbara had an accident," Nate said, wishing he could believe it himself. "According to everyone who saw, she slipped and fell."

"I spoke to Judy Terrel last night," Joel said. "She said Barbara was in a terrible mood that afternoon, and even swore at her. In all the years we've been married, I never heard her use one off-color word. She used to have fits if I said 'damn,' for God's sake. And Judy tells me she used the word 'fuck'?"

"Everyone has their bad days," Nate said uneasily. "What are you thinking?"

"That Barbara was driven to that accident," Joel said. "Something upset her—something so terrible that she lost control and fell from that damned thing up there. I'm going to find out who's responsible."

Nate sighed. "I really couldn't tell you, Mr. Warner. But it *was* an accident. It wasn't anyone's fault."

Joel glared at him.

"It's never anyone's fault, is it?" he asked bitterly.

He turned and left the stage. Nate watched him, his suspicions about the accident stronger than ever. Even an outsider sensed something was wrong.

"I've got to find out what it is," he said out loud.

From behind him, a little girl took a step forward but stopped. Her outstretched arms dropped to her sides. It wasn't time yet.

After rehearsal Adrian took a seat next to Nate.

"I was right," Nate said. "He does suspect something about Barbara's death."

"Do you think he'll do an investigation?" Adrian asked.

"He said he would," Nate replied.

"We don't have to tell him anything," Adrian said. "We can declare this theater off limits to outsiders."

Nate shook his head.

"Oh, no," he said. "Then Joel will believe we really have something to hide. The only way we can convince him Barbara's death was completely accidental is by being cooperative."

"It's bound to cause a lot of bad publicity anyhow. I just hope to God he doesn't cause us to miss our opening."

"Nothing," Nate said, "could ever do that."

Adrian took his hand.

"We know the crew members won't tell him anything," she said. "Nor the cast."

"But wait a minute," Nate said. "What about Denny? And Georgia is quite the blabbermouth. Maybe we ought to go there and talk to them."

"Good idea," Adrian said.

Nate closed his black book.

"Well, one thing's for sure," he said. "Denny's safe at home now. Nothing can happen to him."

But Denny was not safe. At that very moment he was grasping the edges of his dinner tray, looking into the eyes of the little girl who stood before him. She was angry, and her anger terrified him.

"He went away for a whole week," she said. "They all went away, and when they came back, they were happy. I don't want them to be happy!"

There was a malevolence in her voice that made Denny stiffen. Was he going to start falling again?

"But they're back now," Bonnie said. "And pretty soon they're going to pay. *She's* going to pay. That stupid lady named Adrian!"

"Adrian?" Denny choked uncertainly.

"She interferes," Bonnie snapped. "I don't want her to have him!"

"Who?"

Bonnie simply shook her head.

"You're all going to die," she said. "Even you, Denny. I thought you were my friend, but you aren't."

"Yes, I am!" Denny insisted, panicking.

"Liar!"

She heard footsteps and her eyes darted towards the door. Denny leaned back against his pillow, grateful his mother was coming. When she opened the door, Bonnie disappeared.

"Who were you talking to?" she asked.

"No one, Mom," the boy said.

Georgia looked around the room, then at the still full dinner tray.

"Well, eat your supper, darling," she said. "You need your strength."

She started to leave, but Denny called, "Mom, could you stay a while?"

"Why, darling?"

Denny shrugged, unable to answer that. He knew his mother, who fussed over him endlessly, would stay if he wanted. But he couldn't tell her. Finally, he picked up his fork and started eating.

"It's okay," he said.

"Well, all right," Georgia said. "You call if you need anything."

"Yes, ma'am."

Georgia's eyebrows went up. He hadn't called her "ma'am" since they had left South Carolina. Still, she didn't think anything was wrong. Denny was eating hungrily—a good sign. He'd be back on stage soon enough, for sure.

After she'd left again, Bonnie reappeared, and pulled the fork from Denny's hand.

"Listen to me," she said. "You are going to forget what happened. When they ask you about the air passages, you are going to say you did it yourself!"

"But I didn't," Denny protested.

"Shut up! You listen, or I'll make the dark come again, and I'll make you fall."

Denny cringed.

"You lied," Bonnie said. "You went into the air passage by yourself and lied so your mommy wouldn't put you in a dark closet! Say you lied, or I'll make you fall again!"

Denny swallowed and said softly, "I lied."

Suddenly, the child was gone, and Denny was left staring at his tray in total confusion. He felt disoriented, as if some of the last moments had been lost. But that happened a lot since his stay at the hospital. And that was why he hadn't returned to work yet. Rubbing his eyes, he looked around for his fork to start eating again.

For some reason, it was on the floor. Had it dropped there? Denny let it go and picked up a spoon.

His mother opened the door. She smiled and said, "You have visitors, Denny."

"Who, Mom?"

"Why, it's Nate and Adrian," Georgia said. "Come on, darling. Put on your robe and come into the living room."

She took the tray away, noting he'd only eaten half his food. Well, she'd see to it that he had more a little later. Right now, she thought he might be happy to see his director. Denny adored Nate. But for some reason he seemed afraid to leave his bed.

"Denny?"

"Mom, I don't feel very good."

"What's wrong, darling?"

"My—my stomach."

"You're hungry," Georgia said with a nod. "You can finish this nice piece of cornbread in the living room."

Finally, the little boy got up and pulled on the grown-up looking red velour robe the cast had sent him. He shuffled into the living room. Adrian watched him carefully, afraid of another outburst.

"How do you feel?" she asked as the boy climbed into a lounge chair.

"Okay," Denny lied. His mother came over to him and kissed his forehead.

"He's so happy to be home again," Georgia said, smiling at him. "Home and safe."

Somehow, Denny didn't feel very safe. But he didn't tell the adults this. They'd only fuss over him and say it was part of his illness.

Nate looked at Georgia and said, "You heard about Barbara Warner, didn't you?"

"Oh, yes," Georgia said. "How awful!"

"Well," Adrian said, "her husband is asking the cast and crew a lot of questions about the accident. We want to make sure Denny is very careful in answering him."

"I won't have anyone questioning my little boy," Georgia said firmly, putting her arm around Denny's shoulder.

"Good," Nate said. "I doubt Joel will get to Denny, anyway. But we wanted to be certain."

Adrian smiled at the small figure curled up in the massive lounge chair.

"Denny, we missed you during the previews."

"We sure did," Nate said. "Your understudy did just fine, but you would have done better."

Denny's eyes lit up.

"Really?"

"Really," Nate said. "And I want you to get well quickly so that you can come back to the theater."

Denny looked down, suddenly grim. For a moment, Nate and Adrian tensed, afraid he was about to go into another attack. But the room stayed silent except for the clicking of an ornate clock on the mantel.

"I don't think you're going to let me back," he said.

"Yes, we are," Nate said.

Denny shook his head and swallowed.

"No, you don't understand," he said. "I did a terrible thing. I—I . . ."

He chewed at his lips, then blurted out, "I crawled into that air passage by myself! I just blamed Adrian so I wouldn't get in trouble!"

Georgia gasped, and Nate and Adrian exchanged looks. Nate was surprised at the outburst but kept an even tone when he asked Denny to go on.

"I—I don't remember very well," Denny said. "I think I was exploring. I wanted to see where the passage led, and I . . ."

He could not recall climbing into the opening but somehow knew that he had. There was only a vague memory of crawling in darkness, and nothing more.

But he had to tell what he knew as the truth.

"I knew I did a stupid thing," he said. "I knew my mom would really give it to me, so I lied and said Adrian made me do it."

"Why?" Adrian asked, hurt. "Haven't I always been your friend?"

Denny looked up at her, tears in his eyes.

"Sure," he said. "You're really nice, Adrian. I don't know why I did that!"

Georgia brushed his hair back and said in a gentle tone, "It's all right now, darling," she said. "Adrian will forgive you, I'm sure."

"There's nothing to forgive," the actress said.

Nate wasn't buying any of this. Nate knew what it was like to be a frightened child. How often had he been so terrified of a beating that he made up stories to save himself? This child was frightened too. But not of punishment at the hands of his mother. He was afraid of someone else. Someone who had put him up to this.

"Denny," he said finally, "does the name Bonnie mean anything to you?"

Adrian looked at Nate, then back at the small boy who sat cuddled in his robe across the room.

"No," Denny said.

"You don't have any friends named Bonnie?"

He insisted that he didn't.

"Who's Bonnie?" Georgia wanted to know.

"A name he mentioned once at the hospital," Nate said. "It may be a clue as to who made him do all this."

"I did it myself!" Denny cried.

"I don't believe that," Nate said. "You aren't foolish, Denny. You would never have done this on your own."

"But I . . ."

Georgia put her arms around him.

"Easy, darling," she said. "Maybe you ought to go to bed now. It's getting late, and you're upset."

"It's only eight o'clock," Denny said.

"Never mind," Georgia replied, though her tone was not as scolding as usual.

Denny obeyed her, and silently the three adults watched him slink toward his room, his head hanging. He opened the door, then turned and said, "I did it myself."

"We'll talk about it another time," Nate said.

When Denny had shut his door, Nate turned to Adrian and Georgia.

"Someone made Denny tell us this new lie," he said.

"But how?" Georgia asked. "Denny's been alone all night."

Nate shrugged. "I don't know."

"Do you think someone named Bonnie is involved?"

"Maybe," Nate said. "I'm going to start asking around the theater. See if anyone knows someone by that name."

"Oh, please do," Georgia said. "I don't want some maniac running around when my Denny returns to the theater!"

"I promise I will," Nate said.

But he couldn't be certain how he'd go about doing that. How do you catch someone you can't see?

FIFTEEN

No one at the Dysart Theater knew anyone named Bonnie, and Nate found himself at another dead end. He had an important clue—a name—but couldn't seem to go anywhere with it. It was the first of December and his play was opening in less than two weeks, so he had no choice but to let the matter go and concentrate on the morning's rehearsals. He wanted to discuss the next step with Adrian, but at lunchtime Don announced that Joel Warner was waiting in his office.

"Already?" Nate sighed. "All right, tell him I'll be there in a minute."

He wanted Adrian with him, since she was as much a part of all this as he, but she'd made a date to eat with Judy. And, Nate reasoned, Joel probably wouldn't appreciate her being around.

"Mr. Warner," he said as he entered his office. "Have you thought of any new questions since yesterday?"

Nate locked his copy of the script in his desk, then walked over to the office bar. He offered Joel a drink and, as he fixed a scotch on the rocks, listened to his new line of questions.

"Some things have been bothering me," Joel said, taking the drink and making himself comfortable on the leather couch.

"Like what?"

"First, can you tell me how many people are working here?"

Nate sat down behind his desk and propped his elbows on its glass top. He pulled his hands away from each other and shrugged.

"Oh, about forty-two," he said. "Including both the cast and crew. I can look up the exact number, if you'd like."

"That won't be necessary," Joel said. "Have they all been with you since this company opened?"

Nate said that was true.

"You trust them all?"

That was a question the director could not answer immediately. When he'd chosen his staff, he picked them because they had had experience elsewhere. How much did he really know about any of them? He had trusted each one of them to do his or her professional best for the Dysart Theater Company. Yet now he had to face the fact that one of them might be a killer who was trying to destroy him and his life's work.

"Of course I do," he said, finally.

"Then why did it take you so long to answer me?" Joel demanded.

"Look, I don't need to justify..."

Joel picked up his scotch and waved his hand at Nate.

"Never mind," he said. He twirled the ice in his drink. "Let me ask you this—have you ever fired anyone?"

Nate shook his head.

"All my staff have been with me since day one," he told Joel. "With the exception of Don Benson, my new stage manager."

"You had to have the other one replaced after he died," Joel said.

Nate felt a sudden flash of anger. "The other one" had been his best friend! He sat back in his chair with his lips set hard.

"Jim died of a heart attack," he said grimly. "And as far as Don Benson goes, he's a fine man. I *do* trust him."

"What about the people who built this theater?" Joel went on. "Were any of them ever fired?"

"Possibly," Nate said. "I didn't have control over the contracting company."

Joel leaned forward, holding his drink in two hands.

"But if someone had been fired," he said, "for whatever reason, it's possible he could hold a grudge against this theater, isn't it?"

Nate bit his lip, wondering if this might be a new clue.

But he dropped that hope very quickly. The nightmares and voices had started long before the theater was even designed.

"People get fired every day," he said at last. "That doesn't mean they try to get even with their employers by causing trouble."

"This city is full of nuts," Joel said. "In my work, I find them all the time. And some nut might have killed my wife."

"Barbara's death was an accident," Nate said perfunctorily.

Joel's eyes widened.

"The way your wife's death was an accident?"

"How did you know about that?" Nate asked softly.

"I did some research."

"You leave her out of this," Nate warned. "She has nothing to do with it."

"Not directly, no," Joel said. "But I read about her in a back issue of your hometown paper. Said she fell from a scaffolding. Just like Barbara."

"I don't want to talk about that," Nate said forcefully, standing.

But Joel would not relent. If he hit below the belt like this, maybe he could shatter Nate's cool, protective shell. And then he'd learn the truth.

"It's strange how accidents keep happening around you," he taunted. "You were right there when Meg was hurt, too, weren't you?"

A red film came down over Nate's vision, and he lost control of himself. Lunging forward with a terrible roar, he knocked Joel from the couch. His hands wrapped around Joel's neck, the fingers tightening as his rage increased.

"You bastard!" Nate cried, his face reddening.

Joel's fist came up from under Nate's jaw, stunning him momentarily. It was time enough for Joel to pull away from him and hurry toward the door.

"You *are* hiding something!" he said, adjusting his glasses as he gasped for air. "And believe me, I'll be back again to find out what it is!"

Adrian who had been outside the door, jumped out of the way as the reporter hurried down the hall. She turned and saw Nate pick himself up off the floor. His jaw was bruised purple, and he was fingering it gently. Adrian ran and pulled his hand away.

She winced. "What happened?"

When Nate simply shook his head, she pressed on.

"Look, I can't help you deal with these things if you aren't totally honest with me. What did he do that made you so angry?"

Nate rubbed his eyes.

"He started talking about Meg," he said finally. "About how she died."

Hating the memory, he busied himself with picking up ice cubes from the floor.

"Sit down, Nate," Adrian said. "Let me do that."

"I feel okay," Nate said, though his jaw was sore. Still, he could move it, so it wasn't broken.

Adrian went to the bar and opened the ice bucket. With a hand towel, she made an ice pack and carried it back to Nate.

"Don't put it right on the bruise," she said. "There, hold it there. It'll help a little."

"Thanks," Nate said. "What happened to your lunch date?"

"Believe it or don't," Adrian said, smiling, "it's for tomorrow. We got our dates mixed up. And a good thing for that! You look like you need a friend right now."

Nate closed his eyes and nodded.

"It scares the hell out of me when I get that angry," he said.

"That's because you're usually so patient," Adrian said. "It's so out of character for you to get really infuriated that it's frightening."

"I wanted to kill Joel Warner," Nate said. "When he mentioned Meg, I wanted to tear his throat open."

"He shouldn't have touched such a sore spot," Adrian said, rubbing his thigh a little. "Don't worry about him."

"But I do," Nate said. "My father used to fly off the handle like that all the time. I vowed I would never be like that."

"And you aren't," Adrian reassured.

"I was just like my father a few minutes ago," he said. "I was just like the man I hate!"

Adrian put her arms around him.

"Don't even think about that old SOB," she said. "He's dead and gone. And Joel Warner deserved worse from you."

"Sometimes," Nate said softly, playing with Adrian's hair, "I wish my father were alive. He said I'd never make it in show business, but I want to prove he was wrong."

He sighed.

"But, maybe he wasn't."

Adrian pulled away and looked into Nate's blue eyes.

"Don't even talk like that," she said. "This show is going to be a hit, and you know it!"

"But . . ."

"Just look how well we did in Connecticut," Adrian pointed out. "Now, don't start worrying just because Joel Warner is harassing you! You're going to be all right!"

Nate pulled her close and held her tightly, wishing he shared her confidence.

1975

Nate walked down a long, cold hallway, his eyes fixed on a door straight ahead of him. The walls and ceiling and floor were all stark white and unsettling, and overhead, pale green lights shone down on him with chilling beams. He hated this

*place. He hated coming here. And yet he couldn't bear to
imagine never seeing Meg again.*

"She's gotten worse since your last visit, Mr. Dysart," the
nurse beside him said. "She clings to the doll I gave her as if
she were a real baby."

Why did you give her a doll? Nate wondered. *Why torment
her?*

But he said nothing. He stopped at the door to his wife's
room and put his hand on the knob. Before he could think
that he didn't want to see what was inside, he turned it
quickly and opened the door onto a small room.

Meg turned and stared up at him with wide, dark-rimmed
eyes. Her hair, once so beautiful, hung like straw. Her lips
were cracked and pale. But still she smiled, recognizing him.

"Our baby," she sing-songed, holding up the doll.

SIXTEEN

The next afternoon, Adrian asked Nate's chauffeur to take
her to F.A.O. Schwartz. She had decided Nate needed something to get his mind off his worries, if only for a little while.
He'd been very distant all morning, his eyes filled with a
sadness he refused to discuss with her. She decided he ought
to have something to amuse himself. It wouldn't solve any
problems, but maybe it would make him smile.

George let her off on the corner where the toy store sat,
half-hidden behind a cluster of window-shoppers dreaming
about being able to afford the magnificent dollhouses and
huge stuffed toys on display in the windows. Adrian was
caught up in a knot of children as she pushed through the
doors, fighting the rush of Christmas shoppers.

George pulled his double-parked car onto Fifth Avenue
and circled the block on the slim chance he'd find a parking
space. In the rearview mirror, he noticed a familiar-looking
man walking toward the toy store. After a moment he realized it was the reporter, Joel Warner. He decided he'd park
the car as quickly as possible and follow the man into the
store, to make certain he didn't bother Adrian.

Joel had spotted Nate's distinctive Rolls, and after a moment's thought he had turned around and walked toward it. To his surprise, only Adrian St. John got out of the car.

Well, she might be easier to talk to, he decided, remembering Nate's angered outburst as a hand went to his throat.

It took some time to find her amongst the crowds in the store, but at last he spotted Adrian admiring a set of electric trains. Coming up beside her, he said, "I had a set of those when I was a kid. But who can afford them these days?"

Adrian turned around to make a friendly comment, the way anyone would in a cheerful place like a toy store. But when she recognized Joel her smile faded.

"Mr. Warner," she said simply.

"I'd like to speak with you, Ms. St. John," Joel replied.

She shook her head.

"I'm in a hurry," she said. "And I don't want to talk to you. You've caused enough trouble, hurting Nate the way you did!"

Joel's expression turned angry.

"He nearly strangled me," he said. "The man is . . ."

"Under a lot of pressure these days," Adrian said. "And how could you have been so insensitive—bringing up his dead wife?"

Joel followed closely behind her as she moved away from the display.

"I'm not insensitive," Joel said. "I know what he feels like."

Adrian turned to him.

"I'm sorry." She sighed. "I understand how angry you are. But please realize you're pursuing something you'll never find. Barbara died accidentally. Why do you torture yourself?"

"Because I can't believe it," Joel said. "I know that Barbara was not herself before the—what you call—the accident, according to Judy Terrel. Judy was her best friend. She'd never lie!"

"I'm sure she wouldn't," Adrian said. "Look, I'm in a hurry. I've got to get back to rehearsals . . ."

Joel grabbed her arm and held it fast.

"I'm not through," he said. "There's also the parallel between Barbara's death and Meg Dysart's accident that . . ."

But now someone placed a large hand on Joel's shoulder.

"However," George said, "the young lady is through."

"Oh, George," Adrian said. She glanced at Joel, who

removed his hand from her arm. "This is Nate's chauffeur. If you'll excuse me, I really do have to get back to work. We do want to cooperate with you, Mr. Warner. But please don't harass us. You can reach me at the theater."

When Adrian and George reached the car, George opened the door and let her in. As they headed down Fifth Avenue, Adrian looked out the window and debated about stopping elsewhere to get something for Nate anyway. But suddenly, the car started making strange noises. She leaned forward.

"What's that noise?"

"I'm sure I don't know," George said worriedly. "Perhaps I should pull over and . . ."

But there was no chance to pull over. A city bus cut in front of them at an intersection, and George's foot automatically slammed onto the brakes.

They didn't work.

"George!"

In a flash, George jerked the wheel to one side, hearing the front bumper scrape over the side of the bus. As dozens of people watched in horror the big old car flipped over and skidded on its roof into a newspaper stand. It all happened in a matter of seconds, and for a moment there was stunned silence on the street. Then a mob of people were running toward the car. Adrian, completely dazed, saw a dozen faces looking in the upside-down window.

"Are you—are you all right?" George asked weakly.

"I don't know," Adrian answered in a small voice.

Sirens screamed through the air, and a few moments later someone was trying to pry the door open. A woman poked her head in and said, "I'm a doctor. Do you hurt anywhere? Any dizziness? Nausea?"

"I—I don't think so," Adrian said, hardly believing it.

Two policemen came into the picture.

"We're going to help you out of there," one said. "If anything hurts, you tell us."

When at last she was pulled out, Adrian was made to sit on the curb next to the ruined newsstand. Her head dropped between her knees as a wave of nausea came over her. Nearby, the owner of the stand was ranting about suing someone or other for the damage done to his property.

Adrian was vaguely aware of George being laid on a stretcher, then of someone poking at her.

"Does this hurt?"

Adrian shook her head.

"This? Or this?"

"Nothing hurts," Adrian said.

"You might easily have been killed," a cop said. "They sure don't build cars like this old baby any longer. It was that strong frame that saved you."

"How did it happen?" his partner inquired.

"I—I don't know," Adrian said.

The doctor put her hand on Adrian's shoulder.

"I'd like you to be taken to the hospital for observation," she said. "You don't appear to be hurt, but..."

"No, no, I'm fine," Adrian insisted. She got to her feet, though her knees were trembling. "I'd like to go back to work."

"I don't think you..."

"Please!" Adrian cried, needing to be with Nate. "Can someone take me to the Dysart Theater?"

"Sure," one of the cops said. "That's near here. But you'll have to give us a statement, first."

Adrian nodded, then turned to the news dealer and said, "Please contact Nathaniel Dysart at the Dysart Theater. He'll pay for this."

Even as she told what little she remembered to the cop, a tow truck came and pulled the huge black car off the curb, working busily to turn it over. She was given a card telling where she'd find it and was promised it would be fixed within a week's time. At last, holding on to the young policeman's arm, she walked to his car. She said nothing as they drove, feeling too weakened to discuss the accident further. Thank God, she thought, as she entered the theater, there wasn't even a scratch on her.

And when she saw this, the little girl named Bonnie let out a silent scream of rage and knocked over a lamp on the stage.

As the actors looked at each other in wonder Adrian came down the main aisle of the theater.

Nate put his script aside and rushed to her side. All the actors on stage turned, amazed to see her disheveled hair and dirty clothes.

"What happened to you?" Sander demanded.

Adrian ignored him and threw her arms around Nate. In his embrace, the reality of the accident finally hit her, and she began to cry. Nate looked up at Don Benson, busy picking up the lamp, and said, "Take over here."

He led Adrian to his big office and sat her down on the couch, propping a pillow behind her back to make her comfortable. Gradually, between sobs, she told him what had happened.

Nate put his arms around her, thinking it was ironic that for once he was comforting her. But another thought overshadowed this one. He could not help a feeling that this was no accident, the way Barbara's fall had been no accident. He couldn't help a feeling that someone had just tried to kill Adrian too.

The next morning all the newspapers carried stories about the accident. Adrian's name was prominent, and it was mentioned that she was an actress at the Dysart Theater, where a new show would soon be opening. What worried Nate, though, was that all the newspapers chose to mention the other accidents that had been happening to the people in his company—Barbara's fall, Denny's misadventure in the air passages, even the stagehand who had been burned in that fire.

"They even include Jim Orland," Nate said, as he sat next to George's hospital bed.

"You're in the public eye now, sir," George said. "You have to expect this sort of thing. Besides, it may bring in more box-office sales. You know how curious people can be."

"I don't want tickets sold because of other people's misfortunes," Nate snapped. "I want them to come because *Making Good* is worth seeing."

He turned to the inside of the newspaper for the continuation of the story. His eyes scanned the article, then finally he shook his head and said, "Listen to this: 'In light of all the tragedies befalling Nathaniel Dysart's production of the original comedy *Making Good,* one is inclined to wonder if the theater is cursed. What malevolent specter is casting its evil eye over the cast of *Making Good?*'"

Nate crumbled up the paper and tossed it into a metal trash can.

"Damned sensationalism," he growled. "They can't leave people alone, can they? I know there's an explanation for the things that have happened at my theater, but it will be a mortal one when I find it." He waved at the trash can. "That idiot would have you think the damned place is haunted!"

"There are no such things as ghosts, sir," George agreed.

Nate managed a smile for the chauffeur, and changed the subject.

"What did the doctors tell you? Are you going to get out of this place today?"

"I have a slight concussion," George said. "And my wrist is broken. I imagine I did that when I turned the wheel of the car, sir."

"I called the repair shop," Nate said. "They say they can't find anything wrong with the brakes system."

"That's odd, sir," George said. "It was working perfectly earlier in the day, and after a half-century of driving, I ought to know how to use a brake pedal!"

"I certainly don't hold you responsible," Nate assured him. "But I still wish I knew exactly what happened."

"It is frightening, isn't it, sir?" George asked.

Nate did not say anything. It was more frightening, he thought, than George realized.

To look at her, one would never have realized Adrian had been in an accident just the day before. Her hair was neatly pinned up again, and her white wool suit was fresh and clean. Still, there was a weariness in the way she moved. It had been a sleepless night for her. She knew she should have her understudy work today, but since she'd never before missed a rehearsal (until yesterday), she refused to consider the matter. Still, the armchair across her dressing room looked very comfortable. But she knew she must keep going. Her parents were arriving soon, and she didn't want them to know about the accident. Her mother would worry too much.

Adrian glanced at the clock on her vanity. Rehearsals would not start for another ten minutes. Perhaps she could rest a while in that chair.

The dark! The dark hurts!

Adrian looked up. The voice had sounded nearby, yet her room was empty. She sat up a little.

"Is someone there?"

I don't like the dark. You're going to pay for bringing the dark!

Adrian jumped to her feet and hurried to Nate's office. He wasn't there, nor was he on the stage. At last, she found him talking to Mike Woodson about the upcoming opening night. Adrian took his arm, and when he saw the urgency in her manner, he excused himself.

"I just heard a strange voice," Adrian whispered as they walked down the hall. "Talking about the dark, just like that voice you hear."

Nate's eyes widened. "Show me where," he said.

A minute later they entered Adrian's dressing room. She pointed to her vanity chair.

"I was sitting there," she said, "when I heard someone say 'The dark, the dark hurts,' and some other things I can't remember."

"What kind of voice was it?"

Adrian thought a moment, bringing the voice back into her mind.

"Very young," she said. "Like a small child. And she had sort of an accent. Southern, I think, but not as thick as Georgia's."

Nate bit his lip. Quietly, he asked, "Could it have been a southwestern accent?"

"Well, yes," Adrian said, "that's exactly what it was like. She spoke the way people do in western movies."

Nate turned from her and walked across the room, folding his arms. Adrian came up behind him and put her own arms around his shoulders, resting her head against his back.

"It was frightening," she said, "but it was also a kind of relief. If I'm hearing voices, it means you can't be imagining the ones you hear."

"The accent is the same," Nate said. "And the childish voice."

He broke away from Adrian and threw his arms up.

"But where does that lead us? Who the hell is doing this?"

"It's got to be someone in the company," Adrian said. "You know we haven't allowed anyone in the theater since our return from Connecticut, with the exception of Joel Warner. Security is tight. No one could have wandered in off the street."

"But Joel wasn't here when I heard the first voices," Nate said.

"Look, let's put our facts together," Adrian suggested. "We have a person with a childish voice and southwestern accent. Anyone in the company like that?"

Nate shook his head.

"Not that I can recall. But don't forget—someone with acting experience might easily be able to imitate any sort of voice they wanted."

He put his arm around her and started to walk with her from the dressing room. For a moment, the fatigue Adrian had felt earlier caught up with her, and she swayed a little.

"Are you all right?" Nate asked with alarm, steadying her.

"Oh, Nate, I'm fine," Adrian said. "Just a little tired."

"Maybe you ought to rest this morning," Nate said. "That accident yesterday . . ."

"Nate Dysart," Adrian said with a small laugh, "you aren't the only one who can use work as a means of escape. I don't want to spend the morning moping around, thinking about that voice I heard!"

But she did think about it, all during the rehearsal. A vague memory was stirring in her mind, something connected to the horrible words she had heard that morning. And the more she thought of them, the more she was certain she'd heard that voice somewhere before.

"Adrian!"

She looked up, startled, and realized she had lost her place.

"I'm sorry," she said. "Where were we?"

"Nigel was just asking Daisy to play up to the local millionaire," Sander said. "Really, Ms. St. John. If your head was that badly injured in that accident, you shouldn't be here!"

"Thanks for your concern," Adrian said sarcastically. "But I'll be all right."

Suddenly, it had come to her. Several weeks earlier, there had been a strange little girl in her dressing room. A child who had spoken fearfully of the dark, then had seemingly vanished into thin air. At the time she'd assumed she was the daughter of one of the company or crew but now . . .

SEVENTEEN

At the end of the rehearsal Adrian took hold of Nate's arm and held fast to him until everyone had left the stage. Then she said, quietly, "I might have another clue."

"Is that where your mind was during rehearsal?" Nate asked, as they started to walk together down the hall. "You've never missed a cue before, Adrian."

"I'm sorry," she said. "But I couldn't help it."

Nate kissed her lightly.

"I'm not angry," he said. He was speaking partly as her director, partly as the man who loved her. "I'm just concerned. Are you sure you're all right?"

"I'm fine," Adrian said. "It's just that I can't stop thinking about that voice I heard. Nate, I think I might have an idea who it belongs to."

Nate stopped walking and turned to look at her. Was it possible? Quietly, Nate took her hand and said, "Let's go into my office."

But they never reached it. Suddenly, from back in the wings, there was a strange crackling noise, and a split second later the entire upstairs of the theater went dark.

"Oh, no," Adrian groaned, annoyed by the interruption.

Nate turned his head around, though he couldn't see anything, and listened to the sounds of others in the hallway. Recognizing Judy's voice, he called, "Get Mike Woodson, Judy, will you?"

"Sure, Nate," Judy said. "If I can find the stairs!"

Adrian found Nate and put her arms around him. As they stood waiting for the electrician, Nate could not resist searching for Adrian's lips in the darkness to place a warm kiss upon them. She sighed softly, her hand coming up behind his head. His hair felt soft to the touch, and Adrian kneaded it between her fingers for a moment before sliding her hand down to his back. She was massaging his muscles when suddenly a sharp, burning pain ran along her arm. With a cry, she pulled away.

"Something burned me!"

"What?" Nate asked. Without waiting for an answer, he demanded impatiently, "Where the hell is Mike?"

Adrian twisted her arm up to her mouth and blew on the sore spot. It felt something like the sting of a hot iron, and yet what had touched her hadn't been hard like that. It had been soft, almost like a human hand.

Bonnie could see in the dark what the others couldn't, and what she saw next enraged her so that she let out a long, silent scream. Nate was pulling Adrian back into his arms, cooing over her as if she were a child. But in a moment, the little girl collected her senses. She would be stronger than this Adrian. She would win in the end no matter what the woman did—and the end was not far away. Quietly, she disappeared into a blackness even deeper than the one that held Nate and Adrian captive.

When all the lights came up a moment later, Nate could hear cheers throughout the building. He turned to Adrian with concern in his eyes and lifted her arm gently. But there was no sign of a burn.

"Nate, something did burn me," Adrian said, her eyes wide.

"You know I believe you," Nate said. "The important thing is that you aren't seriously hurt. Do you still feel anything?"

"Not at all," Adrian said. "Forget it—or add it to the list of unexplained phenomena that we have. Let's go to your office."

"Somehow we managed," Mike Woodson said, as he waylaid them in the hall, "to blow out a third of all the fuses downstairs. Were you running too many lights at once up here?"

"No more than usual," Nate said. He shrugged perfunctorily, for the benefit of those in the hall watching him. "I guess it was just one of those things."

"Yeah," Mike said. "I'm going to check the control board. There may be something wrong there."

"If you need me," Nate said, "I'll be in my office."

A few minutes later they were interrupted by an urgent knocking. A stagehand reported that Mike had to see Nate. They found Mike in the wings, poking at the control panel—or what was left of it. All the insulation had melted, and the plastic hung like globs of old bubblegum. The bare wires were twisted and mangled, as if someone of unnatural strength had reached in and wrenched them from the unit.

"This could only have been done with intense heat," Mike said.

"A fire?" Nate asked, almost in a panic.

"No, no," Mike assured him. "If I thought there was any danger of that I would have cleared the building. But the walls around here aren't even warm."

Nate felt a cold chill as a feeling of déjà vu ran through him. Intense heat. Fire. A burning theater...

"Maybe someone with a blowtorch," Mike was saying when Nate came out of the daze that had momentarily claimed him. "That's the only thing I could think of."

"Who could do such a thing?" Adrian asked.

Nate was about to ask who could have hurt Barbara or Denny, but he stopped.

"Just do what you can to fix it. I'll expect a progress report tomorrow."

"Someone is trying to ruin me. I've got the building crew working overtime, and now the damned lighting crew. I'm going to have a strike on my hands if this keeps up!" Nate said.

"Don't even think about that," Adrian said. "Let's talk about what we started earlier. Listen, I might have a clue about that voice." Adrian set a drink on the glass top of his desk. She took a sip of her own and let the alcohol warm her. "A few weeks ago, I was in my dressing room, when I noticed a little girl sitting in my armchair. She kept staring at me, so I thought she might be too shy to speak. Anyway, I asked what she was doing there, and she started saying all these strange things about the dark coming."

Nate leaned forward.

"Did she have the accent?"

"I don't recall," Adrian said. "Maybe, since the voice I just heard said the same things."

"What did she look like?"

"Very pretty," Adrian said. She brushed back her hair. "Her hair was pulled to the side with a big white bow—black hair, I recall. And she was wearing a white dress with tiers of ruffles. I remember it so clearly because it was such an unusual..."

She saw that Nate wasn't listening. He stared into his glass, a frown turning his lips, trying to recapture the picture that had flashed in his mind when she described the little girl. He could see a child in a white dress, standing near the theater. No, near the empty lot. He had seen that same child before the theater was built.

But in a moment, a more terrifying thought occurred to him. Nate had also seen the little girl in another place.

In his dreams.

"Adrian," he said, his voice in monotone. "You can't dream about something you've never seen before, can you?"

"I don't think so," Adrian replied. "Why?"

"The little girl in the white ruffled dress is the one I see in my nightmares," he said.

Adrian's eyes widened, but then she shook her head. At first she was a little stunned by the coincidence, but in her way she found a logical explanation.

"Look, you must have seen her somewhere before," she said.

"No," he said. "I swear I never saw her before the dreams."

"Then how do you know it's the same child?"

He spread his hands. "All of this is so bizarre that I'm beginning to think the newspapers were right the other day. Maybe there really is something supernatural going on here."

"Nate, that's impossible, and you know it," Adrian said. "Whether you can remember or not, you surely must have seen the little girl before your dreams."

"I know I didn't," Nate said.

Adrian sighed, not knowing how to comfort him. Finally, she decided to take a businesslike approach. She stood up and walked over to Nate's file cabinet.

"We were going to look up the names of people from the Southwest," she said. "Let's just concentrate on that for now."

Nate put down his glass and came to unlock the files. Though he was aching for an explanation about the little girl, he decided to follow Adrian's advice. He pulled out a folder and carried it to the coffee table. For the next ten minutes he and Adrian skimmed through résumés. At one point, Nate interrupted and said, "How could a child do all this?"

"Maybe it isn't just a child," Adrian said. "Maybe the voices belong to a child—someone small enough to duck away before being caught. But the really bad stuff is the work of a sick-minded adult."

She tossed her last sheet on top of the pile, and Nate returned them to the folder. They had gotten nowhere.

"For a minute there"—Adrian sighed—"I had the idea that we might find an adult from the Southwest, someone who sneaks his or her kid into the theater."

Nate snapped his fingers.

"But," he said, "he could have lied about his origin. We're just going to have to ask around if anyone knows about a little girl wandering through the theater."

"Oh, we can't do that," Adrian said quickly. "We'd upset everybody—and right before opening night. You know how superstitious we actors are. Besides that, we'd give ourselves away. If this monster is to be caught, he must have no warning."

"You're right," Nate said. "But I don't like being left at a dead end like this. Isn't there anyone we can talk to?"

Adrian thought a moment.

"Denny," she said. "Maybe he's thinking more clearly now, and he'll be able to tell us something."

When they arrived at Georgia's apartment, a grandmotherly-looking baby-sitter let them in. Georgia had explained she had a date, and Nate was glad they would have a chance to talk to Denny alone. Like most kids, there were probably things he didn't want his mother to know.

Denny, already in his plush robe and pajamas, hurried to the door to greet them. His eyes lit up when they handed him the present they'd bought, a big book on basketball.

"I'll be in the kitchen if you need me," the sitter said.

Denny carried the book to the couch and sat down with it, flipping through the photographs with delight.

"It's got all my favorite players in it," he said.

"We thought it might make you happy," Nate replied. It was partly a gift, partly a bribe he hoped would help the boy open up to them.

Denny smiled at him. "My mom says I can go back to work, soon."

"Wonderful!" Adrian cried. "We really miss you, Denny."

"Really?" Denny asked. "I thought you'd still be mad at me."

"Denny," Nate said, taking a seat, "we cleared that up last time we were here. We are definitely not mad at you."

Adrian crossed the room and sat beside Denny. Watching her with big eyes, he closed the book and placed it on the coffee table.

"There's something we didn't clear up, though," she said. She looked over at Nate, who picked up her signal and took over.

"Do you remember how we asked if you knew anyone named Bonnie?"

"Uh-huh," Denny said with a nod. "And I still don't."

"Denny, think really hard about that," Nate said. "See, we think someone named Bonnie has been causing—causing trouble at the theater. You may be able to help us."

He knew that children were more likely to be responsive if treated on an equal level with adults. Maybe Denny would think himself privileged to share in the problems facing the theater, instead of being left out just because he was a kid.

But Denny shook his head adamantly.

"I don't know anyone named Bonnie," he insisted.

"Maybe you just don't know her by name," Adrian said. "She's a very little girl with black hair. She wears a white dress with ruffles all over it."

Something was coming back to him, a shadowy picture. The little girl Adrian was describing did sound familiar, but Denny couldn't place her. He closed his eyes and thought deeply. A picture of the backyard came to his mind, with its crates and litter. He was playing basketball. He bumped into someone.

"Bonnie," he said, softly.

"Do you remember now?" Nate asked.

Denny nodded his head slowly. He pictured the little girl in his mind and knew she had come to play with him. He opened his eyes to tell Nate this, but almost immediately his expression went blank, and he fixed a stare on something across the room. Nate and Adrian turned that way, but saw only the darkened television set and an empty chair.

"Denny?"

Adrian went unheard. Denny was only aware of the little girl sitting in the chair next to the TV, her small hands curled around its arms. She was shaking her head at him, and when she spoke her words were for his ears alone.

"She's interfering again," she said. "I have to stop her!"

And then she was gone.

As Nate and Adrian watched in horror Denny's head fell back, and his eyes rolled back until only the whites showed. Then he collapsed across the plaid couch.

"Denny!" Adrian cried.

Nate went to the boy and put a hand on his forehead.

"He's burning up," he said. "Get the sitter and have her call a doctor."

Adrian hurried towards the kitchen. Nate, not knowing what else to do, straightened the boy out on the couch. What had he seen a moment ago? What had frightened him?

Suddenly, Denny began to shiver violently. Nate looked around and found an afghan, which he laid over the child's quaking body as Adrian and the sitter entered the room. Words began to pour from Denny's mouth, at first slurred and unintelligible, then horribly clear.

"The dark, Daddy! Take away the dark!"

Nate felt a chill run over him. It was not Denny's voice, but a little girl's. A little girl with a southwestern accent.

"Take the dark away, Daddy!" Denny screamed. "The fire! The fire! Stop, it hurts!"

Denny sat up abruptly, his eyes wide and glistening, his body stiff. Strange choking noises began to escape from the back of his throat. Then, suddenly, strings of a muslinlike substance began to gush from his mouth. Adrian screamed and backed away. The sitter turned and closed her eyes in horror.

"My God," Nate whispered, unable to move.

The strange matter began to pour from Denny's nostrils, from his ears, and even began to darken the seat of his pajamas. Whatever it was, it seemed to be escaping from every orifice of the child's body.

"What the hell is that?"

An eternity later, yet only a few seconds after the seizure had started, Denny collapsed again.

The room was silent except for the baby-sitter's sobs. Nate and Adrian stared at the mess that covered the plaid couch, a mess that somehow resembled torn-up pieces of cloth soaked in gelatin. A moment passed, then Adrian screamed.

"Nate, look!"

Nate followed the line of her finger. There in the white

mess, a face was looking up at them, a portrait of a small child somehow imprinted on the strange substance. But in the blink of an eye, it was gone.

"That was her," Adrian whispered, tears pouring from her eyes. "That was the little girl!"

Nate could not say anything. He didn't even put his arms around Adrian when she moved closer to him. He just kept staring at Denny, unable to comprehend what had just happened.

Finally, it was the sitter who broke the spell. She walked toward the couch and gingerly touched Denny's neck.

"We have to get him to a hospital," she said quietly.

She looked up at Nate and Adrian.

"Why must little ones suffer?" she asked. "Why must they be tormented?"

"Tormented?" Adrian asked.

The sitter pointed a bony finger at the mess on the couch.

"Ectoplasm," she said. "That horrible stuff is called ectoplasm."

"I—I don't know what that means," Nate said, his voice hollow.

The sitter glared at him.

"Ectoplasm," she said, "is physical evidence of a ghost."

EIGHTEEN

After bringing Denny to the hospital and notifying Georgia, Nate ordered George to take him back to the theater. He and Adrian sat in silence in the back of a Lincoln Continental, and though Adrian desired only to go home and comfort him, she did not argue with his plans. She did not tell him these things were best figured out after a good night's sleep. She did not tell him there must be some logical explanation for what they had seen. Instead, she simply took his hand to let him know she was there.

They entered the theater through the front door, crossing the dimly lit lobby where crystal chandeliers glowed in dreamlike silence. The auditorium was dark but for the ghost light burning center stage. Nate let go of Adrian's hand and walked slowly toward it as she stood behind the back row. Then he began to run, his anger mounting, nearly crashing into the railing that surrounded the orchestra pit. He grabbed hold of it and tossed his head back.

"Who the hell are you?" he cried. *"Who the hell are you?"* Silence.

Nate tightened his fists on the railing, fury emanating from every pore of his body. Someone was trying to ruin him. Someone did not want his life's dream to come true.

"WHO THE HELL ARE YOU? WHAT DO YOU WANT FROM ME? YOU WON'T DESTROY MY WORK! YOU WON'T!"

He screamed and screamed like this until his voice was so hoarse that he began to choke. Yet still the theater was silent. Though she knew he was screaming for her to answer, Bonnie simply stared at Nate, confused by his anger. Why was he angry? He never got angry! Only Mommy did, and then she'd be locked in a dark place until Daddy came to get her out. Daddy was always happy.

"Don't be sad, Daddy."

But Nate did not hear her this time.

"WHY DON'T YOU ANSWER ME?"

Adrian had seen enough. She ran down the center aisle and threw her arms around him, bursting into tears.

"For God's sake, Nate, stop it!" she cried.

Nate groaned and brought his hands up to his face. With a heavy sigh he quieted down and dropped his head to bury it in her soft hair. The two held each other in silence, not knowing what to say to each other, not knowing that they were being watched.

The Dysart Theater was busy the next morning, and no one would have guessed what had taken place there during the night. Nate seemed as calm and professional as ever, interrupting with suggestions and taking notes the way he always did. Only Adrian, who had spent the night comforting him, knew there was something wrong. His no-nonsense voice had an edge to it, and there were times when he seemed not to be paying attention to the action on stage.

"Maybe you ought to let Don take over," she suggested quietly.

Nate merely stared blankly at her and turned back to his script. Adrian decided she'd discuss this with Nate at lunch, but when noon came around, Mike Woodson got to him first and asked to discuss the blackout. Adrian expected to stay there with Nate, but to her surprise, he said, "I'll probably be a while. Why don't you eat without me?"

Adrian considered telling him she would wait, but there was something in his tone that indicated he preferred to be alone. At first she was hurt by his coldness, but then she realized he probably wanted time to think things out for himself.

As she readied herself to go out, she could not help an occasional glance at the armchair of her dressingroom. It remained innocently empty.

Deciding she would bring lunch back and eat in the greenroom, Adrian remembered she had a takeout menu in her vanity drawer. She pulled it open, pushing aside curlers and makeup and souvenirs from old shows. Something small and yellow revealed itself, as a *Playbill* slipped to one side. Adrian reached for it and pulled out a roll of film.

"I can't believe I forgot about this," she whispered.

It was the roll she and Nate had taken of the theater, to see if the strange white flaw would show up again. But then Denny's accident had happened, and in the confusion that followed the film had been forgotten. Adrian recalled the first set of photos that Nate had showed her. The blur had almost resembled a human figure, a ghostlike image.

"Ghostlike image," she said aloud. The words of Denny's sitter came back to her. *Ectoplasm. Physical evidence of a ghost.*

Had the old woman been right? Adrian shook her head. No, she would not believe that. The sitter had been hysterical, a crazy old lady. Of course there was a logical explanation for what had happened to Denny. Perhaps something not even connected to the horror at the theater. The doctors would be able to explain it and give Danny the proper medicines to make him well again.

But she and Nate had both seen that face.

We were upset, she insisted to herself.

Instead of sitting there frightening herself, she would do something constructive. It took half an hour to find a photog-

raphy store that would develop the film within a day, but to
Adrian it would be worth the effort if any clues were found in
the new set of photos.

Nate hardly spoke to her when she returned to rehearsal.
While she and Sander were waiting backstage at one point,
the actor pulled her aside and whispered, "Perhaps you
should tell our director to leave his problems at home.
Whatever they are, they're interfering with the show."

Adrian glowered at him. Of all the people in the company,
superstitious Sander was the last person she wanted to have
know about what had been happening. When she heard her
cue, she hurried on the stage, then remembered she was
supposed to be walking lazily and slowed herself. For the rest
of the afternoon she concentrated on her work. But when it
was over, she walked downstairs to Nate and said carefully,
"Do you want me to come home with you?"

"I have a lot of work to do," Nate said. "I really should be
alone."

He hates being alone, Adrian thought.

"Nate, I . . ."

"Adrian, the show is opening in barely a week's time," Nate
said. "I'm going to be very busy."

Adrian did not say anything more. Nate ducked his head
back down to read his script, almost as if dismissing her.
Sadly, she left. She did not see him again before going home.

Nate sat alone in his office, listlessly flipping through a
copy of *Variety*. He had tried to keep himself busy all day,
had even avoided Adrian, so that he would not have to think
about what had happened the night before. But all day long it
haunted him, and now, alone this way, he could not turn his
thoughts elsewhere. The deaths, the voices, the accidents all
added up to one thing:

Someone wanted him to lose his theater.

"I won't let that happen," he whispered. "Damn whoever
you are, you won't do this to me!"

He ran his hands through his blond hair and leaned back
with a sigh, closing his eyes, letting a memory appear in his
mind. He was in his father's office, and he was wearing a
black suit, though he hated dark clothes. It was just after
Meg's death.

"You've won, Father," he said. *"My production company is closing. I can't do it without Meg."*

"You could never do anything right," the old man sneered. *"Not even making a healthy baby."*

Nate's eyes snapped open, and he stood up abruptly.

"This time, I will succeed," he said. "I'll show you how wrong you were, Daddy. No one will destroy me!"

He was standing, locking his briefcase to take it home, when a knock sounded at his door. Before Nate could answer, it opened, and Georgia Richmond strode into his office. Her eyes were bloodshot, and her cheeks splotchy.

"What the devil happened last night?" she demanded, her voice strained as she stared coldly at him.

"I don't . . ."

Georgia cut him off.

"Denny was perfectly fine yesterday," she said. "Now he's back in the hospital, indefinitely!"

"He had another attack," Nate said quietly. "I—I really don't know why."

"He was so happy yesterday," Georgia blubbered. "My poor Denny!"

Nate watched her for a few moments in silence. She cried openly, making no attempt to control her sobs.

"What exactly did they tell you at the hospital?" he asked finally.

"That Denny became so upset during your visit that he began to throw up," Georgia said. "I don't know what you said to him, but I'm going to tell you one thing. You are forbidden to go anywhere near my child! He's out of the show, and that's *final!*"

Nate didn't argue with her. Quietly, he said, "We'll have to make it official, then."

Georgia sniffled and opened her purse. Pulling out a folder of white papers, she said, "Then let's do it. I've brought my copy of the contract."

"Uh, let me get ours from my files," Nate said. He crossed the room and pulled open a drawer, fishing through it for Denny's contract. But after a moment he stopped and closed his eyes. Then he said, "Are you sure you want to do this? Denny was so happy here—and I'm sure he wants to come back in spite of everything."

"I'm quite sure," Georgia said. "My son's *health* is most important."

"But he worked so hard," Nate protested futilely.

"Oh, my son will have his chance," Georgia said. "I am going to set up some auditions for him as soon as he's better."

"Maybe you shouldn't rush things," Nate said.

He started through the file again.

"Of course Denny will have as much time as he needs to get better," Georgia said. "We're going back to South Carolina. But we'll be back here in New York—or maybe we'll go to California and try for a movie."

Nate turned with the contract and brought it to the coffee table.

"We'll need to make this official," he said. "I'll call my lawyer tomorrow. But our signatures will do for now."

After they were finished, Georgia stood up and said, "I'm sorry it worked out this way. My boy was so happy here."

Nate did not respond but watched her move toward the door and out of the office. He was sorry too. My God, he was sorry. He'd lost three people in his company—Jim, Barbara, and now Denny. But Denny was alive, thank God. Maybe it was all for the best if the child never came back.

The next day, Adrian did not bother asking to share lunch with Nate. She went directly to the photography store, then bought a sandwich at a deli. In her dressing room her lunch remained uneaten as she shuffled through the photographs. They were clear, with no mysterious flaws. She began to relax, but then she turned over the last photograph. It was a picture of the building's front, and a white blur seemed to float above the cornerstone. Adrian studied it for a long time, trying to make something human of the shape. But her eyes kept wandering, as if drawn to something else in the picture. It took a minute for Adrian to realize what it was. The date on the cornerstone was wrong.

It read "1902."

"How can that be?" she demanded of the empty room.

Someone had tampered with the pictures, of course. Nervously, Adrian skimmed through the negatives until she found this one. It also said "1902." There was no indication it had been tampered with. She swept all the photos back into the envelope and went outside to check the cornerstone. It read, quite clearly, "1981."

"Someone *did* manage to change it," she said to herself.

There were about twenty people on line at the ticket office as she reentered the theater through the front door. Adrian knew they were all staring at her, asking each other if that was the actress who'd been in the car crash a few days earlier. But Adrian ignored them. She was in a hurry to get the photos and show them to Nate.

To her surprise, he barely looked at them. He had been so adamant about finding an answer, yet now he didn't seem to even care.

"I'm not surprised to see this," he said.

"How can you say that?" Adrian demanded. "In light of all that's been happening, how can you suddenly be so nonchalant?"

Nate looked up at her.

"Only one thing matters to me," he said, "and that's to see my show open on time without any trouble."

"Of course the show is your main concern," Adrian said. "But you can't pretend none of this is happening!"

"You used to say that," Nate said. "You used to say the voices and nightmares were all products of a tired mind. Well, maybe you were right."

Adrian put her arms around him.

"Oh, no, Nate," she said. "I was wrong, terribly wrong! I heard the voices too. I saw what happened to Den . . ."

Nate pulled away from her.

"I have to get back to the stage," he said, almost impatiently. "Rehearsal is about to begin."

Adrian watched him leave his office, aching to run after him and yet unable. She was shocked by his complete turnaround. But in a way, she understood. This play meant the world to Nate, and he was terrified it was all going to be taken away from him. Nate could not let that happen, and so he threw himself into his work while trying to push away the truth about what had been happening at the theater. Adrian realized he wanted this play to open at any cost.

"And it will open," she said. "I promise it will."

She left the pictures on Nate's desk and went to the rehearsal. As she waited for her cues she pondered the next step. Finally, she decided she might as well start at the beginning and visit Fred Johnson, the architect who, Nate had told her, had designed the theater.

Adrian called ahead to be certain he hadn't left for the day, then fought the crush of an uptown subway. She was so deep in thought that she didn't notice the sandy-haired, mustached man who walked behind her. Joel Warner had followed her from the theater.

When the subway stopped, Joel walked off, a few paces behind Adrian, and followed her into a steel-and-glass skyscraper. Hidden in the rush of people in the lobby, he heard her ask someone which elevator bank went to the fiftieth floor. Then he followed her, taking a different elevator.

Adrian rode up, trying to decide what questions she'd ask. She didn't want to reveal anything, yet she also didn't want to sound ridiculous. She suddenly found herself before the receptionist's desk. The woman was getting ready to go home, and she looked up at Adrian without smiling.

"I'm looking for Fred Johnson," Adrian said.

The woman pointed and gave her an office number down the hall. Adrian thanked her and headed that way. In the meantime, Joel had walked off his own elevator. The receptionist considered her work over for the day, and she did not question his presence.

Adrian was greeted by a thin, dark-haired man.

"Adrian St. John," Fred said as he backed away to let her enter. "I don't like using clichés, but you're prettier than your pictures."

"Thank you," Adrian said, politely. "And thanks for staying late just to see me."

"No problem," Fred assured her.

He indicated a chair for her, and she took it, resting an arm on the bookshelf filled with art volumes next to her.

"I was sorry to hear about your accident," Fred said. "But you seem to be all right. You are, aren't you?"

"I'm fine," Adrian said, though that wasn't entirely true. But for now she straightened herself and got to the point of her visit. "Mr. Johnson, I'd like to ask you some questions about the Dysart Theater."

Fred shrugged. "Go ahead, although I can't imagine what information you'd want from me."

"When you were designing this theater," Adrian began, "do you recall anything strange happening?"

Fred thought a moment, but it had been so long ago that the memory of the design process was a vague one. He finally shook his head.

"Nothing at all," he said. "Why?"

Adrian didn't answer his question. She stood up and walked over to a wall-unit sectioned into deep cubbyholes. Each one contained a half dozen cardboard tubes filled with blueprints. Adrian looked over her shoulder at the architect and said, "Could I see the prints of the theater?"

"Don't see why not," Fred replied, crossing the room.

Adrian hoped there might be a clue in the blueprints. Perhaps she'd find a hidden room or passageway where a small child could hide and call out in the voice she and Nate had heard. But when Fred unrolled them on the drafting table, there was nothing like that to be seen.

"Maybe I could help if I knew what you were looking for," Fred said.

"I'm not sure, exactly," Adrian replied.

She moved the top sheet and studied the next drawing. Somehow, the layout of the basement didn't seem right. Adrian quickly realized no room had been left for the lockers, and that the staircase was on the wrong side.

"Wait a minute," Fred said, taking it from her. "That's an old one. I had done another version of the theater before— using the plans you see there."

"Nate didn't like the original?"

Fred shook his head.

"He was quite happy with it, actually."

"Then why did you bother changing it?"

"I don't really know," Fred answered. He scratched his head. "Actually, I've often tried to figure that out for myself. I suppose the new ideas just came to me, and I decided I preferred them."

"The theater's design—" Adrian said, "that's Art Nouveau, isn't it?"

"Yes, it is," Fred replied. "I thought it was a rather old-fashioned theme for a young man like Mr. Dysart to choose."

Adrian looked up at him.

"Where do you get your ideas?"

"Oh, initially from books," Fred said, pointing to the case of art volumes. "Then I adapt them into my own."

"What book did you use for Nate's theater?"

Fred could not answer that. He hadn't used any books at all, but somehow had gotten every detail of his design from his own head. And yet he had a feeling that, as talented as he was, something was missing here. He had never felt the design was truly his. But of course that was a ridiculous idea, certainly nothing he wanted to mention. He looked at Adrian and made up a lie to satisfy both of them.

"I often visit the library at Lincoln Center," he said. "They have a good deal of theatrical literature. If you are interested in the Art Nouveau style of Mr. Dysart's theater, perhaps they can help you there."

"Thank you," Adrian said. "I'll do that."

She knew he was avoiding telling her something, but she sensed somehow that if he were able to, he would. Could Fred Johnson be controlled by the same person who had Denny in his clutches? Could he, too, have been threatened into silence?

She picked up her purse and smiled a little.

"Thank you for your time," she said, and walked to the door.

"I hope I was of some assistance," Fred said, though he had no idea what this had all been about.

Adrian nodded once and turned the doorknob. Seeing her silhouette through the translucent glass, Joel ducked into the nearby men's room. As he waited for Adrian to leave he thought about what he had just heard. The design of the theater had been changed, for no apparent reason. And Adrian had seemed very upset about this. Joel decided he would confront her again. He opened his small notebook and wrote "Lincoln Center."

The next day, Nate asked Adrian to share lunch with him. He did not seem as cold as previously, and it hurt Adrian to refuse him, but she wanted to get over to the library. That, in the long run, was more important than a lunch date.

"I'm sorry if I was mean to you," Nate said. "I shouldn't

have made you the brunt of my anger. My father did things like that, and I don't ever want to be like him."

Adrian kissed him.

"I understand," she said. "After what happened to Denny..."

Nate cut her off. "I don't want to talk about Denny."

"That's just it," Adrian said. "You don't want to talk. Your attitude has completely turned around since we visited him the other night. Nate, darling, your problems won't go away if you ignore them!"

"Yes, they will," Nate said. "Whoever is tormenting me will stop when he sees I'm not affected by it. Adrian, my show is opening December twelfth. I can't be involved with anything but thoughts of that. It's the most important thing in my life."

"Of course it is, Nate," Adrian said. "But how can..."

"Please," Nate interrupted. "Let's not talk about it, okay? I just thought we'd have a nice, pleasant lunch together."

Adrian shook her head.

"I'm really sorry, Nate," she said. "But I've already made other plans."

She kissed him again.

"I'll see you later."

She walked out of his office, leaving Nate to watch her sadly. At that moment Sander Bernaux came by and noticed they were not together.

"You've missed lunch again," he said. "That's three days in a row—has she lost interest in you?"

Nate turned to him, his expression grim.

"Shut up," he said. "Just shut up."

He slipped back into his office, slamming the door so hard that an echo reverberated down the hallway. Sander shook his head and walked away.

Adrian hesitated in the alley that ran alongside the theater, fidgeting with a bracelet that she wore. The hurt in Nate's eyes had upset her so much that she was tempted to run back and apologize. She understood that his distance had been caused by fear—it was easier to deny trouble than to face it. But she also understood that he needed her, and she was leaving him alone.

"Oh, Nate," she whispered.

She turned around and put her hand on the latch of the

door leading back inside. But then she drew it away and hurried down the alley, carefully avoiding a pile of trash. She was going out to help Nate, and putting off this trip would only delay her plans.

Adrian stood out from the curb with her arm raised, but three taxis in a row ignored her signal. Finally, when she had almost decided to walk, one pulled over. She climbed in and gave the driver her destination. Keeping his eyes on the street for an opening in the lunch-hour traffic, he said, "Cute kid you got there, lady."

Adrian shook her head, confused.

"Excuse me?"

"I said you got a cute..."

The driver glanced over his shoulder and noticed she was alone in the backseat.

"There was a little girl standing next to you in the street," he said. "I just thought she was yours."

Adrian grew cold suddenly. She turned to look at the theater as the car pulled away. There were lots of pedestrians: people were reading posters for *Making Good*, and one or two were entering the theater to buy tickets. But no children.

"This child," Adrian said, turning frontward again. "What did she look like?"

"Hey, kids are kids to me," the cabbie said. "Oh, well, I guess she had kinda dark, shoulder-length hair and a white dress."

She was with me, Adrian thought. *She was with me and I didn't even know it.*

"No," she said finally. "No, that wasn't my child."

She paid the cabbie at Lincoln Center, and got out, walking up a short flight of stairs and crossing the courtyard. The Metropolitan Opera House sat regally at its back, its arched windows revealing an opulent lobby. Adrian thought about Nate's theater and wondered what she hoped to find here. Another piece to fit the puzzle, she supposed, no matter how insignificant.

The librarian directed her toward the books on theatrical architecture. Adrian skimmed over the titles but could not find one covering the proper era. From the corner of her eye she saw a tall man reach for a book on the next shelf. He heaved down the thick volume, nearly staggering under the weight of it.

"This is what you're looking for," Joel Warner told her.

Adrian turned and gaped at him with wide green eyes. She made no attempt to take the book he was holding out to her.

"You again," she said. "Why do you keep following me? There's a law against it, you know."

"It's my job," Joel said, the general answer he gave uncooperative people.

"Your job, Mr. Warner," Adrian said, folding her arms, "is to report the news. I am not someone you can question to the breaking point, the way you do those big businessmen and landlords."

"My job," Joel shot back, "is to find the truth. I know my wife's death was no accident, and I . . ."

Adrian sighed. "Oh, God. We have been through this repeatedly. Nearly a dozen people *saw* her fall. The police, insurance people, everyone involved, said it was most assuredly an accident."

"The fall, perhaps," Joel said. "But my wife wasn't herself before that. Something upset her. Something may even have frightened her to death."

Adrian was going to tell him he was ridiculous, but she decided that was too callous a statement. He was under an enormous emotional stress. Instead she took the book from him.

"What are you doing here, anyway?" Joel asked, as if he had not heard yesterday's conversation with Fred Johnson.

"Reading up on the type of architecture used in the theater," Adrian said.

"Why would an actress care about architecture?"

Adrian looked him in the eye and said quietly, "That's none of your business, Mr. Warner."

She wheeled around and hurried off toward the most occupied section of the library, hoping that Joel would stop bothering her if people were around.

It seemed to work, and as she looked carefully around she could not find the reporter. Soon she was so engrossed in the book that she didn't see Joel take a seat across the room. He sat pretending to browse through a book he'd chosen randomly, watching her.

Adrian's book contained old photographs as well as drawings and paintings of the numerous theaters built in New York in the decades surrounding 1900. There were floor plans, enlarged details, and a lot of text. Adrian recognized familiar-sounding names but could find nothing in particular of interest to her. She sighed wearily and flipped through a few more pages. She didn't want to be late for rehearsal.

Maybe I'm just wasting my time, she thought.

She turned over one more page, and what she saw there made her eyes widen. Across the room, Joel Warner noticed the change in her expression and leaned forward. He saw Adrian run her finger down the page and made out something like "Oh, my God" on her lips.

There were three pictures in front of Adrian. A photograph of a theater's front, a sketch from an old newspaper article, and a print of an oil painting of a stage. Adrian skimmed over the article, which ran under the subtitle "Winston Theater— 1902." She felt a chill run over her and forgot completely about the time.

The facade of the theater featured swirling designs. There were three crystal chandeliers in the lobby, a winding staircase, and etched glass doors. But the stage was what hit Adrian hardest of all. Its curtains were of a swirling, gold-and-white design.

It looked exactly like Nate's theater.

What she read at the end of the chapter made her gasp in horror. According to the author, the Winston Theater had burned to the ground on December 12, 1921.

Exactly sixty years to the day before the opening night of Nate's production.

Because his doctors had been unable to find anything wrong with him, Denny was sent home soon after his visit to the hospital. He sat on the living room couch now, cuddling inside his velour robe, a newspaper opened on his lap. Georgia dusted one of the knickknacks she kept on the TV set and watched him sadly. Words like "mental exhaustion," "therapy," and "psychiatric help" haunted her thoughts. Denny's physician had told Georgia that his illness might have been in his head—a reaction to the hectic life of the theater, perhaps. Georgia decided that she was glad she had broken Denny's contract. Her son's health was more important than *any* job in the theater!

And he did seem healthier these days. Georgia marveled at the resilience that was so natural in children, grateful that Denny had recovered so quickly. To look at him reading there on the couch, no one would ever guess how sick he had been.

"Mom, can I have some hot chocolate?" Denny asked now.

"Sure, honey," Georgia said, putting her dust rag down. "I'll make some for both of us."

While she was in the kitchen Denny turned to the next page of his newspaper in search of the comics and instead found the entertainment page. There was a publicity shot from *Making Good* at the top of the page, in the middle of a long article. Adrian and Sander stood to either side of Nate Dysart. Denny felt a twinge of jealousy to see Nate's hand on the shoulder of his understudy, Johnny Hemlock. Denny was aware that his mother had had a few unkind words to say to Nate after Denny's second visit to the hospital. Maybe Nate was being nice to Johnny because he thought Denny didn't like him anymore! Worried about this, Denny showed the article to his mother.

"I miss everybody," he said.

"I know," Georgia said, sitting beside him. "But I've told you before that you mustn't even think about the theater. I don't want you to get sick again!"

Denny took a sip of his chocolate.

"I feel okay," he insisted. His eyes lit up then, and he asked, "Could I call Nate up on the phone?"

"I don't want you talking to Mr. Dysart," Georgia said.

"But why?"

"Don't argue with me, Denny," Georgia said. "I just don't approve of you talking to that man—after what happened the last time you did!"

"Nate's my friend," Denny protested. "He didn't hurt me."

Georgia's voice took on a shrill quality. "Denny, the subject is closed!"

Forgetting her chocolate, she hurried into the kitchen, unable to deal with her son's innocent questions. Denny gazed at the kitchen door over the rim of his mug, unable to understand why his mother suddenly hated Nate so much. Well, he would find some way to get to his friend. Nate would be happy to know that Denny still liked him.

NINETEEN

"I don't like to be kept waiting, Ms. St. John," Sander said coldly as Adrian raced on stage five minutes late. "Do you realize we're opening in one week?"

"I'm sorry," she gasped, her face red.

She had run all the way from the library, and now it took her a moment to calm down. She shook her head at Nate, who stood off to one side of the stage, talking with Denny's understudy.

"I really have to talk with you," she said, hoping he'd tell the others to "take five."

"We're losing time, Adrian," he said, sounding more like her director at that moment than ever before.

"But I . . ."

Nate walked off the stage to his seat in the front row and called for action. It was as if he hadn't even heard Adrian. Frustrated, she nonetheless played her part, reciting lines that had been drummed into her head for the past five-and-a-half weeks. It was only her "show must go on" training that kept her from crying out her news.

By the time the day ended she was so full of anxiety that she felt ready to burst. Sander came up to her and said, "If you're this nervous for rehearsals, how will you be on opening night?"

Adrian was about to tell him it wasn't stage fright that made her so edgy, but quickly thought the better of it. She smiled bravely.

"I'm just upset because I was late," she said. "I've never done that before."

"And never do it again," Sander said. "It's the sign of an amateur."

"Yes, sir," Adrian said, resisting the urge to salute him. Instead, she walked down to Nate.

"Can we talk now?"

"Well, I wanted to discuss . . ."

"Please, Nate!"

He read the desperation in her eyes and consented finally. They walked together to his office, where he fixed a drink for Adrian.

"You look like you need this," he said. "What was wrong with you today?"

"Oh, Nate," Adrian said, taking the glass from him. "I just learned something that terrifies me."

Nate took a seat behind his desk, not sure he wanted to hear it. But Adrian was already talking.

"I was doing some research in the library this noon," she said. "I found a book on old theaters and I was trying to find out something about the architecture of this one."

"Why would you do that?"

"Because I went to Fred Johnson," she said, "and he couldn't give me a solid reason for building the theater just the way he did. That really bothered me, and I . . ."

Nate leaned forward, resting his arms on the glass top of his desk.

"You went to my architect," he said, "and I didn't know it?"

Adrian dropped her shoulders a bit.

"Nate, I tried to tell you," she said, "but you weren't willing to listen. I understand it was because you were upset by what we saw at Denny's apartment the other night. But I couldn't start denying this theater was in trouble, the way you did. I had to take matters into my own hands!"

Nate shook his head.

"I never denied there was trouble," he said. "I just feel it's best not to give in!"

Adrian took a sip of her drink, then set it down on the coffee table.

"Does the name Winston Theater mean anything to you?" she asked now.

"Should it?"

Adrian nodded. "You're damned right it should. I found a chapter on the Winston Theater in the book I was reading. I understand it was a pretty spiffy place in its day—and it was built in 1902. Remember the photograph?"

"Coincidence," Nate said. "Lots of theaters were built around that time."

"No, darling," Adrian said. "There were three pictures with the article: the building's front, the lobby, and the stage.

Nate, the Dysart Theater is an exact replica of the Winston Theater."

"You can't be sure of that with only three pictures," Nate said. "Fred might have used that particular theater as a model."

Adrian shook her head.

"For God's sake," she said. "All the pieces are falling together and you're acting as if it's no big deal!"

"My opening night is the only big deal I care about," Nate said.

"Nate," Adrian said, "the Winston Theater burned down in 1921. On December twelfth—the same date as our first performance here. Is *that* coincidence? And I learned something else. The address of this theater is exactly the same as the Winston Theater's had been. Is that *another* coincidence?"

Her eyes were wide as she looked at him for an answer. But Nate simply looked behind himself then back at her again and said, "I don't know what to tell you."

"Listen to me," Adrian said. "Something is going to happen here on December twelfth. Everything I've learned points to that conclusion."

"You sound like that sitter the other night," Nate replied. "Are you going to tell me my theater is haunted?"

"It could be!" Adrian cried. "Stranger things have happened in this world. But listen—let's stick to your theory that someone is trying to destroy you. That person could have persuaded Fred Johnson to rebuild the Winston Theater as part of some sick plan. It all fits into place, Nate. I'm telling you this theater can't be occupied that night."

"Adrian," Nate said, "you are talking about something that's going to happen in a matter of days. I can't do anything about it now."

"Yes, you can," Adrian said. "Shows are often closed for a night or two."

"And thousands of dollars are lost," Nate said. "Be realistic, will you? I have backers to pay, not to mention the cast and crew here. I am not going to close the show for even one night, and that's final!"

Adrian opened her mouth to make a reply, but instead, her eyes went wide and her hand flew to her lips.

"Nate, I just thought of something," she said. "My parents will be here that night."

Nate shook his head.

"That's something you'll have to deal with, then," he said.

"How can you be so stubborn?" Adrian cried. "Don't you see the danger we're facing?"

"I won't close my show!"

Their discussion had turned into a shouting match, and out in the hall, Sander Bernaux stood listening. What was going on, he wondered? Why was Adrian so terrified to have the show open on schedule? All Sander's fears about bad luck rushed to his brain, and he began chewing at his fingernails.

"She's making him sad."

Sander turned to see a little girl.

"I beg your pardon?"

"She's making him sad," the child said again. "Make her stop!"

Sander threw his shoulders back.

"I'll do no such thing," he said. "How dare you order me about like that?"

"I don't like you," the child said. "You're going to die, just like the rest of them."

"Impudent brat," Sander growled. He wanted to listen to more of the conversation in Nate's office but couldn't bear having this child staring at him. With a grunt, he walked swiftly away.

Bonnie was inside Nate's office in a second's time, standing near the door unseen. She wanted to kill Adrian right now but didn't make a move. The time was coming quickly enough, and then Adrian would pay with the others.

"Look, Adrian," Nate said finally, his voice lowered considerably. "If it'll make you happy, I'll post security guards all over this theater on opening night. People will wonder about them, and I'll sound pretty ridiculous when I can't explain why they're there."

Adrian wasn't quite sure she liked the idea. So much had happened right under their noses that the idea of security guards seemed a waste of time. And yet she realized Nate was trying to compromise.

"You're my leading lady," Nate said. "In more ways than one. But as far as this theater goes, I call all the shots."

"Nate," Adrian said. "I love you, and you know that. But I'm frightened!"

Nate stood up and crossed the room. Adrian rose from her own seat and held her arms open to accept him into them. He kissed her softly, wanting to chase away her fears and yet so full of his own. Finally, he said, "I will never, ever let anyone hurt you."

He tightened his arms around her, and whispered, without really hearing himself, "I won't lose you the way I lost Meg."

Adrian sighed.

"You won't lose me, Nate," she said. "Not ever."

As frightened as she was by the things she'd learned, she knew she would never leave Nate alone to face them.

Joel walked from the skyscraper where he'd just interviewed a union boss, thinking not of the upcoming strike (the subject of his latest column) but of the things he'd learned in the library earlier. He had taken Adrian's seat after she left and, after reading the opened pages, knew what had frightened her.

The question that seemed to drum most loudly in his mind was why sixty years had passed before the theater was rebuilt. Anyone old enough to remember it would have to be over seventy. And, Joel wondered, what other buildings had stood there in the past six decades. Surely it hadn't remained an empty lot, considering its prime location and property value.

As he headed towards the Fifty-ninth Street subway station he asked himself if there were answers to be found in the history of the land. The Winston Theater was rebuilt for some reason—an evil one, Joel was certain, because no one had ever publicized that the Dysart Theater was its replica. And that meant no one was supposed to know. Obviously, Adrian hadn't, or she wouldn't have been so shocked by the information.

Joel descended a long flight of stairs into the subway. He always thought of Barbara when he rode the underground trains. She had hated them, with their stale smells and graffiti-covered walls. Barbara wanted everything in life to be happy and beautiful, and she often succeeded in making others as cheerful as she was.

But now she was dead, killed not by an accident, as her

colleagues insisted, but by something that was as malevolent
as she had been good.

Adrian was sitting at her kitchen table, eating a store-
bought quiche and trying to figure out what to do about her
parents. She could hardly tell them not to come to New York
for her opening, and if she gave them the real reason, they'd
think she was crazy. Nutty things like this just didn't happen
in small Ohio towns. Suddenly the shrill ring of the phone
interrupted her thoughts. To her surprise, it was her mother's
voice that she heard. But Martha didn't sound as animated as
usual. Adrian prayed nothing had happened at home to add
to her worries.

"I have some bad news, darling," Martha said.

"Mom, what's wrong?"

"Well, I'm afraid your father and I won't be able to make it
to New York after all," Martha said.

Adrian felt something like relief wash over her, but she
kept the emotion out of her voice and asked with concern,
"Why not?"

"Well," Martha said, "you know your father's been having
some heart trouble these past few years, and . . ."

"Oh, my God," Adrian said. "Dad didn't have a heart
attack, did he?"

She heard her mother click her tongue a few times.

"Just a very mild one," she said. "He's out of the hospital.
In fact, they only kept him in overnight."

"Why didn't you call me?"

"Well, I know how busy you've been," Martha said apologetically. "I didn't want to upset you. But I wanted to let you
know we had to cancel our reservations. The doctor said your
father shouldn't be traveling right now."

"He's right," Adrian agreed, unable to believe this coincidence. Now at least she didn't have to worry about them. She
continued the conversation by asking more about her father's
health and inquiring after her brothers. Her youngest brother
came on the line, excited about being chosen for the grade
school basketball team. She had to hear all the details. Her
baby brother was growing up. By the time she hung up, she
felt as if a burden had been lifted from her. Now, if only she

could solve the mystery of Nate's tormentor. But that was impossible.

Much as Adrian wanted to research the theater's history even further, she couldn't. There were so many things to do for the play coming up the next Saturday night that she simply did not have the time. Nate didn't take any leisurely lunch breaks, so it was rare that they could sit down and talk. Maybe Nate was right—the best defense against whoever it was that tormented them was denial.

The day before opening night a mixture of tension and excitement filled the air. Actors could be seen embracing each other in the hallways or on the stage, silently wishing each other good luck. A week had passed since Adrian had learned of the Winston Theater, and nothing bad had happened. Everything on stage and off was going smoothly.

"You see?" Nate said. "After all this time, maybe whoever it was gave up."

"Or maybe you've been too busy to notice anything," Adrian said. "And because of that, he got bored."

Nate grinned at her, the first time he'd done that in days.

"One of the extras tore her dress during a fitting," he said. "And the cat chewed up Don Benson's script."

Adrian laughed, and Nate threw up his arms.

"Problems!" Nate cried. "Everyday, innocent, ordinary problems!" He looked up at the ceiling. "God, I hope this good luck lasts."

"Sander would tell you it's a bad idea to get too cocky before the show goes on," Adrian said.

"I can't help it," Nate said. "This isn't eight weeks of rehearsals behind me, Adrian. It's thirty-two years of dreaming."

He came over to her and put his arms around her. As she held him close and pressed her lips to his Adrian prayed nothing would happen to shatter this happiness.

Bobby and Alec Warner were staring in awe at the bustling sidewalk activity to either side of the bus and eating the big salty pretzels their father had bought for them. Alec was holding the yellow dog Judy had brought home from Barbara's locker. He was really too young to understand it was his mommy's last present to him, but it had become a symbol of security for him, and he never let it out of his sight.

The two boys were with Joel today because their sitter had canceled at the last minute. There had been no time to find a substitute, and so Bobby and Alec had accompanied Joel to his newspaper office.

Joel tried to answer his sons' questions in as animated a voice as possible and hoped they did not figure out that there was something wrong. But he couldn't stop thinking of the Winston Theater and the information he found in back issues of *The New York Times*. His destination now was the Dysart Theater, and he could feel his muscles stiffen with anger in anticipation of his meeting with Nate.

He was holding on to both his sons' hands when they entered the vestibule of the building.

"Bobby," Joel said, "you sit right here and wait for me. When I get back we'll go to the Museum of Natural History."

"Mr. Warner," Nate said simply when he entered the office. Adrian, sitting next to him on the couch, put an arm over his shoulder.

"I haven't come to cause trouble," Joel said, reading the distrust in their eyes. "I just want to ask you some questions."

"All right," Nate said. "Sit down over there, will you? Adrian told me you followed her to the library."

"I had a right to do that," Joel said defensively. "And you will definitely want to hear what I have to tell you—provided you don't know it already."

Adrian leaned forward, entwining her fingers together, and asked quietly, "Did you read about the Winston Theater?"

Joel nodded. "The book you left open on the table," he said. "But that passage wasn't half the story. I went to the archives at the *Times* and read up on the history of the place."

"I know about the fire in 1921," Nate said. "And if you've come to tell me I should close my show..."

"You may want to," Joel interrupted, "after you've heard what I have to say."

Nate looked at Adrian as if asking for support. He'd been so happy a moment ago! But maybe it had been too much to ask for that happiness to last.

"As you know," Joel began, looking at Adrian, "the Winston

Theater, which stood on this very ground, burned down in 1921. According to an article dated December thirteenth—the day after the fire—it was of a mysterious origin. No later article solved the mystery, so I guess it remains an open case to this day. Anyway, it happened at night, after the evening's performance, and for some reason there were several people still in the theater."

"Did they die?" Adrian asked. "Who were they?"

"Only one name was given," Joel said. "And that was of the fire's only victim—a five-year-old child named Bonnie Jackson."

Adrian gasped, and Nate closed his eyes to mutter a swearword.

"The name means something to you?"

"No, no," Adrian said quickly. "How could it?"

Their initial reactions told Joel she was lying. He watched Nate carefully as he spoke; the man was chewing his lips as if to bite clear through them.

"Anyway," he went on, "another theater was built about a year after that one went down. It never had a successful run and finally closed down, bankrupt, in 1934. Now, according to the microfilms I was reading, a restaurant was established there. It, too, burned in a mysterious fire."

"The realtors never told me any of this," Nate said quietly, refusing to believe what he was hearing.

"A hotel was built next," Joel said. "By 1968, the place was a haven for addicts and prostitutes. One day, a hooker opened a fifth-story window and started screaming something about the dark. Next thing people knew, she jumped to her death."

The dark, Nate thought. *My God, she was talking about the dark*.

But still he stared at his hands, listening intently, on the surface not seeming to react.

"They did an investigation and found nothing. The girl hadn't even been on drugs," Joel said. "Finally, the place was torn down two years later. And that property sat barren for over ten years. After a hell of an effort I located the realtor and asked why. But they couldn't tell me."

He stood up and walked to Nate, looking down at him.

"Didn't you ask?" he inquired. "Didn't it seem strange to you that a lot in a prime location like this remained unsold for a decade? Didn't you worry that there was some reason for that?"

"Why would he think to do such a thing?" Adrian demanded. "He's had enough on his mind without worrying about the history of a piece of land!"

"Well, he damned well should have worried about it," Joel snapped. "Every damned building erected here since that fire in 'twenty-one has met with tragedy! He should have known more would happen! He could have prevented my wife's death!"

Nate stood up abruptly now, the blank expression leaving his face. With widened eyes he grabbed hold of Joel's collar and hissed, "I did not murder your wife! I didn't want that to happen to her! I didn't want anything to happen to anyone!"

Joel forced Nate's fingers from his neck and said quietly, "What do you mean you didn't want anything to happen to anyone?"

Adrian came closer to them and put her arms around Nate. "He's upset," she said. "The play is opening tomorrow, and he's got too much in his mind."

But Nate shook his head and stared at his shoes. "Adrian," he said, "the man knows more than we do. There's no use denying that."

Adrian led him back to the couch and forced him to sit down before he spoke again. He looked up at Joel, feeling every nerve ending tingle, wanting to scream and yet forcing himself to remain calm. Joel was already looking at him as if he were a madman, and Nate couldn't risk that. He couldn't have this reporter telling his colleagues that the director/producer of *Making Good* was out of his mind.

"You're right," he said finally. "Something is going on at this theater. I didn't tell you about it because I didn't believe it myself, but now I do."

"You don't have to tell him anything, Nate," Adrian interrupted.

Joel sank into a chair. "He'd better," he said. "I want full cooperation or I'll spread this story over every paper in the city."

"You're very cruel," Adrian said.

"No," Joel answered. "I'm just a man who wants to know the truth. I'm listening, Mr. Dysart."

For the next twenty minutes, Nate found himself telling Joel everything that had happened at the theater. The reporter learned about the voices, about Denny, about the little girl.

"Her name was Bonnie," Nate said. He rubbed his eyes and looked wearily at Joel. "The little girl who died in that fire was also named Bonnie."

"Coincidence," Adrian said.

"I don't know," Nate replied. He wanted to agree with Adrian, but her doubting answer had come out too quickly. "I mean, there may be a connection. It—it isn't the same little girl, of course."

Joel pointed a finger at him.

"But it could be a relative," he said. "Look, the kid's parents survived that fire. If her mother were alive today, she'd be about ninety years old."

"A woman that age couldn't do what's been done here," Nate said.

"No," Joel said, "but her children could."

"Presuming she went on to have other children," Adrian put in.

"Women those days had a baby every year," Joel said. "Now let's take that theory. The woman is about ninety-five. If she had another child at, say, age thirty, that child would be sixty-five right now."

"Still too old," Nate said. "This isn't working."

"But you said it was a child's voice you heard," Joel answered. "And a child you've seen. This new Bonnie could be the original Bonnie's descendant."

Adrian left Nate's side to walk across the room. She paced the floor for a few moments, then threw up her arms.

"This is so impossible," she protested. "You're talking about four generations! How could a need for vengeance last so long?"

"Considering all the things that have happened in this theater," Joel said, "it doesn't surprise me. Look, let's start with Bonnie's mother. She has another child, and she tells this child about Bonnie's death. Her child tells the grandchild, then *that* one tells her own little girl. Crazier things have happened in the world—especially in this big city.

Maybe the family has never been able to avenge the child's death until now."

Nate began shaking his head.

"But why me?" he asked. "Why do they pick on me? Why did they choose me to rebuild this theater?"

"You were in the right place at the wrong time, I guess," Joel suggested. "They heard you wanted to build a new theater and saw to it that you built this one. How they did it doesn't matter right now. The only important thing is that they're planning to avenge the first Bonnie's death on your opening night."

"But why," Adrian asked, "would anyone want revenge? Surely the first fire must have been an accident."

Joel could only shake his head.

Adrian hurried back to the couch and put her arms around Nate.

"I can't believe this," Nate said. "It can't be possible."

"You'd better believe it," Joel said coldly. "Because if anything happens tomorrow night, your hands will be so soaked in blood that you'll never be able to wash them clean."

Denny played basketball with Mikey Smith and Paul Kasson for the first time in weeks, racing around the street outside his apartment building, shooting baskets.

"So, anyway," he said, stopping for a moment as Paul tried to reach the hoop over their heads, "I want to go into the city to see my director so he'll know that I still like him. My mother thinks it was Nate's fault that I got sick when he came here last time. But I know it wasn't!"

"Denny, that's a crazy idea," Mikey said as he knocked the ball from Paul's hands. "This is the first day your mom let you outside, and you think she's gonna let you go all the way into Manhattan tomorrow night?"

"She won't know about it," Denny replied. "My mother never wakes up once she goes to sleep at night—and she's been going to bed around eight-thirty these days. I don't know why. But as long as she's asleep when I sneak out tomorrow night, that's okay by me. I'll be back before she knows it."

The ball dropped from Mikey's hand and rolled to the curb, where it was forgotten.

"So, what do you want from us?" he asked. "I can't sneak out like that."

"Yeah, and I'd probably get caught," Paul added. "I don't want to be grounded over Christmas vacation!"

"Oh, you guys are just chicken!" Denny accused. "Now I know where my real friends are—at the theater!"

He grabbed up his ball from the curb and began to walk home, determined to go into Manhattan the next night even if Mikey and Paul didn't. He really didn't want to go inside just yet—not after it had taken so long to convince his mother that he felt good enough to leave the apartment. But he was mad at his two friends; he had thought they would be with him all the way. He hadn't been wrong—in a moment, Mikey and Paul were at his sides.

"Okay, we'll go," Mikey said. "I'll tell my mother we're going to the movies. But we have to be back home by midnight!"

It amazed Denny that anyone his age would be allowed out that late, but he was delighted. Now he would have someone to share his adventure!

"Thanks," he said. "C'mon, let's play some more basketball."

Denny played as vigorously as he had before his strange illness. Memories of crawling under the stage floor, of being in the hospital, and of a little girl named Bonnie were pushed so far back in his mind that they would probably never be recalled again. At that moment, Denny only cared that he would be seeing his theater friends again.

TWENTY

Bobby, after waiting half an hour for his father, finally grew tired of studying the designs that circled the doors and racing up and down the grand staircase. Pouting, he walked over to a couch and bounced up and down on it, folding his arms. He wished his father would hurry and take them to the museum, like he promised.

"Don't know why he had to come to this dumb place, anyway," he griped.

Little Alec sat in the middle of the rich carpeting with the yellow stuffed dog in his hands, pretending it was walking around him. He banged it along the rug, laughing and making its ears flop up and down. From across the room, Bobby suddenly saw him stop and look up, his eyes wide.

"Watcha starin' at?" he asked, seeing nothing.

Alec did not answer, so Bobby lost interest in him. He did not know that his little brother was staring at a child hardly bigger than himself, standing before him in a white ruffled dress. She smiled at him, and he returned the smile, holding up the dog.

"What are you doing here?" she asked.

"Waiting for Daddy," Alec replied. "See my dog?"

The child nodded. Yes, she saw the dog. She had put it in that woman's locker. And the woman had died. Why were her children here now?

"Want to play?" Alec chirped.

Bonnie tilted her head. It had been a long, long time since anyone had asked her to play. There had been other children, but they had always been afraid. Then Denny—but he wasn't here anymore. And he had not helped her. He had been made to pay for that.

"Yes, I want to play," she said. She sat down. "I want someone to play with forever."

"I play with you," Alec said. "I be your friend."

Bonnie's head went back a little, and she studied him like some long-ago tyrant scrutinizing a subject.

"Come tomorrow night," she said. "Come tomorrow night and I'll make you my friend forever."

She disappeared. Too young to dissociate reality from fantasy, Alec simply waved bye-bye. Bobby saw the gesture and walked over to his brother with an exaggerated swagger.

"Who're you waving at?" he asked. "There's no one else in here."

"Little girl," Alec said. "She wants to play."

Bobby looked around the empty lobby. Then, with an exasperated sigh, he grabbed his brother's hand and pulled him to his feet.

"You've got a weird imagination," he said. "Come on and sit down."

Alec, poking a thumb into his mouth, followed his older brother obediently. He sat down, folding his two arms around the yellow dog, and began to rock back and forth on the couch, finally falling asleep. When Bobby suddenly decided he had to use the little boys' room he debated whether or not to leave his brother. But he finally decided it would be okay. Alec was asleep. He'd be right back. His father wouldn't mind.

As Bobby was climbing the stairs the little girl returned, taking a seat beside Alec. He intrigued her, this child who did not seem to fear her. Maybe, when she had her daddy, she could have a friend too. Then she wouldn't be lonely, and it would never be dark again.

Across the room one of the etched-glass doors swung open. Sander Bernaux saw Alec on the couch, curled around something small and yellow. At first it meant nothing to him, until the child stirred in his sleep and the dog dropped to the floor.

"No!" Sander cried. "No!"

His shouts woke up the little boy, and he sat upright with a gasp. Alec looked at Bonnie, seeing her, though Sander didn't, and then up at the actor.

"You can not have that yellow dog in this theater!" Sander cried. "It's bad luck—horrible luck! And the night before our debut! Get it out of here!"

He snatched it up and started to carry it towards the door. Alec, screaming, shot to his feet and raced after the man, tackling him head-on. The man was trying to steal his doggie!

Bonnie stood up and watched the scene in unemotional silence.

The doors to the vestibule swung open, and as a crowd of ticket-buyers watched in bewilderment, Sander pushed through the front doors and flung the dog into the street. A taxi, colored the same yellow, crushed the toy dog beneath its wheels. Sander gave his head a quick nod, then turned on his heels and walked back inside, as the ticket buyers whispered in shock.

Alec stood in the middle of the lobby, screaming.

This is how Joel found his two-year-old son. Tears were pouring down the boy's reddened cheeks, and he was waving his hands around him in a tantrum. But when he saw his father, he ran up to him to be taken into his arms.

"Took doggie!" Alec whined. "Man threw doggie in street!"

Joel looked at Sander, who was pacing the floor worrying about whatever bad luck had already befallen the production. When Nate and Adrian entered the lobby Sander stopped and announced, "Outsiders should not be allowed in here. That child had a yellow dog in his possession!"

"Big deal," Joel said. "It's a kid's toy!"

"An instrument of evil," Sander said.

Nate looked at both men, then held up a hand and said quietly, "Wait a minute. I think I know what Sander means."

"Then maybe you'd better tell me," Joel said, rocking his son as the boy began to calm down in his father's strong embrace. Joel looked around for Bobby. "Where's your brother?"

Alec shook his head in confusion. He had no idea what was going on.

"The yellow dog," Nate said, "is one of the theater's oldest superstitions. It brings bad luck to a production."

Joel frowned. "You took my son's toy because of some idiotic belief?"

"My beliefs aren't idiotic, sir," Sander said, straightening as if to ready for a fight. "And the dog means much more than my director is telling you."

Shut up, Bonnie called. *Don't say anything more! Don't ruin my plans!*

But Sander didn't hear.

"In medieval plays," Sander continued, "yellow was the color worn by the Devil. And to this day the presence of a yellow dog in the theater means someone in the company is going to die."

Adrian and Nate saw Joel blanch, and Adrian quickly added, "It's just a legend. Surely you don't believe in such things, Mr. Warner?"

Joel shook his head. He squeezed Alec closer to him and kissed the toddler's soft cheek. His son had been playing with that damned dog. He had been playing with the symbol of Barbara's death...

He closed his eyes in disbelief.

"Judy Terrel found that thing in Barbara's locker," he said. "Are you going to tell me now that my wife wasn't murdered?"

The lobby was silent. Even Alec had calmed down, and now he watched the adults quietly, sucking his thumb. He noticed the little girl and waved to her. But she did not wave back. She was watching the mean man who'd thrown his little toy out to the street. And she looked angry.

"I don't know what to tell you," Nate said. "Except what you know already."

"Tell me you're going to close this place down," Joel said.

"No!" Nate snapped. "I won't close my theater! Opening night is tomorrow!"

Joel turned on him. "Is that all you care about?" he demanded. "Your frigging opening night? I don't give a damn about it! I only care about my Barbara—and seeing her killer punished!"

Bobby walked up to his father's side carefully, frightened by his yelling. It was bad timing.

"Where the hell did you go?"

"To—the boys' room," Bobby faltered.

"You couldn't wait a few minutes, at your age?" Joel demanded. "You left your baby brother alone?"

"Dad, I . . ."

But Joel was already delivering an angry whack to his backside. Nate cringed, picturing himself there, receiving punishment harsher than deserved from his own father. Bobby burst into tears, the first he had shed since the funeral. It was Nate who came to his rescue, grabbing Joel's arm before the second blow came down.

"You don't do that in my theater," he said plainly.

Joel stared at him for a moment, then relaxed.

"May I say something?" Adrian asked. "Mr. Warner, you really want to find your wife's—" She looked at the children and hesitated.

Joel nodded, understanding.

"Then let the show open," Adrian said. "The only way we'll succeed is if we let this person come here tomorrow night. And then we'll be able to catch him."

Joel looked down at his sobbing son. He knelt and took Bobby into his arms, closing his eyes and rocking him.

"God, I'm sorry," he whispered. "Daddy's so sorry."

He looked up at Nate.

"All right," he said. "Go ahead with opening night. I want the bastard caught, no matter what the cost!"

When Sander Bernaux entered his dressing room, he at first did not see the small child standing off in one corner, watching him. He sat at his vanity and checked his makeup kit. It was in a disarray, for Sander believed a tidy kit would make him look like an amateur. He had better things to do than worry about neatness.

He poked around the box, and mumbled "ahh," when he found a cellophane-wrapped crayon. He would use a brand-new set of makeup on opening night, as he always did. That again was an old theatrical superstition. Legend had it that once upon a time an actor became so angered at another actor's popularity that he stuck pins in the man's makeup stick. When the actor used it, he cut his handsome face to pieces. So, to this day, many performers insisted upon using unopened, untouched makeup.

The child suddenly reflected in the mirror. Sander swung around and demanded, "Who are you? What are you doing here?"

The little girl simply shook her head.

"Impudent brat," Sander said. "Why must it always be children who cause trouble? I've had enough with that little boy in the lobby!"

"He was nice," Bonnie said. "He wanted to be my friend. You scared him away."

"Nonsense," Sander said. "I merely averted disaster." He waved the back of his hand at her. "Now, get going! I won't have a child contaminating my dressing room!"

Bonnie threw back her head and began to scream.

"Stop that!" Sander ordered.

Bonnie lowered her head and looked into his eyes, her own dark and deep.

"You're a bad man," she said. "You gave them a warning!"

"Warning?" Sander sneered. "What are you talking about? . . . Never mind, I don't care! Get out of here! Go back to wherever you belong."

"You have to pay," Bonnie said. "You have to pay for what you did."

She picked up one of the new makeup crayons. Sander

smacked it away from her hand, then tossed his head and turned away from the sight of the hatred in her eyes.

It was the last mistake he'd ever make in his life.

She came around to the front of his chair, her small body wriggling easily between his knees and the vanity. Before Sander could pull away, she reached up and placed her hands on his cheeks. Sander froze, wanting to scream as horrible pain filled his head, horrible burning pain. But he couldn't move. Her eyes held him paralyzed, her eyes that looked up at him with a power such as he had never imagined existed. He began to tremble. And then everything grew dark and he was falling, falling . . .

"NNNNNOOOOO!!!!"

"You have to pay!" Bonnie screamed. "You must be punished!"

Sander found himself in his chair again, but he was not the same outraged, arrogant man as a moment earlier. Now he was meek, cringing as the child threatened to touch his flesh again. The thought of the pain terrified him. He would do anything to make it stop. He was completely in her power.

"You warned them!" Bonnie cried. "Now they know I'm coming—but they won't stop me! They won't!"

She picked up the new crayon Sander had been saving for opening night. The one he had not yet opened. She thrust it at him.

"Put on your makeup, darling," she said. "Put on your makeup for your first act."

Sander took the tube but did not turn his gaze from her. In the back of his mind, he knew this was not opening night. He knew there were no performances, and that rehearsals were over for the day. Yet still he unwrapped the plastic, obeying her, terrified of the pain and unable to fight.

"After you've done that," Bonnie said, her voice mimicking her mother's voice, "you'll go in the dark closet. You will go there because you were bad."

A memory came to her, and through glazed eyes Sander saw her cringe.

"Put it on," she said again, pointing to the crayon.

Sander raised it to his face and began rubbing it in. Habit made him turn from the child to the mirror, and he watched himself work. He wondered vaguely why there were red streaks on his face, why there were fine lines of stinging pain.

"Harder," Bonnie hissed. "You aren't putting in on dark enough!"

Without thought, Sander pressed harder and deeper. He did not seem to care that he was slashing his face to pieces with a nail that had somehow been embedded in a brand-new makeup crayon.

TWENTY-ONE
December 12, 1981

Opening night had come at last. In spite of all the tragedies, in spite of the fears Nate had been unable to push away from himself, it was really here. People were already filing into the lobby, excited about being at a fashionable premiere. Reporters took notes on how the elite crowd dressed and the elegant Dysart Theater. They asked to come backstage, but Nate understood about first night jitters and wouldn't subject his cast to reporters before the performance.

While the crews took over the stage for a last double-check of their work, Nate made his way to each and every actor or actress, giving them a few words of encouragement. He was relieved to note that none of them seemed to detect the slight edge in his voice.

Let me get through this night, he prayed even as he patted one of the extras encouragingly on the shoulder.

He moved on to Sander Bernaux's dressing room. He smiled in spite of himself to see that the number on it was fourteen, although the room before it was numbered twelve. There was never a thirteen on anyone's dressing room door, let alone superstitious Sander's. Nate knocked, but there was no answer.

"He should be putting on his makeup," Nate thought. He knocked again, and when he was not acknowledged he tried the doorknob. It was locked.

A thought flashed through Nate's mind—he hadn't seen Sander since they were all in the lobby yesterday.

But he quickly shook his head to drive away any fears that

might surface. Sander just wasn't answering his door, that was all. Nate wouldn't put such eccentric behavior past him.

He walked on to Adrian's room, quickly forgetting Sander. He found her sitting before her vanity, dressed in a red and gold kimono, fussing with her red hair. He kissed her neck, which was free of makeup for the moment.

"How do you feel?" he asked.

"Nervous," she said. "And not just about my first Broadway play. The important thing is, how do *you* feel?"

Nate shrugged and pulled up a seat next to hers, speaking as she got ready for the first scene.

"I don't know," he said. "The way things are happening tonight, with everyone so excited and so much going on, I can almost believe none of the past weeks was real. None of the bad stuff, anyway."

"You know it was real, though," Adrian said gently.

"Yeah," Nate said, studying his hands.

Adrian unwrapped a makeup crayon.

"Have you seen any of the security guards yet?" she asked.

"They've been here for two hours," Nate said. "You wouldn't know it, though. They're dressed just like everyone else."

Adrian nodded. "That's good."

"I came up with a pretty logical reason for them being here," Nate said. "I told them that some of the women in the audience would be wearing expensive jewels, and that I was taking every precaution to make certain no one was robbed."

"Makes sense," Adrian said. She turned to him. "Kiss me before I'm not kissable any more," she said.

Nate put his arms around her and kissed her half-made-up face. For a moment, it seemed he would never let her go.

"Everything's going to be all right," she said. "With all those guards, our mysterious Bonnie won't be able to make a move. We'll catch her, and this nightmare will end."

Nate straightened up and backed away.

"Don't even think about that," he said, though he knew it would be heavy on her mind the entire night. "You're not Adrian St. John anymore. You're Daisy Bertrand. And Daisy doesn't have a care in the world."

We should all be so lucky, he thought.

"I'll knock 'em dead," Adrian said.

Nate kissed her again.

"Hey," Adrian said, pulling away, "you've got other actors to encourage. You'd better get going."

"I'll see you on stage at five-to-eight," Nate said. "I'm going to give everyone a pep talk."

"Shades of Knute Rockne," Adrian couldn't help teasing.

Nate finally left her, feeling just a little stronger. He was met in the hallway by Don, who held a clipboard and a pen in one hand. One of the stage manager's jobs was to be certain everyone was here, but he had been unable to locate Sander.

"His dressing room door was locked," Nate said. "He has to be in there."

"But he isn't answering," Don protested.

"You know Sander," Nate replied. "With all his superstitions, he's probably going through some preshow ritual."

"I still wish he'd just say he was in there," Don answered. "For a guy as respected in the theater as he is, Sander Bernaux is damned strange."

Nate patted his shoulder.

"Don't worry," he said. "He'll show up."

He *had* to show up!

But when Don had brought all the cast on stage for Nate's speech, he whispered in the director's ear that Sander still wasn't here. Nate felt something sour in his stomach. *Don't let it be starting,* he prayed. But for the sake of the actors around him, he bit his lip and steadied his expression.

"It seems Sander Bernaux has taken ill," he said.

A moan ran through the group, and Adrian raised her hand to her mouth. Nate looked at her only momentarily, as if to say she shouldn't indicate something more serious was wrong.

"Not to worry," he said. He pointed to Sander's understudy. "Think you can handle a first-night performance?"

"Of course I can," the understudy said.

"Good," Nate replied. "Don, do me a favor and announce that the part of Nigel Bertrand will be played by Patrick Smith."

Don walked over to the microphone, and in a moment the cast heard his clear voice. They also heard a rush of protests from the audience, but these lasted only a moment. Nate, satisfied no one was going to leave, began his speech.

"We've worked damned hard these past weeks," he said. "All of us. And what happens tonight is the proof of the pudding. I know you're all going to do your best. Remember to pause for effect after the jokes we discussed, but also remember some of them have to be shot out quickly. And another thing—those people out there will probably be talking about Sander's absence, so speak up during the first scene. You should feel your voices in your stomachs."

He gave everyone a final word of encouragement and wished them all luck, then walked off the stage. Actors and actresses hurried back to their dressing rooms to await their cues, and Adrian caught up to Nate in a hallway.

"What happened to Sander?" she whispered.

"I don't know," he said quietly. "Don Benson hasn't been able to find him. Don't worry. You'll get yourself too worked up to go on stage if you worry."

But she did worry, and to stop herself from bursting into tears Adrian threw her arms around Nate and kissed him warmly.

In the upstairs lobby of the theater Joel Warner bent to take a drink from a gilded water fountain. He moved through the crowd of people heading towards their seats and pulled his ticket out of the pocket of his best suit. From the corner of his eye he could see a man watching the crowd with a deadpan expression, and knew this was one of Nate's guards. Well, hell, he thought. I hope they do some good.

His throat was suddenly dry again. Joel was more nervous about this night than outward appearances revealed, and he had been unable to stop coughing. He walked back to the fountain for another drink. As he was bent over, a small child came up beside him. Joel straightened, fishing through his pockets at the same time for a mint. But his hand stopped moving when he saw the little girl.

She was clothed in a ruffled dress, and her black hair was pulled aside with a big white bow. Her feet were clad in white Mary Janes. She watched him with hateful eyes.

"Who are you?" Joel asked quietly, so that none of the others in the lobby could hear.

"You're going to die tonight," the child said. "You're going to pay with the rest of them when the dark comes again."

Suddenly, inexplicably, she vanished before his eyes. Joel took a step forward, his hands outstretched. He couldn't possibly have seen her, could he?

He didn't stop to think of an answer but broke into a run. Taking the curving staircase two steps at a time, he pushed by several latecomers and ran to the lobby. A door marked No Admittance indicated the hallway that led to Nate's office. He had found the child named Bonnie! He had to warn Nate that the show must not be started!

But a burly man grabbed him by the arm.

"No one is permitted backstage during the performance," he said.

"I have to see Nate Dysart," Joel answered. The man simply shook his head, so Joel pulled out one of his cards. "I'm a reporter. I have to see him."

"All you reporters want to see Mr. Dysart," he was told. "Sorry, but no can do."

Joel wrenched from the bigger man's grip.

"You're one of the guards he hired, aren't you?" he asked. "Look, I found the little girl. She's in the upstairs lobby. I have to tell Nate!"

"What little girl?" the guard asked. "What are you talking about?"

A few people looked their way, then decided they didn't want to be late for the curtain and walked through the etched-glass doors.

"Didn't Mr. Dysart tell you about the little girl?" Joel asked worriedly. The guard shook his head. "Look, she's the one who's going to cause the trouble tonight! You have to stop her!"

"Stop a little girl?" the guard asked incredulously. He took hold of Joel's arm again. "Come on upstairs with me, pal. We've got a nice little room where you can rest."

Joel struggled to get away, but the man's grip was too strong.

"You don't know what you're doing!" he protested. "You can't hold me like this!"

"Wanna see me try?"

The lobby was empty now except for the two men. No one saw Joel being pulled up the stairs. No one but a little girl who was waiting for the right moment to set her plans for revenge into motion.

Don Benson made a final check of the stage to make certain everyone was in their places. He whispered to Mike Woodson and was assured once again the lights were working just fine. Then, at Don's signal, Mike took down the house lights and brought up the footlights. As the audience clapped in anticipation, the curtain rolled up. Nate, standing just behind his stage manager, watched Adrian cross the stage. She was holding a newspaper, and in her Brooklynite, Daisy-Bertrand voice she said, "Will ya just looka what they got in the papers today?"

Nate watched in silence as the first act progressed, feeling a wave of satisfaction run over him as he heard the audience laughing at just the right moments. But after a few moments it was all lost to him. He closed his eyes and was brought back to a time when Meg was still alive, when he had that little off-Broadway production company.

He was with Jim Orland and Meg, standing on a bare stage.

"In just about two months," he was saying, "we're going to put on a show like New York's never seen."

"It's going to be wonderful," Meg said.

In the dark wings of the Dysart Theater, Nate's head went up and down.

Yes, Meg, he thought. *It's going to be wonderful.*

She should have been here today, to share this with him. And Jim Orland should have been here. And Denny and Barbara...

His father should have been here too, to see that his son was going to be a success after all.

In a small upstairs sitting room Joel Warner paced the floor and tried to reason with the guard.

"You don't understand," he said. "You were hired to make certain nothing happened tonight."

"That's right, pal," the guard said, lighting a cigarette. He offered one to Joel, but the reporter shook his head.

"And nothing's going to happen," he said. "So long as I've got my eye on you."

"But it isn't me you should be watching!"

"No kidding?"

"And nothing's going to happen," he said. "So long as I've got my eye on you."

"But it isn't me you should be watching!"

"No kidding?"

"There's a little girl," Joel said, for perhaps the hundredth time.

The guard sucked deeply on the cigarette and held in the smoke as he laughed.

"You want me to believe a kid is going to cause trouble here?"

"She's probably working with someone."

"Where is she now, then?"

Joel gestured towards the door.

"Out there somewhere," he said. "She . . ."

He noticed the amused look on the guard's face and shut his mouth. Damn it all, why did he have to run into a moron like this one? He sank down to a couch and folded his arms. For the time being there was no use in arguing. He would have to think of another plan of action.

Denny's hand squeezed the doorknob for nearly fifteen minutes before daring to turn it. Finally, convinced by her snoring that his mother was sleeping soundly, he left the apartment. He had momentary doubts about this, anticipating what might happen if he was caught. But then he remembered his friends at the Dysart Theater, that it was their big opening night, and hurried for the building's rickety old elevator. He knew that he'd miss the whole first act, but that was okay as long as he was there for most of the play. Nate would understand.

"Anyone see you?" Mikey asked when they met in front of Denny's building.

"Uh-uh," Denny said. "It's okay."

Paul rubbed his arms. "Let's get going. I'm freezing to death!"

The three boys walked in the direction of the nearest theater, where Mike and Paul had told their parents they would be for the next few hours. But just before they reached it, they descended a dark stairway into the subway station below. Except for a young couple heading into Manhattan on a date, they were alone.

To the sound of thundering applause, the curtain came down on the first act. Don called "Strike!" the signal for the stagehands to change the sets for act two. No one in the clapping audience heard him. Adrian rushed into Nate's arms and kissed him. The other actors hardly noticed her, each one too intent on the fifteen-minute intermission to care what another member of the company was doing. Adrian squeezed Nate tightly.

"We're halfway through," she said. "Halfway through, and nothing has happened. And they *loved* us!"

"You were wonderful," Nate said, rubbing her back. He could feel perspiration through her cotton dress, the result of working under hot stage lights. But he also knew she had been nervous on that stage, anticipating what could happen at any moment.

"Maybe we were wrong," she said. "Maybe there is no danger."

Nate kissed her again.

"Forget it," he said. "Just go back to your dressing room and relax."

As they were walking hand-in-hand, Don came up to them with Sander's agent, Tom Selton. Both men looked very worried.

"I tried to get backstage when I heard Sander wouldn't be performing," Tom said. "But some goon of a fellow wouldn't let me."

"I'm sorry," Nate said. "What can you tell me about Sander?"

"I haven't been able to reach him at his apartment since yesterday morning," Tom said, "when I called him to give him a word of encouragement. He told me then he was on his way to the theater."

"Yes, he was here yesterday," Nate said.

"Well, apparently," Tom said, "he never came home. We were supposed to go out for a few drinks last night, but Sander didn't show up."

Hearing this, Adrian took Nate's hand, a gesture not lost on Tom.

"Is something wrong here?"

"I don't know," Nate said. "What do you suppose happened to him?"

Let it be nothing, he thought. *Dear God, let it be nothing.*

"My client never missed a performance in all the years I've been working with him," Tom said. "This just isn't like him."

Don looked down the hallway.

"I say we check Sander's dressing room again," he suggested. "Maybe he's got a bad case of stage fright and couldn't answer us before."

"Not my client," Tom said. "Not Sander Bernaux. He's one of Broadway's greatest actors!"

"I saw him cringe at the sight of a cat once," Adrian said.

Nate, not wanting anyone to see the trembling that had begun to creep under his skin, hurried towards the actor's dressing room. They spent a few minutes knocking on his door and calling to him, until Adrian finally had to leave.

"Let's break the lock," Tom said. "If he's not in there, we'll know he may not be answering his phone at home. Then I'll go there and find out what's going on."

Don stopped an actress who was passing by and asked if she had a hairpin. She pulled one out and gave it to him, then headed towards the stage. Don bent the pin open and worked it into the hole beneath the glass doorknob.

"This old-fashioned lock should give way easily enough," he said.

In a moment, the door clicked open. Don switched on the light and led the other two men into Sander's dressing room. It was empty. The makeup on his dresser sat in its usual disarray, and there were papers thrown around the floor. Nate bent down and picked up a copy of *Variety*. Absentmindedly, he neatened the pages and put the paper down on top of a costume trunk.

"Well, he's obviously not here," Tom said. He looked at his watch. "I'll go over to his apartment."

"Call me if he's there," Nate said.

Tom left Don and Nate alone. Don looked around the room for a moment, wondering how any one individual could make such a mess, then said, "Do you think something's happened to Sander?"

Nate shook his head quickly. No. Nothing could have happened! Not on his opening night!

"Well, Tom will call us," Don said. "I've got to get back to the stage. Intermission'll be over in a minute."

In the lobby the lights flickered to signal curtain time.

Joel's own little prison went dark and brightened again. And he realized he had wasted over an hour.

"You have no right to hold me here," he said. "Do you know who I am?"

"I read your articles all the time, Mr. Warner," the guard said. "It doesn't give you the right to cause trouble."

"But I'm not..."

Suddenly, the lights went out again. And this time they did not turn right back on. Downstairs in the wings Don Benson looked out at the house and saw the audience was seated in darkness. He turned to Mike.

"Hey," he whispered. "Get the lights up!"

Mike punched buttons and flicked switches, but nothing happened. In a flash, the stage lights also went out. Confused and excited whispers ran through the groups of people on the stage and in the audience. Mike cursed under his breath.

"Damn! We've got another blackout!"

"Keep working on it," Don said. "I'll take care of the audience."

He hurried across the stage and through the curtains. Though he knew the audience couldn't see him, he called for attention and told them there was a power failure.

"But don't worry," he called out. "We'll be getting on with the play in just a few moments. Thank you for your cooperation."

In Sander's dressing room Nate had spent the last few minutes thinking about Meg and Jim. When the lights went out, he stood up from Sander's chair and moved towards the door to find out what was wrong. But as he approached it, he heard it slam shut. And then, a familiar childish voice said, "It's time. It's time, Daddy."

Nate backed up a pace.

"Who is that?" he demanded. "Who are you?"

His eyes adjusted to the dim light flickering into the room from the neon sign of the hotel next door, and Nate saw a little girl standing before him. She was smiling.

"Who are you?" he demanded again.

"I'm your little girl," Bonnie said. "Don't you know me?"

Nate shook his head.

"I have no little girl!" he cried. "What kind of sick joke is this?"

Bonnie took a step forward, her arms outstretched.

"I want us to be together again, Daddy," she said, taking both his hands.

But though Nate could see her hands in his, he could not feel them. With an angered cry he jerked away, stumbling backwards and falling against the closet door. It bounced open. Nate pulled himself away from it, grabbing the room's curtains, letting in more light from outside.

Light that revealed Sander Bernaux's hideously mutilated face.

"No," Nate whispered, too stunned to scream. He dropped to his knees. "My God, no..."

"He had to pay, Daddy," Bonnie said, her voice sweet. "He had to pay."

There was a noose around Sander's neck, and his body hung freely from a high bar in the closet. His face was a mass of blood and gore, a mixture of red and pale, pale green. His tongue protruded from his mouth, his eyes stared wildly; streaks of dried blood stained his face, blood that had dripped from deep cuts in his forehead.

"He was a bad man, Daddy," Bonnie said, taking Nate's hand as the director stared in wide-eyed silence at Sander's body. "He tried to interfere, but I wouldn't let him."

Nate didn't hear her. Somehow, all he could think of at the moment was his father. He could hear the laughter of the old man, high-pitched, hysterical laughter. And he could hear the words his father used so often when speaking to him.

"Failure! Failure!"

Maybe I am a failure, Daddy. Maybe I'm not supposed to be happy. Maybe things aren't supposed to go my way . . .

He felt two hands press on his shoulders. The little girl had come up behind him, and unlike the moments when she'd held his hands, he was aware of her palms touching him.

"Don't cry, Daddy," Bonnie said. "This is a happy time. We're going to be together again!"

Nate wanted to run away from her. He wanted to stand up and run out of here and get Adrian away from this place. He wanted to warn the others before it was too late.

But he could not move. Bonnie's small hands held him down like steel bolts. Slowly, he was falling into her power.

"The time has come, Daddy," she whispered.

*   *   *

Judy Terrel came running up to Mike Woodson as he worked on the control box, breathing heavily. Forcing herself to whisper, she hissed, "My God, we've got a fire backstage—and it's spreading!"

"Get the fire department here," Mike ordered.

"But the phones..."

"Run next door, Judy!" Mike yelled. He turned to the people standing near him. "Get fire extinguishers!"

He could smell smoke and, when he turned, saw the reflection of flames that poured over the sets and props behind the back curtain. It all happened in a matter of seconds when the flames suddenly shot out and overtook the wooden, painted sets on stage. Even as the actors ran to save themselves or to get fire extinguishers, the audience noticed the flames and smoke. Terrified screams filled the dark auditorium.

"Fire! Fire!"

Adrian hurried toward Nate's office, thinking that you were never supposed to yell "fire" in a crowded theater. Where was Nate? She hadn't seen him backstage. Was he hurt somewhere? Did he need her?

"NATE?"

Someone bumped into her in the darkness. She felt a sudden rush of cold when the back door was forced open as everyone made their way out of the theater. A shaft of moonlight barely illuminated the crowded hallway, and Adrian used it as a guide to find her way.

"NATE, WHERE ARE YOU?"

Even as she ran along the hallways, crying out for Nate, the members of the audience were making their own mad dashes to safety. The walls and ceiling had come to a point of such intense heat that they burst into flame simultaneously. Pieces of the wooden ceiling dropped on the screaming, rushing throng of people. Black smoke curled up and caressed the gilded wainscotting and balcony trim.

"Help me!" a man screamed.

"My children! My children!"

One young man knocked another aside to move ahead more quickly. The latter picked himself up off the floor just in time to miss being stepped on. But an elderly woman was not so lucky, and as the crowd pressed toward the doors she fell forward. A thousand feet trampled her, a thousand ears ignored her screams.

The mock columns to either side of the room ripped away from the wall, no longer supported by wooden beams. A series of loud crashes echoed throughout the building as they fell to the floor. A man was knocked down and pinned under it. He reached forward with a curling hand.

"Get it off of me!" he gasped. "Get it off!"

Then his gasp turned into a scream and his scream into a sickly choking sound as the smoke made its way down his throat.

Denny and his friends pounded up the stairs to the street, glad the ride was over. In typical subway style the train had stalled for twenty minutes, cutting short the time they could spend in Manhattan. Eager to get to the theater, they ran along the street, dodging crowds of people. They didn't pay attention to the sirens of a passing fire truck until Denny realized it had turned down the block where Nate's theater was.

"C'mon!" he cried.

When they rounded the corner, it was to see the crews from several other trucks already trying to put out the fire that was claiming the Dysart Theater. The three watched the scene in awe, too engrossed by the fire to think that the delay on the subway might have saved their lives.

The fire department had worked quickly to get its hoses into action and to save as many lives as possible. Some of the cast and crew had come out to the street from the side alley. Everyone was trying to comfort each other as they watched the beautiful Dysart Theater's destruction.

In the crazed chaos, no one heard Joel's cries.

"What the hell is going on out there?" he demanded of the guard. "Why do I smell smoke!"

"I don't know," the guard said. "But I'm going to get us out of here."

He fumbled for his key and pressed his fingers on the door to locate the keyhole in the blackness. The key slid in and turned, but nothing happened.

The guard began to rattle the door.

"What's wrong?" Joel asked.

"It's jammed," was the panicked reply. "I can't get it open!"

Joel pulled him away and tried the door himself, to no avail. Then he started pounding on the wood, screaming.

"GET US OUT OF HERE! WE'RE TRAPPED! HELP! HELP!"

But no one heard him.

Not Adrian, who raced through the smoke-filled building in a desperate search for Nate.

Not Mike Woodson or Judy Terrel, who finally left the theater to the fire department and ran to safety.

Not the casting director, Virginia, who paused only a second in her flight to lift the theater's cat, the screeching Cartier, into her arms.

Not the fire fighters, nor the other actors and stagehands, nor the people still trying to get out of the theater.

Only Nate Dysart heard him, a voice faraway and faint. But he did not move to help him. He was frozen, staring at Sander Bernaux, holding the little girl named Bonnie.

"You have to remember me, Daddy," Bonnie said. "You have to remember the night I died."

She put her head on his shoulder.

"It was so, so long ago . . ."

TWENTY-TWO

Bonnie placed her hands gently on Nate's cheeks, hands that earlier had brought horrid pain to those who had angered the little girl. But Nate felt no pain—only the loving touch of a small child. Bonnie looked at him and saw not a Broadway producer, nor a man born some thirty years after her death. She knew him not as Nate dysart but as Philip Jackson, the daddy she had been taken from sixty years earlier on a fateful December night.

And now her daddy was back again, his reincarnated spirit locked within the mind of Nate Dysart, only now to be released on the anniversary of Bonnie's death. She kissed Nate's forehead and whispered, "Remember, Daddy. Remember what happened to me."

Nate felt himself being lifted up, and the room he was in

faded away. He was floating, floating through a long, dark tunnel. Faint voices reached his ears, sounding muffled and contorted like a tape recorder running backwards. There were screams and there was laughter. Flashes of light and pockets of deep blackness swirled around him, images wavered before his eyes like pictures in an old family album. There was the mansion, there his first car, there a toy boat...

For a long time he floated that way, experiencing again the phenomena of an entire lifetime, seeing images of his childhood, of Meg, of his father, of...

Suddenly, he was on his feet in a darkened room. He felt a small child's arms around his knees and said, "You just wait here. I'll be right back."

But the voice wasn't his. Nate moved to touch the tiny girl who hugged him...

... but it was Philip Jackson who stroked Bonnie's soft hair.

By way of a power only evil could conjure up, Nathaniel Philip Dysart became Philip Nathaniel Jackson. He had gone back sixty years in time to relive the night his daughter, Bonnie Jackson, had died. Nate watched the scenario like a person watching a play. And yet, strangely, he felt himself as part of the action, as if he were sharing Phil's body. It seemed as if his being had been split in two—one half as Nate Dysart, observer, the other as Phil Jackson, participant.

Phil Jackson stomped along the blackened hallway that led away from Bonnie's dressing room, waving the gun he held as his anger grew. In the deep darkness, his sense of hearing was sharpened, and he easily found his wife when he heard her whispering behind one of the doors. He put a hand on the glass knob, hesitated, then burst into the room.

Through the light of a hurricane lamp, Phil stared at Margaret. She was trying desperately to pull up the bodice of her silk dress. Her mouth gaped open when she saw the gun. Her beads (Phil had given them to her last Christmas) were tossed carelessly, almost contemptuously, on the floor. Nervously, Aaron followed Phil's gaze to the necklace, then he stopped fastening his suspenders and bent to pick it up.

"Phil!" Margaret cried, finding her voice at last. "What are you doing with that gun?"

Phil said nothing in response. With his lips set hard, he

walked across the room and delivered a hard backhand to his wife's jaw. Margaret screamed and fell back on the couch.

"How dare you?" Aaron demanded, stepping between them. He knocked the gun from Phil's hand, sending it flying across the room.

Without warning, Phil ran a blow to Aaron's stomach, sending him to the floor. Margaret's lover doubled up in pain, clutching his middle.

"You lousy little bitch," Phil hissed, enunciating each angered word. "What the hell do you mean, endangering Bonnie's life so you can have your fun with that bastard?"

"Phil, Aaron and I were only..."

Margaret had started to sit up, but Phil slapped her again. She brought a slender hand up to her reddened cheek.

"I found Bonnie locked in a closet," Phil said. "What did she do this time, Margaret? Did she scuff her shoes again? Did she spill her milk?"

"Phil..."

He couldn't resist another smack, hating her now more than he ever had. She had hurt his baby. She had thought screwing with Aaron was more important than Bonnie's welfare.

"Oh, wait," he drawled, his slicked-down hair glistening in the light of the hurricane lamp. "I know! Bonnie figured out you were up to no-good, huh? You locked her up so she wouldn't get in your way!"

Once again, he struck her. Aaron had got to his feet, and he tried to grab Phil's arm. With a gasp Margaret stood up and ran from the room.

Phil broke away from Aaron's grip, picked up both the gun and the hurricane lamp, and ran out into the hallway. He saw his wife turning a corner up ahead and hurried toward her.

"That child is more trouble than she's worth. You keep her! I hate her!"

"Margaret..."

But she began walking toward Bonnie's dressing room, shouting.

"BONNIE JACKSON, HOW DARE YOU BAD-MOUTH ME?"

"DON'T YOU HURT HER!"

Phil yelled at his wife even as she pushed open the door to

Bonnie's room. But it was empty! Phil followed her in and moved the hurricane lamp around, seeing no sign of his little girl. Across the room, the closet gaped like a demon's mouth—waiting to devour a little girl.

"Son-of-a-bitch," Phil whispered, leaving the room. He looked up and down the hallway. "BONNIE! BONNIE WHERE ARE YOU?"

The theater was silent. So silent that the sound of footsteps behind him made Phil turn with a gasp. Frustrated that it was Aaron and not Bonnie, for a moment he lost control and fired the gun. Aaron grabbed his arm where the bullet had grazed him, barely making a burn on his shirt.

"You're insane!" he cried.

Phil moved quickly along the hallway, shouting, praying, his heart pounding so hard it hurt his chest. What had happened to Bonnie? Was she hurt? Was she even able to answer him?

"BONNIE!"

He came to the stage and held up his lamp. Ropes and sandbags cast weird shadows in the light, but it did not find Bonnie for him. Phil looked up beyond the crystal chandelier at the mezzanine, but no one was there. Unless Bonnie was hiding, too frightened to let him know where she was . . .

"Let's try upstairs," he suggested to Margaret.

Just at that moment, Aaron Milland walked on stage. He took Margaret's arm and said, "I'm leaving."

"Aaron, no!"

"This isn't my problem," Aaron said. "I want no part of you, or your daughter!"

Margaret, stunned by the changed attitude of the man who'd said he loved her just a few minutes earlier, watched Aaron storm from the theater. But she made no attempt to follow him. Instead, she turned and ran after Phil.

She found him on stage. "You ruined everything!" she shouted. "For once in my life I was happy, and you and that kid ruined everything!"

"You really do hate Bonnie, don't you?" Phil asked, incredulously.

"I never wanted a baby, and you know it," Margaret said. "*I* was supposed to be the actress in this family. But what happened? You got me pregnant at eighteen years old, and I was ruined!"

"That wasn't Bonnie's fault," Phil protested. "You could have..."

"God damn it, yes it *was* her fault!"

Suddenly, she grabbed the hurricane lamp, and in an effort to vent her anger threw it with all her might at the gold-and-white curtains that rose majestically to the striplights above.

"NNNNOOO!!!"

Phil's angry cry tore through the air even as the flames from the lamp devoured the curtains. He took a step forward, his hands outstretched, as if he could put the fire out. Then he caught hold of his senses and hurried off the stage.

Flames poured with lightning speed over the wood and curtains and ropes, destroying everything in sight, spreading wildly. Margaret ran toward a nearby office to phone the fire department, as Phil ran off in the opposite direction. He had to find Bonnie!

"BONNIE? BONNIE, FOR GOD'S SAKE, WHERE ARE YOU?!"

The hallway began to fill with black smoke. Tears stung Phil's eyes as he stumbled along the hallway, guided by the light of the rapidly spreading fire. He crashed into the lobby, already thick with smoke, coughing and yelling.

"BONNIE?"

The winding staircase beckoned him, and he raced up it, taking the steps two at a time. A quick, desperate search of the upstairs proved Bonnie wasn't hiding anywhere. Phil didn't even stop to catch his breath as he raced back down the stairs again, burning his hands on the metal railing, which had heated up in the last few moments. As he crashed to the bottom floor a line of flames raced along the ceiling above him, and one of the lobby's chandeliers collapsed. Axes began to pound on the stage door.

Moments later, a dozen firemen broke into the building. They helped Margaret to safety, trying to calm the hysterical woman.

"Margaret, I can't find Bonnie!"

But Margaret could only scream.

Phil hated her more at that moment than any other time in his life. With a loud cry that seemed to rip open his already pained throat, he pushed a fireman aside and ran to the hallway that led backstage. His daughter was hiding somewhere, of course. She was hiding because she was terrified of her mother.

"BONNIE?"

Just a few yards away, in the orchestra pit, five-year-old Bonnie Jackson coughed and regained consciousness. Weakly, with the last breath in her smoke-filled lungs, she cried out, *"Daddy?"*

Phil stopped in his tracks. The voice sounded so faraway that he didn't dare believe it wasn't a trick of the crackling flames.

"BONNIE?!"

He raced onto the stage. The ghost light had been knocked over, and unable to see in the darkness, Phil tripped over it and fell into the orchestra pit. His arms flung out and touched something small and warm.

"Bonnie!"

He gathered the little girl up into his arms, tears of joy racing down his flushed cheeks. But the joy was soon shattered.

Bonnie didn't respond to his hugs and kisses.

His little girl was dead.

"NNNNNOOOOO!!!!!"

Phil Jackson threw back his head and let out a scream of anger.

And at the same time, Nate Dysart also screamed, sitting once again in Sander's dressing room. Sixty years of time had flown by in a split second, and the present had taken over.

Nate screamed in terror, rocking the little girl in his lap. In that brief moment, he came to understand what he had been trying to know all these months. His theater was haunted by a little girl who should never have died, a little girl who was still looking for her daddy. And Nate was that daddy—Phil Jackson's reincarnated spirit. Bonnie had come back to the site of the theater to find him.

"Bonnie . . ." he whispered, somehow hearing Phil Jackson's voice.

"Daddy, don't cry," Bonnie said, her voice sweet. "We're together again. The dark isn't here anymore!"

Nate didn't hear her. As Phil Jackson he remembered. His

wife, Margaret, had died several months later in an asylum. By some freak of time and fate, Nate's wife Meg had also died in a mental institution, driven there by Nathaniel Sr. after the loss of her baby. Meg's maiden name had been Margaret Jackson . . . and Phil, the father who had so loved Bonnie that she looked for him even beyond mortal life, had shot himself in the head.

Nate brought his hands up to his own head and remembered the suicide attempt he'd made after losing Meg.

"Nate!"

The spell was broken when he heard someone shouting his name. He looked up to see Adrian in the doorway, staring wide-eyed at him as he held Bonnie on his lap.

"Nate, what are you doing?" she demanded. "That's her! That's the little girl!"

Suddenly, Adrian caught sight of Sander Bernaux's corpse, swinging from a rod in the dark closet, illuminated by the hotel lights outside. She covered her mouth with her hand and screamed in horror.

"Nate, what's happening here?"

Now Bonnie crawled from Nate's lap, a strange, bestial growl escaping from her small mouth. She lunged at Adrian, knocking her to the floor.

"DON'T!" Adrian cried in a panic.

"You won't take him away from me!" Bonnie cried. "You won't! You won't!"

She placed her hands on Adrian's face, sending intense burning pains over the woman's skin. Adrian screamed and struggled, unable to understand why Nate didn't help her.

"Nate, *please!*"

Nate sensed something was wrong as he watched the woman and child struggling, but under Bonnie's spell he could not move.

"*Nate!*"

The pain raced over Adrian's body, burning her and yet making her quake as if it were freezing in the room. Nate watched her struggle as if she were a figure on a movie screen, as if she were not a flesh-and-blood woman, a part of his life.

"NATE FOR GOD'S SAKE STOP HER!!!"

Abruptly, like the crash of thunder, the hypnotic vacuum

Nate had been in exploded. He saw Adrian writhing in pain.
He saw the woman he loved being tormented.

"NO!"

He stood up and looked at Bonnie.

"STOP THAT RIGHT NOW!"

Shocked, Bonnie turned away from Adrian and looked
innocently into Nate's eyes. Adrian, sickened, wrapped her
arms around herself as the pain slowly subsided.

"Daddy?"

"What *are* you?" Adrian demanded.

Nate shook his head, locking eyes with the small child.

"Daddy, she was bad," Bonnie said. "She wants to take you
away from me!"

"No . . ."

"Nate, what is she talking about? Who is she?"

Nate ignored her. He took a step toward Bonnie.

"What do you want from me?"

"You're my daddy," Bonnie said. "I want you to come with
me."

"No," Nate said. "No, I'm not your daddy."

Bonnie threw back her head and screamed.

"You are! You are!"

"No!" Nate cried. "Your real daddy died a long, long time
ago! I am *not* Phil Jackson!"

Adrian's eyes dripped huge tears as she watched this,
unable to understand or believe what was going on.

"Please come with me, Daddy," Bonnie pleaded.

"I'm Nate Dysart," Nate said firmly. "I am not your
daddy!"

"I want you to come with me!"

It wasn't right! The little girl couldn't believe his words. All
these years in darkness, all the plans she had made. How
could they fail now? How could he reject her so coldly?

"Daddy . . ."

Nate put his hands on her shoulders.

"Your daddy died a long time ago," he said again. "Maybe
his spirit is in me—I don't know. But I do know I have a long
life ahead of me. I'm not ready to give that up!"

"Nate, for God's sake," Adrian choked, rubbing her eyes.

Bonnie stared into his eyes.

"You're supposed to love me, Daddy," Bonnie said. "You're supposed to come with me now."

"No!" Nate snapped. "I don't want to come with you! I don't want to die! I am not your daddy—no matter what I was in 1921, I am *not* your daddy!"

Adrian moved inside the room and took his arm.

"Nate, I can see flames in the hallway!" she cried, pulling him.

"Bonnie," Nate said, his voice strangely calm, "you'll be with your daddy, one day. But the time isn't right now. And I'm not coming with you!"

"Then I'll wait, Daddy," Bonnie said. "I'll wait. Because I know you always come for me."

"I don't..."

She pulled him down a little and kissed his cheek.

"You always come, Daddy," she said. "I'll wait."

And then, suddenly, she was gone. Nate and Adrian stared at the spot where she'd just been, stunned. Then Adrian pulled Nate with all her might from the room. Flames were just reaching the doorway, flames that spread mercilessly in spite of the fire department's work. Nate and Adrian raced away from them, stumbling down the dimly lit hallway toward the back door.

A few seconds later they crashed into the backyard. The icy December wind struck Nate like a slap in the face, bringing him to his senses. He collapsed onto the frost-covered ground, his ears bombarded with the sounds of screams and sirens.

"Oh, Nate," Adrian said weakly. "What happened in there? Who was that child?"

Nate couldn't tell her right now. He began to cough, his lungs giving in to the smoke. Trembling, he turned away and buried his head in Adrian's chest. For a long time they sat in silence, protected from the smoke by a wind that blew in toward the front of the theater.

The theater...

Nate looked up at the building that had once been his pride and joy. But it had brought only pain to him, and in a strange sort of way he was relieved to see it haloed now in flame and smoke.

"She was looking for her father," he said softly. "She thought I was her father."

"Nate?"

Adrian kissed the top of his head, smelling smoke in his hair. She didn't understand what had just happened, but to her the most important thing was that they were safe.

"I looked everywhere for you, darling," she said. "Why didn't you answer me?"

Nate couldn't tell her he'd been in another dimension, unable to hear her.

"Just hold me, Adrian," he said. "Just tell me everything's going to be all right."

"I have to know what happened in there," Adrian said.

"She was a ghost," Nate said, as if that were the most natural statement in the world. "Bonnie was a ghost who walked the halls of my theater looking for her daddy."

"Nate . . ."

Adrian wanted to say that was impossible but stopped herself.

"Nate, let's not talk about her," she said. "No one would believe us. No one has to know what happened."

"But Joel Warner knows about her," Nate protested.

Adrian closed her eyes and gently told Nate the news.

"He's dead, Nate," she said. "He died from the smoke upstairs."

"Oh no . . ."

"Two other people died too," Adrian said. "And God only knows what happened to Sander in there! Let it be, Nate. If you start talking about ghosts, the police will think *you* set the fire! They'll put you away, Nate!"

Put you away . . .

The way Nathaniel Sr. had put Meg away . . .

"I don't want to die," Nate said weakly.

"You aren't going to die, Nate," Adrian said, crushing him to her. "You aren't ever, ever going to be hurt again!"

She rested her cheek on top of his head and stared at the shell of the Dysart Theater. As its life came to an end, she knew that the horror, too, was over.

EPILOGUE
Summer, 1986

So much had happened in the last five years. As if he had been reborn after the fire, everything had taken a turn for the better in Nate's life. He was married to Adrian now, the father of twin boys, and heading up a theater company he'd started in 1983. Much of the profits that he made went to compensate the families of those who had died in the fire. But money didn't really mean very much to Nate. He had everything he wanted in his little family.

Well, almost everything. It had seemed, after all the investigations were over and the fire declared accidental, that everything would be all right. No one even looked his way regarding Sander Bernaux's death. It was believed to have been a suicide, and the note lost in the badly burned dressing room. And so, with no worries, Nate should have been happy. But somehow, he knew something was missing from his life.

Though he loved his sons dearly, he couldn't stop thinking about the little girl named Bonnie. It amazed Nate, a man who had hated his father, that a child could so *love* her father that she'd haunt the earth for six decades in search of him. He often wondered, as he looked back on that December night, if he had done the right thing by rejecting her. And he always decided that he had. Life was too precious to him to be thrown away. His sons, Joey and Jimmy, were a constant source of joy to him. And they, he vowed, would never know the heartaches and cruelties he'd experienced in his own childhood.

Yet, still, the idea of having a little daughter became an obsession with him. But Adrian was at the height of her career and couldn't afford time off for another pregnancy. Still she understood Nate's feelings, and after many discussions and arguments, had finally consented to adopt. So today, on a warm July afternoon, they were heading toward the Goldmountain Foundling's Home for a prearranged meeting with its director.

"You don't know how excited I am," Nate said, squeezing Adrian's hand. "Just think—we might have a little girl soon!"

Adrian laughed. "It'll be a new experience for me, coming from a family with nine brothers!"

They arrived at the gate of the home, and George swung their Lincoln onto its gravel driveway. A few minutes later they were in an office, telling a stocky woman why they wanted to adopt another child when they had a pair of toddler boys at home.

At the end of the meeting, the woman smiled and said, "Well, there don't seem to be any problems, Mr. and Mrs. Dysart. We've looked thoroughly into your background. Now, would you like to look at some of our children?"

Nate grinned.

"Please," he said.

They were led out to a huge backyard, where several dozen youngsters played on swings and slides and chased each other through the garden. Nate put his arm around Adrian's shoulder and watched them in silence for a long time. They all seemed very happy.

But there was one little girl who sat apart from the group, swinging lazily in a tire that hung from an oak-tree branch. She was dressed in a red sunsuit, and her dark braids flicked over her slight shoulders. She turned, as if hearing a signal from Nate's mind, and stared into his eyes with big, black ones of her own. Nate smiled slightly at her.

"Who is that?" Adrian asked. "She's certainly a shy little thing."

"Strangest thing about that child," the woman replied. "She was left with us about five years ago, when she was a very tiny infant. No one ever came to claim her."

"But she's beautiful," Nate said, tilting his head to one side as he watched her play. "Why hasn't she been adopted yet?"

The woman signed. "The poor dear has problems. She's terribly shy, and she has a tremendous fear of the dark. Wakes up from nightmares almost every . . ."

But Nate wasn't listening. The word "dark" kept bouncing

back and forth in his mind. This little girl was afraid of the dark. Just like Bonnie . . .

"Nate. It's a coincidence," Adrian whispered.

He turned to the woman.

"May I speak with her?"

"Why, of course!" the woman said. She hoped they would like the child and would adopt her.

She walked across the yard and took the little girl by the hand, leading her to Nate and Adrian. The child was hesitant, staring down at her feet. Nate got on his knees and put his hands on her shoulders. He said nothing but only smiled. And in a moment the child returned the smile. She looked into his eyes, her eyes filled with great innocence, and in a sweet voice she said, "My name is Bonnie. Are you going to be my new daddy?"

ABOUT THE AUTHOR

Clare McNally attended the Fashion Institute of Technology in New York City where she studied advertising and communications. She has worked on a children's wear magazine, freelanced as an advertising copywriter and edited a technical magazine. She now devotes all her time to writing novels. Her first occult thriller was GHOST HOUSE, followed by GHOST HOUSE REVENGE. She is currently hard at work on her fourth novel of supernatural terror.

Ms. McNally lives on Long Island with her husband.

From the author of
THE LITTLE GIRL WHO LIVES
DOWN THE LANE,
a terrifying novel of a mother's
ultimate nightmare

ROCKABYE
by Laird Koenig

One minute ago, Susannah Bartok's precious
two-year-old son Laddie was giggling beside her,
adorable in his red cap and mittens. Now, suddenly, he's gone—yanked away into the icy night
by an unseen madman. Outraged and desperate,
Susannah rushes into the cold city on a frantic
search, tormented by the agonizing reality that
her little boy is out there ... defenseless ...
facing God-knows-what ...

Hair-raising happenings
that guarantee nightmares!

You'll be fascinated by unearthly events, intrigued by stories of weird and bizarre occurrences, startled by terrifying tales that border fact and fiction, truth and fantasy. Look for these titles or use the handy coupon below. Go beyond time and space into the strange mysteries of all times!

☐	22634	THE AMITYVILLE HORROR by Jay Anson	$3.50
☐	20707	HAUNTED HOUSES by Winer & Osborn	$2.75
☐	20757	GHOST HOUSE by Clare McNally	$2.75
☐	23065	GHOST HOUSE REVENGE by Clare McNally	$2.95
☐	20701	THE EXORCIST by William Blatty	$3.50
☐	14036	HALLOWEEN by Curtis Richards	$2.50
☐	20535	50 GREAT GHOST STORIES by John Canning, ed.	$2.95
☐	20799	50 GREAT HORROR STORIES by John Canning, ed.	$2.95

DON'T MISS
THESE CURRENT
Bantam Bestsellers

- [ ] 22656 **NO TIME FOR TEARS** Cynthia Freeman $3.95
- [ ] 22580 **PEACE BREAKS OUT** John Knowles $2.95
- [ ] 22740 **HALLOWEEN** Curtis Richards $2.95
- [ ] 20922 **SHADOW OF CAIN** $3.95
  Vincent Bugliosi & Ken Hurwitz
- [ ] 20822 **THE GLITTER DOME** Joseph Wambaugh $3.95
- [ ] 20943 **THE EARHART MISSION** Peter Tanous $2.75
- [ ] 20924 **THE PEOPLE'S ALMANAC 3** $4.50
  Wallechinsky & Wallace
- [ ] 20558 **THE LORD GOD MADE THEM ALL** $3.95
  James Herriot
- [ ] 20662 **THE CLOWNS OF GOD** Morris West $3.95
- [ ] 20181 **CHALLENGE (Spirit of America!)** $3.50
  Charles Whited
- [ ] 14894 **FIRELORD** Parke Godwin $3.50
- [ ] 13419 **THE CHAINS** Gerald Green $3.50
- [ ] 20581 **FROM THE BITTER LAND** Maisie Mosco $3.25
- [ ] 01368 **EMBERS OF DAWN** Patricia Matthews $6.95
- [ ] 13101 **THE BOOK OF LISTS #2** $3.50
  Wallechinsky & Wallaces
- [ ] 20164 **HOW TO MASTER VIDEO GAMES** $2.95
  Tom Hirschfeld
- [ ] 20560 **CHIEFS** Stuart Woods $3.75
- [ ] 14716 **THE LORDS OF DISCIPLINE** Pat Conroy $3.75
- [ ] 20387 **THE COMPLETE MONEY MARKET GUIDE** $3.50
  William Donaghue
- [ ] 20134 **THE PRITIKIN PROGRAM FOR DIET** $3.95
  AND EXERCISE Nathan Pritikin w/
  Patrick McGrady, Jr.
- [ ] 20356 **THE GUINESS BOOK OF WORLD** $3.95
  RECORDS 20th ed. The McWhirters
- [ ] 23024 **MORE OF PAUL HARVEY'S THE REST** $2.95
  OF THE STORY Paul Aurandt

Buy them at your local bookstore or use this handy coupon for ordering:

Bantam Books, Inc., Dept. FB, 414 East Golf Road, Des Plaines, Ill. 60016

Please send me the books I have checked above. I am enclosing $_____
(please add $1.25 to cover postage and handling). Send check or money order
—no cash or C.O.D.'s please.

Mr/Mrs/Miss_____

Address_____

City_____State/Zip_____

FB—11/82

Please allow four to six weeks for delivery. This offer expires 5/83.